Last Lift
from Crete

Historical Fiction Published by McBooks Press

ALEXANDER KENT

Midshipman Bolitho
Stand Into Danger
In Gallant Company
Sloop of War
To Glory We Steer
Command a King's Ship
Passage to Mutiny
With All Despatch
Form Line of Battle!
Enemy in Sight!
The Flag Captain
Signal—Close Action!
The Inshore Squadron
A Tradition of Victory
Success to the Brave
Colours Aloft!
Honour This Day
The Only Victor
Beyond the Reef
The Darkening Sea
For My Country's Freedom
Cross of St George
Sword of Honour
Second to None
Relentless Pursuit
Man of War

DOUGLAS REEMAN

Badge of Glory
First to Land
The Horizon
Dust on the Sea
Knife Edge

Twelve Seconds to Live
Battlecruiser
The White Guns
A Prayer for the Ship
For Valour

DAVID DONACHIE

The Devil's Own Luck
The Dying Trade
A Hanging Matter
An Element of Chance
The Scent of Betrayal
A Game of Bones

On a Making Tide
Tested by Fate
Breaking the Line

DUDLEY POPE

Ramage
Ramage & The Drumbeat
Ramage & The Freebooters
Governor Ramage R.N.
Ramage's Prize
Ramage & The Guillotine
Ramage's Diamond
Ramage's Mutiny
Ramage & The Rebels
The Ramage Touch
Ramage's Signal
Ramage & The Renegades
Ramage's Devil
Ramage's Trial
Ramage's Challenge
Ramage at Trafalgar
Ramage & The Saracens
Ramage & The Dido

ALEXANDER FULLERTON

Storm Force to Narvik
Last Lift to Crete
All the Drowning Seas

JAMES L. NELSON

The Only Life That Mattered

PHILIP MCCUTCHAN

Halfhyde at the Bight of Benin
Halfhyde's Island
Halfhyde and the
  Guns of Arrest
Halfhyde to the Narrows
Halfhyde for the Queen
Halfhyde Ordered South
Halfhyde on Zanatu

V.A. STUART

Victors and Lords
The Sepoy Mutiny
Massacre at Cawnpore
The Cannons of Lucknow
The Heroic Garrison

The Valiant Sailors
The Brave Captains
Hazard's Command
Hazard of Huntress
Hazard in Circassia
Victory at Sebastopol
Guns to the Far East
Escape from Hell

R.F. DELDERFIELD

Too Few for Drums
Seven Men of Gascony

DEWEY LAMBDIN

The French Admiral
Jester's Fortune
What Lies Buried

C.N. PARKINSON

The Guernseyman
Devil to Pay
The Fireship
Touch and Go
So Near So Far
Dead Reckoning

The Life and Times of
  Horatio Hornblower

JAN NEEDLE

A Fine Boy for Killing
The Wicked Trade
The Spithead Nymph

IRV C. ROGERS

Motoo Eetee

NICHOLAS NICASTRO

The Eighteenth Captain
Between Two Fires

FREDERICK MARRYAT

Frank Mildmay OR
  The Naval Officer
The King's Own
Mr Midshipman Easy
Newton Forster OR
  The Merchant Service
Snarleyyow OR
  The Dog Fiend
The Privateersman
The Phantom Ship

W. CLARK RUSSELL

Wreck of the Grosvenor
Yarn of Old Harbour Town

RAFAEL SABATINI

Captain Blood

MICHAEL SCOTT

Tom Cringle's Log

A.D. HOWDEN SMITH

Porto Bello Gold

Last Lift from Crete

ALEXANDER FULLERTON

THE NICHOLAS EVERARD
WORLD WAR II SAGA, BOOK 2

MCBOOKS PRESS, INC.
ITHACA, NEW YORK

Published by McBooks Press 2005
Copyright © Alexander Fullerton 1980
First published in Great Britain by Michael Joseph Limited

Cover illustration adapted from an image by Chris Mayger.
*Every effort has been made to secure permission
from copyright holders to reproduce this image.*

Library of Congress Cataloging-in-Publication Data

Fullerton, Alexander, 1924–
   Last lift from Crete / by Alexander Fullerton.
      p. cm. — (The Nicholas Everard WWII saga : bk 2)
   ISBN 1-59013-093-6 (trade pbk. : alk. paper)
   1. Everard, Nick (Fictitious character)—Fiction. 2. World War, 1939-1945—
Greece—Crete—Fiction. 3. World War, 1939-1945—Naval operations,
British—Fiction. 4. Great Britain—History, Naval—20th century—Fiction.
5. British—Greece—Fiction. 6. Crete (Greece)—Fiction. I. Title.
   PR6056.U435L375 2005
   823'.914—dc22

                                             2004024058

Distributed to the trade by National Book Network, Inc.
15200 NBN Way, Blue Ridge Summit, PA 17214
800-462-6420

Additional copies of this book may be ordered from any bookstore or directly
from McBooks Press, Inc., ID Booth Building, 520 North Meadow St.,
Ithaca, NY 14850. Please include $4.00 postage and handling with mail
orders. New York State residents must add sales tax to total remittance
(books & shipping). All McBooks Press publications can also be ordered by
calling toll-free 1-888-BOOKS11 (1-888-266-5711).
Please call to request a free catalog.

Visit the McBooks Press website at www.mcbooks.com.

Printed in the United States of America

9   8   7   6   5   4   3   2   1

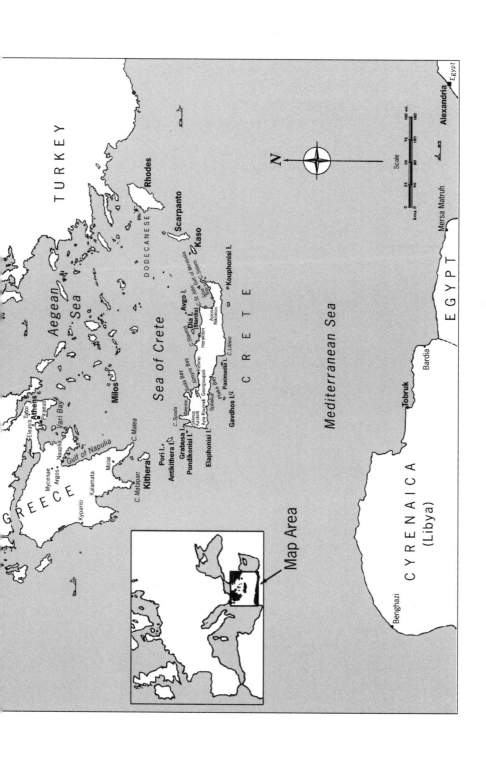

CHAPTER ONE

. . .

A dark shape looming up ahead with the quarter-moon behind it was the rearmost enemy, tail-end Charlie of a convoy of transports almost at its destination and stupidly relaxed, feeling safe, waddling like a brood of ducks into the shelter of the land and keeping, Nick Everard deduced, a bloody awful look-out. *Tuareg's* turbines thrummed in the quiet Mediterranean night, her ventilator fans hoarsely sucking the cool air, her steel's vibration like the tremble of excitement in a thoroughbred as she stemmed white-swirled sea in *Blackfoot's* wake. Astern, *Masai* and *Afghan* followed, and in all four ships tin-hatted guns' crews and torpedomen stood by their weapons. The British destroyers had come down from the north, found the convoy exactly where they'd expected it to be, and sheered away to starboard to come up on it from astern with the moon where it would be most useful—as it was now, throwing the enemy ships into silhouette. At that first sighting, when the flotilla of Tribals had turned away westward, the Italian escort commander should have seen them: having failed to, he'd sealed his convoy's fate.

His own, too, with any luck. *Tuareg's* captain, Commander Sir Nicholas Everard, Bart., DSO, DSC, RN, felt almost sorry for him. Almost: and if there'd been time for sympathy . . . Rocky Pratt, the destroyer's navigating officer, reported quietly, "*Blackfoot's* altering to port, sir."

Nick swung his glasses to the flotilla leader, saw her low stern sliding to the right, pushing round the mound of white wake seemingly glued to it. And from the director control tower's voicepipe another report came now: Harry Houston's emotionless tones informing him, "Two escorts in sight to port of the convoy, sir."

From the level of this bridge the Italian destroyers were not yet visible, but they'd have been spotted from *Blackfoot* half a minute ago and they'd be the reason for her swing to port. Nick stooped to the wheel-house voicepipe: "Port ten." Bringing his ship round in *Blackfoot's* track. There were supposed to be three escorts shepherding this convoy—according to the report from a Fleet Air Arm reconnaissance flight—and as two of them were on the convoy's seaward side you could reasonably assume that the third, most likely the senior man, would be up front. He told the helmsman—CPO Habgood, *Tuareg's* coxswain and senior rating—"Midships and meet her."

"Midships and meet her, sir. Wheel's amidships . . . Ten o' starboard—"

"Steady!"

"Steady, sir. Oh-eight-three."

"Steer that." His voice and the coxswain's were both low, echoey in the metal tube, backed by the hum of the ventilator fans and engine noise, the ship's vibration, and the constant underlying rush of sea along her sides. He could see two of the transports quite clearly now as *Blackfoot* overhauled them and *Tuareg* followed her: farther ahead, up-moon, a less distinct huddle of blackness would be the other three. Five transports, the Walrus recce report had said: they'd been much farther west then, having crossed the Sicilian narrows and then hugged the coast around the Gulf of Sirte, and they'd be deep-laded with troops, weapons, ammunition, and stores for Rommel's eastward drive. Those stupid bas-tards *must* be blind . . . The night air was cool with a hint of land-smell in it, the sweetish tang of the desert littoral. He told Houston through the voicepipe to the director, "Your first target is the nearest transport. Open fire when *Blackfoot* does. As we move up, shift to the next with-out waiting for my orders."

"Aye aye, sir."

"Be ready with torpedoes either side, Sub."

"Standing by, sir." That was Ashcourt, the RN sub-lieutenant, at the torpedo control panel. It probably hadn't been necessary to tell him he'd need to be looking both ways at once: the reminder had been precautionary, a warning to a young officer who hadn't seen all that much action yet—except against the Stukas, which was a different thing

altogether—against becoming mesmerized by whatever might be happening in one particular direction . . . It was extraordinary how familiar
and how—could the word be "pleasurable"?—was this tension that bound
them all, the silent ultra-tense expectancy, the careful hold on pre-action
nerves. There was a thrill in it, a sense of arrival after long preparation,
interminable waiting; he thought, his mind going back to take in another
war as well as the first eighteen months of this one, *It was always like this,
probably always will be* . . . The flash and thunder of *Blackfoot's* guns came
as a relief and brought a reek of cordite flying back over his own bridge:
Blackfoot had engaged the Italian destroyer over her own port bow and
Tuareg's guns flamed and roared now, one half-second later, to starboard,
blinding light giving a photo-flash view of the ship's side and the smoking out-trained barrels of the twin four-sevens, then darkness utterly black
for about a second before the salvo struck below the transport's bridge
and in her waist. The guns had fired again and the pompoms were in it
now, raking the already blazing ship with their streams of two-pounder
shells. Explosions on her stern would be shell-bursts from *Afghan* or *Masai*
or both: there was a constant din of firing and *Tuareg's* four-sevens had
shifted their point of aim to the target's side, the waterline, while on her
waist-deck you could see motor transport, jeep-like trucks, burning
fiercely. There'd be some petrol there perhaps, to help things along.
Glancing away to port Nick saw the Italian destroyer stopped and on
fire, *Blackfoot* leaving her and engaging a new target somewhere ahead;
he yelled up to Houston, "Shift to the next transport, don't waste time
on that escort." And into the other pipe, "Steer five degrees to starboard."
He told Ashcourt, "Enemy destroyer on red three-five. One fish into
her"—*Tuareg's* guns fired, and he paused fractionally until he could almost
hear his own voice again—"as we pass, Sub."

"Aye aye, sir!"

"Three-six-oh revolutions."

"Three-six-oh revs, sir!"

Ahead, it looked as if *Blackfoot* was now in action with *two* Italians:
Reggie Marsh, Captain (D), might be in need of some assistance. Three-

six-oh revs would give *Tuareg* 34 knots, about her maximum, even if she wouldn't have time in covering that short gap of sea to work up to such a speed. The second transport was burning: she'd swung away to starboard and Houston was pumping shells into her stern as they swept past her, vibration worse and noise increasing as revs built up: and now he'd shifted target to the next ship, the third in the line. Way back astern, tail-end Charlie was a blazing wreck, a firework display as minor explosions shook her apart. The burning and immobile destroyer was coming up to port and about to be given its comeuppance. *Tuareg's* guns were hard at it, with a fast rhythm to the firing now, pompoms just as busy and very noisy and the point-fives rattling away as well, arcing tracer traversing a seascape lit by gun-flashes, shell-bursts, burning ships. Dramatic, even beautiful, if you'd an eye for this sort of thing and time to take it in. Ashcourt had reported, "One torpedo fired to port, sir." Another salvo crashed out, guns trained abaft the beam now as they moved up to join the flotilla leader, leaving three ships now well on fire. Nick told Houston, "Shift target. Two enemy destroyers engaging *Blackfoot* ahead of us. Take the nearest." *Masai* and *Afghan* would be pushing on to round up the rest of the convoy: the ones astern could be finished off later if they were still afloat, but those which hadn't yet been attended to had—predictably—turned away to starboard, running for the beach. They wouldn't get there. Explosion to port: a vertical column of black water illuminated by the Italian destroyer's fires. Ashcourt exultant: "That fish hit, sir!" There'd have been answers called for if it hadn't. But *Blackfoot* had been hit too: Nick had had his glasses on her and seen a shell burst abreast her for'ard funnel: then *Tuareg's* "A" and "B" guns fired, at the nearer of the two Italian destroyers. It was coming *this* way, with *its* for'ard guns spurting flame: shells scrunched whistling overhead and some of *Tuareg's* burst shatteringly in the forefront of the Italian's bridge. He was swinging away to starboard, turning very slowly—for lack of steerage way, Nick thought. More hits blossoming amidships and one of his boats ablaze in its davits lighting his upperworks in flaring yellow. A shell clanged off *Tuareg's* foc's'l, hurtled away without exploding, and "X" and "Y" guns were in action now, trained about as far for'ard as they'd go, and the pompoms opening up again as well. Nick had been concerned not to expose his beam to enemy torpedoes, but the Italian's bridge was all flame now and the fires were spreading aft very quickly as he turned into the north-west wind; only one of his after guns was firing. Nick told Ashcourt, "I'm going to turn hard a-starboard. Give him one fish when your sight comes on."

"Aye aye, sir!"

Into the wheelhouse voicepipe: "Starboard—"

That last salvo from the four-sevens hit the Italian amidships, all four shells close together. With his face lowered to the voicepipe Nick saw, under the rim of his tin hat, the flash of one shell bursting on the torpedo tubes and then the eruption from inside as the others penetrated and exploded in the boiler-room. Deep, thunderous explosion: no flames, only a dark mushrooming cloud of smoke or steam or both billowing up, enfolding. From the outer pipe he heard Houston's flatly-spoken order to the guns, "Cease firing." He finished his own order to the coxswain in an amended form: "Starboard ten. Two hundred revolutions."

"Starboard ten, sir. Two hundred—"

"Belay that last order, Sub." No need for a torpedo now. *Blackfoot's* other opponent was done for, too: the Italian's stern was awash, bridge smashed, guns silent, flames dancing here and there. The sea would soon drown those flames. The flotilla leader was turning away, about fifteen hundred yards north-east of *Tuareg*, turning towards the continuing action eastward, inshore. Benghazi lay north-east and about six miles away: eastward there'd be about four miles of sea with deep water right up to the coast. Benghazi had been in British hands until only about a month ago: Wavell had flung the Italians out of it early in February, lost it to the new German drive two months later. The Germans were outside Tobruk now. Nick had his glasses on *Blackfoot* and he couldn't see anything wrong with her, any damage from that hit.

"Midships. Steer one-two-oh."

The guns' crews were cheering, for some reason.

"Midships, sir. Wheel's amidships, sir. Two hundred revolutions passed and repeated."

"Our joker's sunk, sir."

Rocky Pratt was referring to the destroyer they'd been engaging, the one whose boilers had gone up: that explosion would almost certainly have blown her sides out too. Anyway, she'd disappeared, and it would account for those cheers from the gundecks. CPO Habgood's voice floated from the tube: "Course one-two-oh, sir."

Nick had his glasses on the transport which had been third from the rear—the centre ship of the convoy, in fact—and was now alone, with the first two burning and sinking a long way astern of her. This one's fires seemed to be dying down: she'd had less attention given to her, probably, because there'd been some urgency to push on quickly and prevent the escape of the other two. He saw now, as he inspected her through the binoculars, that she was getting under way, a white bow-wave seeming to flicker in the dark as she began to move ahead.

"Starboard fifteen. Three-six-oh revolutions." Straightening from the voicepipe, hearing his coxswain's repetition of those orders, he saw that *Blackfoot* was calling him up by light. Beyond her, gunfire and the flashes of shell-bursts still broke the darkness. The moon was hidden at this moment: he heard the turbines' rising note, the slap of sea against his ship's side as she swung.

"Signalman?"

"Aye, sir!" A flash from the port-side Aldis proved that *Tuareg*'s V/S department weren't asleep. Nick called down to Habgood, "Midships and meet her," and transferred quickly to the other voicepipe. "Bridge, direc-tor!" Houston answered, "Director," and he told him, "Target that steamer ahead of us. When we're closer I'll come round to port."

"I'll engage with 'A' and 'B' now, sir."

"A" and "B" were the two for'ard mountings; turning would allow the after ones, "X" and "Y," to bear as well. From *Masai*'s and *Afghan*'s area of operations the deep *crump* of an explosion and a single leap of flame was probably a torpedo ending one Italian's bid to escape—or to put his cargo on the beach where at least some of it might have been salvaged by the Wehrmacht.

"Steady as you go, Cox'n. One-four-oh revolutions."

No need for high speed now: 140 would produce about 12 knots. He heard the fire-gongs clang, down for'ard, a split second before the guns flamed and split his eardrums—that was how it felt—and in the ensuing, ringing silence before the shells smashed into their target, Yeoman Whiffen reported, "From Captain (D), sir: *Your last bird was only winged, I see.*"

The explosion was magnificent. A great shoot of fire, vertical at first but starring outwards: orange and yellow with a shade of green—a delicate, chartreuse tint—in its centre. Black objects hurtling skyward, disappearing as they passed out of the multicoloured circle of illumination, reappearing in the form of splashes, some of them very large: that was a cargo of ammunition going up, ammunition that would *not* be thrown at Wavell's army. He saw a truck airborne, silhouetted against a sheet of copper-coloured fire: it seemed to rise slowly, turning end-for-end, and then begin to fall just as gradually, as if it wanted to stay up but couldn't quite make the effort: it fell into a bed of black smoke that was swelling now with the central fire contracting to an orange core inside it.

He ducked to the voicepipe: "Port twenty." Then to Houston in the tower, "You hit the jackpot that time." He didn't hear the ex-bank official's answer, only Petty Officer Whiffen's question, "Any reply to Captain (D), sir?"

Burning or burnt-out wrecks: sea loppy, broken up by the wind and patched with moonlight where it leaked through scudding clouds. There was one point of burning inshore but no gunfire now; the entire convoy must have been accounted for, and the flotilla would shortly be re-forming. There'd be time, possibly, to scout around for survivors.

Nick told the yeoman, "No. No reply." That column of flame had been as much answer as Reggie Marsh could need. Marsh had been a fool of a man when Nick had been his senior—*and* had had to kick his arse for him, more than once—back in 1929; and he was still—Nick suspected, privately—not exactly bright . . . But there were other things to think about, here and now—such as the fact that picking up survivors mightn't be all that easy. *Tuareg* had one of her two motorboats left, and its engine wasn't reliable; the other motorboat, the whaler, and the dinghy had been lost or smashed during the last fortnight while the Mediterranean Fleet had been struggling to get an army off the beaches of southern Greece. The other ships in this flotilla were about as badly off: *Afghan* didn't have a boat at all. There'd be replacements to be had from the dockyard in Alexandria, presumably, but this flotilla had come directly from Suda Bay in Crete and the odds were they'd be going straight back there now, to help in the final stages of the Greek evacuation. It wasn't anything to look forward to.

"From Captain (D), sir: *Order One, executive.*"

"Right." Bending to the wheelhouse pipe, he ordered, "Midships the wheel." Straightening, hearing CPO Habgood's acknowledgement, he focused his glasses on *Blackfoot,* to estimate her speed: "Order One" meant line ahead, and he had to take *Tuareg* into station astern of her. Re-forming, and *not* bothering to look for survivors? It had been a clean sweep, anyway: five transports and three escorts reported, five plus three destroyed.

"Steer one-two-five."

"One-two-five, sir!"

He didn't see how the army, now it had been pushed out of Greece, was going to hold on in Crete. That was the intention now, but he couldn't see it happening. Since the beginning of this year—it was May now, actually May Day of 1941, and had been for the last hour or so—since January the Luftwaffe had been building up its strength in the Mediterranean. *Fliegercorps* X had come first, moving into Sicily to put the heat on Malta: and now *Fliegercorps* VIII was operating in Greece and over the Aegean, commanded—according to the last WIR, War Intelligence Report, by a man called von Richthofen, cousin to the fighter ace of the '14–'18 war. He had nearly a thousand front-line aircraft in his command, and from this flotilla's recent experience you could reckon about half of them were dive-bombers. How many aircraft did we have in Crete now, Nick wondered, a dozen?

"Three hundred revolutions. Steer five degrees to starboard."

Blackfoot's shaded lamp was passing a message to *Afghan* and *Masai:* you saw only a faint blue leak of its radiance, from this angle. Telling them to rejoin, re-form, probably. One transport was still burning, so far inshore that it might be on the beach, he thought; the absence of other fires suggested that all the other targets had been sunk. It felt good, made a welcome change, to have dished out some punishment, after weeks of being on the receiving end, giving the Stukas and Ju88s target practice . . . Sheer exhaustion was a major problem for both men and ships: they'd spent March putting the army into Greece, and now April taking it out again: and at the same time there'd been this immensely long desert coast to look after, and Malta to be fed and the Italian fleet to be contained—plus a few lesser tasks.

"Sub—tell the first lieutenant I'd like a word."

"Aye aye, sir." Ashcourt could pass the message aft over his torpedo-control telephone. Tony Dalgleish, *Tuareg's* second-in-command, had a roving commission at action stations but his base was the after-control position on the searchlight platform. In less than a minute he'd arrived in the bridge.

"Nice party that, sir."

"Nothing came near us, did it?"

"One scratch on the foc's'l where a dud bounced off. Nothing else. It's put new heart into the lads, sir. Could you hear them cheering?"

With extra sweaters under his duffel-coat as well as the regulation Mae West, Dalgleish looked about twice his normal size. He was a lieutenant-commander, young-seeming for the rank: dry-mannered, self-contained. Nick said, "We seem to be re-forming. I don't know if we'll be looking for survivors or not, but you'd better be ready for it anyway. Motorboat, scrambling nets, lines, and warn Gallwey. I shan't use the boat unless we have to."

It might be necessary. Wounded men couldn't be expected to climb nets or ladders.

"Doc's all set up for it, sir." Surgeon-Lieutenant Gallwey, RNVR was the doctor. Dalgleish asked, "Will we be going back to Suda, d'you expect?"

Nick called down, "One-eight-oh revolutions. Follow *Blackfoot* now, Cox'n." *Tuareg* was sliding up into station on the flotilla leader. Straightening from the pipe, he said, "We might be sent to Alex. After all, tonight's the last of the pick-ups, or supposed to be." The last troop-lifts off Greek beaches, he meant: according to the signals, and reading between the lines of some of them, you could guess that any soldiers they didn't get out tonight wouldn't get out at all.

Pratt called from the front of the bridge, "*Masai* and *Afghan* red one-oh, sir, rejoining." And *Blackfoot* had begun to flash again, in *this* direction.

Dalgleish muttered, "I'll go down and—"

"Wait. See what this is about."

If he was in Reggie Marsh's shoes, Nick thought, he wouldn't hang around looking for survivors. Not only because of the lack of boats—which really wasn't much of an excuse—but more because they were on an enemy-held coast with enemy-occupied airfields, and the priority must be to get as far offshore as possible before daylight brought the bombers over. Not to mention the even closer danger of E-boats, which by now the enemy might have brought up to Benghazi.

"From Captain (D): *Nine blue,* sir."

"Nine blue" meant "alter course in succession ninety degrees to port." In other words *Blackfoot* would shortly turn left and wanted *Tuareg* to follow in her wake. The other two would then be roughly on the starboard beam and they'd steer across to tag on in line astern.

"Executive signal, sir!"

"Very good." And he could see the leader turning: the sudden heel of that slim, black shape, the sharp elbow in the white wake. He bent to the pipe: "Steady as you go."

Cancelling his last order, which had been for the coxswain to follow the ship ahead . . . The new course would be 040. It could be either for a straight dash across the Mediterranean to the Antikithera Channel and into the Aegean, or a course to round the bulge of Cyrenaica and then head east for Alexandria. He heard a telephone buzz in the front of the bridge: Rocky Pratt began to back out of the chart alcove but PO Whiffen was there ahead of him, snatching the phone off its hook.

"Repeat that last bit?"

Whiffen had edged into his own hooded table's light, with the phone at his ear, reaching inside the canvas flap to scribble on a signal pad.

Nick, watching *Blackfoot's* wake, called down, "Port fifteen."

"Port fifteen, sir!"

Whiffen called, "Signal from D.37 to C-in-C, sir, reporting convoy and escorts destroyed, flotilla withdrawing north-eastward. Then reply, C-in-C to D.37: *Well done. Proceed to rendezvous with First Battle Squadron noon May 1 in position 180 Cape Littino 25.* Time of Origin—"

"All right, Yeoman."

Cape Littino was on the south coast of Crete, about halfway along.

"Fifteen of port wheel on, sir!"

Watching the turn, Nick thought about that signal—which would have been received in cipher and translated into plain language in the plot, one level below this bridge and adjoining the signals office, by young Chalk, the RNVR sub-lieutenant . . . "Midships." He straightened again: "How is a course of oh-four-oh for that rendezvous position, Pilot?" Ducking back to the pipe: "Meet her!"

"Meet her, sir!"

"Follow *Blackfoot.*"

Pratt answered that last question: "Need to come round to about oh-six-four when we're round the bulge, sir."

"Distance?"

"Two-eighty miles, sir."

With about ten hours in hand, it would mean making a good 28 knots all the way. Hard on fuel consumption; but they'd be able to replenish from the big ships when they reached them—or from the oiler in Suda Bay, if it had got there, replacing the one that had been sunk a few days ago . . . First Battle Squadron consisted of the battleships *Barham* and *Valiant* with the aircraft carrier *Formidable* and a bunch of escorting destroyers, all under Rear-Admiral Rawlings. They were up there first to provide cover for a big convoy that was being run from Suda Bay to Alexandria, and then to support, in case of interference by Italian surface ships, the last three lifts of troops from Greece.

"From Captain (D), sir: *Speed three zero, executive.*"

He called down, "Three-one-zero revolutions." Then he asked Pratt, "Remind me, Pilot, would you—there's the Suda convoy going to Alex, but what are the three Greek pick-ups?"

"Well, *Hotspur* and *Havock* are collecting a load from Milos, sir, and *Hero* with *Isis* and *Kimberley* are fetching some from Kalamata. The other's—well, you know, *Carnarvon* and—"

"Yes. Thank you." He certainly did know about *Carnarvon*'s trip. She was a light AA cruiser and a new arrival on this station, up through Suez from the Red Sea, and his own young half-brother, Jack Everard, was serving in her. Being fresh, in good order compared to most of the Mediterranean ships, she and the destroyers *Highflier* and *Halberdier* had been given the trickiest of the final troop-lifting jobs to do: right up at Nauplia, where the last lift was supposed to have been the one two nights ago, to bring out a rearguard battalion of New Zealanders.

Dalgleish murmured, "We aren't looking for swimmers, I don't think."

"No. Sorry, Number One." He'd forgotten he'd told him to wait. And leaving men in the water wasn't a *happy* necessity: it just did happen to be a necessity sometimes. At least one didn't turn machine-guns on them, as the Luftwaffe did. He told his first lieutenant, "Soon as we're off the coast a bit, one watch can get their heads down. Say in half an hour." They'd sleep at their action stations, while the other half of the ship's company stayed awake.

Dalgleish said, "I'll have the galley organize some hot soup meanwhile."

"Splendid. And don't forget the bridge."

Dalgleish cleared his throat. "What they all need really, sir, is a night or two in harbour."

That throat-clearance was a habit of his first lieutenant's, Nick had noticed, before advancing an opinion. But what he'd said then was more a statement of fact than an opinion: in the last seven weeks they'd had— what, three nights in harbour? It wasn't anything that anyone could help: the fleet had been at full stretch even before the Greek adventure started . . . He breathed cold air, taking deep breaths of it to freshen mind as well as body. The wind was almost on the beam, not enough of it to make the sea more than choppy, but at 30 knots it was bringing bursts of spray that swept across the foc's'l, slashed and drummed against the for'ard gunshields and the forefront of the bridge. *Blackfoot* was still easy enough to see, with the mound of wake bright under her counter, but the moon had hidden itself behind thickening cloud. A bit of cloud-cover for tomorrow, for those last trips out of the Aegean, might be worth praying for.

He didn't want to keep thinking about *Carnarvon*—or rather, about Jack. For a mixture of reasons, some of them old, private history, and some he couldn't easily have explained even to himself, he'd have preferred to have had the boy anywhere but on this station.

Jack Everard—lieutenant, Royal Navy—had just checked his anchor-bearings on *Carnarvon's* softly-lit gyro repeater. The cruiser's captain, Howard Napier, lowered the binoculars through which he'd been staring at the Dutch ship, the *Gelderland*. Napier was a tall man, about Jack's own height, and slim, wide-shouldered: normally rather quiet-spoken, easy-mannered, he was fidgety now with impatience.

"Might send someone over there, sir?" Bell-Reid, Napier's second-in-command, suggested it. Talking about the *Gelderland,* the transport, and exasperated at the unexplained, inexcusable delay . . .

Napier put his glasses up again: "What the *bloody* hell's the matter with him?"

The Dutch ship hadn't moved or even begun to prepare to move: one of her lifeboats was still in the water—you could see the falls dangling there, on her quarter—and there'd been no activity at all on her foc'sl, at the anchor gear. Napier had twice signalled to her captain to weigh anchor: the signals had been acknowledged but nothing had happened. *Carnarvon's* own boats were hoisted, her messdecks were full of New Zealanders—most of whom had simply collapsed and fallen asleep, still in tin hats and boots and with the packs strapped on their backs— and the three destroyers had already weighed and moved out south-eastward to wait a mile or two down the gulf.

It was vital to get out of the Stukas' backyard before daylight, at least to get far enough south to have some hope of air cover from the RAF in Crete. *Gelderland's* best speed was 16 knots, 17 if they sat on all the safety-valves and prayed: so there'd be seven hours' steaming from here to the Kithera Channel. If they started now, this minute, they'd be there at about 1030. With Morning Civil Twilight coming at 0528 you could reckon on broad daylight well before 6:00, so even now it would be a miracle if they didn't get *some* attention from the Luftwaffe.

Jack Everard told himself, *We might not. They might not find us . . .* He checked the time: 3:25. At the same moment Napier swung round, lowering his binoculars.

"Very well. Everard—go over to the Dutchman and give him my direct order to pull his anchor up and sail immediately." He looked at the commander: "Which boat, John?"

"Motorboat's still turned out port side, sir." Bell-Reid raised his voice: "Bosun's Mate, call away the second motorboat!"

"Take whatever action's necessary, Everard. Just get him moving."

"Aye aye, sir!" He was already on his way, rattling down the steel ladder. Two more ladders after that one: skimming down them at a speed that came with long practice, hearing the shrill pipe and the wailing cry, "Aw-a-ay second motorboat's crew! Aw-a-ay second motorboat's crew!" It was abreast the foremost funnel, just abaft the bridge superstructure, and as he burst out of the screen door Jack saw the boat's coxswain and three crewmen there ahead of him, already climbing up into the boat where it hung in its out-turned davits.

Tom Overton, the cruiser's first lieutenant, arrived at the same moment from the foc's'l where he'd have been standing by with his cable party, ready to weigh anchor; he was mustering the lowerers, one leading hand and two seamen to each fall. Climbing up into the boat, Jack heard Overton's order, "Turns for lowering!" Bell-Reid was bawling down at him from the after end of the signal bridge, telling him to get a move on; Overton called back patiently, "Aye aye, sir!" and added in a quieter tone, "Start the falls." In the boat's stern-sheets Jack felt the jerky start, the boat dropping a few inches; then the next order, "Lower away," sent them down fast towards the sea. The motorboat's coxswain, a leading seaman, asked him where they were going; Jack told him, "To the Dutchman. Find out why he hasn't pulled his hook up."

Then they were in the water and the engine puttered into life, with Overton's shout of "Light-to!" up above their heads and down here the bowman and stern-sheetman hauling at the falls to get some slack so they could unhook the boat. He told the coxswain, "Near side of her, long as there's a ladder. Fast as you like."

Several hours of Stukas, he thought. It would be his baptism of dive-bombing. Even to himself he was unwilling to admit that the prospect did, truly, chill him.

There was a first time for everyone, of course, and it was the time you dreaded most. Brother Nick had told him, *Not so bad once it starts . . .* Well, he'd heard the same line from other people too: but Brother Nick acting big-brotherly, acting kind, for God's sake!

"There's plenty of ladders there, sir. 'Alf a dozen of 'em!"

Ladders the Dutch had put over for embarking New Zealanders, who'd been brought off from the open beach in lifeboats and naval whalers in tow of motorboats: the harbour was blocked by the wreck of the assault ship *Ulster Prince,* who'd grounded during a previous night's lift and then, at daylight, become a sitting target for the Stukas. How would Nick handle *this* job? Jack wondered. He'd be sure of himself, he'd know instinctively how to take command . . . Jack told the coxswain, pointing, "That one." It dangled below the *Gelderland's* bridge, a long chain-sides ladder with flat wooden rungs, reaching to the water. He heard a voice raised, on deck above him somewhere, then a flicker of torchlight grew into a beam directed vertically down the ladder as the boat slid up to it.

"Wait alongside, Cox'n." The ladder was an awkward thing to climb. But it would have been worse for the soldiers, weighed down with packs and weapons and just about dropping from exhaustion. The Germans were only a few miles behind them, they'd said.

"Is your captain on the bridge?"

An elderly seaman in a blue jersey, the man with the torch, had tried to help him over the rail. As if he thought a twenty-two-year-old RN lieutenant might be some kind of cripple. He'd got into the habit, perhaps, dragging pongoes aboard earlier on.

"Kapitein?"

"Yes. On bridge?"

The man didn't look too bright. Jack went inside the superstructure, pushing through a double flap of blackout canvas: the sailor gabbled something, following him in, and one word stood out.

"In his cabin?"

"Ja. I show." In his quarters, when his ship was supposed to be getting under way? The sailor had passed him and he was banging on a polished hardwood door: he'd opened it, and stepped aside.

Now, Jack thought. Act like Nick might . . . "Captain?"

A squat, pale-skinned man with a close-shorn grey head: *Gelderland's* captain wore white flannels and a food-stained reefer jacket. Jack had a fleeting memory of the Royal Naval College at Dartmouth, the daily working rig: except that if a cadet had appeared in flannels even half that dirty he'd have been flogged.

"I am Kapitein. Anton Beukenkamp. What you want?"

"You're to weigh anchor and sail, Captain. *Now.* We've signalled you twice. What's—"

"I wait." Beukenkamp had tobacco-juice stains running from the corners of his mouth, a left eye that wandered, and he was so short and broad he made Jack feel like a flagpole. "Little while, must wait. Peoples coming—from shore, peoples . . ."

"My captain"—Jack pointed in the direction of *Carnarvon's* berth— "the force commander, Captain Napier, orders you to weigh immediately. Otherwise—"

"No, mister, please!"

A woman in a red dress: long, greasy black hair and swarthy skin: she'd emerged from what must have been the sleeping-cabin. Beukenkamp muttered defensively, "This lady—her peoples—her brother and uncle and also—"

"You've been waiting for—for *this lady's* family?"

"I have boat inshore, you see." Incredibly, the man was trying to smile about it. "Coming very soon now, I think."

It was unbelievable. Thousands of lives, several ships, the whole operation . . . The gypsy woman was jabbering in what sounded like Greek. Jack cut across the babble to tell the captain, "Sail now, this minute. Otherwise we put the lady ashore, put you under arrest, and take over your ship. D'you want to be shot, Captain? Because if you don't move now—"

"My boat . . ."

"You'll have to leave it."

"But—I *ask* you . . ."

"Give the order, Captain!"

He made sure it was actually happening: that Beukenkamp was on his bridge, main engines rung-on, capstan turning on the foc's'l. Then he went down into the boat and waited, lying-off, until he saw the Dutchman's anchor break clear of the surface streaming mud, and then a swirl of movement at the stern as his screws began to turn.

"Back to the ship, Cox'n."

In *Carnarvon's* bridge, he told his CO what had been going on. Napier said, "When we get back to Alex, I'll see if I can't have him shot."

"I did mention it as a possibility, sir." He thought, *If* we get back to Alex . . . You could hear the cruiser's cable clanking up, and smell the stench of the mud that it was shedding as it rose.

Napier added, "You did a good job, Everard. Never mind his boat's crew—they're on *his* conscience . . . Why, look at that!"

Some kind of flare-up—and now the thump of an explosion—a few miles inland, to the north. There was a spreading glow with a halo to it, diffuse and orange-tinted. Fading now . . . Bell-Reid suggested, "Probably the railway junction. One of the pongoes did say they'd mined it."

It was ten minutes to four. It would be daylight by, say, 0550. Two hours, at perhaps a little better than 16 knots; they'd have covered at the most 35 miles before the bombing started. More than that if the Luftwaffe didn't find them at first light, of course; but luck of that sort wasn't anything to count on.

Jack went to the chart. He was acting as navigator now. He'd been appointed to this ship as an ordinary watchkeeper, but the navigator had been landed in Aden suffering from stomach ulcers and Napier had shuffled the jobs around. He was keen to get the same navigator back when the ulcers were cleared up, and if he'd had a new man appointed he'd have made that impossible. Jack let down the canvas flap behind him, leant over the chart and switched on the inside light, marked the EP, estimated position, 35 miles down the pencil track. He saw they'd be just about on latitude 37 north: which to all intents and purposes was beyond the range of any RAF or Fleet Air Arm support. Even if there were any on *36* north, which wasn't by any means a certainty.

He switched off the light and backed out. There was a yell from Tom Overton down on the foc's'l, and the commander, who was looking down over the front of the bridge, reported, "Clear anchor, sir."

"Half ahead together. Port twenty."

Following astern of the *Gelderland*. Time—he checked it, took a reading of the log and entered both figures in his notebook—was 0358. One hour later than it should have been.

• • •

"Morning, sir."

"Morning, Pilot. All well?"

"No problems, sir."

Rocky Pratt, his navigator, had the watch. A former P&O Line deck officer, Pratt was short and stocky, and gnome-like now with the hood of his duffel pulled up. It was cold enough to need it, in this pre-dawn hour: *too* cold, Nick thought, for the first day of May. Wind was still from the north-west, which meant that with the ship on a course of 063 it was slightly abaft the beam, and *Tuareg* was rolling as she thrashed along in *Blackfoot's* wake. He'd slept, in his fold-away canvas bridge chair, from 3:30 to just after 5:00; hoisting himself on to the high seat now and feeling like something recently disinterred, he almost wished he hadn't. You had to get some rest when there was a chance to, though, or you'd be at half-cock when you needed to be wide awake: so he'd dozed somewhat uneasily with the Cyrenaican land-bulge only fifteen to twenty miles away to starboard, and now as dawn approached he was fit—or would be, in a minute—to cope with whatever daylight might bring. There were airstrips, for instance, on that desert coastline, and the aircraft on them now were German, whereas the RAF had a total of 21 serviceable Hurricanes in the whole of the Western Desert and there was an army as well as a fleet needing air support.

Even Norway hadn't taught the powers in London that ships couldn't operate for long under skies dominated by the enemy. Until the Norwegian fiasco nobody had really thought about it: which was partly why most destroyers' guns—*Tuareg's* included—could only elevate to forty degrees. Fat lot of use that was, against bombers diving almost vertically. Luckily these Tribals had multiple pompoms as well, which was *something* to ward off Stukas with: and when the opportunity occurred there was an intention of replacing the twin four-sevens at "X" position with a four-inch high-angle mounting. But many of the older ships— of the H-class, for instance—had nothing but point-five machine-guns for close-range protection. That was all he, Nick Everard, had had in *Intent,* in the Namsos fjords when he'd been trapped there with the

Germans invading Norway and his ship crippled, immobilized: if the dive-bombers had found her she'd have been there still, as scrap-iron. He'd been lucky, though, he'd been able to bring her out and do some worthwhile damage to the enemy en route. Then, back in England, he'd been hauled over the coals because in an earlier action he hadn't prevented another destroyer committing harakiri.

When he'd first got back, there'd been congratulations and applause. The Press had made an overnight hero of him: so much so that the new Prime Minister had expressed a wish to have Commander Everard brought before him. It was at this interview that Nick's troubles must have started. Winston had remarked that it was saddening to see a campaign which had opened with such an impressive performance by the Navy going so dismally now on land; Nick had agreed, adding that the soldiers, sent in so late and so ill-equipped and unsupported against the Luftwaffe, really hadn't ever had a dog's chance. It so happened that he had a great admiration for General Carton de Wiart, VC, and he'd spoken as much as anything out of respect for him; he'd also been speaking the plain truth, but forgetting that the Prime Minister in his former role of First Lord of the Admiralty and as a member of Chamberlain's cabinet had been closely concerned with the mounting of the Norwegian expedition.

At the time, all he got was a cold stare. But 24 hours later he was facing an inquisition in the Admiralty. It wasn't an "official" inquiry: it started with "Look here, Everard, we need your help. There've been some questions asked, and we have to produce some answers . . ."

So he was still a commander. He'd hoped, after the Norwegian success, to have won a fourth stripe and a flotilla, to make up the leeway he'd lost by retiring from the Navy in 1930. He'd spent eight years "outside," and now he was back in the rank he'd reached in 1926, just before his thirtieth birthday.

All right—so he'd been an idiot . . .

Eastward, there was a silvery streak on the horizon and, above it, a faintly lighter section of sky. No cloud: last night's hope of cloud-cover for today had been wishful thinking. He swung round to see what was happening in the bridge behind him: he'd been lost in his thoughts, searching the horizon with his glasses but seeing and hearing nothing close at hand. Houston, the gunnery control officer, touched his cap.

"Morning, sir."

"Morning, Harry."

Houston was an RNVR lieutenant. He was of medium height, like Nick himself, but corpulent. Nick was broad, strongly built, but Harry Houston was fat: if he put on any more weight, Dalgleish had warned him recently, they might have to get rid of him because he wouldn't be able to shoe-horn himself into the director tower. He was going aft now, to the ladder that led up to it. Ashcourt, the RN sub-lieutenant, was yawning over the torpedo control panel. He was tall and slim, willowy; if he'd been dark instead of fair he'd have been rather a Jack Everard type, Nick thought. Yeoman Whiffen was in the port after corner of the bridge, lecturing the young signalman of the watch. And now Tony Dalgleish, the first lieutenant, hoisted himself off the up-ladder into the bridge's after end and came for'ard, nodding to Rocky Pratt who was at the binnacle. Dalgleish stopped beside his captain.

"Morning, sir. Darned cold."

"Be less so, Number One, if you had a coat on."

"Oh, soon warm up." Dalgleish was wearing a polo-neck sweater under his reefer jacket. He reached to the alarm buzzer, held his thumb ready over it. "Close the hands up, sir?"

"Yes, please."

The noise of the alarm was muted up here, but a harsh, sleep-penetrating racket down in the messdecks. Dalgleish kept it going in short sharp bursts for about half a minute. Then he turned away. "I'll go on down, sir."

"Make sure they know this isn't just routine. There's an airfield at Benghazi, and we stirred things up last night."

"Aye aye, sir."

Ashcourt was testing his communications with Mr Walsh, the gunner

(T), whose action station was at his torpedo tubes aft, and from the director tower Houston would be lining up his sights with the receivers at each of the four, twin, four-seven gun-mountings. He'd be checking his connections with the TS too, the transmitting station two decks down and below "B" gun; and higher than Houston's steel box up there, above his head and a bit aft, Petty Officer Wellbeloved and Able Seaman Sitwell would have settled into the combined rangefinder and HA director; they'd be testing their circuits too.

Reports were coming in now. Main armament closed up and cleared away, circuits tested. Torpedo tubes and depthcharge crews closed up, communications tested. Close-range weapons closed up . . . Dalgleish would be moving round the ship, seeing that men on the upper deck were wearing their anti-flash gear, lifebelts, and tin hats, and that everyone was alert and ready, wide awake. Nick reached for his own helmet and put it on. Light was flushing up that eastern sky, greying upward from an horizon which in that quarter—on the starboard bow—could just be made out now with the naked eye. Light growing steadily: you could see the sky's greyness reflected on the sea now, on that bow. This was the period when light was confusing and attack most likely, and when the range of visibility suddenly expanded so that an enemy who hadn't seemed to have been there one minute might be in gun-range the next. Nick, Pratt, and Ashcourt all had binoculars up, searching sea and sky: farther aft the look-outs, two men on each side in the bays where the eighteen-inch searchlights stood like huge, closed eyes, were dark, tin-hatted silhouettes slowly turning as each swept his own ninety-degree sector through high-powered glasses. And overhead the director tower trained slowly round, like the head of some animal wary of its surroundings.

In London, it would be dark for another hour or more. He wondered if the bombers had been over again: nights were London's *bad* time, while here they provided intervals of near-safety. He hoped Fiona was all right. *Please, God* . . . Here, light would come rapidly, in a minute: and it would be exactly like this two hundred miles away in the Aegean, where *Carnarvon* must be hurrying her convoy down from Nauplia. There, too, the curtain would be going up on a new Stuka-infested day.

CHAPTER TWO
· · ·

In Carnarvon*'s bridge* McCowan, the gunnery lieutenant, banged a telephone back on to its hook and told Captain Napier, "All quarters closed up and cleared away, sir." McCowan was a thin, bony-faced man in his middle twenties, with deepset eyes and wiry black hair; he was a Scot but he didn't sound like one. Ahead of the cruiser the Dutch transport lumbered stolidly south south-eastward, following *Halberdier* and with the other two destroyers, *Huntress* and *Highflier,* on her bow and beam to port. The mainland of Greece was a humpy grey division, touched by early daylight now, between sea and sky to starboard; a quarter of an hour ago, when Cape Turkoviglia had been abeam, the convoy's distance offshore had been as little as three thousand yards. It was twice that now, but the closeness of land was Napier's reason for having kept his destroyers only ahead and on the seaward side; by hugging the coast he was making the trip as short as possible, and as soon as it was fully light he'd be shifting the escorts into a more regular formation.

Pretty soon now, in fact. It was already almost day. They were well out of the Gulf of Nauplia but for another hour that land would be close to starboard.

"I'll go up, sir." Up to the ADP, McCowan meant. The letters stood for Air Defence Position; it was the partly enclosed platform up on the tripod foremast above the bridge, with the rangefinder-director above that. When *Carnarvon* had been launched in 1918 as an ordinary light cruiser the ADP had been known as the Spotting Top, but in an extensive refit from 1939 into 1940 she'd been re-equipped as an AA cruiser, with high-angle four-inch guns and a whole lot of modern fire-control devices in that ADP.

It was light enough now for Jack Everard to be able to see *Gelderland* easily without glasses, and *Highflier* and *Huntress* as silhouettes against the flush of dawn. The wind was a light breeze on the starboard quarter, but here in the land's shelter the sea was flat with that dawn shine on it: it was going to be a beautiful, classic Aegean day. Bell-Reid must have had the same thought: he murmured with binoculars at his eyes, "Splendid flying weather. Wonder if they'd let me change sides."

"You'd make a rotten Nazi . . . Pilot, what's that?"

Napier was pointing at a white lighthouse on a minor headland. About a minute ago Jack had been studying the chart, memorizing landmarks, and he was able to trot out the answer: "It's a light called Aspro Kortia, sir."

"Sounds like something for a headache."

"The inlet to the south of it is Port Kyparisi."

Bell-Reid snorted—derisively, perhaps—a comment on a young man showing off, offering more information than had been asked for. Bell-Reid was a caustic and impatient man, entirely different from the quiet, easygoing Howard Napier, whose last pre-war post had been as naval attaché in an embassy.

Irvine, a bearded RNR lieutenant who was action officer of the watch, was at the binnacle. Jack Everard lingered near the chart table; as navigator his duties were divided between bridge and plot. Napier—perched up on his bridge chair—and Bell-Reid and the midshipman of the watch, Brighouse, all had their glasses up, probing the circle of visibility as it expanded. Elsewhere in the bridge were the chief yeoman of signals, a leading signalman and a bridge messenger; right aft at the base of the tripod mast which formed a circular steel shelter housing the Tannoy broadcast equipment, a very young Royal Marine bugler conversed in whispers with the commander's "doggie"—an ordinary seaman by the name of Webster—while behind them, leaning against the shelter, loomed the bow-legged figure of Able Seaman Noble, the captain's servant.

Jack took his eyes off the Dutch ship and glanced again at the coastline. It was a bleak, barren-looking landscape. Within days it would be overrun by Germans. To port, the sea was like a mirror throwing light into the sky: the stars had vanished and there was a loom of brilliance from just over the horizon. An empty, cloudless sky, half-lit: the question in all their minds was how long it would *stay* empty.

"Chief Yeoman!"

"Sir!"

CPO Hegarty came forward: he was a smallish man with a flat, sharp chin like a paint-scraper. Napier told him, "Hoist: *Destroyers form close screen round convoy.*"

"Aye aye, sir!" Hegarty went aft, yelling down to his men on the flagdeck, one level below the bridge, for the flags he wanted to have bent on, then leaning over the back end of the bridge and watching to see each one whipped out of its pigeon-hole in the big, grey-painted locker. The signalmen could tell from the toggle-fittings on each flag which was the top or bottom of it . . .

"Hoist!" The string of bunting ran up swiftly, led by the yellow-blue-yellow of the destroyer flag, and the destroyers' red-and-white answering pendants shot up in acknowledgement within seconds, pausing momentarily at the dip and then rushing close-up to the yardarms, signifying "signal understood." Napier called, "Executive please, Chief Yeoman," and Hegarty roared, "Haul down!" The hoist tumbled, to be gathered in on the flagdeck and the flags restowed in their slots. *Highflier* and *Huntress* were on the move at once, *Highflier* increasing speed and angling inwards to close up on the Dutch ship's port beam, *Huntress* also cracking on more revs and at the same time going over to starboard, heeling to the turn, passing ahead of the Dutchman and astern of *Halberdier* in order to take station on the landward side.

To all intents and purposes it was day now. That eastern glow had acquired a hard, hot centre growing upwards out of a strip of sea so bright you couldn't look straight at it without being blinded.

Bell-Reid asked Napier, "Might send one watch to breakfast, sir?"

Napier didn't answer immediately. He'd lowered his binoculars and he was looking around, swinging his high chair around as he examined the sky astern and on the quarters.

"Yes." He nodded to the commander. "And get 'em up again and the others down there as fast as it can be done. You go down too, John; I'll have mine up here." He glanced at Jack. "And you, Everard. Don't take longer than you need."

On his way down, Jack met Overton, the first lieutenant, coming up to take over from Willie Irvine as OOW. Tom Overton's action job was damage-control, below decks, and on this trip he was also responsible for looking after the army passengers. He smiled amiably at Jack: "Nice quiet morning, eh?"

Quite a pleasant old goof . . .

The breakfast on offer consisted of cornflakes, scrambled eggs made of egg-powder, and toast and marmalade; in the interests of speed he decided to do without cornflakes. The wardroom was littered with bed-rolls, and some of them still contained slumbering New Zealanders. Jack sat down opposite Bell-Reid, who was chatting over his shoulder to a major with a bandaged head.

"Steward'll give you chaps some breakfast in half an hour or so. We have to be rude and eat first so we can be ready to receive the Luftwaffe."

"Don't worry about us, Commander." The major put a hand to his lightly bearded jaw. "Might even get to shave before I eat."

"Use my cabin. The steward can show you where it is, and you'll find all you need there . . . Here, come and sit, have some coffee to go on with. Jenkins!"

"Coming sir." The steward was at the hatch at the end of the long, rather narrow wardroom. There was a sideboard under the hatch, connecting to the pantry. Bell-Reid told the soldier as he pulled a chair out, "Leading Steward Jenkins will attend to all your wants. He'll be single-handed once we're closed up, because we need the others else-where, but just tell him what you want. Right, Jenkins?"

"Do me best, sir." He was a large, happy-looking man; he told Jack over Bell-Reid's head, "Your eggs is coming, sir."

"Good. Make it snappy, please." He nodded to the soldier. "How d'you do, sir. I'm Everard."

"Our navigating officer." Bell-Reid told Jack, "This is Major Haskins, OC troops."

"Glad to know you, Everard. Reckon to find the way home, do you?"

"Oh, with a bit of luck . . ."

"No fooling." Melhuish, the surgeon commander, flopped into a nearby chair. A boozy-looking man with greying hair. "Luck's the word for it. He spins a coin, then we bounce our way off the headlands. I've just been up for a breather, and we're practically on the bloody beach." He looked at Jack. "Didn't know that, did you?"

"You don't mean there's land in sight?"

They all laughed—except for Bell-Reid, who only raised an eyebrow. Robson, a lieutenant-commander and electrical specialist, asked Melhuish, "How are your patients doing?"

He meant the military wounded. Melhuish told him, "All respond-ing nicely, touch wood."

Jack had his eggs now. The powdered stuff had seemed uneatable when it had first appeared, but you got used to it: surprising what you *could* get used to. Including, he wondered, Stukas? He asked Major Haskins, "Must have been pretty awful, the last few days?"

"Well." The New Zealander sipped at his coffee. "I'll admit there've been happier times."

"On the Corinth Canal, we heard—"

"Christ, *that.*" He shook his bandaged head. It was like a turban only with short hair bristling from the top of it. "That was *something.*"

A very large, younger man, a captain with one arm in a sling, came and stood behind him and took over the answering as Haskins seemed to dry up. The newcomer told Jack, "They sent 88s over first to draw

our ack-ack so they could spot the batteries. Then Stukas came after to
dive-bomb the guns first and then our positions, fifty or sixty bloody
Stukas routing around like mad dogs and I'd say maybe a hundred
Messerschmitts strafing anything that moved. It just went on and on like
that. I tell you it was plain *unbelievable,* and when they had us about
cooked, the gliders and paratroops came over and went down behind
us." He turned away. "Damn right it was something. Something like I
hope to God I never—"

The action-alarm bell silenced that single voice. The bell was ringing short-long, short-long, as for aircraft alarm, action stations.

Jack was getting out through the doorway and the bell was still
sounding off when the four-inch guns opened fire overhead: the noise
of them, down here inside the ship, was something you felt as well as
heard, as if it jarred the bone of your skull. Like an incredibly violent
impact of iron on iron: solid, ringing. But he was up the ladder now
and out of the screen door, turning for'ard, hearing a burst of fire from
the multiple pompoms at the other end of the ship as he ran that way:
the four-inch fired again and he felt the blast from the midships mounting as he passed below it. Up the ladder at the foc's'l break, level with
the second funnel and between the whaler and the starboard motorboat,
then in the door to the bridge superstructure, taking the ladder several
steps at a time, racing up towards whatever . . .

The guns had ceased fire. He was in the bridge, and he could see no
aircraft anywhere. Napier told Bell-Reid, who'd arrived a few yards
behind, "One Messerschmitt—a 110, the twin-engined kind. It came out
of the sun"—he pointed—"and we didn't see it in time to get a barrage going. It aimed two bombs at *Gelderland* and missed by fifty yards
or more."

Bell-Reid, panting from the fast hundred-yard run, leant against the
side of the bridge, shielding his eyes and staring towards the sun. AB
Noble came lurching from the ladder, bringing a tray with the captain's
breakfast on it.

"Sorry I got 'eld up, sir. Trouble was—"

"Doesn't matter, Noble." Napier told Bell-Reid, "We'll stay closed up now. Action messing henceforth."

Jack was checking the ship's position by land bearings, and Irvine was saying to Overton, "I've got the weight, sir. Many thanks for my breakfast."

"My dear boy." Overton stepped down from the binnacle platform, the slightly raised bit in the centre of the bridge. He was a lieutenant-commander but before the war he'd twice been passed over for promotion, and he was older than Bell-Reid. His only burning enthusiasm was for golf.

Course 159: revs for 16.5 knots. Halberdier, the leading destroyer, was in sight to the left of the Dutchman, who must have swung off course during that surprise attack. There was nothing for *Carnarvon* to do about it: *Gelderland* was the one out of station and it was up to Anton Beukenkamp to get back into it. One might imagine that the Messerschmitt's visit would at least have got him out of bed?

Glancing round, Jack saw the snotty, Brighouse, leaning against the starboard searchlight sight and picking his teeth with a matchstick. Brighouse was an untidy, rather hairy little lad, with small sharp eyes and an insolent manner, and Jack wondered whether brother Nick might not have been something like Brighouse when he'd been a snotty. According to Nick's own stories he'd been constantly in trouble—disciplinary trouble—in his early years at sea. It would certainly delight this little brute, Jack thought, to be told he might have anything in common with a brass-hat baronet who had a DSO and two DSCs . . .

Coming up from Suda Bay they'd had air cover—Fulmars—until dusk, and until dusk they'd steered a course well away from the Nauplia direction, so as to mislead the enemy in case one of his recce flights did get past the Fulmars and see the ships. The point of an air escort was more to keep the Hun reconnaissance flights away than to shoot down attackers *after* you'd been spotted.

But the Luftwaffe would know where they were *now,* all right.

Napier was in his bridge chair; he was munching his breakfast, but his eyes were on the sky. Bell-Reid was leaning against the port side of the bridge, thumbing tobacco into his pipe. Jack checked the time: it was 6:58.

"All guns follow ADP!"

There was a loudspeaker in the bridge so that Napier could hear what Jock McCowan's team up on the foremast were saying to the guns. He could have it switched on or off, loud or quiet, and when he wanted to he could chip in on his own sound-powered telephone line to McCowan. But the voice from the speaker had been that of Paymaster Lieutenant Clutterbuck, whom McCowan had trained to operate the HACS, high-angle control system. Clutterbuck had been telling the layers and trainers at the cruiser's four, twin four-inch guns to line up the pointers in their dials with the pointers which were controlled electrically from the sight in the ADP.

A red air-warning flag fluttered at *Carnarvon's* yardarm. Bell-Reid murmured, his glasses trained almost right into the sun, "Twelve of 'em. Four flights of three. About six thousand feet."

Twin-engined, black against the sky, and with the sun behind and under them: Junkers 88s. Clutterbuck would have a chance to go through the HACS drill this time. The system involved the feeding of information such as height, range, course, speed, and angle-of-sight to a machine down below called a Fuse Keeping Clock, which then provided the guns with fuse-settings and aim-off, but it wasn't often of much use because attacks tended to be made in a less orderly way: aircraft jinked, dived, dodged about. There was a type 285 RDF set up there as part of the system, but it was no good for anything but ranging; you had to see your target and then point the aerial at it. It was mounted on the director above the ADP platform and it looked like three broomsticks with small cross-pieces all down their length.

"Open fire!"

Highflier had opened up with her four-sevens at that moment. Some of the H class—including *Huntress*—had been fitted with three-inch AA

guns in place of their after tubes, but this one hadn't. The low-angle
four-sevens could really engage only approaching aircraft, or put a barrage over other ships. Now *Carnarvon's* high-angle four-inch opened fire,
brown smoke and cordite fumes blowing back from "A" gun, down
for'ard; the Ju88s seemed to be rising across the sky as they came over
on a straight course towards the ships. Shell-bursts were opening below
them and to the right. You saw the smoke-puffs appear and only afterwards, if surrounding noise permitted, you heard the thudding sounds
of the bursts: by which time there were a lot more of them, all the ships
shooting fast now, the sky a mass of shell-bursts and the bombers not
wavering at all, coming on and rising into the littered sky-bowl overhead. The first flight of three had gone into shallow dives—going for
Gelderland, the biggest and most obvious target for their bombs.

"Pompom open fire!"

Noise-level leapt as the multiple pompom, eight-barrelled, added its
fast thump-thump-thumping to the general din. It was immediately
below and in front of the bridge, where in former days the old cruiser
had had her "B" gun-mounting. The destroyers were shooting at the
succeeding flights of bombers, the ones still coming in behind this first
bunch, but *Carnarvon's* guns were throwing a barrage over the Dutchman
and ahead of the three front-running Junkers, who seemed to be flying
straight into the mass of shell-bursts. Tracer was flaring up from
Gelderland's own close-range weapons; by the look of it, one Bofors and
several lighter machine-guns. You could see the black-cross markings on
the bombers' wings and the shine of the early sun on them, and then
the bombs falling away, a tight black rain of high-explosive slanting seaward, quite slow-moving it seemed when they first started but then
speeding—obeying, Jack mentally noted, the formula of 32-feet-per-
second, the acceleration due to gravity: hardly surprising that one lost
sight of them.

Paymaster Lieutenant Clutterbuck's even tones ordered
Carnarvon's four-inch to shift target and engage the second flight of
Junkers. Jack could visualize him up there with his pale face and bluish

jaw, pale eyes blinking surprisedly through his spectacles: he wondered if they steamed up—the spectacles—as they did when Clutterbuck drank pink gin. Either the Dutch ship had discovered she had reserves of speed or *Carnarvon* had slowed down: Irvine bent to the voicepipe and called down, "Up four revolutions," just as Napier turned to draw his attention to the increasing gap and three geysers of water—four—towered astern of the Dutchman, momentarily blotting him from sight. Another stick fell short, closer to *Highflier* than to *Gelderland,* and the rest were out ahead, a short avenue of waterspouts out on the transport's bow. Three more flights to come.

"'X' and 'Y' guns shift target, Messerschmitts green one-five-oh, blue barrage, *fire!*" Clutterbuck's voice sharp and urgent . . . The number three look-out on the starboard side had seen the new threat at the same time as the paymaster had given tongue: he was up on his feet, pointing and shouting, no words audible, only a mouth open in the middle of ginger beard. They were fighter-bombers, 110s, slanting in low, curving over towards *Carnarvon.* The starboard point-fives were letting rip, tracer streaming out on the quarter and seeming to curve away behind the oncoming planes: Bell-Reid had rushed to the back of the bridge to tell that look-out to get down—he was bawling now at everyone to take cover—*down!* There wasn't really any cover but you could duck, throw yourself flat in the stupendous noise as the Germans tore over with their guns flaming, hammering, sparks flying from the side of the bridge and torn steel where a nest of voicepipes had been smashed.

Everyone was getting up now: but Napier had never left his seat. Clutterbuck's voice was cool, back to normal as he told "X" and "Y" to follow ADP. Bomb-splashes were lifting in quick succession beyond the Dutch ship. The Messerschmitts had flown over *Huntress,* raking her with machine-gun fire as they crossed and then banked the other way to swing left, swooping upwards with the land behind them: bombs were falling from the third flight of Ju88s, and *Carnarvon's* four-inch were shifting to engage the last flight as it approached. And one Messerschmitt had been hit: there'd been a burst beside it as it turned, and the end of the raised wing disintegrated, the aircraft rolling over and going down, upside-down and falling sideways towards new bomb-splashes rising ahead of *Gelderland*—the Dutch ship was steaming into them, passing through them with salt water raining down across her. More bombs were falling close to *Halberdier.* A dozen things happening at once, and in all directions . . .

The Messerschmitt had gone into the sea: it must have been *Huntress,* he thought, who'd got that one: and she'd suffered, there was movement around her "B" gun, it looked like men had been hit and were being lowered from the gundeck. The gun was still in action, though. Napier called out, pointing, "*That'll* larn 'im!" He was pointing up at a Ju88 trailing smoke, losing height and diverging to starboard while his two companions held to their straight course. There were flames coming out of him now as well as smoke. Clutterbuck's voice came out of the speaker: "Check, check, check . . ." The other Messerschmitt had turned back over the land, climbing as it circled northward. Below *Carnarvon's* bridge the pompom gunners were cheering: that Junkers was in a dive, all flame and smoke, and it was going to crash in Greece, not in the sea. Either the pompom crew were just glad to see it, or they reckoned *they'd* hit it. Looking at his watch, Jack saw they'd been in action for six or seven minutes. It had felt more like half an hour: it was all one, now, a smear of violence wrapped in noise, but at the time each picture had been frozen in your mind as in a frame. It felt marvellous to have it over, threat and noise so suddenly removed: he felt an urge to laugh, chat . . .

Napier looked around at Bell-Reid and pointed up towards the ADP: he said, "They were beginning to get the hang of it."

Bell-Reid was inspecting the side of the bridge, the smashed voice-pipes to the plot, captain's sea-cabin and signals office. He glanced round at Napier and nodded, and Clutterbuck's voice came booming from the loudspeaker, "Alarm port! All guns follow ADP, red one-seven-oh, angle of sight two-oh, large formation of Ju87s, closing!"

Christ. Not a bloody *moment* . . . And Junkers 87s were Stukas. Jack thought, putting it to himself calmly, rationally, that his advisors had been

right, that there always *was* a first time, and the anticipation was probably worse than the actual experience. He told himself, There'll be *hours*
of this . . .

"Red barrage . . ."

Red was the long fuse-setting, blue the short one. There was a fuse-
setting machine at each gun and also a few shells with these pre-set
standard fuses, dabbed with coloured paint to make them easily recognizable, in the ready-use racks. *Highflier* had opened fire with her four-
sevens: and Jack had the attackers in his glasses. His first sight of Stukas:
a big group of them, squat and evil-looking. Like vampire bats, he
thought: not that he'd ever seen a vampire bat . . . They were splitting
up, some circling off one way and some the other, just one pair flying
straight towards the convoy, shell-bursts opening in front of them, brown-
ish puff-balls flowering in irregular batches and the Stukas racing in
through them and between them, ignoring them, bat-like and yellow-
nosed, beginning to weave now as the anti-aircraft barrage thickened:
some of the others who'd swung off to circle the ships at a safe distance
were turning in.

He looked over to the other side, saw it was happening there as well.
Huntress on that side was throwing a barrage ahead of the ones approaching from that landward side: the whole sky was already pock-marked
with shell-bursts and full of weaving, jinking bombers. Clutterbuck had
ordered a switch to blue barrage and *Carnarvon's* were bursting over the
Gelderland, roofing her with a layer of explosions through which no pilot
in his right mind would consider flying: but Jack saw the first two Stukas
suddenly tip over and go screaming down in steep dives towards the
Dutch ship, their sirens screaming through the racket of the guns, which
was now one continuous roar. There were more Stukas coming in from
starboard, pompoms and point-fives blazing at them, the Dutch close-
range guns all busy, *Huntress* making a violent course-alteration as a plane
dropped down at her like a plunging eagle. He saw bombs falling towards
the *Gelderland* and the first Stuka pulling away out of its dive, streaking
away to the right with the second one following some way behind it.

He hadn't seen that one's bomb go but it burst now, the sea erupting on the Dutch ship's bow so close it could as easily have hit as missed. Stukas everywhere you looked, weaving between bursts of shells and streams of tracer: one on fire spinning away to port and another diving over *Carnarvon,* coming down right on top of her and almost vertically. Napier shouted, "Port twenty-five!" and Irvine passed the order down the pipe to CPO Partridge: crouching with his beard touching the voicepipe's rim he watched the Stuka, seeing shells bursting all around it as it came rushing in that dead-straight dive with its angled wings and the undercarriage like a vulture's legs and claws: a bomb dropping from it was turning over and over with the sun's glitter on its fins, Irvine scowling up at it and Jack Everard guessing it was going to land in this bridge—and nothing anyone could do about it. The noise was enclosing, isolating; *Carnarvon* was swinging fast to port, heeling as her rudder dragged her round, and the bomb went into the sea off her starboard bow, a sheet of water leaping and the thud of the explosion like a hard kick in her belly. Napier shouted, "Bring us back on course!" Irvine called down, "Midships," and Partridge acknowledged the order, then confirmed, "Wheel's amidships, sir." Irvine told him, "Starboard twenty."

The destroyers were under helm too most of the time, but the barrage over the Dutch ship never slackened much. It was keeping the Stukas high, or high-ish, and the Dutchman's own close-range weapons were helping too, but another Stuka was diving on her now and higher up were two more just at this moment tilting their yellow noses down. Bell-Reid was talking into a telephone, getting reports from below about possible damage from those near-misses. Napier was on the phone to the ADP, conferring with Jock McCowan; bombs were splashing in astern of the Dutch ship, and one Stuka was careering away landward just a few feet above the water, passing so close to *Huntress* they could have thrown spuds at it. Another was coming down—*now*—on top of the Dutchman and one on *Carnarvon,* and *Highflier* was swinging hard a-starboard with a bomb-splash rising just ahead of her: he saw the muzzle-flashes of her for'ard four-sevens as she shifted target and began to put a barrage over *Carnarvon* to ward off this attacking Stuka. It was silvery-grey against bright smoke-stained sky, yellow-snouted, disgusting, screaming hate: Irvine was ready at the voicepipe, waiting for Napier's order, when a shell burst close to that yellow nose and the machine exploded, wiped out in mid-air in a spread of smoke-trails and debris. A Stuka was pulling out of its dive over *Gelderland,* its bomb on ·the way down, tracer arcing up to converge on the plane as it flattened and presented a broader and perhaps temporarily slower-moving target; *Huntress,* inside her station and very close to the Dutchman, was turning her point-fives on it. And that bomb had hit the *Gelderland* . . .

Port side aft: a burst of flame and smoke, and the Stuka was flying out of all that concentration of close-range weaponry, escaping landward. There was another one too, going for her now, approaching in a shallower dive from the other quarter, astern of *Huntress.* The Dutch ship was still plugging on and seemed not to have slackened speed. Clutterbuck had directed *Carnarvon's* two after four-inch to go for the shallow-diving Stuka, and Napier had come to the binnacle himself: he called down, "Port twenty-five!" He was staying there: Irvine had moved over, off the step. The pompoms were roaring away at a new one coming in from the port bow, diving steeply across *Highflier,* screaming down with its sights obviously on the cruiser's bridge. The for'ard and midships four-inch were pumping a barrage into the sky right in front of that yellow nose: for a moment you couldn't see it for shell-bursts, but then it was in sight again and still diving on its target—*this* target. Napier called down, "Midships and meet her!" His object was to steady her on a course directly towards the diving bomber: if its pilot was to have a chance of hitting with his bomb he'd have to steepen his dive, take it even nearer to the vertical and thus to suicide: he'd chosen not to, he was pulling out prematurely—which was his only alternative—and the multiple pompoms' concentration of two-pounder shells was reaching eagerly towards him as he levelled across the stream of it: *and shells were hitting* . . . Clutterbuck's voice came urgently from the speaker: "Shift target right, green one hundred, Stuka over *Gelderland* . . ."

.   .   .

The one the pompoms had hit had gone into the sea in a sheet of flame. The other, the last to come, had dropped its bomb short of *Gelderland* and broken away landward, pursued at first by shell-bursts and machine-gun fire from *Huntress.*

Now it was quiet again and the sky was empty. Smoke leaked thinly from the Dutch ship's stern, but the fire was out and the bomb didn't seem to have hurt her much. The convoy was maintaining its previous course and speed: they were two-thirds of the way across the twenty-mile half-moon formed by the coast of the Elos Peninsula. In about twenty minutes Cape Malea would be abeam to starboard, and from there roughly three hours' steaming would see them into the Antikithera Channel, at the western end of Crete. But long before that, Jack guessed, with any luck at all and if there were any RAF or Fleet Air Arm planes at all left in Crete . . .

It was a lovely thought. *Too* lovely, and dangerous to reckon on. The odds were, he told himself, that before they saw a Hurricane they'd see a lot more Stukas. The German airfields were so close that the bombers had only to fly back and land, refuel and refill their bomb racks, and come back for another go. Over and over again: yellow-nosed bastards in pursuit of Iron Crosses.

Bell-Reid had gone for a tour of the ship. He'd chat to guns' crews and ammo-supply and damage-control parties, look in at the marines in the TS, have a word to the engineers and give the pongo passengers news of what was happening up top. Guns' crews meanwhile would be clearing away the clutter of empty shellcases, replenishing the racks with fused shells, relaxing tired muscles, lighting cigarettes, and drinking the dark brown liquid that sailors called "tea;" the pompom and point-five gunners would be re-ammunitioning, oiling, and cleaning their some-what temperamental weapons.

It might start again at any moment: that it would start again before long was inevitable. So far they'd been lucky. Only poor *Huntress* had suffered any casualties: two dead and one wounded at her "B" gun-mounting. Jack had a feeling that *Carnarvon's* and *Gelderland's* luck couldn't last: sooner or later the other side would get some. But looking round the bridge he noticed the snotty, Brighouse, scratching like a dog and looking bored, and beside the bridge shelter the Marine bugler—Sykes, that one's name was, and he looked even younger than the midshipman—was laughing at some remark made by Durkin, the leading signalman. Jack thought, If *they* can stand it . . . But there was no question, none at all, of *not* standing it. Not to be able to stand the stress of action because of some defect in oneself had been the fear, the nightmare of the recent years: if one could give it the boot, there *was* no fear.

Like hell there wasn't.

Well, not real fear: not that deep, recurrent dread . . .

No, he assured himself, not that kind. He smiled, making a private joke of it to himself: *Just pure terror, that's all.*

Half-brother Nick, he knew, expected him to lose his nerve. Nick had a private theory about Jack being a reincarnation or facsimile of the older, dead half-brother, Nick's own elder brother David who'd gone into a blue funk at Jutland—gone *mad* at Jutland, and then drowned . . . Nick had told the story, years ago, to their father Sir John Everard. He'd apologized for it since, or half-apologized, admitting he'd only burst out with it in a rage, stung by the old man's goading. All anyone knew for certain was that David's ship had been sunk and that afterwards the ship's chaplain, a survivor, had told their uncle, Admiral Sir Hugh Everard, that David had died a hero's death trying to save wounded men. Sarah, Jack's own mother, swore this must be the truth. She'd known her stepson David and admired him, adored him. Nick had spoken out of spite, she said, because he'd always resented David for being the older son and their father's heir. It was the shock that Nick had given her husband, Sir John, with that pack of lies about poor David, that had given the old man his first heart-attack and finally killed him. Jack had been only a little boy, then, his half-brother Nick already a grown man.

Sarah had added, "In any case, you aren't really at *all* like David!" But he was: there was an oil painting at Mullbergh of David in naval full-dress, and some old sepia snapshots that she hadn't wanted him to see. She'd persisted, "If there's some superficial resemblance, that doesn't mean you're . . ."

"No." He'd tried to make it easy for her. "No, of course not."

The second lot of Stukas, the ones who'd arrived just when the convoy had been altering course to 170 degrees, had made their attacks and been beaten off; *Highflier* had been near-missed, stopped for about one hair-raising minute and then got going again, to everyone's intense relief. Napier had signalled to her: *Are you all right?* and she'd flashed back: *Never better, thank you, it was just a temporary indisposition.* And in *Carnarvon* three men of "Q" gun's crew—"Q" was the midships four-inch mounting—and Sub-Lieutenant Ramsden, RNVR, who was the officer of the quarters there, had been hit by machine-gun fire from a Junkers strafing them. That had been the end of it so far as the 87s were concerned, but just as they'd finished and the last of them had winged away, a crowd of 88s had appeared, coming from the same direction—from over the land on the quarter. They'd made their shallow-diving runs, a few quite low but mostly fairly well up, and the action had been quite hot for a while but ended with the convoy still intact and plugging on, no ships damaged and no aircraft hit. Then there'd been a breather—quite a good one, ten or twelve minutes—before this last Stuka attack had started. Now it was eight minutes past nine and there'd been a whole quarter of an hour of peace. *Carnarvon* was back where she belonged, close astern of the Dutch ship, and the destroyers were in station ahead and on either beam. The sea's surface was ruffled by a light wind on the quarter; it was coming to them through the Elaphonisos Channel, the gap between the mainland and Kithera Island. The lighthouse on Anti Dragonera bore 243 degrees, nine miles away; he could still see Cape Malea, and the 0900 fix using these two landmarks showed they had 35 miles to cover, to reach the Antikithera Channel.

Bell-Reid suggested, puffing at his pipe of pusser's best—Admiralty-issue tobacco—"Shot their bolt, d'you think, sir?"

"Doubt it. If I know anything about 'em they'll be grinding their teeth with fury, by this time, and mad to get back at us." He was looking at the sky over the Grecian mainland. He added, "Although it's conceivable we might get some help from our own air boys before much longer." He'd sent a request for air support, after that first attack. He shrugged: "*Conceivable* . . . Pilot, how far are we from Maleme airfield now?"

Jack went to the chart and measured the distance. Maleme was in north-west Crete, about ten miles west of Suda Bay.

"Fifty-three miles, sir."

"Close enough, you'd think." Bell-Reid pointed with the stem of his pipe at the *Gelderland*. "And by this time, mark you, we'd be clear out of it, if it hadn't been for that bloody woman."

A telephone buzzed: Midshipman Brighouse, who was nearest to it, snatched it off its hook. "Bridge." Then: "Hold on, sir." He looked at the captain: "PMO would like to speak to you, sir."

Napier slid off his seat and went across the bridge; PMO stood for Principal Medical Officer. Jack Everard was thinking that the attacks *might* be over: the Germans might reckon they'd be under their own air cover by now. So even if the RAF didn't show up soon, the Stukas might stay away. Napier said, "I see. Thank you, Doctor." Jack thought about the Stukas not coming back. Pigs might fly, too . . . Napier told Bell-Reid as he went back to his chair and got up on it, "Ramsden's dead. The loading number, Richardson, has only a slim chance. The other two will be all right."

"Aircraft, right astern!"

Number three look-out on the port side had yelled it. Napier reached down for his telephone to McCowan: before his hand had closed on it Clutterbuck's voice came sharply from the speaker: "Alarm astern! All guns follow ADP, aircraft, angle of sight two-five—red barrage, load, load, load!"

Then he came through again: "Aircraft astern are Stukas."

Napier murmured, settling his tin hat on his head, "On battle bowlers." He beckoned: "Pilot, let's concoct another signal. Pad?" Jack got one from the chart table, and a pencil. Napier began, "Same addressees as last time. Prefix 'Most Immediate.' Start—*Since my*—time of origin of the last one—"

"Oh-seven-nineteen."

"Since my oh-seven-nineteen I have been under almost constant air attack. New force of Stukas is now arriving. My position—whatever—"

The two after four-inch mountings had opened fire: Clutterbuck was ordering "A" and "Q" to load with the shorter, blue barrage settings.

Napier went on quickly, "Put in the position: then, *course one seventy speed 16"*—he paused as the guns fired again—"and time of origin. Fix that up and send it in plain language."

"Aye aye, sir." Jack yelled for the chief yeoman as he ducked to the chart, filled in the missing bits and added time of origin 0921. Hegarty was waiting: he tore the top sheet off the pad and passed it to him. All the guns were firing now: coming up from the chart table, Jack saw Stukas overhead and on both sides, shell-bursts under them and all around them: one bomber diving now at *Gelderland,* and the pompoms had opened up just as it turned its snout down. He recalled a thought he'd had earlier, about luck changing, the unlikelihood of having a monopoly of it: and it was as if he'd seen it before it happened, knew beyond doubt that it was about to happen: *a hit on the Dutch ship, in her bridge superstructure . . .* Then another in the sea just over, a near-miss, but already her bridge was a mass of flame, and she was swinging out to port with a third bomber going for her, dropping on her in shrill cruelty. Every gun—*Carnarvon's, Halberdier's, Highflier's* and *Huntress's*—was in action to shield the transport from this fresh attack, but she'd been hit again, a column of smoke and flame bursting upwards from her forepart as she circled, out of control. *Highflier* was turning outwards to give the Dutch ship sea-room, *Huntress* beginning to turn too, in towards her. There were Stukas everywhere and the sky was plastered with shell-bursts, laced with tracer. Napier had taken over at the binnacle: Irvine moved around to stand beside his vacated seat within reach of the telephone to the ADP. The noise of the pompoms was head-splitting as they fired vertically at a diving bomber and the bridge caught all the sound of it. *Gelderland* was still circling, with smoke and flames pouring out of her. Napier was stooping to the voicepipe to pass a helm order and at the same time looking upwards, seeing the Stuka coming down at them—vicious, horrible . . . The pompoms were hitting him or it was the Stuka's guns firing, or both, there were flame-spurts anyway in that blur of movement: flames expanding suddenly, whooshing out: but the *thing*, still diving, still had its bombs . . . Noise a crescendo, mind-numbing: there was a moment's passing, scorching heat and then the Stuka had plunged into the sea a dozen yards from the cruiser's side and exploded as it went in: sea cascaded across the ship.

The Dutch ship must have got her rudder centred because she'd stopped circling, but she was going the wrong way, back along the convoy's tracks so that she was steaming into the wind and it was helping to drive the flames aft, spreading the fires along her decks. *Carnarvon* was under helm, turning to stay with her: *Highflier* had gone right round to port and was beyond her, on her starboard beam, and *Halberdier* had also gone about. *Halberdier* was having to defend herself at this moment, speeding up and zigzagging to dodge a Stuka in its dive, but her four-sevens were still contributing to the barrage over *Gelderland*. *Gelderland* was slowing—stopping . . . Jack focused his glasses on her and saw that the only section of her not on fire was her stern part, roughly one-fifth of her at that end, and both tiers of deck there were thronged with men. Some of them were trying to get her boats away: only four boats, if there were two intact on the other side, where he couldn't see; the others were in the flames. The two he could see, still high in their davits, were already full—*too* full . . . Stukas were diving on her again: and now one racing across her stern with its machine-guns blazing, and men in khaki jumping from that stern into the sea. He saw a Stuka diving now to bomb, straight into the barrage, through it: bomb falling away and the plane curving out and away below the shell-bursts: behind it the bomb struck *Gelderland* amidships bursting inside her, the ship's guts spilling skywards. More men were jumping from her stern into the sea as the flames spread back towards them: she was listing to starboard and at a standstill and another Stuka plummeting down above her.

"Midships. Signalman . . ."

Carnarvon was moving up on the doomed ship's port quarter. Ringing with noise . . . Eardrums mercifully part-numbed, but down below in the enclosed compartments it must, he thought, be unbearable. *Huntress,* who'd turned in from what had been the convoy's starboard side, was now astern of the cruiser and closing up towards her, a bit out on the starboard quarter. *Highflier* was on *Gelderland's* starboard beam and *Halberdier,* circling back now, was right astern of her. A Stuka was tearing across over *Halberdier* with its machine-guns sparking and the destroyer's point-fives missing astern of it, the tracer's curve seeming to fall back on itself and the Stuka away and clear, lifting higher as it flew off northward. Napier had shouted to Durkin, the leading signalman, "Make to *Highflier* by light: *Close* Gelderland *and pick up swimmers."* The order was going to her now in dots and dashes from the starboard Aldis lamp. He'd ordered port wheel and an increase in revs, and called the chief yeoman and given him a signal for the other two destroyers: *Act independently while* Highflier *collects survivors.* They would circle, dodging, using their guns to shelter the rescue operation as far as was possible. But the noise of the guns was slackening: just as he noticed it, it increased again, every weapon back in it suddenly, as one last Stuka came screaming down and every gun that could bear concentrated on that one target, one last enemy symbolizing all of them, all the ferocity of the past few hours.

Jack Everard watched it with a kind of astonishment in his own *enjoyment* of it: enjoyment coming from anticipation, the *certainty* that the Stuka would be hit, explode, go like those others had in a flash and roar of bombs, gas-tank, human blood, and bone: watching, expectant, *longing* for the sight of it . . . The Stuka came straight as a dart, loathsome, a vulture plunging on an already dying victim: the bomb fell away and he saw the levelling-out process begin, knowing it was the stage at which several of them had been destroyed. But the plane wasn't touched and its bomb struck, hideously, landing on that packed stern deck. Bodies and objects flying outwards from the burst . . . The Dutch ship was *all* flame now, and the Stuka was racing away north-westward across the blue Aegean.

"Midships. Slow ahead together."

There were no enemies overhead and the guns were silent. You could hear clangs from the gundecks and splashes alongside as the crews ditched shellcases; from across the water came the roar and crackle of that giant floating bonfire. She was listing now, lying almost on her side. Napier called down, "Stop both engines." Jack Everard was stooped against the side of the bridge in order to rest his elbows on it and hold the glasses steady despite his hands' tendency to shake. He was counting heads, or trying to, as *Highflier* nosed up towards the swimmers, *Halberdier* joining her now in the rescue work. *Highflier* had a scrambling-net down on this near side; she'd slipped her whaler and she had men standing by with lines all along her sides from stem to stern. He trained his glasses left, to *Gelderland* herself. The whole ship was on fire: at her stern one lifeboat, suspended vertically from only one fall, was resting against the ship's raised side, lying on it, and the boat itself was smouldering. Then he caught his breath: he was seeing arms, some bare and some in khaki shirt-sleeves, waving from open scuttles in the Dutch ship's side. Signalling for help, rescue. But she was going. He saw the final movement start, the downward wash and froth of sea as she rolled right over, turning her keel up first and then the stern lifting before she slid bow-first into something like 500 fathoms.

Gelderland had sunk at 0937. It had taken *Highflier* and *Halberdier* half an hour to gather the survivors, and at 1010 the force had got under way on course 170 at 25 knots, which was *Carnarvon's* best speed. *Highflier* had 84 survivors from the Dutch ship and *Halberdier* had 31. At Nauplia *Gelderland* had embarked twelve hundred soldiers.

At 1025 two aircraft had appeared ahead and were identified as Hurricanes. They'd hung around, patrolling to the northward, for about an hour, and when the ships were in the channel between Crete and Antikithera Island one of the aircraft had flashed a message to *Carnarvon: Have to leave you now. Good luck.* They'd flown off eastward, presumably to Maleme. It had been half-past eleven when they'd left, and at that time the force had been steering due south with Agria Grabusa, the north-western point of Crete, seven miles abeam to port. At 1220, by which time Elaphonisi lighthouse was coming up on the port bow, a signal thumped up in the pneumatic tube from the office down below; the yeoman of the watch, PO Tomkins, extracted it and brought it to the captain.

Napier read it, then held it out to his navigator. "We're to rendezvous with the First Battle Squadron ten miles south of Gavdo at 1430. How does that look?"

Jack went to the chart to check distances and courses. He had in mind that there was a much earlier signal on the log—it had been repeated to *Carnarvon* for information—ordering the 37th Destroyer Flotilla to meet the battle fleet south of Cape Littino at noon. Thirty-seventh DF was the Tribal flotilla with brother Nick's *Tuareg* in it, and presumably that rendezvous would have been effected by now. There'd be *Barham, Valiant, Formidable,* plus the destroyers they'd had with them already, and now this bunch, and presumably after they'd joined up they'd all be heading back to Alexandria.

He told Napier, "We can hold these revs, sir, and alter to one-three-five when Elaphonisi bears oh-five-eight. That'll be in about ten minutes."

"Good." Napier looked round. "Yeoman—bend on, but do not hoist yet: *Course one-three-five.*" He told Jack, "Warn me when we have three degrees to go on that bearing, would you?"

Jack nodded. "Sir." He moved to the pelorus, where he could keep an eye on it. He saw that Napier was still looking at him, either critically or thoughtfully.

"Everard," speaking quietly . . . "it's not the end of the world, you know."

"No, sir." Lining up the sight on that lighthouse. "I know."

You didn't have to talk about it. Everyone in the ship felt the same despondency. Napier added, lifting his binoculars, "It's the end of Demon, though." "Demon" had been the code-name for the Greek evacuation. He added, training his glasses slowly left to study the rocky coastline and the Cretan mountains that rose behind it, "The Germans will be going for *this* place now."

CHAPTER THREE

· · ·

Tuareg was rolling in quite a lively fashion as, with *Masai* and *Afghan* following, she zigzagged astern of *Blackfoot* towards the Kaso Strait. Tribal-class destroyers did tend to roll, in any kind of a beam sea; but it was a small fault to put up with, Nick thought, for the pleasure of driving such a lovely ship. Resting his eyes from binoculars, he was looking for'ard over the front edge of the bridge. The flare of "B" gundeck hid "A" gun from his sight; beyond "B's" twin muzzles and that jutting flare was the narrow foc'sl and sharp prow splitting the sea ahead, carving deeply into it and sending it curling out and back, the white of the broken water vividly bright against varying shades of blue. Harry Houston, who was officer of the watch, informed him from the step behind the binnacle, "You have a—ah—visitor, sir."

Nick was on his bridge seat, a wooden-based affair in the port fore corner behind the chart-table alcove: glancing round he saw the young Royal Marine captain, Brownlees, lurching for'ard from the ladder, grabbing hold of fittings here and there for support as he approached. Captain Brownlees looked uneasily aware of the destroyer's motion.

"I wondered if we might take a shufti at that chart now, sir, as you suggested earlier. Hope you don't mind me barging up like this."

"You've timed it well. We'll be going to action stations in twenty minutes." He told Houston as he slid off the seat, "I'll be in the chartroom."

A haze of land on the port bow was the mountainous eastern end of Crete, and a more nebulous but higher haze to starboard was the ridge of mountain which ran like a spine along the lizard-like shape of Scarpanto. A smaller island, Kaso, lay this side of Scarpanto, but it was lower as well as smaller and from this distance you couldn't see it. The flotilla had sailed from Alexandria at 6:00 this morning—having got into harbour at 10:00 the night before and spent several hours fuelling and ammunitioning. They'd steamed all day at 20 knots, and at 8 pm this evening, by which time they'd have passed through that Kaso gap, they'd be stopping the A/S zigzag and increasing to 30 knots for the night dash to their target area.

Putting in marines, he thought, who in a few days' time would have to be brought out again. He didn't mention the thought to Brownlees.

"Is *that* Crete?"

The Marine was pointing. Nick, pausing near the head of the bridge ladder, nodded. "Yes. And the high ground on the other bow—there— is Scarpanto. Italian."

"Scarpanto where they've based a Stuka group?"

"Right. Not a bad reason for going to action stations before we get too close to it, would you say?"

"Perhaps"—Brownlees staggered, caught at something—"perhaps you've a point, sir."

There'd been no let-up for the fleet since Operation Demon had ended three weeks ago. It had been logical and obvious that Crete would be the Germans' next objective: so Crete had to be supplied, and the waters to the north of it patrolled; and down in the south Tobruk was under siege and there was a desert army to be supported. Two destroyers, for instance, operated what was known as the spud run out of Alexandria up-coast to Tobruk every single night with ammunition and stores, leaving for return to Alex the same night with the army's wounded. You couldn't let yourself be caught on that coast in daylight now.

And just as the Greek evacuation ended—fifty thousand men had been lifted, most of them from open beaches—London had decided to run a convoy from Gibraltar right through to Alexandria, bringing tanks and aircraft for the defence of Egypt. A German panzer division had been identified in the desert, and without tank reinforcements Wavell would have been at a hopeless disadvantage. The Admiralty had pointed out that with powerful Luftwaffe forces now based in Sicily—Malta was under day-long, day-after-day attack—the chances of getting a convoy through without appalling losses were extremely slim: Churchill had overridden the objection, insisted on the convoy being sent. Incredibly, it had turned out well: low cloud and bad visibility, conditions never heard of in the Mediterranean at this time of year, had come like a gift of God to protect a wild gamble. It had been a complicated operation, code-named "Tiger": Admiral Sir Andrew Cunningham hadn't just sailed his Mediterranean Fleet to meet the convoy, he'd also run two convoys of his own into Malta and carried out two bombardments, *en passant,* of Benghazi, and he'd brought the tank convoy from Gibraltar into Alexandria harbour on 12 May.

The fleet had benefited from "Tiger." With the convoy had come reinforcements, the battleship *Queen Elizabeth* and the cruisers *Naiad* and *Fiji.*

After five days of heavy air attacks on the airstrips and on Suda Bay, the German military assault on Crete had opened 36 hours ago with parachute and glider landings. Twenty-four hours before that, all RAF and Fleet Air Arm operations finished. On 15 May there'd been three Gladiators, three Fulmars, and three Hurricanes working from Maleme: they'd fought virtually to the last man and the last aircraft, and now the fleet had no air support at all, no hope of any—only the certainty of German air assault from fields at Scarpanto, Tatoi, Eleusis, Mycene, Molai, and Argos. And from Crete itself too, when they captured Maleme—which they might have done already. After the first day's fighting they'd already had part of the airfield in their hands. Other airborne forces were fighting furiously for the airstrips at Retimo and Heraklion.

Brownlees unfolded his own map. He'd wanted to see the naval angle, relate map to chart. There were about one hundred and fifty marines in each of the four destroyers, and their colonel was in *Blackfoot*.

"We're to be landed about"—he pointed—"here?"

"Right in that corner. Almyro Bay—also called Almirou Bay, on some charts. I'll show you the detail in a moment on a different one, but you'll be landing beside a village called Yeorgioupoleos . . . Look, here's Retimo. Alternative spellings Rethimnon or Rhithymno, take your pick. But it has an airstrip—fairly primitive, I gather—about here."

The marine nodded. "Germans are on a hill that commands both the airstrip and the road south-west out of Retimo. On and around it. There's to be an attack by Aussies from Retimo itself at the same time as we barge up the other way . . . Why are we having to start so far west?"

"Is five miles *far*, for leathernecks?"

Brownlees smiled patiently. "I'm thinking of the delay, possible hold-ups."

"It's the best spot. The only one, probably. The pilot"—he reached to a shelf above the table and tapped the spine of *Mediterranean Pilot vol. IV*—"this tells us that for five miles east of our village there's a wide coastal bank with hidden rocks in it. Then it gets openly rocky from about where your hill is right up to Retimo." He pulled the marine's map closer and bent over it. "I wonder why we haven't planned to bombard the German positions—lob starshell over that hill and then plaster it with HE before your attack. It wouldn't have presented any problems."

Brownlees shrugged. "Colonel mightn't go for that. Rather do it softly, softly, I should guess."

Nick thought that if he'd been in Reggie Marsh's place when the orders came . . . Well, he hadn't been, and wasn't. He pulled another chart out from under the one they'd been looking at. "Now—here's your landing area . . ."

"Speed 30 knots, sir!"

"Very good."

Blackfoot was flying the signal. Nick leant out to port and looked astern, saw *Masai's* and *Afghan's* answering pendants going up. *Tuareg's* was already close-up. Cape Sidaro, Crete's north-east corner, would be abeam before much longer; Kaso was behind them, about twenty miles on the starboard quarter. They'd come through without even a sniff from the Luftwaffe. Not that one should count chickens yet: it was 8:00, and it would be an hour before it was dark enough to start feeling safe.

"Executive, sir!"

He glanced at Pratt, who called down to the wheelhouse, "Three-one-oh revolutions." Now he was taking bearings: and Ashcourt had got a pad ready, to write the figures down for him. The ship was still at action stations, and would be until the light went. Pratt said, "Paximadia, two-eight-one. Plaka, two-one-three." Then he took the beam bearing last, because that was the one that changed fastest: "Sidaro, two-five-three." He straightened from the pelorus and put a hand out for the pad. "Thanks."

"My pleasure."

"Your pleasures don't bear thinking about, chum."

"Don't they, hell. They're all I have to keep me warm."

"Sub."

He turned quickly. "Sir?"

"Go down and bring me the pilot, would you."

Nick met Pratt's glance, and winked. But he did want the book of sailing directions. Sooner or later—it was a certainty, he felt, not speculation—they'd be told to start getting the army out of Crete, and he might as well start familiarizing himself with details of the few small ports and the coastline.

It would be a matter of taking them off beaches again, he supposed. Such ports as existed—Suda Bay, Retimo, Heraklion—were all on the island's north coast; and even at this stage it was chancy enough to be on the northern side in daylight. All right, so you'd make your pick-ups in the dark: but you'd have to get to the embarkation point in darkness, load the troops—which wasn't always the smoothest, fastest evolution—

and then back either to Kaso in the east or to Antikithera in the west: two or three hours' steaming at full speed, and you'd still be in those straits at daylight, with no air cover and your ships crammed with soldiers. Like the Dutch transport that young Jack had seen go down.

Nick had seen Jack in Alexandria, just before they'd sailed for "Tiger," the convoy operation. He'd been—well, his usual self. Polite, but under the politeness, hostile. Or defensive? Yes, defensive: and you couldn't blame him for that. Nick *didn't* blame him: only wished, as he'd wished for years, that he could cut through the barriers.

Was every man allowed one truly colossal failure?

"*Blackfoot's* altering to port, sir."

Cutting the corner. Midnight was zero-hour for landing the marines; a few minutes saved now might prove valuable later. Nick told Pratt, "Follow him round." Pratt was a reliable navigator and a good man to have around. He'd make a good first lieutenant before long. There'd be plenty of opportunities coming, with the rate at which destroyers, sloops, and corvettes were beginning to pour out of the yards at home. None too soon, at that.

But Jack, Sarah's son . . .

It was a safe way to label him, in your mind. Your stepmother's son, when his name was Everard, was obviously your half-brother; people took it for granted. You couldn't tell anyone the truth, ever, but out of your own need to be honest or loyal—something like that—you couldn't deny it, deny him either. Nick hadn't been able to get close to him, help him, or really talk to him; Sarah had made it impossible, and he'd been forced to accept the situation—accept, without really understanding it even now, her fierce, long-standing hatred. Only Nick and Sarah knew that Jack was his own son, not his father's. It was Sarah who'd worked the deception, fooled the old man completely and left him, Nick, to guess in silence at how she'd managed it.

It was now 2200 and pitch dark. Standia Island three and a half miles abeam to port. Everyone in the bridge was dressed for the cold. The

Mediterranean Fleet had shifted into summer whites several weeks ago, but once the sun went down there wasn't much feel of summer.

Beside Nick in the dark bridge, Dalgleish said, "Must be a lot of ships plugging around tonight."

"Yes." Nick asked Pratt, "Are we on the ball with recognition lights?"

"All checked, sir."

There were lights fixed to the lower edges of the foreyard, and a locked steel box in the chartroom where you could change the combination. To challenge an unidentified ship at night you pressed a key here in the bridge, and the pre-set sequence of colours flashed out at her. You'd have your guns loaded and trained before you made the challenge.

As Dalgleish had remarked, something like half the Mediterranean Fleet was in the Aegean tonight. A lot of ships: and also a truly vast number of aircraft squatting, ready bombed-up and fuelled, on the German airfields all around, waiting for first light, knowing they'd have the sky all to themselves. A Stuka pilot's dream of heaven: plenty of targets and no airborne opposition. They'd be getting in a good night's rest—to be fresh and eager for the dawn.

The Luftwaffe had made only one kill today; they'd bombed and sunk the destroyer *Juno,* who'd been with Admiral King's Force C. But there'd been air attacks all through the daylight hours, and the cruiser *Ajax* had been damaged by near-misses. *Ajax*—with *Orion* and *Dido* and destroyers—was part of Force D, under Admiral Glennie. By the sound of things, tomorrow would see a lot more action—there'd been reports of German troop convoys from the Piraeus and from Milos Island heading south for Crete, and several squadrons were being deployed to search and intercept.

Including—later tonight—this flotilla. After they'd put the marines ashore, the Tribals were to make a sweep north-westward before turning down to pass through Kithera and join the battle-fleet—Force A1 as it was now being called—under Admiral Rawlings with his flag in *Warspite.* The C-in-C, directing operations from Alexandria, was keeping a force of big ships in that south-west area in case the Italian fleet should so far forget itself as to venture out to sea.

Carnarvon, Jack's cruiser, was down there with the battle squadron.

What else had been happening . . . Well, the 14th Destroyer Flotilla had bombarded Scarpanto airfield last night, the cruisers *Gloucester* and *Fiji*—Force B—had made a night sweep up to Cape Matapan, and King's Force C had had a brush with Italian torpedo-boats in the Kaso Strait. During the day *Gloucester* and *Fiji* had joined Rawlings's battleships, and so had Glennie's Force D, *Orion* and company; and tonight Forces B, C, and D would all be up here in the Aegean looking for those invasion convoys. Force C had been scheduled to pass northward through Kaso about two hours astern of this flotilla; the three groups had orders to foregather off Heraklion at dawn, after their night sweeps, and hunt north-westward towards Milos Island.

In daylight, with no air cover. Evidently all risks were to be accepted, to stop seaborne invasion forces reaching Crete.

"Captain, sir. Signal . . ."

"Read it to me, Yeoman, or tell me what it's about."

He didn't want to ruin his night-vision by going to the light. PO Whiffen told him, "Bad news, sir. Gerry's got Maleme airfield. It's a general signal to all ships."

"Gerry" could fly in his heavy stuff now, in the big Junkers 52 transport planes. Men, weapons, ammunition, stores: he'd got the back door open and he could expand, consolidate. Even if the fleet *did* stop all surface invasion forces—which they would, of course.

"Messenger!"

"Sir?"

"Give him that signal, Yeoman. Harris, take it down to the wardroom and show it to the captain of marines."

Twenty-three-fifty: *Tuareg* lay stopped and silent four hundred yards off-shore, and only about half that, a cable's length, from the little island of Ayios Nikolaos. On the shore opposite the island, which had a church

on it and a rough, narrow causeway connecting it to the beach, a huddle of white buildings which comprised the village of Yeorgioupoleos
gleamed in the darkness. Rocky Pratt was hunched at the gyro repeater,
checking shore bearings, and the echo-sounder was humming as it
recorded the depth of water under the ship's keel; in this sheltered bay,
with every star reflected in its surface, it would have been a waste of
time to anchor. It would have been noisy, too. Crete wasn't a German
stronghold—not yet—but there were pockets of invaders everywhere
and the marines were treating this landing as a raid into potentially
enemy territory.

For the last twenty or thirty minutes—since about the time they'd
turned for the run down into Almyro Bay—there'd been outbreaks of
gunfire to seaward. The sound of it came from the north-west, where
the flotilla would be heading when this landing job was done. Admiral
Glennie's ships, he guessed: they'd have been sweeping eastward on a
track to the north of the Tribals' westward one, and they must have run
into something . . . He thought, waiting for the all-clear signal from the
shore, *Come on, come on* . . .

The boats were alongside, full of men and ready to shove off. On
the port side one motorboat—with Sub-Lieutenant Chalk, RNVR, in
charge—had the whaler astern of it in tow, and to starboard the other
motorboat waited on its own. All the boats had been scrounged or "borrowed" from Alexandria dockyard by Dalgleish—who was down there
on the iron deck now, waiting to send them away. Nick had his glasses
trained on the islet, the causeway, and the land behind it, and Ashcourt
was at the after end of the bridge acting as a link between Nick and
Dalgleish. Half a cable's length to starboard *Blackfoot* was a low, rakish
silhouette, and *Masai* lay beyond her; one motorboat-load of marines
had already gone inshore from *Blackfoot* to check that the immediate
surroundings were clear of Germans, and the destroyers were at action
stations, their guns ready to respond instantaneously to any opposition.

Afghan was guardship, two miles out in the bay and keeping an Asdic listening watch. She'd come in and land her troops when the first of these three finished and moved out to take her place.

Ashore, across that gap of starlit water, nothing moved. Gunfire in the west—ashore—was a sporadic crackling like the sound of fireworks at a distance. It was quite different from the heavier explosions that came from seaward—*still* came, although less frequently.

Ayios Nikolaos . . . Ayios, according to the pilot, meaning "saint." Where the causeway reached the beach was the mouth of a river, the Almiros, and its westward-reaching valley carried a track which later curved northward to the southern shore of Suda Bay. Suda, which Winston Churchill had thought should be turned into a Mediterranean version of Scapa Flow, an impregnable naval base. Royal Marines were improvising defences for it now, marines of the MNBDO, Mobile Naval Base Defence Organization, under a General Weston.

Nick saw the all-clear: a morse "K" on a blue lamp from the shore. And now a second later it had been repeated from the island. He told Ashcourt, "Away boats!"

Ashcourt called down to Dalgleish, "Away boats, sir!"

Nick asked Pratt, "Depth all right still?"

"Yes, sir. We seem to be static." Pratt added, "That action's still—"

"I know, Pilot, I've got ears . . ."

Pratt had been talking about that gunfire: and Nick was wanting to finish this quickly, get out there . . . The motorboat from the starboard side was chugging out ahead of the ship, waiting for the other one with its whaler. Nick had given orders that they were to stay together, move to and fro as one unit. Motorboats' engines were notoriously unreliable, and by doing it this way you ensured that if a boat broke down there'd be only a minimal delay before it was added to the tow. As a last resort, if both power-boats failed, the whaler had its oars and would tow *them*. There were fifteen marines in the 27-foot whaler, thirty in each of the motorboats, so two round trips would complete the job. The boats were all clear now, moving shoreward, and he could see the other destroyers' boats off to starboard, the phosphorescence at their sterns and their dark shapes against the shiny surface. *Blackfoot's* and *Masai's* would be landing on the north side of the islet, while *Tuareg's* had this side to themselves. In both approaches, the seaward extremity of the island had to be widely skirted, because of off-lying rocks; *Tuareg's* boats had farther to go than the others had, but the lack of competition for landing space ought to give their coxswains an advantage.

Apart from the desire to get out to sea and to where the action was, he wanted *Tuareg's* boats to finish first: in particular, to beat *Blackfoot's*. He'd have made sure of it, he knew, if he'd put Ashcourt in charge of the operation, instead of young Chalk; Ashcourt had two years' experience of boat-handling as an RN midshipman behind him, whereas Chalk had come straight from Oxford via the Joint Universities' Recruiting Board. He needed experience, the feel of responsibility, though, and it was in the ship's interests as well as his that he should get it. Besides, with a first-class killick coxswain in each boat he couldn't go far wrong.

"Boats returning, sir!"

Ashcourt sounded as if he'd caught the regatta spirit too. Or he was thinking about that gunfire. Anyway, those *were Tuareg's* boats: the others must still be behind Ayios Nikolaos.

Blackfoot's having put the advance party ashore hadn't given her any advantage, because the marine colonel had a few extra men in his contingent anyway. And unless *Tuareg's* boats did something silly now—like breaking down—they'd win easily: they were more than halfway from the shore, and the first of the others had only just come in sight.

"Sub, tell the first lieutenant to stand by with the second flight." He went to the engine-room voicepipe and told Redmayne, the engineer lieutenant, "About three minutes, Chief, then I'll be turning the ship." The boats were making their approaches; down on the iron deck Dalgleish, aided by Mr Walsh the gunner (T) and PO Mercer the chief buffer, would have the rest of the landing-force ready at the top of the nets.

Nick thought that if he'd been in Reggie Marsh's boots, he'd have been flashing to *Afghan* now, telling Pete Taverner to start moving in.

There'd been no flashes or colour in the sky, nothing visible to accompany that gunfire. No sound for the last few minutes, either.

Reggie Marsh had had a pat on the back, apparently, for snapping up that convoy off Benghazi, at the beginning of the month. Aubrey Wishart, who was a rear-admiral on A. B. Cunningham's staff in Alexandria, and who'd been a close friend of Nick's for more than thirty years—since a somewhat hazardous submarine patrol to the Golden Horn, back in 1918—Wishart had told him that the C-in-C had been impressed by the neatness of that interception and the clean-sweep of the convoy.

Well, it *had* been an efficiently handled affair. Perhaps Reggie Marsh wasn't as muddle-headed as he'd been in earlier days. Perhaps one should accept him now at apparent current value, forget the longer-standing, less favourable impressions?

Tuareg's boats were going to beat *Blackfoot's* hollow. They were clear of the ship, heading away shorewards and going well, and the other two destroyers' boats were only just getting in alongside. Dalgleish—or rather Mercer, his right-hand man—would be getting the scrambling nets up now and overhauling the boats' falls, ready for all three to be hooked on and hoisted. *Tuareg* would be under way and gathering speed seaward the moment those boats' keels were clear of the water.

"Sub, tell the first lieutenant I'm about to turn the ship." He went to the wheelhouse voicepipe. "Port twenty-five. Slow astern starboard." Straightening, he asked Pratt, "All right for water?"

"Three and a half fathoms, sir. Fine as long as we don't go any closer in."

That was why he was turning her astern. The ship was trembling now as the one screw churned, driving a swirl of water up her starboard side. He could see her stem against the land, moving to the right as she began to swing around with stern way on.

"Slow ahead port."

Pratt said, "We've made Captain (D) look a bit slow off the mark, sir."

"We had the best billet, Pilot." He stooped to the pipe again.

"Midships." *Tuareg* was turning nicely, spinning on her heel. For ten minutes now the only gunfire had been from the land fighting, the westerly direction. He guessed that the sea action, whatever it had been, must have been about thirty miles offshore. Ashcourt reported, "First lieutenant says they're standing by and ready to hoist the boats, sir."

"Very good." He told Pratt, "See if you can spot *Afghan* out there." And into the voicepipe, "Stop both engines, Cox'n."

"Stop both, sir . . . Both engines stopped, sir!"

The swirl of sea would settle now, leaving calm water in which the boats would shoot up to the dangling falls and hook on.

Oh-two-thirty: one watch slept around their weapons or at their stations below decks, while the other half of the ship's company stayed awake. Pratt was sleeping in the chartroom and Nick had told Dalgleish to get his head down in his—Nick's—sea-cabin, which was next to the chartroom, just one ladder down from the bridge. Ashcourt was at the binnacle as officer of the watch.

The flotilla had formed up six miles east of Cape Malea three-quarters of an hour ago; they'd idled northward across Almyro Bay while *Afghan* had been landing her quota of Royal Marines and then come racing out to rejoin them. The four Tribals were in line-abreast now, steaming at 30 knots on a course of 336 degrees, north-north-westerly. Marsh in *Blackfoot,* had put *Afghan* to port of him and *Masai* to starboard, with *Tuareg* out on the sweep's starboard wing; *Afghan* and *Masai* kept station on *Blackfoot* and *Tuareg* kept station on *Masai.* The ships were five cables, half a sea mile, apart from each other. If it had been a decision for Nick to have made he'd have had one-mile or even three-thousand-yard gaps, to widen the coverage of the sweep; there was no moon, but stars gave light enough for the flotilla to keep in visual touch without much difficulty.

Nick thought he *should* try to dismiss his reservations about Reggie Marsh. They were based, after all, only on recollections of the man as he'd been more than ten years ago. Pete Taverner of *Afghan* and

Johnny Smeake of *Masai* seemed to think well enough of him as their Captain (D), and he passed muster—presumably—with the great A. B. Cunningham . . .

Poor old ABC. It irked him badly, Aubrey Wishart had told Nick, that he had to run this widespread battle from a shoreside headquarters. He'd sneered at it as "soft-arsed accommodation" . . . Cunningham was 100 per cent seaman and seagoing commander: but obviously with so many ships involved and over such an area, with the desert coast and Malta to look after as well as the Aegean, and the Italian fleet still a *potential* menace lurking in its harbours, and having to keep in close touch with Army HQ in Cairo as well as with what existed of the RAF —it was obvious that he couldn't be stuck out at sea.

About now, Nick guessed, the flotilla was passing through roughly the area where that action must have been. It was a reasonable guess that Admiral Glennie with *Dido* and *Orion* and the other ships of Force D might have run into an invasion convoy and disposed of it, then continued their eastward sweep. Whether that made it more or less likely that this flotilla would meet any other invasion groups farther north was an open question; but the orders were that they should sweep as far as a position 36 degrees 30 north, 23 degrees 45 west—it was the midpoint of a line drawn between Cape Malea and Milos Island—and then come about to course 190 degrees so as to be down in the Antikithera Channel by first light.

Having, as likely as not, seen damn-all.

He planned to take an hour or two's rest after they'd turned to the southerly course, which would be at about 0400. Dalgleish and Pratt could be up here then, and he'd sleep in his bridge chair and be back on his feet, rested and fit for another day's work, by dawn action stations.

In the cocoon of ship and sea noise, using binoculars to study a hazy, vague horizon while the four Tribals' hulls lathered white tracks northward into the Aegean, your mind could slide from one thing to another without interrupting the concentrated effort of looking out. He was thinking again about Jack: Jack saying, when he'd consented to dine on board *Tuareg* as Nick's guest in Alex about three weeks ago, something about war reducing men to the state of wild animals. It was the Stuka attacks he'd been thinking about, the impression of ferocity, blood-lust.

"Oh, those people could teach wild animals a thing or two," Nick had agreed with him. "But several million decent people in Europe, in countries they've invaded, have been shut up in cages in conditions you wouldn't inflict on any animal. Those Stukas you didn't like the look of have already flattened cities and bombed columns of helpless refugees. They've struck at countries who were falling over backwards to stay clear of war—it's like a gang of thugs walking up to innocent passers-by and attacking them. They're gangsters. You either surrender, or look the other way until it's your turn, or you fight."

"I'm not saying we shouldn't be fighting. I'm only saying—well, it's a revelation; people who preach that war's foul are right—even the Oxford Union—"

"No, Jack. The foulness is in instigating war, making it necessary, not in standing up against it. It would be degrading *not* to be fighting them."

"Well, as things are, certainly. But . . ." Shaking his head, perhaps confused by the contradictions of it . . . Nick wondering whether Jack remembered anything of the David-at-Jutland business, the truth he'd told their father—wishing immediately afterwards and ever since that he'd kept his mouth shut—whether Jack could have remembered it, and if so, whether he'd have allowed it to worry him. Because the physical likeness to David was unmistakable. Even his manner, his way of looking at you . . .

But perhaps he'd changed, in recent weeks? Wasn't there a degree of new self-assurance behind that defensive reserve? And the talk about war—wasn't it possibly the nearest thing to a conversation they'd ever had?

Hopes, to counter fears . . .

But they hadn't talked all the time about war. Jack heard regularly from his mother, with reports of Mullbergh, the Everard house and estate in Yorkshire, and some items from her letters he'd been prepared to pass on. Sarah, and Jack when he was at home, lived in the Dower house; Mullbergh and its land was Nick's now. It had been taken over by the War Office as some sort of training centre, while Sarah kept an eye on the management of the four farms and also accommodated some girls of the Women's Land Army in her Dower house. It had been an exceptionally hard winter: when she'd last written, at the end of April, the whole West Riding had still been deep in snow.

And London lay in partial ruin, with bombers over night after night. But *Blithe Spirit* and *Arsenic and Old Lace* were still showing to capacity audiences, and Carroll Gibbons and his orchestra still played at the Savoy. There had been a Communist-organized demonstration at the Savoy a few months ago: because Cabinet ministers, foreign press, representatives, and diplomats still ate well there despite shortages and rationing. The Communists, whose Soviet masters were, of course, allies of the Nazis, were calling it a "bosses" war.

"Object in the water green four-oh, sir!"

He swung his glasses to it . . .

"Looks like a caïque, sir."

Nick thought Ashcourt was right. And there was no bow-wave or wake; so it was stopped, and probably damaged. About three thousand yards away.

"Bring her round, Sub."

"Starboard fifteen!"

"Signalman—make to *Masai: Investigating object bearing*"—he checked the bearing quickly and roughly—*"bearing oh-one-five."*

Ashcourt said into the voicepipe, "Midships."

"Midships, sir . . . Wheel's amidships, sir."

"Steer oh-one-five."

No need to rouse the other watch. The invasion troops had been reported as coming in convoys of caïques, and this was as likely as not one of them, but it was alone and quite probably holed, half full of water: that was how it looked. He'd been hearing the clacking of the lamp, and now the familiar rhythm of the AR end-of-message sign:

Blackfoot would probably have read the signal, and if she hadn't *Masai* would, anyway, be passing it on. He told the signalman, "Stand by the eighteen-inch, starboard side."

The searchlight, he meant. There was an eighteen-inch diameter light on each side of the bridge and a twenty-four-inch one on the platform aft . . . That "object" *was* a caïque: almost certainly a victim of the action they'd heard earlier. But not necessarily: caïques had been used extensively during the Greek evacuation, ferrying troops from shore to ships, and this one could have drifted from any of the islands . . . The purpose in taking a close look at it now was to check whether there might be anyone alive in it.

"Messenger—go to my sea-cabin and shake the first lieutenant." He glanced round to see what the rest of the flotilla was doing. *Masai* was following, about a mile astern, and he could see *Blackfoot,* when he used binoculars, in silhouette; Marsh hadn't altered course, but he'd reduced speed.

About half a mile to go. Nick told Ashcourt, "Two hundred revs, Sub. Steer to leave it close to starboard."

"Aye aye, sir." Ashcourt called down, "Two hundred revs. Steer three degrees to port."

"Ship green nine-oh, sir!"

A second look-out amplified: "Destroyer, sir!"

He was at the binnacle, displacing Ashcourt. "Sound surface alarm, Sub." He called down, "Full ahead together, starboard ten."

Dalgleish was in the bridge: "Challenge, sir?"

Nick told him, "No. Stand by the searchlight sight." He wouldn't expose its beam until he told him to, he'd just have it trained ready to illuminate the target: which was showing two red and two white lights, fixed, on its foreyard. The surface alarm S's were jarring through the ship, and Nick was telling Houston in the director, "Unidentified ship starboard—"

"I'm on it, sir. Eyetie, I think." The merchant banker up on the foremast was talking into his headset before Nick had moved from the voicepipe: "All guns with SAP load, load, load . . ." Nick called, "Signalman, make to *Blackfoot: Enemy destroyer bearing one-one-oh.*"

"Searchlight ready, sir."

"Searchlight *on!*"

The light's beam sprang out across the sea, fixed immediately on an Italian torpedo-boat of the *Partenope* or *Climene* class. Short, high foc's'l, long and lower afterpart, single funnel. Afterpart all smashed: mainmast gone, wreckage where the deckhouse and a stern gun-mounting should have been . . . the fire-gongs clanged, and the four-sevens flashed and roared. Eyes blinded, ears stunned. Fire-gongs again, a distant tinny sound, and shells exploding, orange explosions in the Italian's bridge, an Italian caught up in his second action of the night. Those hits had set his bridge on fire: but he was speeding up—you saw the bow-wave rising—and coming round to port: the gun on his stubby foc's'l spurting flame. Just that *one* gun, all he had left: it would be a 3.9. He'd reversed his helm—turning away now, *Tuareg's* four-sevens firing fast, plastering him. It was conceivable he was turning to fire torpedoes.

"Starboard fifteen."

If torpedoes were coming, *Tuareg* would point her nose between them, comb their tracks. *Masai* was coming up to port with her "A" and "B" guns in action: it was astonishing that the diminutive Italian could take this much punishment and remain afloat. Well, he wouldn't, not for much longer. *Tuareg's* two for'ard mountings were the only ones that would bear now she'd pointed her stem at the enemy, but with *Masai* in it as well that still amounted to four, twin four-sevens pumping semi-armour-piercing shells at the six- or seven-hundred-ton torpedo-boat.

"Midships."

"Midships, sir . . . Wheel's amidships, sir!"

If he'd turned to fire torpedoes, he'd done it. He was coming round to port now. Bridge and midships section burning brightly.

"Port fifteen."

"Port fifteen, sir!"

Houston called down the voicepipe to tell him he couldn't fire: the Italian was about to pass between *Tuareg* and *Masai*. Giving himself a few minutes' extra life: he'd kept that wheel on and spun right round— like a speedboat, dodging shells.

Dalgleish shouted, "He's going to ram *Masai!*"

The Italian had flung his wheel hard a-starboard just as he entered the gap between the two Tribals: choosing *Masai* probably because she was the nearer. *Masai's* "X" and "Y" guns fired right over her just before the crash came, and shells whirred only a few feet over *Tuareg's* bridge as Nick called down, "Midships!" The Italian had struck *Masai* right aft as she swung hard in an effort to avoid him, and now the two ships were locked together, circling, *Masai's* way carrying them both along, circling like dancers, flames on the Italian dazzling bright and a wide streak of their reflection reaching to *Tuareg* across a couple of hundred yards of sea. Movement slowing: all guns silent. *Masai* had stopped her engines: or her screws were done for. Near one would have been any- way. Losing the forward impetus, she'd ceased the process of tearing her own stern off with the Italian embedded in it.

"Meet her. Steer north. Slow ahead both engines."

The Italian was sinking, sagging low in the sea, probably only sup- ported by her stem's grip on *Masai*. The sea was washing across her afterpart, rising in a pale fog of steam where it lapped her fires. *Masai* seemed to be on an even keel: it looked from here as if the damage would be all in the stern twenty feet of her: just the tiller flat, the steering-gear compartment, then. The port screw and shaft *might* have survived: but one screw and no steering wouldn't be much help . . . He ducked to the voicepipe: "Starboard ten." Up again, with his glasses on that stern, in time to see a sudden lurch and an upheaval of white foam: the Italian had broken loose, dragged out by the weight of his flooded hull. As the torpedo-boat slipped back he saw its bow lift vertically before it disappeared.

"I'll want the loud-hailer, Yeoman." It had only to be fetched and plugged in. He stooped: "Midships." He put his glasses back on *Masai's* stern: the only way she'd get home, he guessed, would be under tow. She'd float, all right; there was a watertight bulkhead immediately for'ard of the tiller flat, and even if that one was ruptured there was another through the centreline of "Y" gun-mounting's support. It was a matter either of towing her, or of taking her crew off and sinking her. Towing would mean a slow-speed withdrawal southwards, and a lot of Stuka attention from first light onwards—with a towing ship who couldn't dodge.

It was a decision for Reggie Marsh.

CHAPTER FOUR

. . .

"One-three-five revolutions on, sir." Pratt reported it from the binnacle. Those were revs for about 12 knots: Nick was building the speed up gradually, with Dalgleish on the quarterdeck watching the tow and the strain on it. *Tuareg* had a shackle of chain cable out astern, and *Masai's* towing wire was shackled to it, the weight of the cable acting as a spring to absorb the stresses on the wire and on the gear on *Tuareg's* stern and *Masai's* foc'sl.

Sub-Lieutenant Chalk, on the bridge end of the depthcharge telephone, reported, "First lieutenant says all's well, sir."

An absence of any protests from *Masai* indicated that she had no problems either, from the last step-up in speed. Nick let it settle down for a few minutes, then told Pratt, "One-five-oh revs."

Thirteen knots.

It was past 4 am. *Tuareg* was towing *Masai* on a course of 227 degrees, south-westward, with thirty miles to go to the Antikithera Channel. Not that reaching Antikithera would mean any lessening of the Stuka threat: with no air cover and with the Luftwaffe ranging freely over the whole area in enormous strength, you'd be bombed as thoroughly down there as you would be here. It was simply a step in the right direction, the direction of the long route south.

"One-five-oh revs on, sir."

Marsh had made a wrong decision, Nick thought. The right one would have been to take *Masai*'s crew out of her and sink her, then carry on with the ordered northward sweep before turning south to join the battle squadron. All right, so it would have resulted in one fleet destroyer lost. But in terms of this battle for Crete she was already lost: she'd be out of action for many months. This effort to get her away turned her from a loss into a liability; air attacks were inevitable from dawn onward, and with the sitting-duck target of two unmanoeuvrable destroyers chained together, and tied to a straight course and a set speed, the hungry Stukas would be competing for sky-space to get at them. So there'd be a distinct possibility of losing more than just *Masai,* and in present circumstances here in the eastern Mediterranean that was a risk no one could afford.

"One-six-oh revolutions."

Blackfoot was on the beam to starboard, *Afghan* to port. Marsh had wirelessed a signal a quarter of an hour ago, to C-in-C and repeated to the various force commanders now at sea, telling him what had happened and that the flotilla was withdrawing via the Antikithera Channel; he'd given an 0400 position, their course, and speed 12 knots.

"Signalman."

"Sir?"

"Lever . . . Make to *Masai: Are you quite comfy?*"

When the attacks started, he thought, *Masai* might not be able to use her after guns. Almost certainly not "Y" gun, the quarterdeck mounting, with the strain it might impose on the stern bulkhead. She'd lost her starboard screw and she had no steering: rudder gone, tiller flat smashed and flooded. The port screw and shaft were undamaged, but that wasn't going to help her without steering. The signalman was just finishing that message. Nick went to where young Chalk was propped in the bridge's starboard for'ard corner with the depthcharge or A/S telephone in his hand; its lead came up from the door of the tiny Asdic cabinet, so that when you were hunting a submarine you could stand behind the operator and talk over the line to Mr Walsh the gunner (T) back aft at the chutes and throwers. He took the telephone from Chalk and asked Dalgleish how the tow was looking. You looked for the cable's sag in the water, and for vibration: you could put your hand on it and feel any change. "Think we can stand a bit more?"

"Certainly looks all right, sir."

"Good." He put the phone back on its hook. The signalman told him, "Reply from *Masai*, sir: *Snug as a bug. Let's step on the gas.*"

Nick told Pratt, "One-seven-five revolutions."

The wind was about Force 2 and north-west; there was hardly any movement on the ship. When they were through Antikithera, of course, conditions might be quite different. He thought, *Sufficient unto the day* . . .

There'd be some evils to *this* day, he guessed.

Pratt had been checking the automatic log, timing its ticks against his stopwatch; he told Nick, "Fifteen through the water, sir."

Not bad, with a two-thousand-ton destroyer in tow.

"Let's go up another notch. One-eight-five."

Four-thirty, nearly. Dawn in about an hour. With so many ships in and around the Aegean, the Luftwaffe would be out in force. They'd every reason to be: the Germans wanted to push surface convoys into Crete, and while the Royal Navy was in these waters they weren't able to. It would be a straight fight between something like two thousand German aircraft and a couple of dozen British ships, more than half of which were already suffering from defects that in normal times would have put them in dock. Engine-room staffs were having to improvise and make-do, handle their own problems as best they could—anything to keep the ships at sea. Ships' companies weren't exactly fresh either: for a long time nobody had been to sea without being bombed, and as they were only allowed into harbour for long enough to refuel, re-ammunition, and top up with fresh water and stores, they'd begun to

equate salt water with high explosive. What with that and the lack of
sleep, it was hardly surprising that one saw, here and there, signs of strain.

Thinking of the dawn and of the bombers jogged him into a change
of mind. He'd been hoping to work the speed up to 20 knots, but it
struck him now that 15 to 16, which they were already doing, wasn't
at all bad. The round figure of 20 wasn't worth running risks for: one
of those risks being the backwash effect, *Masai's* exposed after bulkhead
and the forces sucking at it as she was pulled through the water, a suc-
tion force directly related to the speed. If that bulkhead collapsed it
would mean not only more damage to *Masai* and perhaps some lives
lost, but the sudden jerk and increase in weight would almost surely part
the tow; then you'd be at a standstill, picking it up and making it fast
again just as the light came—and the bombers.

He reached past Chalk for the A/S phone again. "Number One?"

"'Alf a mo,' sir." Then Dalgleish came on. "Sir?"

"I'm going to settle for these revs. Leave one hand to keep an eye
on the tow." He hung up the telephone and told Chalk, "You can leave
it now." Chalk was sturdy, freckle-faced, boyish-looking. Nick told him,
"You did a good job with the boats, Sub."

He grinned: "Thank you, sir."

Pratt said, "Just under 16 knots, sir."

"It'll do." He called to the signalman, "Lever, make to *Masai: I think
this is fast enough.* Then to *Blackfoot: Intend maintaining present speed.*"

Marsh could object if he wanted to. But there'd been a night in the
English Channel in 1917 when Nick had been first lieutenant of the
destroyer *Mackerel* and his captain, Edward Wyatt—who died a few
months later on the mole at Zeebrugge—had been greedy for more
speed than the ship's shattered bow could stand. He could remember
vividly the lurch and rumble as the bulkhead went: and he could see,
as clearly as if he was standing in front of him now, the face of the man
who'd been trapped in the for'ard messdeck when the sea burst in. A
chief petty officer by the name of Swan.

He often thought of Swan. And of others like him.

It was a relief to have come to that quite ordinary, logical decision. So much so that he realized he must be more tired than he'd recognized. He saw Dalgleish just coming from the ladder. With him and Pratt up here—and they'd both had a stand-off—and with dawn about an hour ahead and then hours, even a whole day if it lasted that long, of the Luftwaffe . . . He made up his mind that half an hour's cat-napping in the chair would be better than no rest at all.

"I'm going to have a snooze, Number One. Give me a shake at 5:15, and we'll close the hands up at 5:20."

"Aye aye, sir." Dalgleish poked Rocky Pratt. "I'll see this bloke stays awake."

Someone else had arrived behind him: as he came forward into the bridge, Nick saw that it was Simon Gallwey, the doctor.

"Can't you sleep, Doc?"

"They won't let me, sir. Cruel men keep bringing me signals to decode. Like this one." He had a sheet of signal pad in his hand. Nick thought, *Twenty-five minutes now, if I'm lucky* . . . He took the signal to the chart table, elbowed his way inside its canvas hood and switched the light on.

It was to D37—Marsh—from Admiral Rawlings, commanding the battle squadron somewhere down in the south-west; it informed Marsh that *Carnarvon* was being detached to join them five miles west of Cape Grabusa at 0600.

Well. Perhaps they had a chance of getting away with it, now. He came out, and handed the signal to Pratt.

"We're having company. *Carnarvon's* meeting us in the Antikithera soon after dawn."

Pratt clasped the sheet of paper to his heart . . . "Saved, saved!"

Laughter in the back of the bridge. But the AA cruiser's eight high-angle guns *would* make a difference.

Fighting to wake up, to crawl out from under a deadweight of heavy sleep . . . The voice broke in again: "Five-fifteen, sir." The voice was like a rope let down to you: you needed to grab hold of it before sleep closed over your head again, to let the rope haul you up into the light and air. Or you could let go, slip back, forget . . .

"Captain, sir—it's 5:15, sir!"

The rendezvous with *Carnarvon* was set for 0600. But the signal Marsh had sent earlier had given this flotilla's speed-of-advance as 12 knots, not 16. Unless he'd amplified it since then. If Rawlings's staff man had based his orders on that information, the flotilla would be eight— no, six—miles farther south than anyone expected.

But it wouldn't make all that much difference.

"Captain, sir, it's five—"

"Yes, I know. Thank you, Number One."

Collecting thoughts . . . This was Thursday. Thursday, 22 May 1941 . . .

"Kye, sir?"

"Thank you. What the doctor ordered."

It was marvellous—the "kye," or cocoa—thick, hot, and sweet, life-restoring . . . Marsh might have sent another signal amending the speed he'd given before. Otherwise there could be a delay in effecting the rendezvous. In full daylight six miles wouldn't make much difference at all, but it wouldn't be fully light until just before the time they were supposed to meet.

Before long all ships would be fitted with RDF, new types that were being developed and which even destroyers would be getting—so one heard—in a year or so. It would remove a hell of a lot of problems if they did get it. The Americans were working on it too, but they called it "radar."

He'd finished the kye, at the cost of a burnt tongue, and he felt alive again. Pulling off the hood of his duffel-coat, and reaching down beside the chair for his cap . . . It was a cap he'd owned in 1926, and the oak-leaves on its peak were distinctly the worse for wear. The badge was tarnished too, and he could feel ragged ends of gold wire with his thumb. This was his seagoing hat: he also had a new one, smart and shiny, which had been posted by Messrs Gieves to him at a pub in Hampshire where, last autumn, he'd spent a few days with Fiona. She'd opened the parcel during breakfast in bed: then put the cap on her dark, tousled head and pranced around the room stark naked, uttering what she'd imagined to be nautical phrases.

But think about Stukas now: not about Fiona Gascoyne with her clothes off. Fiona had *her* bombers to cope with, too: the night raiders on London, where she was stationed in the MTC—ambulances, despatches, driving for the Army or civilian ministries. He thought rather frequently about Fiona, nowadays: ever since a chance meeting in a restaurant, each of them with someone else—an accidental meeting but a watershed in their relationship . . .

He got up out of his chair, and stretched. He hoped to God she was all right, after the 11 May raid. The Germans had sent five hundred bombers over, and set seven hundred acres of London on fire. He hoped and prayed to God he'd hear from her soon.

"Tow all right?"

"No change, sir, and no problems. May I close the hands up?"

"Go ahead. Pilot, did you check the rendezvous position?"

"Yes, I did, sir." Pratt told him, "We'll be six or seven miles to the south of it, at this rate."

"He hasn't amended that signal, then."

"No, sir. There's nothing new of any interest on the log."

Thinking it out—the flotilla would be passing through the rendezvous position at, say, twenty minutes to six, and at that time *Carnarvon,* if she was coming at her flat-out speed of 25 knots, would be something between six and ten miles to the west. It would be pretty well light by that time, and they'd be looking out for each other, so they should make contact all right. Marsh probably hadn't wanted to go on the air again: the more signals you sent, the more clearly you advertised your presence. Although the Germans had to know, surely, that the whole area was crawling with ships, that any bombers taking to the air this morning were bound to find targets?

On that basis, they wouldn't be hanging around their airfields waiting for reconnaissance reports. They'd be airborne at first light, and bottlenecks like Kaso and Antikithera would be obvious places to take an early look.

"Ship is at action stations, sir." Dalgleish had been taking reports through telephones and voicepipes. "I'll go on aft."

There was a familiar greying in the east. Cape Spada was in that direction, about nine miles away, and the sun would rise there, behind the land. Much closer than Spada and roughly on the beam now, south-eastward, Cape Grabusa was a mound of black rock which was staying inky-black while its surroundings lightened.

"When should we be altering, Pilot?"

"If it was up to me, sir, when Grabusa lighthouse bears oh-eight-four. That'll be in about twenty minutes. Then one-nine-five would clear Pondikonisi."

Pondikonisi was a small off-lying island. *Blackfoot* would be ordering the change of course, when it pleased Reggie M. Just on 5:30 now.

The Italian commanding that torpedo-boat had displayed a lot of guts, last night. Whatever they had as the equivalent of a VC, he deserved one. As a nation they weren't militarily impressive; they weren't really significant—at Matapan for instance, two months ago, when the ten-thousand-ton cruiser *Pola* had been immobilized by a torpedo from one of *Formidable*'s aircraft, destroyers found her lying in a state of helpless panic, her upper deck littered with baggage, bottles, and drunken sailors. How to deal with her had been something of an embarrassment, but eventually she'd been sent to the bottom—joining the heavy cruisers *Zara* and *Fiume* and two destroyers—and nine hundred of her crew were saved. Rescue work was interrupted by German aircraft—Ju88s—and had to be broken off; so A. B. Cunningham signalled the Italian admiralty telling them where to find the rest of their survivors, and they sent out a hospital ship which for some reason the Germans didn't attack. But there'd been some other interesting signals exchanged between the destroyer flotilla who picked up the nine hundred Italians, and the Commander-in-Chief in *Warspite*. One had reported: *Prisoners when asked why they had failed to fire at us replied that they thought if they did we would fire back.* Then, when ABC had called for details of any wounded men picked up, he was told: *State of prisoners: six cot cases, fifty slightly injured, one senior officer has piles.* The Commander-in-Chief flashed in reply: *I am not surprised.*

But the *Pola* and last night's torpedo-boat seemed hardly to have belonged to the same navy.

Five-thirty-five. In a quarter of an hour it would be daylight. Start of the bad time here, end of the bad time in London . . .

When Nick had got back from Norway, his uncle Hugh had been in London, wreathed in smiles at his nephew's recent successes. Admiral Sir Hugh Everard had retired years before the war, but like many other retired admirals he'd rejoined as a convoy commodore. He was doing that now, in the Atlantic: no sinecure, for a man of seventy. He'd been dressed in his new rank of Commodore RNR when Nick had met him in London, in the late spring of last year. Hugh had asked him to lunch, and produced another guest as well, a wren third officer called Virginia Casler. She was small, blonde, smart, and very pretty, and she was working in the Admiralty; Hugh had come across her at the time when there'd been no news of Nick or of his destroyer *Intent,* when everyone had been assuming the worst. Hugh Everard had been highly impressed by the WRNS third officer, and when the great news had arrived— *Intent* still afloat and with a string of successes behind her—the gaunt old admiral and the curvy little blonde had gone out to celebrate; and Hugh had resolved to introduce Nick to her when the chance came. Match-making, Nick had guessed; the old boy had been on at him for years about settling down with a new wife.

But the night before this luncheon, his first night in London, he'd spent with Fiona. He'd arrived late, learnt that there was no room for him at his club, telephoned her and found she was alone. (He wouldn't have taken a chance on it. She wasn't a one-man girl: she'd been married, not too successfully, to a rich man nearly twice her age, and when he'd died she'd decided that the one thing she wasn't going to do was

tie herself down again in any hurry. Nick had happily accepted this situation: he'd concluded a long time ago, after the divorce from Ilyana,
that he wasn't cut out to be a husband.) He'd asked her, in her flat that
night, to join him next evening for dinner and a nightclub, but she'd
said she couldn't because she'd be on duty. So he invited Ginny Casler
instead, and Ginny said she'd love to, which was fine. A "stunner" was
how Hugh Everard had described her, when he'd been asking Nick for
lunch: he'd also referred to her as a "corker."

Nick booked a table for that evening at the *Jardin des Gourmets*.
London's ordeal by bombing hadn't yet started, in May 1940, and all the
restaurants and nightspots were still open and intact. The table they'd
reserved for him was one of a pair at the far end of the long, rather
narrow dining-room: there were just those two "banquette" tables facing this way, down the room's length as you approached them. He
hadn't been taking much notice of his surroundings as he and Ginny
followed the waiter to it; it was only when the man had pulled one end
out for Ginny to slip in behind it that he noticed the occupants of the
other one—Fiona Gascoyne, with an RAF wing commander.

There'd been no reason to be upset about it: he'd known she went
out with a lot of other men. Why shouldn't she? He was surprised she'd
made that excuse, though: there'd been no reason to. Looking at her,
showing his surprise, seeing her take in all there was to see of Ginny
Casler in one swift feline appraisal before she glanced back at him—
puzzled, almost—he'd felt a new element in the air between them: there
was something disturbing about it but at the same time exciting, a feeling—which he couldn't have described there and then—of make or
break. Afterwards he'd wondered if he and Fiona hadn't been struck
simultaneously and separately by the same feeling: that it was—surprisingly—wrong to see each other out with other people. The corollary,
of course, would be that they belonged together.

In the next few days he'd telephoned her several times, both to her
flat and to the MTC headquarters in Graham Terrace, but failed to catch
her. Then he had to go back up to the Clyde, where he'd left *Intent* in

dock. He was on his way north when news came that the Dutch army had surrendered; and for the next fortnight there was a whole series of evacuations from various points in Norway. By that time *Intent* was fit for sea again, and he was bringing her into Harwich after a fast dash around the top of Scotland when a BBC broadcast announced the collapse of Belgium. There was just about time to refuel, and they were away to take part in the Dunkirk evacuation. After that there was hardly any leave for anyone: invasion was expected at any time, the Battle of Britain was being fought over southern England, and the flotillas and squadrons waited with intentions that were entirely clear: whether the air battle was won or lost, the Navy would die in the Channel before a live German landed on an English beach.

The all-night raids on London started at the end of August; in his destroyer during the patrols and anti-invasion sweeps and bombardments of the invasion-launching ports, he prayed for Fiona to be alive each morning. It wasn't until October that he had some leave—before taking over *Tuareg* in Portsmouth—and spent nearly all of it with her in Hampshire. They'd laughed about that chance meeting in the *Jardin:* she explained that she *had* been on the duty roster, but another girl had persuaded her to swap, for some reason, and then this friend-of-a-friend had called: and she hadn't known where Nick was . . . That she'd bothered to explain was unusual, out of character with their relationship as it had been. And on their last night together he'd been woken by her crying on his shoulder. She'd asked him, "You *will* come back, Nick? Please? Promise me?" He'd thought of her expression when he'd seen her in the restaurant, remembered how he'd felt and felt now even more, and he'd had a sickening glimpse of what it would be like not to have her to come back to.

Nearly fifteen hundred people had been killed in London on the night of 10/11 May.

There'd be a letter from her soon. There might be one now, at this moment, lying in the Fleet Mail Office or in *Woolwich,* the destroyer flotillas' depot ship in Alexandria. Even if there wasn't, she might still have written: mails were unreliable, particularly out of London. And at least she didn't ride a motorbike now. Without any help from Germans she'd twice nearly killed herself on that machine . . .

The light was coming rapidly, pouring up from behind a range of mountains which slanted jaggedly southwards from the low cape to port. It was 5:45: they were in the position ordered for the rendezvous with *Carnarvon*.

If the cruiser was inside visibility range, she ought to see them before they saw her. She'd have them silhouetted against the dawn—if the land's shadow didn't hide them—and she had a greater looking-out range from that old spotting-top of hers.

Pratt said, "Should be altering at any time now, sir."

It was up to Marsh: and as if he'd heard what Pratt had said, *Blackfoot* started flashing. Nick was looking out that way, in the faint hope of an early sight of *Carnarvon,* and he saw it start: and Whiffen had his sig-nalman ready and waiting for it, so that the answering clash of *Tuareg*'s lamp came with pleasing promptitude.

"You must have a carrying voice, Pilot."

"Perhaps Captain (D) and I are on the same wavelength, sir."

Ashcourt, beside his torpedo-control panel on the starboard side, read the message aloud as it came rippling over in fast dots and dashes: *Alter course to one-nine-seven. I will wait here for* Carnarvon *and then catch you up.*

Tuareg's signalman had rapped out a "K" in acknowledgement. Pratt said, "There's an answer to the speed discrepancy, sir."

Nick glanced at him: it was light enough to see the navigator's slightly rueful smile, as if he was thinking that Marsh had been a jump ahead of them all the time.

"Bring her round gently to one-nine-seven, Pilot."

Nick could hardly believe Marsh was doing this. What if there was some delay in *Carnarvon*'s arrival, and the Stukas found him first? The only effective weapon ships had in this battle against dive-bombers was *collective* firepower. A single destroyer with low-angle main armament, alone and unsupported, didn't stand a chance.

•   •   •

"How far are we from them now, Pilot?"

Jack Everard went down to the chart to check on it. *Carnarvon's* best speed now was 22 knots. She was no chicken, and a month's hard driving plus quite a few near-missing bombs to shake bits loose had taken its toll despite extraordinary efforts by her engineers. She'd been on the move and at sea, without any break at all lasting more than a few hours, since she'd arrived in the Mediterranean near the end of "Demon." She'd had *one* whole night in harbour—in Alexandria, just before "Tiger," the convoy trip to Malta and back. There were three other AA cruisers on the station—*Coventry, Carlisle,* and *Calcutta*—and all four of them were wanted here, there, and everywhere else, simultaneously.

At 4:50 this morning, after a breakdown lasting half an hour, the engineer commander had told Napier, "If you can keep her down to revs for not more than 22 knots, sir, I can keep her running for a week or two. If we have to exceed that for more than a few minutes I can't answer for the consequences."

It wasn't light enough for chart-work: Jack pulled the screen down behind him and switched the light on. About time he replaced this chart anyway; the bridge charts always got harder use than the ones in the chartroom, and there were so many rubbed-out workings from the past month's operations that the paper had barely any surface left on it. *Carnarvon* was steering a course of 106 degrees, aiming to meet the 37th Flotilla at 0700 instead of the ordered 0600 rendezvous farther north; Napier knew that the Tribals would push on southwards, and he'd had to make the adjustment for his ship's reduced speed. It did mean the destroyers would be on their own for the first hour of daylight, but that was beyond his control; he'd be joining them eight or nine miles south of Pondikonisi at seven instead of four miles north of it at six.

Jack came up from the chart and told him, "At their 0600 position they'll bear oh-seven-eight, range 26 miles, sir."

Napier looked ten years older than he had a month ago. Thinner, greyer, eyes deeper set.

So long as the Stukas didn't arrive too soon, Jack thought, everything should turn out all right. Even if they did find them, the four Tribals would be able to fend for themselves for a while, with luck. They'd be handicapped, of course, by only two of them being free to take avoiding action; *Tuareg* and *Masai,* confined to a steady speed and straight course, would obviously be the bombers' target.

But brother Nick, for God's sake, was more than capable of looking after himself . . .

By five-past six it was daylight. The Cretan mountains, thirty or forty miles ahead, were an uneven scar of indigo against a burning sky. Clear sky: in that quarter, burning bright. Here in the cruiser's bridge, unshaven faces with binoculars at their eyes. From the constant looking-out your eyes acquired rims, circular depressions that you could feel with your fingertips.

Bell-Reid muttered, "Enemy's late this morning. Ought to be ashamed of themselves. A good German's never late."

"Let's not object too loudly." Napier's glasses traversed slowly across the horizon on the bow. "And you know what they used to call a *good* German."

A dead one . . . There'd be a few floating around, too, after last night. Just after 4:00 this morning there'd been a signal to C-in-C from Force D, Admiral Glennie with *Dido, Orion,* and *Ajax,* reporting that earlier in the night they'd run into an invasion convoy of caïques and steamers and one Italian escort, and destroyed it. Glennie was withdrawing westward now, towards Rawlings and the battle squadron, because his cruisers were low in ammunition; Admiral King's Force C was thus alone in the Aegean, carrying out the C-in-C's earlier orders to conduct a daylight sweep from Heraklion northwards to Milos Island, looking for more invasion convoys. The one thing they could be absolutely sure of finding was Stukas.

Other signals on the log showed that the 14th Destroyer Flotilla, the ships who'd bombarded Scarpanto airfield two nights ago, were heading for the Kaso Strait from Alexandria, where they'd have fuelled and ammunitioned; and the 10th, comprising three rather ancient Australian destroyers, was on its way from Alex to join Admiral Rawlings. Also the 5th—Louis Mountbatten's flotilla, which Cunningham had been keeping in Malta as a raiding force against Rommel's supply convoys from Italy to the desert—had sailed from Valetta last night and would be joining Rawlings during the forenoon.

Able Seaman Noble brought Napier a cup of coffee. He muttered in that low growl of his, turning pale slit-eyes up towards the sky, "Gerries must be 'aving a lie-in, sir."

"Long may it continue. If there's any more of that, Noble, perhaps you'd spare the commander a cup."

"Aye aye, sir." Noble asked Bell-Reid, "One lump in coffee is it, sir?"

Bell-Reid nodded, and said to Napier, "Very kind, sir."

Napier's ADP telephone buzzed, and he reached down for it. "Captain." He was listening, and at the same time drawing himself up on the seat, tall in the saddle to get a better view of the horizon on the port bow or the dark blue mountains crowning it. "Are you sure of that bearing?"

He put the phone down and told Jack Everard, "McCowan reports what he says looks like the flotilla on bearing oh-nine-five, but one ship less than there ought to be. We don't expect 'em to be as far south yet, do we?"

Jack told him—the Tribals should have been thirty degrees on the bow, not ten.

"That's where they are, anyway." Napier pointed. "And McCowan's got an RDF range of fourteen miles. Visibility's poor against the land, I dare say they're all there . . . Giving 'em 12 knots, what's an adjusted course to intercept?"

He went to the chart and worked it out. On the present showing he'd have given them about 15 knots, not 12.

"One-four-oh, sir, to bring us up with them at 0700. But they may alter course before that, in the process of rounding Elaphonisi."

Napier told Willy Irvine, "Come round to one-four-oh."

"Aye aye, sir." The black beard touched the voicepipe's rim: "Starboard ten."

Jack checked the time of the alteration: it was 6:22.

"Aircraft astern, sir!"

One of the look-outs had yelled it. Nick slid off his seat: he told Yeoman Whiffen, "Red warning flag," and joined Pratt at the binnacle. Ashcourt had gone to that look-out, to check on the report. Nick told Harry Houston up the director voicepipe, "Alarm astern, aircraft. Be ready with your barrage and for God's sake watch the sun."

They liked to make use of the sun when it was low. It was lifting over the mountains: like an enormous, blinding searchlight aimed into the destroyer's bridge.

Ashcourt shouted from where he was leaning over the look-out bay, "Long way off, sir, hard to see. They're circling, I think—can't see 'em at all now . . ."

They'd be circling over or round *Blackfoot*. Like bloody vultures, Nick thought. He heard "B" gun's fire-gong clang, and there was a split second in which to notice that the barrels of both the for'ard mountings were tilted up to port—into the sun—and then four guns had thunderclapped, recoiled smoking, and the second gun in each mounting fired, and it was continuous now, a fast barrage straight into that blind sector. With his eyes squeezed three-quarters shut Nick tried to see their attackers, but he couldn't: the guns were shooting fast and steadily, and it wasn't just Houston being edgy because the other ships were in action too; *Afghan* slanting across ahead from starboard to port with her guns cocked high spurting flame, disgorging smoke; and *Masai* on the end of her lead also giving tongue, at least with her for'ard guns. And now he heard it—the Stuka's siren, the banshee howl that was supposed to break men's nerves. With the tow astern, there was nothing to do except keep shooting. Every gun was doing that: pompoms thump-thumping, point-fives clattering. There was one four-barrelled pompom between the funnels and another on the platform aft which also supported the big searchlight and the after-control position: over all the din, the growing volume of the Stuka's shriek.

"Flashing, starboard side, sir!"

Carnarvon, at last . . . He put his glasses up. The winking light was on the beam and a long way off: Mason, a leading signalman, was at the starboard eighteen-inch, sending his single answering flash just as a bomb splashed into the sea ahead and the Stuka levelled, tilting on to his starboard wingtip as he swung away towards the north.

"What's happened to the bunch astern?" He was asking Ashcourt—who like everyone else had been concentrating on things nearer at hand. That last one had come from nowhere: out of the sun, of course, but one minute it hadn't been visible and the next it had been in its dive. There was another one behind it too . . . If Ashcourt had heard that question, he hadn't answered it. The guns were thundering again, and the cordite stink was as eye-watering as the sun, smoke flaring over in brown throat-filling gusts with each salvo from the for'ard guns. Pratt yelled in his ear, "From *Carnarvon,* sir: *Joining you at my best speed which is 22 knots. Are you one ship short?*" A Stuka was screaming in, black and bat-like, just to the right of the sun's blaze: it was banking, to come in on *Masai's* beam, in a dive quite shallow by Stuka standards—making full use of the sun, of course. The port-side point-fives had opened up as the range closed in: *Tuareg* had quadruple point-five machine-guns each side of the bridge, on the wings of the signal deck, one level down. Petty Officer Whiffen was looking at him with a question mark on his broad, pink face; Nick shouted, "Make to *Carnarvon:* Blackfoot *is ten miles astern and under attack. Her need may be greater than ours.*" The Stuka was howling in, gun noise rising to a peak, starboard point-fives joining in for a snap shot as the machine roared low over *Masai* and a bomb went into the sea to starboard of her; the four-sevens were still shooting after the plane as it pulled away. Nick called up the voicepipe to the director tower and told Harry Houston not to waste shells on enemies who'd completed their attacks, that it was vital to conserve ammunition.

Because it was going to be a long, long day. If *Carnarvon* got a move on they might last through it. *Might.* The silence came, lasted about 25 seconds before the next attack developed, a batch of a dozen 88s coming up high astern. Houston could give the HACS a run this time, with planes coming straight and high as peacetime expectations had allowed for: you could estimate height, speed, inclination, wind, et cetera, feed it down to the machine below decks—a machine presided over, like the Admiralty Fire Control Table next door to it, by Petty Officer Eustace Roddick, Gunner's Mate—and the machine would feed back its instructions to the layers, trainers, fuse-setters at the guns. The system's pre-war designers had only reckoned on aircraft being able to fly at 125 knots, so all the figures had to be doubled (roughly) to make the equation come out right: and there was a long sheet of paper stuck on to the machine to extend its scale.

Astern, *Masai* had opened fire. Nick got up on his seat for extra height-of-eye, and trained his glasses westward to where *Carnarvon* had until now been only a flashing searchlight. At first he couldn't pick up anything: *Tuareg*'s "X" and "Y" guns opened fire, the hard crashes of the explosions drowning nearer sounds, and there was other gunfire—*Masai*'s astern and *Afghan*'s from the landward bow. Now he had the cruiser in his glasses, he'd moved them to the right and picked up her foretop, bridge, and both funnel-tops: as he'd expected, she'd gone round to port, steering to close *Blackfoot*. Gunfire was one continuous blast again as he got down off the seat, and Pratt was shouting something, pointing astern: his expression was one of alarm and Nick thought the tow must have gone. It wasn't that, thank God: the navigator had yelled, "*Blackfoot* is coming up astern, sir!" Thank God again: for tiny, though very much belated, sparks of sense. But probably *much* too bloody late. The Junkers 88s were coming up astern too, not only *Blackfoot*: they were almost overhead now—twin-engined, black, big-looking against the bright morning sky: the other half of the formation had circled away eastward and were turning in now to make their attack from the direction of the land. Nick leant out over the side of the bridge and put his glasses up for a glimpse of Marsh's ship chasing up astern, but all he was looking at was gunsmoke hanging over his own ship and *Masai*. The report must have come down from the director, which had the advantage of being above most smoke and all but the biggest splashes. He'd thought of the tow first when Pratt had shouted because it was what he most feared— a hit on *Tuareg* aft or *Masai* for'ard, to snap the wire or the cable. Then they'd be done for. Bombs raised humps of sea all up the port side and on the bow; the pompoms were pumping away at the 88s overhead and the four-sevens were engaging the next crowd, the detachment coming in on the beam.

He went to the binnacle, rested a hand on Rocky Pratt's shoulder as he checked ship's head and glanced at the revolution indicators: everything was as it should have been. The first flight of 88s had gone on over and swung north and the other lot was rising across the sky from the Crete side: going into their dives now, more downhill runs than dives. He saw shell-bursts high astern, right up and way back behind *Masai*'s masthead, a couple of miles back, and those bursts led his eye to Stukas, two flights, one of five and one of four: he heard the whistle of the 88s' bombs falling, saw the first go up to port—short—in a thick upheaval of dark sea, and a second, then four others closer and a batch of four still nearer but off *Masai*'s stern: then the much closer rush of the next one coming and a thought flashing through his mind, *Here comes ours* . . . Pratt's face in shock, mouth open and eyes upward then momentarily screwed shut: water-mountains rose to starboard, thirty yards clear, explosions like blows against the Tribal's hull and more bombs falling farther off, receding like huge footprints splashing in puddles as some vast beast plodded on. Pratt was looking up over the stern as the first of the newly-arrived Stukas went into their dives, one pair starting down while others circled left and right: he thought, *They have to hit us some time; they'll go on all day until they do* . . . Ashcourt came from the back of the bridge and told him, "Captain (D)'s about three miles astern, sir; he's on fire and he seems to have slowed—he *was* coming up quite fast but—"

Gunfire drowned the end of it as the pompoms opened on the diving Stukas.

"Going to be too late. Why the blazes he had to go and—" Napier shook his head, bit off words spoken in sudden anger. He had his glasses on *Blackfoot,* who'd just been hit again. She was about four miles ahead of the cruiser. She'd slowed down and smoke was belching from her afterpart, but that last hit had been on the for'ard part of the bridge.

Clutterbuck's voice boomed from the speaker: "'X' and 'Y' shift target, Stukas red one-three-oh angle of sight four-oh, blue barrage—"

"Port twenty!"

"Port twenty, sir . . ."

Napier was at the binnacle: he'd taken over the ship from Irvine a few minutes ago, about the time they'd started having to fight off their own Stukas. McCowan still had "A" gun, the mounting for'ard, throwing shells up over *Blackfoot.* When she'd slowed and they'd turned directly towards her, to get in close and try to save her, the other three guns wouldn't bear. In any case the cruiser had to protect herself as well. Now with the swing to port he was using "Q" again, as well as "A," keeping only the after mountings and the pompoms for self-defence.

"Midships and meet her."

He'd turn his ship back now: the jink had been to fox the Stukas, at least make their job less easy. There was a cloud of them in and out of a haze of smoke over *Tuareg* and the other Tribals: like flies round a distant runner's head. *Tuareg* couldn't do any dodging, with *Masai* strung on astern of her. Napier had ordered starboard wheel, and Clutterbuck was telling "Q" to follow ADP; the multiple pompoms were trained as far aft as they'd go, blazing at the yellow face of a diving 87. *Blackfoot* had been very badly hit . . .

She was about twenty degrees on the cruiser's port bow as Napier checked the counter-swing, steadying on this interception course which also allowed the midships gun to bear. Jack's glasses had been focused on the Tribal leader and he'd watched a Stuka pressing its attack home

almost to deck level, breaking out of its dive only when the Pilot must
have been certain his bombs must hit. Amidships, somewhere abaft the
bridge, a yellow-orange brilliance sparked and bloomed inside out-
spreading petals of black smoke, then the smoke was all you could see,
the destroyer's forepart protruding from it and her "B" gun still firing
at maximum elevation, its small flame-spurts winking in the shredding
eddies of the smoke. There was something both desperate and pathetic
in that one gun's puny-looking effort. Napier had doubled to the voicepipe again, a bomb had thumped into the sea to starboard and a Stuka
had dived straight in after it, its siren shrieking right up to the moment
of explosive impact: another, trailing smoke, was wobbling away just a
few feet above the water, and the cruiser's guns were blazing furiously
at two others screaming down. Jack looked back towards *Blackfoot* as
Napier steadied the ship directly towards her: and *Blackfoot* had blown
up. The sound reached him as confirmation just as his mind grasped
what had happened, watching the huge expanding cloud which had hidden her and a Stuka branching out through its upper fringes, arcing away
towards the mountains: a stab of flame quickly smothered in the centre
of the cloud was the Stuka's bomb exploding on a ship already killed.

Napier called down, "Starboard twenty." Grim-faced, knowing his
duty now: to get his ship and her guns to the others, leave the dead to
bury the dead, seek the salvation of the living. "Midships." A Stuka was
boring down on the quarter and Clutterbuck had all the guns poked
up at it, spitting flame and smoke and noise: Clutterbuck who at breakfast yesterday had blinked pale-faced across the wardroom table, that
strangely calm, deliberate way he had of blinking through shiny steel-
framed glasses while he buttered a piece of toast and piled Oxford marmalade on it from his own private jar, and answered a remark which
Jack had made to the effect that gunnery control, even a half-arsed
procedure like *HA* gunnery control, was a peculiar employment for a
paybob.

In fact, half the fleet were using paymasters for the job. Brand-new
RNVR officers, straight out of the knife-and-fork course at *King Alfred,*

were being drafted to Whale Island for a course of instruction in the
new art, but there weren't many such people at large yet.

"Peculiar, do you say?" Clutterbuck had raised an eyebrow towards
the paymaster commander, his boss. "Not if you give the matter a
moment's thought, my dear Everard. It's a job requiring gumption, d'you
see. Brains. It's not at *all* a job for bone-headed, bloody, salt-horse ullages
such as—"

He'd stopped short as his eyes had met those of Commander Bell-
Reid, who was a salt horse if there'd ever been one. Clutterbuck had
smiled disarmingly. "Good morning, sir."

Crescendo of gunfire: then Clutterbuck's voice from the speaker
intoning the ritual, "Check, check, check," and an isolated last shot from
one of the stern mountings. Silence, now.

Blackfoot had disappeared, and *Carnarvon*'s attendant Stukas had—for
the moment—left them. Fine on the cruiser's bow the cluster of surviving Tribals was almost stern-on, the air above it murky with shell-
bursts: sunlight flashed there on circling and diving Stukas. About five
miles away, Jack thought. Chasing after them now at 22 knots, less the
12 knots or more that the destroyers would be making southwards,
would close the gap at no more than ten sea-miles per hour; so it was
going to take a minimum of half an hour.

Nick hadn't seen *Blackfoot* go. Houston had reported it, from his perch
in the director. Gloom wasn't much lessened, if at all, by having been
aware for some time of the possibility, even likelihood, of it happening,
but one's own predicament left little time for ruminating on the fate of
others. One was aware of the loss of a fine ship and of some proportion of her company of two hundred and thirty men, and that it had
not been necessary. *Tuareg* was leader now, because Nick was the senior
of the remaining COs; and now that the Luftwaffe had eliminated
Blackfoot he knew that *Tuareg* and *Masai* would become the priority target in this area.

Not quite yet, though. There was a lull in progress, and every second of it was being used: clearing gundecks of the litter of shellcases, over-hauling guns, getting up stocks of ready-use ammunition, and setting more barrage fuses.

The Luftwaffe would be busy too, refilling their bombers' tanks and bomb racks.

He'd sent young Chalk aft to make himself useful to Dalgleish. With the tow to keep an eye on as well as his other responsibilities, Dalgleish could probably use some help.

"Alarm port—aircraft, red nine-oh!"

Houston was on them too: the director had just swung round, set-tled on the port beam, and the barrels of "A" and "B" guns had swung to the same bearing. You could see them now slowly lifting as the angle of sight increased, and shifting in small amounts this way and that as lay-ers and trainers followed the pointers in their dials, pointers that moved in step with the one in the director-layer's dial up in the tower. Nick had the Stukas in his glasses now, and it was the biggest group he'd seen this week. Three flights of six planes each, then a space and then another three flights of six.

Pratt muttered, lowering his glasses, "Bastards could do with some thinning out." He glanced round into the bridge behind him casually, then sharply: "Sub, put your bloody hat on!"

Ashcourt grinned as he reached for his tin helmet. Pratt turned back, grumbling, "Cooling his fat head."

Afghan, weaving ahead of them, opened fire. Fire-gongs rang down on *Tuareg's* gundecks and the show was on the road again, the guns' crashes and the ringing in her steel and in men's heads and, up around the oncoming yellow-snouted bombers, puff-balls opening like brown woolly fists with the Stukas streaking on, flying straight and level at the moment so that Houston had the HA director above him controlling the guns, shooting by the book, an AA shoot at this stage and not a bar-rage. After each salvo there was a pause, and just as deafness seemed to be easing off in your eardrums there'd be another thunderclap, and just as regularly a new group of shell-bursts that broke open against the blue background of the sky, adding to those from *Afghan* and *Masai*. Now they were splitting up, some one way and some the other, others coming on but weaving, jinking, rate of fire increasing as the guns switched to barrage fire. Deafness was cumulative, building while the action lasted. The first two planes were tipping over, lowering their yellow noses as if to inspect for the first time the shell-bursts that were plastering the air they were about to dive through. He saw one explode: a flash, black smoke-burst, cloud of debris scattering: only one plane diving now: the next pair tearing in, dodging and bucketing through the bursts, this front-runner half-hidden in them, its siren's ear-splitting note rising as it swept down at the ships. Pompoms giving all they had, point-fives stammering from both sides. Ammunition wouldn't last the day out if this went on—it wouldn't even last till noon. The Stuka was hit, flaming, on its back and falling away to port, but there were two others— no, *four*, two beyond them—in their dives and no pause in the barrage, in the huge expenditure of shells, two more bombers coming in shallowly from astern and yet another brace steeply from right ahead, so there was no question of shooting at individual attackers—except at close range, for the pompoms and point-fives. The best you could do was fill the air with shells and pray for the things to fly into them.

A bomb had gone up astern of *Masai*: about eight Stukas were diving on her and half a dozen on *Tuareg*, one levelling out over *Afghan* now with its bomb raising the sea ahead of her as she swung hard a-starboard: you glimpsed pieces at a time, saw bits here and bits there through a blanket of noise and smoke: behind it was the recurrent and sick certainty that it couldn't last. *Afghan*, being free to dodge, was not a favourite target and she was having a comparatively easy time, contributing her firepower mostly to the barrage above this tow. Flame shot up in a streak like a gas-jet, and as the top of it seemed to pinch inwards a fireball rose from that: burning gas—ammunition, a cordite fire? *Masai*— from her stern, where a bomb had burst. Smoke now erupting: her after magazine, he guessed. Magazine and shellroom, respectively port and starboard sides, were under the "X" gun-mounting, and immediately for'ard of that was an oil-fuel tank. He had to think it out, get facts and probabilities straight in his mind, thinking of what *Masai's* position would be now and what could be done about it, if anything. The tiller-flat bulkhead was already exposed to the sea, and that would have been an internal explosion about 25 feet for'ard of it. But it was whether the bulkhead for'ard of the explosion held that would decide whether she sank or floated.

The bombers' siren-screams were howls of exaltation piercing bedlam: another Stuka had gone down burning, spinning, and the sea was lifting all around as planes hurtled in from all angles and all directions, plummeting through the cloud of shell-bursts screaming for blood to dip their yellow beaks in. One disintegrating, flung over as a shell burst under it, two others weaving as they flew off towards the mountains, one of them trailing smoke: and one right ahead now, coming down near-vertically, pompoms blasting up at it from all three destroyers. It was beginning to pull out, bomb falling clear, shiny like a toy with the flicker of the sun on it as it turned over in the air: the Stuka had flown into converging streams of pompom shells, and flames were licking round its cockpit. The bomb went into the sea but so close to *Masai's* stem that its fins might have scraped it: sea mushroomed up from the explosion, raining across both ships: Nick felt *Tuareg's* sudden lunge and it was the thing he'd dreaded, the tow parting.

CHAPTER FIVE

· · ·

"Stop both engines. Port twenty-five." Over the blare of guns he heard the swelling volume of a Stuka's siren: it wasn't his business, it was Houston's and the gunners'. He yelled at Pratt, "Tell them to slip the

tow!" Pratt was at the A/S telephone. The pompoms had allowed him to make that audible but now they drowned the voicepipe acknowledgements from CPO Habgood: a Stuka was pulling out of its dive higher than usual, he heard the whistling rush of its bomb and then the hard *whumpf* of it exploding in the sea, not in his field of view but too close for comfort. Then in slackening gunfire he caught Pratt's shouted report, "All gone aft, sir!" That meant the tow, they'd knocked the slip off: he told the coxswain, "Half ahead together, three hundred revolutions. Midships." The stop-engines order had been a precaution against getting wire wrapped round the screws: if there was a wire trailing and a screw turning that was what invariably happened, and this wouldn't have been the best time or place for it; but with the slip knocked off, the cable would have gone straight down, taking the wire with it into about four thousand feet of water. Taking stock now: tow gone, *Masai* on fire aft, stopped and down by the stern: *Masai* was a dead loss, in fact. He had no options, really. He called down, "Starboard ten." The crippled Tribal was on his port quarter, two cables' lengths away, with *Afghan* circling round her stern, guns just ceasing fire as a Stuka—the last of this batch, perhaps—batted away towards the land. Nick shouted to Mason, the signalman, "Make to *Masai: Prepare to abandon ship over your starboard side for'ard. I am coming alongside bow to bow.*" He beckoned Ashcourt: "Go down and tell the first lieutenant I'll be putting the starboard side of this bridge alongside the starboard side of hers. I want her people over like greased lightning and straight below. Then—"

"Alarm starboard—Stukas green five-oh!"

"—then stay down there and help, Sub."

"Aye aye, sir." Ashcourt took off. Nick told Pratt, "Warn the doctor." It was only a matter of calling down the voicepipe to the plot, but *Masai* had been hit by two bombs and Gallwey would surely have some customers and might get some more during the transfer operation, if this was a new attack about to start. He looked up and saw them, another drove of Ju87s coming high and bloodthirsty over Crete, obviously from

Scarpanto. Only half a minute between assaults now: the Luftwaffe's orga-nization must be sharpening up. He stooped to the pipe: "Starboard twenty." He told CPO Habgood, "Cox'n, I'm circling to go alongside *Masai* and take her ship's company off. There'll be some close manoeu-vring and I expect we'll have some Stuka interference while we're at it."

"Aye, sir. Twenty of starboard wheel on, sir."

Nick explained to Houston what he was doing: he made it brief because Houston was about to get busy again. Even when they were alongside *Masai* the guns could still be used—all except the starboard point-fives, which otherwise might blow the heads off men in both bridges. And Houston would need to be careful which way he pointed "A" and "B" guns. *Masai* had acknowledged the signal and *Afghan,* on her port beam, had just opened fire at the approaching bombers.

"Midships. One-two-oh revolutions."

Tuareg's four-sevens opened up. About two dozen Stukas up there, in three groups. "Steer oh-one-oh . . ." There was more way on the ship than he'd have been happy with in normal circumstances, but it was essential to get alongside fast, get those men out of *Masai* before things got worse. It wasn't the easiest thing to do while you were being dive-bombed.

"Course oh-one-oh, sir, one-two-oh revolutions."

It was time to cut the speed. "Slow ahead together." Gunfire getting faster, heavier; above the noise of it, like the beginning of some weird descant, he heard the first Stuka in its dive. He wondered whether there'd be many survivors from poor *Blackfoot.* Or any at all. The German flyers didn't seem to like survivors, judging by the prevalence of machine-gun attacks on men helpless in the water. It seemed pointless as well as barbarous: they must be very young, he thought, mindless, really rather horrible people. It could be that they were under orders to terrify, break their enemies' spirit, shatter morale. There was another theory, that the pilots were fed drugs of some kind. But no time now for speculation: pompoms had opened fire.

"Steer two degrees to starboard."

Masai's for'ard guns were hard at it. A Stuka swept so low as it levelled that it passed right through the narrowing gap between the two ships, then banked to the left and curved away down *Tuareg's* port side, getting a parting burst from the point-fives as it swept past. There was a medley of sirens overhead and all the guns were cocked up and blazing. He bent to the voicepipe again: "Stop starboard." *Tuareg* was sliding up almost stem to stem with *Masai:* by doing it this way he was reducing the risk of new explosions in the other destroyer's stern spreading fire or damage to his own ship: and he was keeping his screws well clear of trouble too. By now Johnny Smeake should have most of his men waiting under cover, ready to rush out of the screen door at the foc'sl break and flood over into *Tuareg.* Habgood reported that the starboard telegraph was to "stop." Gunfire was at its peak, about as loud and continuous as it could get, and the ship was ringing to the percussions: by the noise of sirens there must have been two or three Stukas diving now. Looking quickly over the side of the bridge, down at the foc'sl deck, he saw Tony Dalgleish and Petty Officer Mercer, the buffer, standing with heaving lines looped ready in their hands: two other men, one a killick called Sherratt, were dragging up a coil of steel wire rope. He saw Chalk down there, and a man securing a line to the end of a ribbed gangplank: two other planks were ready near it.

"Slow astern both engines."

"Slow astern both, sir!"

Bombs were exploding in the sea astern. This wasn't going to turn out too badly, he thought . . . "Stop starboard."

"Stop starboard, sir . . ."

"Stop port!"

A bit more of a bump than one would normally have been proud of: but the object hadn't been to show off any ship-handling ability, only to get there as quickly as was possible without bumping hard enough for the ships to be thrown apart again. Lines, wires, and planks had gone over, and sailors were boarding thick and fast. Johnny Smeake in *Masai's* bridge was waving and shouting something: Nick waved back but he couldn't hear Smeake's words. He looked down to see two wires made fast: and that at one of the gangplanks a line of *Masai's* men were forming with a gunner's mate organizing them and shells being passed from hand to hand: there was an outsize stoker on the plank as link man. It was four-seven HA ammunition and boxes of pompom, all worth its weight in gold. Pratt pointed northward and shouted something about *Carnarvon* coming: a Stuka was shrieking down, wild fury in the hideous noise, guns doing their best to shout it down, *Masai's* "A" and "B" guns cocked up to port and barraging in front of a group of about six weaving, high-up bombers. *Afghan* was out on that side too, and all three ships' pompoms were pumping vertically at the closer, more immediate threats, the planes already in their dives. Nick was looking down at the foc'sl deck again, at the rapid transference of men and ammunition: he heard the bombs coming—two Stukas diving simultaneously . . . The first eruption was right ahead, not more than ten yards from *Tuareg's* stem and about five from *Masai's* burning afterpart: the second plumped in well clear, farther out on the other side. There'd been the usual thick upflinging of sea as the first bomb splashed in and exploded: now a wall of sea flung back against the bow and into the gap between the ships, sluicing aft. The ammunition handler on the plank staggered, swaying wildly with a shell clasped in his arms: like a high-wire artist, he was on one foot and doubling backwards, but he'd somehow managed to throw the shell towards *Tuareg*—or it had simply happened, ejected from his grasp by his own strenuous efforts to avoid falling between the two ships and being crushed—and PO Mercer, leaning out from *Tuareg's* side, had caught it. It weighed fifty pounds, that shell. The other man was sitting on the plank, his long legs dangling in the gap then whipping up out of the way as he saw his danger a second before the two destroyers lurched back together. A roar of cheers was drowned in gunfire and the shrieking of more diving Stukas: Nick shouted to Whiffen, his yeoman, to get the loud-hailer rigged so he could tell Johnny Smeake to send the rest of his men over, forget the ammunition.

• • •

From *Carnarvon's* bridge all you could see of *Tuareg* and *Masai* was a muddle of bomb-splashes, smoke, shell-bursts, and diving bombers. *Afghan* was more easily visible as she dodged around the other ships at high speed, zigging to and fro to foil her own attackers while keeping far enough from the maelstrom in the centre to be able to keep her four-sevens barraging over it.

Stukas hadn't bothered the cruiser much. They'd made a few attacks, but with her high-angle four-inch guns she wasn't as soft a target as the destroyers were, and the Germans tended to pull out of their dives well up, which considerably reduced their accuracy. During the last ten minutes there'd been a procession of flights of Ju88s coming over, and this had kept everyone busy; but they'd left now, having churned the sea up all around, and McCowan had switched all his guns to a long-range barrage above the Tribals, twenty degrees on the port bow; Napier was steering this course so as to allow all the guns to bear.

The director telephone was calling: nobody heard it, but Brighouse, the snotty, saw its light flashing and jumped to snatch it off its hook and offer it to the captain. Bell-Reid stared at Brighouse with his bushy eyebrows raised, as if amazed that the lad should have done something useful. Jack thought again of the possibility that brother Nick might, a long time ago, have been rather Brighousian . . . He was feeling no anxiety for Nick, no more than one would have felt for anyone else in that fairly desperate situation: less, in fact, because he'd little doubt that when the smoke cleared *Tuareg* and her captain would emerge like muddied players from the bottom of a rugger scrum. Nick was a sort of india-rubber character, a bouncer-back: and didn't he expect everyone else to be just as tough, just as uncaring?

Sarah said he was like flint. She said Nick was so inconsiderate, so lacking in normal human compassion that it was astonishing his marriage had lasted the few years it had . . .

Napier still had the director telephone at his ear: now, pushing it back on its hook, he was looking round and beckoning to the chief yeoman.

Hegarty moved over quickly: his narrow face under the tin hat sharp, terrier-like. Napier told him, "That's *Tuareg*, there." He pointed at the right-hand edge of the smother of smoke and ships; Jack put his own glasses up again, and he could see *Tuareg* drawing out to starboard. Napier told the yeoman, "Make to her: *Course one-eight-oh, 22 knots.*" Hegarty had scrawled it on his pad: he began to shout it back, but the pompoms opened fire and drowned his voice. A Messerschmitt 109, a single-engined fighter, roared over from port to starboard, machine-guns racketing. Now another: and a third . . . Bell-Reid was using a telephone to get a first-aid party up to attend to a casualty in the pompom's crew, and a replacement for him. The fighters had come over without anyone having sighted them, and now Bell-Reid was at the after end of the bridge blasting the port-side look-outs. Messerschmitts making a pass at the Tribals now . . . Putting his glasses on *Tuareg* again, Jack saw the single flash of her light telling *Carnarvon*'s signalman to go ahead, send his message. *Tuareg* had gone astern until she was clear of *Masai* and now she was circling away, gathering speed under helm, her pompoms engaging the oncoming fighters and her four-sevens in action too, pumping shells up at Stukas diving on *Afghan*: she looked magnificent, angry, and defiant. One of the Messerschmitts had flopped into the sea on the far side of *Afghan*: *Afghan*'s bird, by the look of it, he guessed.

A sudden upheaval took his eyes back to *Masai,* as a flash and a spout of water shot up beside her. That had been a torpedo, he realized, from *Tuareg.* Gunfire drowned the sound of it: the high, dark column of sea collapsed right across the abandoned ship, and literally within seconds she'd gone down.

Forenoon wearing on, sun high and hot now, blue sea, blue sky. Mean course south-east: the three ships were zigzagging in unison, following an ordered pattern of regular course alterations to fox any lurking submarines. There'd been only one attack—ineffectual, by high-flying Ju88s—since the force had left the Antikithera Channel.

The engineer commander had just been up to report to Napier on the machinery problems he was having to cope with now. Jack, thinking of engine-rooms and other cramped compartments below decks, wondered whether it would be as unpleasant as he imagined, to be shut down in the ship's guts during action. He imagined that to be below the waterline, hearing the noise of battle and knowing you had two or three decks and armoured hatches between you and the daylight would be fairly nightmarish . . .

Perhaps it was only a fear of the unknown. Perhaps one's imagination would always balk at the idea of being shut-in below decks. And in fact it was something he'd never be called upon to experience. One could be glad of that, to be spared it, but also regret that since one would never be put to any such test it would remain a potential weakness, a suspected Achilles' heel.

He had a fleeting thought of Nick, of brother Nick's expectations, the David syndrome. He told himself quickly, *Don't think about it. There's no point . . .*

"What?" He glanced round: startled, as if the interrupter might have read his thoughts. It was PO Tomkins, bringing him the signal log, which Napier and Bell-Reid had already perused. Jack rested it on top of the binnacle, leafed through the wad of signals.

Admiral King's Force C, up in the Aegean still, had been under attack since 7:00 this morning. Three solid hours of dive-bombing: and it was still going on. *Calcutta*—an AA cruiser like *Carnarvon*—had sighted a transport, and it had been sunk by King's destroyers; now the force had "numerous small vessels" and one Italian destroyer in sight: the destroyer was laying a smokescreen to protect its convoy's retreat northward and the cruisers *Perth* and *Naiad* were pursuing. All this under constant bombing.

Admiral Glennie's cruisers—*Dido, Orion,* and *Ajax,* who'd destroyed the invasion convoy last night—had joined up with Admiral Rawlings's battle squadron west of Kithera. But there was a signal from C-in-C with time of origin 0716 recalling Glennie's force to Alexandria. There was also one from C-in-C to Force B—the cruisers *Gloucester* and *Fiji* with two destroyers, *Greyhound* and *Griffin*—ordering them to a position off Heraklion. They'd been steering west, though, at 0700, and under heavy air attack; *Fiji* had been damaged by near-misses. *Gloucester* had reported that she had only 18 per cent of her outfit of ammunition remaining.

There was also a copy of Napier's signal earlier on about the loss of *Blackfoot* and *Masai* in the Antikithera Channel, reporting too that *Carnarvon's* maximum speed was now down to 22 knots.

Like a peacetime cruise, Nick thought. He'd been down to his sea-cabin for a shave, earlier on, and he was on the bridge now with Ashcourt as officer of the watch. Even if it had been Dalgleish or Pratt at the binnacle he'd have been up here: he was very much aware that as they slanted across the Mediterranean on this south-easterly course they were drawing nearer to Scarpanto and its nest of Stukas all the time. They'd be closest to it at 1600, when they'd be one hundred and forty miles south-west of it, and after that the range would be increasing until dusk.

He heard the zigzag bell ring, down in the wheelhouse, and *Tuareg* heeled very gently to five degrees of starboard rudder as the quartermaster of the watch brought her round to the next leg of the pattern. He had the diagram down there in front of him, the book of zigzag patterns open at the one *Carnarvon's* captain had selected. On this one you lost 15 per cent of speed-made-good; but it was a lot better than being torpedoed, which was what tended to happen to ships that steered straight courses.

He slid up on to his seat, and thought about Fiona. Human problems tended to get buried, when you were having to concentrate on staying alive, afloat. The problems stayed in men's minds but at the back of them, possibly influencing them indirectly in some ways but in storage until pressures eased. Problems like—he lit a cigarette—Fiona's silence.

If anything happened to her, an MTC friend of hers, a Mrs Stilwell, would have written to him. *Was to have* written to him. Fiona had promised to arrange it: and similarly there was a letter addressed to her, back in HMS *Woolwich* the depot ship, that would be posted only if *Tuareg* ran into bad luck. The idea had been to set each other's mind at rest: he could hear her telling him now. *If you don't hear, don't worry . . .*

Pretty silly instruction to give anyone, that had been.

He wondered about marrying Fiona. Not that either of them had ever referred to such a thing, but—well, it could come to marriage. Because . . . all right, because it was what he wanted: wanted—his worry for her brought it out and faced him with it clearly—very much indeed.

Old Hugh Everard might not take too happily to the idea. Hugh was a splendid man, but he was also rather strait-laced, a product of his own age: none the worse for that, but Fiona might be too modernly sophisticated for his taste. Once he got to know her it would be all right, but he wouldn't fall for her as easily as he had for Ginny Casler. He'd try to, he'd do his best to like her, for Nick's sake; they'd always been close, more like father and son than uncle and nephew. Many years ago, when Nick had been something of a rebel and the Navy hadn't thought much of him, Hugh had given him his one big chance: he'd grabbed it, and had some luck, and as sole surviving officer of the destroyer *Lanyard* he'd brought her back—so badly damaged that she'd been unrecognizable—from Jutland. If it hadn't been for that helping hand, Nick knew he wouldn't ever have got anywhere at all.

Sarah? Sarah would hate any woman that Nick married. Any woman he *knew*, she'd loathe. No good trying to reason it out: it was simply how Sarah was. Perhaps because he'd married Ilyana? Because he should have stayed single, Sarah's devoted and remorseful slave?

The zigzag bell rang again, and the quartermaster applied port rudder. Lowering his glasses, Nick watched the stem swinging, slicing round through blue water and edging it with white. On the beam, *Afghan* was also under helm, and on *Tuareg's* quarter *Carnarvon* was taking part in the same stately waltz.

• • •

When Jack came up from lunch there were some new messages on the log. At 1225 Admiral King, still up in the Aegean with his Force C, had signalled Rawlings to the effect that he was in urgent need of support against the ceaseless air attacks. King had broken off his pursuit of the invasion convoy some time before that, earlier in the forenoon, and turned his ships to head for a rendezvous with Rawlings in the southwest; but the attacks had continued and his flagship, the cruiser *Naiad,* had been damaged. Her speed had been cut to 16 knots, she had two turrets out of action and some internal flooding.

Carlisle, sister-ship to *Carnarvon,* had been bombed in her bridge and her captain had been killed.

Jack glanced up from the log. He could imagine how things must be up there. Like all the attacks they'd been through themselves, only a lot more intense and with no breaks in the action, bombers on them all the time, hour after hour. It would be totally exhausting as well as nerve-racking. Napier, on his high seat and with a luncheon tray in front of him, was staring at Jack across the bridge, probably to see his reaction to those signals. Napier called over his shoulder, "Noble, you can take this now."

The tray, he meant. He was reaching for a cigarette. A thump from the pneumatic tube announced the arrival of yet another signal from the office down below. Petty Officer Hillier, the signal yeoman of the watch, was removing it from the carrier; Napier watched him through narrowed, deepset eyes as he flicked a lighter to the cigarette. Behind him, where a tall snotty named Burk was taking over the bridge watch from a short one called Wesley, you could see weld-marks where voice-pipes had been patched up by the ERAs after that Messerschmitt had jumped *Carnarvon* during a Nauplia lift.

Hillier had clipped the new signal to the log and taken it to Napier, who was studying it. He nodded, expelling smoke. "Show it to the navigating officer, please."

And another thump in the tube . . . Jack took the log from Hillier

as he passed: the signal on top was from Rawlings to King and to the
C-in-C: Rawlings was taking his battle squadron into the Aegean to
support Force C. Jack, imagining the scene up there again, thought how
extremely lucky *Carnarvon* was to be out of it, gently shepherding the
two Tribals home to Alex. PO Hillier had taken the new signal straight
to Napier: he told him, "It's addressed to us, sir."

Carnarvon was to leave the destroyers, and proceed at her best speed
to join the battle squadron, Force A1, via the Antikithera Channel.

"Course, Pilot?"

He was already at the chart, getting it: and thinking, *I should have
touched wood* . . . He answered Napier, "Three-two-oh, sir."

"Yeoman, make to *Tuareg: Proceed independently to Alexandria. I have
been ordered to return to Antikithera.*"

Tuareg wouldn't have had those signals, because she didn't carry the
code books for them. As a destroyer and a private ship, not a flotilla
leader, she'd only take in plain-language signals and ones intended for
her or for other destroyers. Durkin, a killick signalman, was already at
the lamp and calling *Tuareg.*

Napier told Bertie Tyler, who was officer of the watch, "Come round
to port to three-two-oh."

"Aye aye, sir." Tyler lowered his tanned face to the voicepipe. "Port
fifteen."

Jack took a reading of the log and noted the time, and went to the
chart to mark it up. Seventy-five miles to Antikithera: best part of three
and a half hours. By that time they might tie up with the battle squadron
and Force C as they came *out* of the Aegean.

One-thirty pm . . . Nick watched the cruiser swinging away on to a
north-westerly course, the course for Cape Elaphonisi and the Antikithera
Channel, the Stukas' playground. He glanced round, and told the signalman on watch, "Make to *Afghan: Speed 30 knots.*"

He'd cut the revs again after dark. It would be necessary to idle away some of the dark hours anyway, because you couldn't enter harbour until the sweepers had cleared the channel at first light. German aircraft were in the habit of planting mines at night in the Great Pass, the Alexandria approach. But it would be as well to get past the Scarpanto airfield's close radius as quickly as possible, now that *Carnarvon*'s reduced speed wasn't tying them down.

"Make that executive, signalman."

Lever was already passing the speed order. Nick told Pratt as the lamp stopped its clattering, "Three-one-oh revs, Pilot."

Behind him a voice murmured, "Burning the midday oil, are we?" Johnny Smeake, *Masai*'s captain. Pratt had called down for the speed increase. Smeake was a commander, recently promoted. "Mind me cluttering up your bridge?"

"You're welcome."

The former captain of *Masai* was fair-haired, skinny, with eyes that looked gleamingly blue in the reddish colouring of his skin. It was the kind of face that turned red when others tanned. Nick asked him, "Your chaps all being looked after?"

"Doing us proud, thank you." He'd taken the loss of his ship hard, though. He said now, "Should have sunk her last night, you know. Pointless, trying to tow her out. I was glad of it at the time—who wouldn't be, but . . ."

"Yes."

The point didn't have to be elaborated. Very few of *Blackfoot*'s company could be alive at this moment. Smeake turned away, stared out over the quarter at the cruiser's diminishing shape. "Going back for another dose of it. Won't be too healthy up there by this time." He looked at Nick—"My chaps are going to be okay, incidentally. Mending well. Frightfully lucky, all things considered."

Only three of the *Masai*'s crew had been wounded, and none killed. It did seem like a lot of luck. Smeake added, "Wonder what they'll find for us to do now." He brought out a cigarette case: "Smoke?" Nick shook his head. Smeake said, "Bloody shame, only two ships left out of four. If there'd been one more—mine—we'd still have looked more or less like a flotilla, and they might have given it to you."

Oddly enough, that thought *had* occurred. Nick said, as if it didn't much matter to him, "They'll tag us on to some other lot." Chalk was just coming off the ladder and there was a signal in his hand. Bad news, Nick thought, guessing it from the boy's expression.

"*Greyhound*'s been sunk, sir, and *Warspite*'s been badly damaged. Two plain-language signals—"

"Let me see them."

Warspite, thirty-thousand-ton battleship, was Admiral Rawlings's flagship. She was more than that, she was floating history, a famous and distinguished ship. But the import here and now was that Rawlings and his battleships must have linked up with King's Force C, which meant that Force C must have run into very serious trouble, or Rawlings wouldn't have taken his ships into that rain of bombs: and it was obvious now why they'd turned *Carnarvon* back.

"Then there's this one, sir."

Plain language again: an order from Flag Officer Force C to the destroyers *Kandahar* and *Kingston* to go and rescue survivors from *Greyhound.*

You could guess how it would be: Men in the water, German aircraft diving to machine-gun them, ships under constant air attack, struggling to get them out of it, but facing the huge risk of presenting stationary targets when they stopped at each boat or raft or individual swimmer . . . The signal office telephone buzzed, and Nick took it off its hook: "Bridge."

"Plain language signal, sir, Flag Officer Force C to *Fiji,* sending her to the support of *Kandahar* and *Kingston.*"

He put the phone down. In bits and pieces and from a distance that felt almost criminally safe, he was witnessing what sounded unpleasantly like the beginnings of defeat. Like a tide starting to come in: swirls here and eddies there, a movement gathering momentum and force, compounding on itself, building a sense of looming disaster. Personal issues flickered inside the wider, vast ones . . . With an effort, he pulled himself together. He told himself that he was overtired, overstrained: that this was a time for strength, purpose, not for letting one's imagination drift: that he was a professional and that in the long run professionalism and staying power, not drugged Stuka pilots, would win and come out alive.

"What was it?"

"Fiji." He told Smeake, "Being sent to support—"

"Alarm port! Red eight-oh—Stukas, sir!"

One of the port-side look-outs had shouted it. Nick had caught the first two words and his thumb was already on the button stabbing out "As" for air action stations. At the same time he was looking out on the port beam and seeing those unpleasant, mosquito-like things glinting in the sky, a small high cloud of them coming from Scarpanto.

Four-thirty pm . . .

Carnarvon pounded steadily north-westward. There was still a long way to go to Cape Elaphonisi but the ship was already at action stations. Twenty miles was no distance to a Stuka, and just over the horizon Stukas would be as thick as flies.

An hour ago the cruiser *Gloucester* had been hit. Badly, by the sound of it. Half an hour before it happened there'd been a signal ordering her and *Fiji* to withdraw from the area where they'd been sent—separately, one after the other—to support attempts at rescuing *Greyhound* survivors. Both cruisers, as Napier had observed to Bell-Reid, must by that time have been extremely short of ammunition for their four-inch AA guns.

Things looked pretty bloody awful. Jack was at the chart putting on it such information as could be gleaned from the recent signals. All the heat of the action seemed to be in the Kithera area: *Greyhound* had been sunk near Pori Island, which was about five miles north-west of Antikithera. The air attacks were constant, with no let-up at all, and it had been like that since early morning. Hour after hour: bombers over-head all the time . . .

Gloucester was obviously in a bad way. She'd reported boiler damage and reduced speed and suffered a series of internal explosions. *Fiji*, who'd been damaged earlier in the day, was standing by her, and they were both under constant attack.

Bell-Reid growled, "No air cover, and now no ammunition. Luftwaffe must think it's Christmas." He rounded on Buchanan, the engineer com-mander, who'd just arrived in the bridge and was hurrying towards Napier. "Can't you make this tub go faster?"

"Going too fast already." The commander (E) wasn't joking. Tin-hatted and wearing a lifebelt outside his white boiler-suit, he stopped beside the captain's seat. "Sir, I'm sorry to have to tell you this, but—"

"I can't slow down any more, Chief. There's all hell loose up there, and we're wanted in a hurry."

One of the signals on the log was from the C-in-C to all ships at sea: *Stick it out. Keep in V/S touch. Navy must not let Army down. No enemy forces must reach Crete by sea.*

Buchanan cleared his throat. He said quietly, "If we don't slow down, sir, we won't get there at all. I'm extremely sorry, and we've been doing everything we can, but—"

"What speed?"

Napier's question cut across the apology: Buchanan looked surprised, as if he'd expected a longer argument.

"Fifteen knots maximum, sir. If we exceed that, we'll break down altogether. Then . . ."

He'd shrugged, glancing skyward. Napier growled, "The consequences of a breakdown, Chief, I do not need to have pointed out."

"Sorry, sir."

He shook his head. Grey-faced, ill-looking. "All right, Chief." He told Willy Irvine, who'd been waiting for the order, "Revs for 15 knots."

"Aye aye, sir." Irvine called down, "One-eight-oh revolutions." CPO Hegarty was removing a new signal from the carrier; on his way towards

Napier he paused to let the engineer commander, leaving the bridge, pass ahead of him.

The pointers were dropping in the rev indicators; the chief quartermaster reported from the wheelhouse, "One-eight-oh revolutions passed and repeated, sir."

Napier said, looking up from the new signal to meet Bell-Reid's questioning stare, "*Valiant*'s been hit by two bombs. Only superficial damage, thank God."

Valiant was the one battleship with Rawlings. Like *Warspite* she was *Queen Elizabeth* class and another Jutland veteran. They'd all had at least one expensive face-lift since *that* war, of course . . . As the speed fell off, *Carnarvon* felt as if she was crawling. Napier told Hegarty, "Take down a signal, Chief Yeoman. To Flag Officer Force C, Flag Officer Force A1, and C-in-C. From *Carnarvon*. *Engine defects have reduced my speed to 15 knots. Present position—course* . . . In code, please."

Hegarty came down to the chart table, where Jack was getting the position for him, a bearing and distance from Cape Elaphonisi. The course was still 320 degrees. It would be dark, Jack thought, before they got close enough to anyone to be of use to them: and before that they'd almost certainly get a ration of attention from the Stukas. He wondered whether *Tuareg* and *Afghan* were getting any as they passed through the Scarpanto area. Yet another signal had come up: Napier glanced back almost fearfully as CPO Hegarty, who'd sent *Carnarvon*'s signal down for ciphering and transmission, went to unload the tube—beating Midshipman Brighouse to it by a whisker. Hegarty glanced at the signal as he crossed the bridge with it, and Jack thought he saw him flinch. Then he was passing it to Napier.

Napier had glanced at it; now he was holding the signal out to Bell-Reid. He saw Jack staring at him and he looked away with a slight shake of the head. Bell-Reid was scowling down at the flimsy sheet of paper with the blue-pencil scrawl on it: Bell-Reid furious, Napier sad. Hegarty murmured to Jack as he squeezed past, "*Gloucester*, sir. She's sunk."

· · ·

There had been nine Stukas in that afternoon attack, and eight of them had flown back to Scarpanto after they'd dropped their bombs. One had fallen to *Afghan*'s four-sevens during the approach run, before any of them started diving, and the early loss had seemed to put the others off their stroke, so that the attacks weren't pressed home as hard as usual. Perhaps that one had been the leader.

Houston was officer of the watch, with young Chalk as his number two: Chalk had no watchkeeping certificate yet, of course; he'd learn the trade by standing watches with the more experienced officers. Nick had sent half the ship's company below again because he thought it was unlikely there'd be any more Stuka visits now; it was getting on for 7:30, Scarpanto was nearly two hundred miles away and the 87s would have bigger and better targets well inside that range. In an hour and a half it would be dusk.

The end of a rotten day. He thought perhaps they hadn't seen—or heard—the last of it yet. He was at the chart, making such sense as he could of the scraps of information that had been coming in.

They'd had A. B. Cunningham's exhortation about not letting the army down; then the news of *Gloucester*'s sinking. More recently there'd been a signal to some of Force C's destroyers, telling them to rendezvous with the cruiser *Fiji* 24 miles north-west of Cape Elaphonisi: *Fiji* had been steering south then at 27 knots. Until *Gloucester* had sunk, those two cruisers had been together. And the battle squadron, one could deduce from other plain-language messages, must be about thirty miles west of *Fiji*'s position and steering either south-east or south-west, still trailed by swarms of Stukas. He guessed that *Carnarvon* would have joined the battle squadron by this time, and that they'd all be heading north again as soon as it was dark, to resume the anti-invasion sweeps.

Depending, of course, on which ships had any ammunition left. *Gloucester* must have been down to about her last shell when they'd sunk her, and *Fiji* couldn't have much left. The destroyers would be low on fuel too; the need for bursts of high speed when you were dodging bombers sent consumption soaring. There'd be quite a few ships who *couldn't* be sent back into the Aegean: it was the dawn you had to be wary of, being caught up there short of oil and out of ammunition . . . Dawn was a bad time anyway, he thought. Dusk—days were worth living through for the dusk at the end of them. Even a day like this one.

"Captain, sir."

He glanced round, knowing from that throaty voice that he'd find himself looking at the broad, cheerful countenance of PO Whiffen. But this evening it wasn't all that cheerful: and he had a signal in his hand.

"It's *Fiji*, sir."

"What about her?"

Guessing it: just giving himself time to adjust to more bad news.

"Hit an' stopped, sir. *Kandahar* an' *Kingston's* standin' by her."

London believed that a fleet could operate four hundred miles from its base in the face of total enemy air superiority. Or they were pretending to believe it, because they hadn't the aircraft to send out or didn't want to spare them from the defence of Britain. Which might be difficult to argue with, but brought one back to the basic, underlying failure, the failure to be ready for a war which everyone who wasn't blind had seen coming.

Chalk looked twitchy, and even genial Harry Houston had a graveyard look. Nick told them as he came up from the chart, "It's what we're *for*, you know."

Houston nodded. As a former merchant banker he ought to know something about risks, Nick thought. What annoyed him about their obvious gloom was that they were showing what he was feeling and *not* showing. Houston murmured, "But *Gloucester* was such a lovely ship. Practically brand new, and . . ." He checked, shaking his head.

Fiji was even newer. Nick didn't bother to mention it, but *Fiji* had been launched in 1939, two years later than *Gloucester*. Houston said, "Rather a good chum of mine in her." He glanced round, as Dalgleish came towards them from the ladder.

"News isn't so hot, sir."

"No." But it could get worse, he thought, and it very likely would. "Are you up here to take over, Number One?"

"Thought I might, sir. Unless our city slicker here doesn't want any supper. I did hear he was going on a diet."

Houston glared at him. "I heard *you* were seen in Mary's House, last time in."

Mary's House was one of Alexandria's more exclusive brothels. Nick snapped, "Shut up, both of you . . ." He was too tired and it had been too foul a day to stand listening to their backchat. One minute they were glum as hell, the next pulling each other's legs like children. Compared to him, he thought, they *were* practically children . . . He told Houston, "When you go down, tell Mr Walsh I want his return of ammo expenditure tonight, not after we get in in the morning. You might give him a hand with it." Mr Walsh, the torpedo gunner, was responsible for the magazines: and Houston might as well work a bit of fat off. Nick looked at Dalgleish, "And everything else, Number One, is to be on the top line before we dock. I want a word with Chief, too, about his defect list. We'll almost certainly be coming straight out again, and I don't want any hold-ups. All right?"

"Aye aye, sir."

"Tell Chief I want the tanks dipped *now.*" Dalgleish nodded. Nick added, "I'll be in my sea-cabin." He glanced at Chalk. "When you go down, Sub, tell my steward I'm hungry, will you?"

He was eating supper in the cupboard-sized cabin below the bridge when Petty Officer Whiffen brought him the news that *Fiji* had sunk. Lying stopped, she'd been attacked again. The destroyers *Kandahar* and *Kingston* were picking up survivors. Then five minutes later there was another signal: it was an order to the destroyers *Hero* and *Decoy* to go to Ayia Roumeli at the western end of Crete's south coast and bring off the Greek king and the British minister and his wife, and various other personages. There was no harbour or jetty at Roumeli, he knew, so these important people would have to be taken off the open beach:

and to get there they must have trekked on foot or perhaps mule-back right across the mountains.

The word "evacuation" hadn't been used yet. Not publicly.

CHAPTER SIX
. . .

The mine-sweepers had come out at first light to sweep the two-mile length of the Great Pass, Alexandria's main entrance and exit channel, and now *Tuareg* was leading *Afghan* down it with the early sun a hot glare fine on the port bow. At this range you could smell Alexandria quite distinctly: the smell was a blend of many compounds, but you'd get a fair approximation to it by mixing horse manure with rotting vegetables, joss-sticks, and swamp water. It was quite a different aroma from Port Said's, which had more blocked drains and cheap perfume in it, or from Haifa's, which with an offshore wind was loaded with the scent of wet hides. It wasn't exactly a *nice* smell, Alexandria's, but it was a comforting one in its familiarity and its promise—almost certainly illusory, in present circumstances—of rest and relaxation.

Two mines had been exploded on the sweepers' trip out northwestward, and they'd just set off another right on the edge of the channel, between North Shoal and the port-hand buoy half a mile beyond it. Dead fish floated belly-up where that one had gone off; *Tuareg* was passing through them now at 15 knots, her pendant numbers fluttering from the port yardarm. She'd identified herself already, from much farther out, to the Port War Signal Station.

Over the jagged stone top of the outer breakwater, which was a couple of miles long, the upperworks of the demilitarized French warships stood out as a foreground to the more distant montage of roofs, cranes, masts, and minarets, all vague in the soupy haze of building heat. Drawing the teeth of the French squadron without bloodshed or much worsened relations had been an individual achievement of A. B. Cunningham's, last July. If Cunningham hadn't decided to ignore at least one utterly inept instruction from Whitehall there *would* have been bloodshed—as there had been at Oran—and quite possibly Alexandria would have been blocked with scuttled French ships as well. They looked pretty now, with the new day gleaming on them. Pretty, and also sad. But at least they were afloat and intact. There was one battleship—the old *Lorraine*—four cruisers and three destroyers; the French admiral's flagship was the heavy cruiser *Duquesne*.

Looking farther to the left, over the northern part of the long break-water, the lighthouse of Ras-el-Tin was a white finger trembling in the haze. Most of the naval administrative offices were in the buildings grouped near that lighthouse. Beyond it to the north-east lay the walled palace of King Farouk.

"How's her head, Pilot?"

Pratt glanced quickly down at the gyro compass . . . "One-one-three, sir." It was as it should have been: Nick had thought she was slightly askew to the line of the channel. Pratt added self-righteously, "We're between the centreline and the southern edge, sir."

About three thousand yards astern of *Afghan*, Admiral Glennie's cruiser flagship *Dido* was leading *Orion* and *Ajax* into the top end of the Great Pass. Nick hadn't any idea what might be happening now in Cretan waters or in the Aegean; there'd been no signals that *Tuareg*'s code-books could have coped with, and nothing of interest in plain language. The only ships the Tribals had encountered during the dark hours had been a northbound force comprising the assault ship *Glenroy* escorted by the AA cruiser *Coventry* and the sloops *Flamingo* and *Auckland* . . . The stunning, really frightful news had come last night in a BBC broadcast, and it had nothing to do with Crete. It rang now in his mind, that calm newsreader's voice: *The Admiralty regrets to announce the loss with all hands of the battle-cruiser* Hood . . . *Hood* had been sunk in the Denmark Strait by *Bismarck*. She'd blown up, apparently, just as three other battle-cruisers had blown up at Jutland a quarter of a century ago. Coming on top of yesterday's losses in the Aegean, there'd been a shock effect to the news: it left you winded, groping for some reason to believe that things weren't quite as hopeless as they seemed.

"Shall I come round now, sir?"

Tuareg was passing the last of the port-hand buoys; the course to the harbour entrance would be 090 degrees, due east. He nodded to Pratt: "Yes, please," and told Dalgleish, "Fall the hands in, Number One. I'll berth starboard-side to."

"Aye aye, sir." Dalgleish moved aft. "Bosun's Mate—pipe hands fall in for entering harbour."

Special Sea Dutymen had been closed up ten minutes ago; the rest of the ship's company would have been getting themselves cleaned and smartened for the formality of entering harbour. *Tuareg* and *Afghan* would be berthing one each side of an oiler that was moored near the coaling arm, on the Gabbari side of the harbour near the battleships' berths. Near ABC's headquarters too: he might well have his telescope focused on the destroyers as they slid by. Later they'd have to shift berth from the oiler to buoys farther in, near the depot ship, and have their ammunition brought out to them in lighters.

At some early stage, mail should be delivered to them. Dreading disappointment, really frightened that there'd be no letter from her, he was trying not to think about it . . .

"Course is oh-nine-oh, sir."

"Very good."

The next turn would be to port, to about 015 degrees, to enter the gap between the outer breakwater and the quarantine mole. At that point Nick would take over the conning of the ship. He looked astern, and saw *Afghan* following round. Two returning, where four had left. These would be sad days for A. B. Cunningham—sending his ships out, seeing fewer and damaged ships come back, wishing to God he could be at sea with them himself, and caring as fiercely as everyone knew he did for both men and ships. *Tuareg* was crossing the foot of the other channel, the Boghaz Pass, where the mine-sweepers were doing their stint now; the Boghaz was the more northerly-leading channel, the one you'd take if you were leaving harbour bound for Port Said or the Levant.

Johnny Smeake asked him, "Mind if I hang around up here?"

Nick glanced round: he hadn't immediately recognized the voice.

"Johnny—no, of course I don't mind. Make yourself at home."

"Thank you." Smeake flicked a half-smoked cigarette away to lee-ward. "Never thought I'd be coming back in someone else's ship."

Aubrey Wishart glanced at Fiona's portrait as he answered Nick's offer of some coffee. "Thanks, but I've just had a bucketful." He stooped, peered closely at her. "Must say, Nick, you do pick 'em."

There was mail on board, two sacks of it that had come over from *Woolwich*, the depot ship, by skimmer. Nick had seen the little grey-hulled speedboat coming bouncing round the end of the coaling arm just as Wishart, in the Commander-in-Chief's barge, had been approaching *Tuareg's* gangway; he'd been waiting to receive the rear-admiral with the pipe and side-party due to him, while oiling continued on the other side. A. B. Cunningham's barge was a thing of beauty, green-painted and orna-mented at the main cabin's sides amidships with brass dolphins that gleamed golden in the sun, and crewed by sailors whose boathook drill was impres-sively precise. *Tuareg* had only been secured at the oiler for about five min-utes before the barge had come into sight, sliding out from behind the far side of *Queen Elizabeth,* the flagship; at first it had looked as if the C-in-C himself had been about to pay them a visit—until keen eyes had checked that ABC's tin "Flag" wasn't mounted in its socket for'ard.

Queen Elizabeth was moored with her stern to the jetty at Gabbari, just a few hundred yards away, and ABC's headquarters was the rectan-gular building behind the quay to which the jetty led. Wishart had mur-mured to Nick as he'd followed him in through the screen door, "Been let out of school for ten minutes. Thought we might have a chat. You've had a rough time, I gather."

They'd be sorting the mail in the ship's office now, under the super-vision of young Chalk. Most of the noise, shouting and clattering that one could hear, came from the oiling operation—the stokers and the oiler's men. This day-cabin—with the sleeping-cabin and bathroom aft of it—was on the ship's starboard side at upper deck level, in the raised after superstructure. The scuttles looked out on to the oiler's deck and, across that, to *Afghan*.

Wishart lowered himself into an Admiralty-pattern armchair, and shook his head at Nick's offer of a cigarette. He was a big man, heavily built, with shrewd eyes behind a genial expression; if it hadn't been for the war, he'd have been retired by this time. He looked tired, and Nick thought there were more lines in his face than there had been a few months ago. Wishart explained, "Trying to cut down. One smokes too much, ashore. Can't stay long anyway, old lad. As you can imagine, we're slightly on the hop."

Nick asked him, "Can you tell me what orders I'm getting now?"

"Yes. You've got today and tonight to lick your wounds. You'll sail at 0600 tomorrow, escorting *Glenshiel* to Plaka Bay with Special Service troops. You'll be senior officer of the escort, which will consist of you, *Afghan*, *Highflier*, and *Huntress*."

A whole day in harbour . . . It was all he needed to know until, later in the day, the operation orders would come in sealed envelopes, by hand of officer, to the captains of the ships involved.

He reached for the bell. "If you'd excuse me, I'll pass on the glad tidings." One watch could go ashore this evening, if the men wanted to. If they had any sense, he thought, they'd stay aboard and get some sleep. The engine-room department would be busy anyway, attending to the numerous defects that couldn't be worked on when the ship was at sea. Leading Steward McEvoy knocked, and came in; Nick told him, "Ask the first lieutenant to spare a moment, please."

"Sir." The door clicked shut. McEvoy was Nick's personal attendant; the other two stewards, the wardroom pair—one of them a petty officer—were Maltese.

Nick asked Wishart, "How are things up there now?"

"Well, starting with your relations—*Carnarvon*'s on her way here at

12 knots. Engine-trouble. Repairable, her plumber says, but she's going to be *hors de combat* for a day or two. Which is *not* all that convenient. Before long we won't have many ships *un*damaged . . ." He shook his head. "We've recalled Force C—at about midnight, that was—and now the battle squadron too. It's slightly complicated, because Rawlings sent Lord Louis's flotilla to look for more *Gloucester* and *Fiji* survivors and then sweep the north-west coast, and one of 'em—*Kipling*—had trouble with her steering-gear. So she's lame too, and Rawlings was taking his ships up to Kithera to meet the rest of that flotilla as it came south. Should all have been extricated by now, with luck."

"So everyone's recalled to Alex?"

"Except for what's heading north. And *Jaguar* and *Defender,* who're running ammunition into Suda. But—yes, mostly. No point leaving 'em up there when they're out of ammo, is there."

"Carnarvon?"

"She got a real bollocking yesterday evening, not far short of Elaphonisi. Near-missed three or four times, apparently. She'll be here tomorrow at first light."

Dalgleish arrived. Nick told him, "We're under sailing orders for six tomorrow morning. Tell Chief, please. So long as ammunitioning's completed you can give leave to one watch from 1600 to midnight."

Dalgleish nodded. "That's marvellous, sir." The whole day and night in harbour, he meant. "Here's your mail, sir."

Nick took the bunch of envelopes—about eight or ten, he guessed—and put it down on the corner of the table without looking at it more than he could help. It scared him, that the answer was so close, that he had only to put his hand out again and collapse the pile to see what was in it—or what wasn't.

"Thank you, Number One."

Wishart said, "Perhaps you'd tell the barge's cox'n that I'll be out there in three minutes."

"Aye aye, sir."

"You might mention it to Commander Smeake too."

Nick asked, when Dalgleish had gone, "By the fact we're carrying troops to Plaka, do I gather there's no immediate likelihood of having to bring the army *out* yet?"

Aubrey Wishart hesitated, his eyes on the pillars of sunlight slanting through the scuttles. Dust-specks swirled in them: the Egyptian flies avoided them, buzzing and circling in the darker areas. There was a reek of oil-fuel. Wishart shook his head. "No." Nick was still keeping his eyes away from those letters. "In strict confidence, old lad, you can't assume it. If we were evacuating, we'd aim to do it from Heraklion, from Sphakia, and from Plaka Bay. The Suda Bay lot would cross to Sphakia, and the Aussies from Retimo would cross to Plaka: those garrisons would fall back across the mountains and we'd lift them from their respective beaches—90 per cent of it from Sphakia, probably. But you see, the beaches and the withdrawal routes do have to be secured." He sighed. "I *will* have a cigarette, if you've one to spare."

Nick opened the box and pushed it across the table. "So in fact we're preparing to evacuate?"

"On the contrary. Orders from London are that Crete is to be held at all costs."

"Does London understand anything about the Crete situation?"

"That might be a very pertinent question, Nick. But—" he leant forward as Nick flicked a lighter for the cigarette. "Thanks. Things aren't going at all well ashore. Morse, who's NOIC at Suda, is pretty sure we can't last. The army are fighting like mad dogs, but they're in the same boat we're in—they can't fight dive-bombers with bayonets. Every time they get the upper hand—and they've had it, several times—in come the blasted Stukas. They've really done incredibly well, but in the long run it's the bloody air that counts." He nodded. "*Only* that. If we'd had a few squadrons of Hurricanes and proper airfields to operate from, we'd have had the Boche licked hollow." He sent a cloud of smoke spiralling through a wedge of sunlight. "The tide could still turn, you know. I'm not saying we *will* evacuate. Certainly Whitehall's still expecting miracles."

"ABC must have his problems."

"Believe me, Nick, he's got 'em coming out of his ears."

"Getting the pongoes out of that island is going to be a lot trickier than Dunkirk was. Distance, lack of air cover . . ."

"It'll be perfectly bloody, old lad." Wishart paused, thinking about it. Then he added, smiling, "Not *much* worse than sneaking through the Dardanelles minefields in a shaky old E-class, though?"

"It might be. As I remember it, we all got quite a bit of zizz-time in. In *this* lark sleep's what you *don't* get. You have to be closed up at action stations three-quarters of the time, and when you take a chance and let one watch get their heads down the Stukas seem to hear of it and come running. I imagine the whole fleet's about shagged out."

"It is. ABC's only too well aware of it."

"Well, we'll pull it off, of course we will, but—how many pongoes will there be to lift?"

"About twenty-two thousand . . . Now, listen. What I came to tell you, Nick, is that ABC wants to see you. Lunch—in *QE,* 12:45 for 1:00. To spare your chaps the effort, I'll have one of *QE'*s boats sent for you at 12:30. All right?"

An invitation—or command—to lunch with ABC in his flagship was very *much* all right.

"It won't be formal or elaborate. And the C-in-C may not be present for much of the time. Lorrimer of *Glenshiel* will be there, though, and perhaps one or two others. Creswell, possibly—you know him, don't you?"

He did, from way back. Hector Creswell was now Rear-Admiral (Alexandria), in charge of the port and its security and all movements in and out; but he was a destroyer man, he'd had the first Tribal—*Afridi*—that came off the stocks, and he'd been Captain (D) of the flotilla of Tribals that Philip Vian had now.

Wishart said, "Now I must push off . . . I'm taking Smeake ashore to tell his story, did I mention that?"

"Yes, you did."

He'd also said there'd be a tender coming to collect *Masai's* ship's company, who'd be accommodated in a transit camp.

"Sorry. Going daft. Tell you the truth, *we* don't get all that much sleep, either." They were both on their feet, and Nick was looking down at the letters, seeing the edge of one dark blue envelope that could— just *could*—be from Fiona. Wishart was saying, "Tell you frankly, old lad, I know you're at the sharp end of it, but I'd rather be in your shoes than mine. Except—"

He'd cut himself short, remembering something else . . . "One thing. At lunch, don't mention *Juno.*"

"Why not?"

"You know she was sunk, day before yesterday? With King's ships, Force C?" Nick had nodded. "Well, her first lieutenant was Walter Starkie, and he was lost with her. He was married to ABC's favourite niece, and his previous job was as the old man's flag lieutenant. He thought the world of him, and—" Wishart frowned. "It's been quite a blow to him. On top of all the other things, *Gloucester* and . . ." He stopped, put a hand on Nick's shoulder. "One thing you'd like to know. When your troubles were in full flood yesterday—*Blackfoot* and all that— your name was mentioned as being the senior CO left in the flotilla, and ABC asked me why you were still a commander, with your record."

Nick smiled. "I liked him before you told me that."

"He knew a certain amount about you, anyway. I answered that it was because you were an outspoken cuss with a penchant for insulting Prime Ministers."

Nick wondered what he *had* said.

"In fact I told him the bare facts as I know them. Norway—he knew all about that—and the interview you had afterwards with Winston. He's—er—" Wishart smiled—"rather on your side. He's had a number of extraordinarily offensive signals from that quarter. Now look, I must be off."

On the quarterdeck, the side-party fell in quickly as the rear-admiral appeared. Half a minute later Nick lowered his arm from the salute as the last wail of PO Mercer's bosun's call faded into silence. He watched the green barge slide away, its powerful twin engines rumbling as it turned out from the destroyer's side. What Aubrey Wishart had told him was distinctly encouraging: and it was also an honour to be invited for lunch aboard the flagship. On top of which, there was a dark blue envelope on the table in his cabin, and he could go back there alone now and—

Redmayne, *Tuareg*'s engineer lieutenant, saluted him.

"Tanks'll be full in another thirty minutes, sir."

"All right, Chief. After we get to the buoy, you can get cracking. You'll make good use of this break, I imagine."

Redmayne—thickset, a rugger player and a graduate of Keyham engineering college—held up two thick, crossed fingers. "I'll have her running like a two-year-old. Twist of wire here, lump of chewing-gum there . . ." His grin faded. "But we're lucky—whole day and night in—aren't we, sir?"

"Most of the fleet's on its way south. Besides, they have this job for us tomorrow."

"Is it to Suda, sir?"

"You know better than to ask me that, Chief." He went in quickly through the screen door: he'd seen the coxswain hovering, and whatever Habgood wanted, Dalgleish could deal with it.

Redmayne said, "No shore leave for *my* department. I need every man jack of 'em."

Dalgleish shrugged. "So long as I have at least a dozen stokers to help with ammunitioning, old cock."

"Sorry."

"What are you apologizing for?"

"Sorry I can't spare any stokers." The engineer's eyes were coldly belligerent. "Out of the question, I'm afraid."

"Now listen to me, Chief, God damn it—"

Nick shut the cabin door behind him, went to the table and picked up the wad of letters and lettercards. He stood, shuffling them like playing cards and discarding the chaff—a Gieves bill, a letter from his bank, another with a Sheffield postmark that would be from the Mullbergh estate's solicitors. And a couple more of even less interest . . . End of obvious chaff. Now, one from Paul, recognizable by the slanting, very even handwriting, and with its PASSED BY CENSOR stamp on the front. He hadn't looked at the dark blue one yet: by sleight-of-hand he'd fiddled it to the bottom of the pack without seeing its face . . . There was an air lettercard from his uncle Hugh: that small, neat hand identified it immediately. For the time being, he dropped it on top of the others, and looked at the blue one.

He sat down slowly. He felt winded, knocked sideways by disappointment deepening into fright. Sure that it would be from Fiona, he'd been saving up the pleasure, the thrill of confirming it: but he'd never seen this handwriting before. London postmark: he thought, *Mrs Stilwell* . . . But it had been sent to him care of Mullbergh: *she* wouldn't—

Turning it over, to look at the "sender's name and address" space, he saw the name: Miss K. Torp.

Kari Torp, for heaven's sake! Claus Torp's daughter, and formerly of Namsos, Norway. It had been in Norway—in a fjord called—memory slipping . . . Folia? Off Vestfjord, the approach to Narvik. That was where he'd last seen Kari Torp.

She'd addressed the letter to him at Mullbergh, and Nick's old butler, Barstow, had re-addressed it in his shaky copperplate to HMS *Tuareg*, c/o GPO, London. Barstow, well into his seventies now, was staying on at Mullbergh during the army's occupation of the house, looking after the small wing that Nick had insisted on keeping for himself and Paul. At least that bit of the house wouldn't be trampled by pongoes' heavy boots: and Barstow, who was of the same vintage as Nick's late father and had been in service at Mullbergh since the beginning of the century, had a roof over his head and a wage to live on.

Well. At least there'd been nothing from Mrs Stilwell.

By the time he'd read all the mail, oiling was finished and it was time to shift *Tuareg* to her buoy. Then he walked round the ship, looking into most compartments and chatting with everyone he met, in the course of it keeping an eye open for signs of stress. There were signs, all right, but none that were chronic, he thought. It was a relief to hear all the usual jokes, all the usual grouses disguised as jokes. He asked Leading Seaman Duggan, "Going ashore this evening, Duggan?"

"Might stretch me legs, sir."

Duggan was a CS rating—Continuous Service, as opposed to HO for Hostilities Only—and bright, likely to make Acting PO after his year as a killick. Goodall, a three-badge Able Seaman and pompom gunner, explained that Duggan's presence ashore that evening was essential, since the Afghans had challenged the Tuaregs to a darts match, and Duggan was the *Tuareg* star player.

"I'd have thought you'd all want to get your heads down."

"Well." Goodall shrugged. "Change is as good as a rest, sir, they say."

At stand-easy, the break from work in mid-forenoon, he had a glass of squash in the wardroom. The ammunition lighter hadn't turned up yet, and with the amount of sea-time they'd been putting in there'd been few opportunities recently of meeting his officers *en famille*. He asked Mr Walsh, the gunner (T), "Is Chief arranging for those cannons to be mounted?"

"We're 'oping so, sir." Chief was at work, down in the engine-room. Mr Walsh, with his seamed, reddish complexion and balding head, looked at least as old as Nick, although he was still in his middle thirties. He'd glanced sideways at Dalgleish. "Not too mad keen on it, but—"

"It'll be done this afternoon, sir," confirmed Dalgleish. "The ERAs *have* got their hands full, but Chief reckons to get some help from Woolwich."

The job was to mount two pairs of Vickers GO machine-guns, one each side of the searchlight pedestal, between the after pompoms and "X" gun. The four machine-guns had been removed from a badly damaged trawler, and the depot ship's armourers had already mounted them in pairs by the time Mr Walsh—who had a nose for treasures lying in dark corners—had discovered them in some workshop and arranged a deal. A lot of destroyers had mounted extra close-range weapons—Brens, Lewis, Spandaus, Hotchkiss, and a dozen other varieties, all makes and nationalities and mostly scrounged in the desert ports of Mersa and Tobruk, which the Tribals had never visited long enough for anyone to get ashore and tour the arms dumps.

Mr Walsh asked Nick, "Who'll man 'em, sir?"

"I'd say your after tubes' crew could look after one of them. Not getting much to do these days, are they?" It was a fact: when the enemy came in bombers, torpedoes weren't in great demand. "Let 'em take turns at it, if you like." He looked past Dalgleish—at young Chalk, hovering diffidently in the background. "You need a change too, Sub. Been cooped up in the plot long enough, I think." He asked Pratt, "Sinclair could work the ARL on his own now, couldn't he? And help Doc with ciphers?"

Rocky Pratt agreed. Sinclair was a CW candidate, and the ARL was the inertial navigation system, a machine wired to the gyro and to the Chernikeeff log so as to trace a record of the ship's track on a plotting diagram. Nick told Chalk, "Your action station is now with the first lieutenant at the after-control position. Under his direction you can use the other Vickers, or act as OOQ, as circumstances demand." Chalk seemed pleased about it. Nick told Dalgleish, "Roddick had better clue him up—and the torpedomen, Mr Walsh—before we sail. How to use the guns and how to clear them when they jam. All right?"

He put down his empty squash glass. Dalgleish began to talk about machine-guns and other close-range weapons: Oerlikons, which everyone was crying for but weren't in adequate supply yet, and Bofors, to which the same thing applied. Nick gave the impression of listening to the discussion, while he thought about Fiona. The relief at not hearing from Mrs Stilwell had faded into renewed worry at not hearing from Fiona herself. It was a whole month since he'd had a letter from her.

The newspapers and magazines that had arrived in that mail had come by surface transport round the Cape, and they were weeks old, so there was no mention of the big raid on London on the night of 10/11 May. There'd been a talk about it on the BBC, though, which Johnny Smeake had heard and told Nick about, in which the point had been made that more people had been killed in that one night in London than had died in the San Francisco earthquake of 1906. But—again according to the BBC—there'd been no raids of any size *since* that night. The suspicion was that the enemy might be saving up for another huge one.

Kari Torp had written, *I am in England, and I am being taught some things to make me useful, which my father has said is about time too . . .* She'd given him the Norwegian embassy in London as a contact or forwarding address, and reminded him of his promise, made in a Norwegian fjord, to take her to the London theatres. Her father was at sea again and very well, she said. But as to her being made "useful," she'd been *extremely* useful up in Namsenfjord, he remembered. She'd acted as local pilot for *Intent* all through those narrow, twisting fjordlets, in pitch darkness and under the noses of the Germans. She was a pretty astonishing female, when you thought about it: and an astonishingly pretty one too.

Not in the way that Fiona was. Fiona wasn't just pretty, she was exquisite. Why the *hell* she hadn't written . . .

Paul was enjoying his submarine training course at Blyth. The trainees, a mixture of RN, RNR and RNVR sub-lieutenants and a handful of lieutenants, were accommodated in Nissen huts inside a wired perimeter; he felt a bit like a POW, he wrote, except that the mess was Duty Free and there was entertainment to be had "ashore," in Whitley Bay just down the coast and farther down at Newcastle. The work intrigued him, and he thought he was doing reasonably well.

Uncle Hugh had written cheerfully too; but everyone knew what it was like now in the Atlantic, where in the month of March alone over half a million tons of British shipping had been lost to U-boats, raiders, and long-range aircraft. And when you thought of the Atlantic conditions—and the fact that it wasn't just one trip now and then but one after another, on and on, in all weathers and all through the year—rereading his uncle's letter and reaching with his free hand for a cigarette,

Nick thought, *What a job for a man of seventy* . . . And arising from that, *What have any of us got to grouse about?*

A bugle-call floated across the water: some big ship ordering "Hands to dinner." Noon. Time to change into Number Sixes, ready for his lunch aboard the flagship.

Andrew Cunningham said, "So you're the fellow who ticks off Prime Ministers."

"Quite inadvertently, sir."

The blue eyes smiled, humour-lines deepening on each side of the straight, decisive mouth. Tanned skin, short grey hair. "Don't spoil it. You've had my admiration ever since I heard about it." He glanced at Aubrey Wishart. "*Envy* might be the word." Now he'd turned to shake hands with Captain Lorrimer of the assault ship *Glenshiel*. "You'll be lunching without me, I'm afraid. I've a stream of bloody nonsense pouring out of London—as well as some more essential business . . ." He'd checked, looking back at Nick. "Has Admiral Wishart told you what's happened to the 5th Flotilla?"

"No, sir?"

"*Kelly* and *Kashmir* were both sunk by Stukas at about half past eight this morning. *Kipling*'s been picking up survivors all forenoon, with bombers on her all the time."

Kelly was the 5th Flotilla leader, Lord Mountbatten's ship.

"Would you like my job, Everard?"

He shook his head. "No, sir."

"Well, I'd like yours."

"I believe you, sir."

"Yes." Staring at him. The blue eyes had a penetrative quality. "We'll see you in a better one before long, I dare say. For the time being, we've all got our work cut out, haven't we? Your ship's company in good heart?"

"They're well up to scratch, sir."

"Good." He'd nodded, turned to Lorrimer. "Everard'll get you there and back all right. Only doubtful point's the weather—I'm told there's a blow coming. Anyway, you'll manage. Sorry I can't stay now—Wishart here'll play host for me." Scanning them both again . . . "Good luck."

"Sir—"

"Yes?"

Nick asked him, "Is Lord Louis—"

"Oh, yes. He's in *Kipling*, drying out."

Wishart murmured, when the door had shut behind their Commander-in-Chief, "He's—well, he's splendid, d'you know?"

Lorrimer said, "We're damn lucky to have him, if you ask me."

"What I was saying earlier, Nick—I'd give my right arm to be at sea, except for the fact that that's the man I'm working for." He smiled, lowered his voice so the stewards wouldn't hear: "Did you know he was given an adverse report after his course on Whale Island, in days of yore?"

"He *was?*"

"Conduct generally unsatisfactory, it said. He's got it framed."

CHAPTER SEVEN

· · ·

Tuareg steadied, aiming her rakish bow up the line of the Great Pass out of Alexandria. Mine-sweepers moving out west-north-westward, a mile ahead of her and with the first light of a new day growing out that way with them, were trembling mirage-distorted objects floating in a shivery, bluish haze. Saturday, 24 May. Nick heard CPO Habgood's report float from the voicepipe: "Course two-nine-three, sir," and Rocky Pratt's quiet acknowledgement. On *Tuareg*'s quarter and a cable's length away, right in the glare of the sun that was scorching up out of Egypt, *Afghan* was nosing into the swept channel, under helm to turn in *Tuareg*'s wake; astern of her at the same two-hundred-yard intervals came *Huntress* and *Highflier.* Farther back still, half a mile astern of *Highflier,* the assault ship *Glenshiel* was just emerging from the harbour, wallowing out through the gap between the breakwaters, bulky and gaudy in her camouflage.

The Glen-class assault ships were converted merchantmen, and in the Greek evacuation they'd proved invaluable. But they'd been sent out here on orders from Winston Churchill, bringing "Lay Force"—commandos under Brigadier Laycock—with the idea of capturing the Dodecanese Islands, Rhodes in particular. Among the officers of Lay Force were Geoffrey Keyes, Randolph Churchill, and Evelyn Waugh.

ETA Plaka Bay was 0200 Sunday morning. None of the destroyers was carrying troops: late yesterday it had been decided to send only about half the force that had originally been intended for this Plaka Bay landing, and that half could very comfortably be accommodated in the assault ship. What was more, her twelve landing-craft—LCAs—would be able to land the six hundred and fifty commandos in one single flight, if Lorrimer and the men's colonel chose to do it that way. Nick thought it might have been to make up numbers in two other expeditions that their own force had been reduced; *Abdiel,* the 40-knot mine-layer, had sailed during the night with a detachment for Suda Bay, and three destroyers—*Isis,* with *Hero* and the Australian *Nizam*—would be leaving Alexandria during the forenoon with Special Service troops to be put down at Selinos Kastelli, at Crete's western end.

Rawlings's battle squadron and King's force and the 14th Destroyer Flotilla were all in Alex harbour now. With the battle squadron had come *Hero* and *Decoy,* their passengers including the King of Greece.

One other force would be sailing from Egypt this morning. There'd been Intelligence reports of an Italian-manned invasion fleet from the Dodecanese Islands heading for Sitia Bay in north-east Crete, so Cunningham was sending *Ajax* and *Dido* with the destroyers *Kimberley* and *Hotspur* to search for it. They were due to sail at 0800, pass through the Kaso Strait and sweep the coastline in the Sitia area, and if they met no enemy they were to push on westward and bombard the Maleme airfield.

It was by no means certain, Nick guessed, that *Glenshiel's* soldiers would get ashore. The rather similar force—*Glenroy,* escorted by the AA cruiser *Coventry* and two sloops—which had been on its way yesterday to Timbaki, some twenty miles from Plaka Bay, had been carrying nine hundred men of the Queen's Royals, but after a conference with General Wavell about the intensity of the air attacks and the chances of the assault ship being sunk with the troops in her, ABC had ordered the force to return to Alexandria. Then, during the afternoon, someone in London— it was tempting and not difficult to guess who—had stepped in over the C-in-C's head and sent a signal direct to *Glenroy* that she was to reverse her course again and continue to Crete. *Glenroy's* captain, Captain Sir James Paget, put his ship about again. But as this would have brought her to the Cretan coast at daybreak, which would have been suicidal, Cunningham reasserted his authority and ordered the force to withdraw.

Ashcourt arrived in the bridge and reported that the foc's'l was secured for sea. Hands had fallen out as soon as the ship had passed the break-water. Nick glanced up over his shoulder, then round at PO Whiffen: he told him, "Down pendants." In the dancing heatwaves astern, all the ships were now in the swept channel. Within a few minutes *Tuareg* would be out of it, passing the sweepers who were already waiting at the top end to let this force get by. They'd found no mines this morning.

Nick saw his ship's pendants, her signal letter and numbers, tumble from the yardarm. There was no sign yet of the blow that had been forecast. He thought it might well be localized, a strictly Aegean wind, and according to the Sailing Directions the most likely wind in Cretan waters at this time of year would be from the north-west. This didn't guarantee there'd be shelter in Plaka Bay on the south coast, because one also knew that squalls driving through the valleys could strike sud-denly and savagely; there was no place on that coast that was really shel-tered. Nor would flat-bottomed landing-craft be very handy, he imagined, in bad weather.

Well, it might *not* blow.

Dalgleish joined him. "Upper deck's secured for sea, sir. May I fall out Special Sea Dutymen?"

"Yes, please. And let's have a demonstration of the new guns. As soon as we've cleared the channel and before we form up, chuck something over for them to shoot at."

"Aye aye, sir."

"We've lost a motorboat—is that what you told me?"

The one Dalgleish had scrounged some time ago had been reclaimed by its rightful owners. Dalgleish nodded. "But we've an extra whaler in its place."

"How about the others—*Afghan* and—"

"She's the same as us—one motorboat, two whalers. Same with *Huntress. Highflier's* been craftier; she's won herself a motor-cutter."

"Where'd they steal that?"

He didn't know. But there'd been a bit of a free-for-all over boats, after so many had been lost on the Greek beaches. Nick was thinking that a motor-cutter, 32 feet long, would be a tight fit in a twenty-five-footer's davits. They must have adapted the stowage somehow: and that boat would hold up to fifty men, at a pinch.

Five minutes after Dalgleish had left the bridge some empty paint-drums were thrown overboard, and *Tuareg* circled to give each pair of guns in turn a few bursts at the floating targets. After an unimpressive start they got the hang of it, and with his third burst Chalk just about cut his drum in half. One of the other pair jammed, but the torpedo-man cleared it quickly and then sank his target. Nick told Dalgleish over the telephone, "Secure from target practice." Hanging up, he told Pratt, "Come up to two-four-oh revs." The destroyers were deploying into their screening positions across *Glenshiel's* bow, Asdics were closed up and pinging and *Glenshiel* had the signal flying for "Commence zigzag." The force had three hundred and fifty miles to cover, and at dusk they'd be only a hundred miles from Scarpanto; but they'd be in range of the Stuka base long before the light went.

"'Commence zigzag' signal down, sir!"

"Port five. Continue the ordered zigzag, Quartermaster." The telegraphman would have started the clock as the wheel went over. Nick, with his glasses on the still hazy horizon on the bow, spotted crosstrees: then more, a ship's superstructure strangely distorted by the mirage. He'd suspected it would turn out to be *Carnarvon* and now, seeing a C-class cruiser's spotting-top sort itself out of that peculiar object, he knew it was. A minute later recognition signals were being exchanged. There was a destroyer, one of the H-class, with her. Astern of *Tuareg*, *Glenshiel* was flashing to the cruiser: *Good morning. Please book me a table at the Auberge Bleu for next Saturday night.* After a few seconds the reply came winking: *Shall I warn Fifi to expect you?*

Lorrimer and *Carnarvon's* captain must be close friends. Nick couldn't see—using his glasses as they passed the cruiser—any external damage. There were two tall figures in the front of her bridge, and either of them could have been Jack. Two days in harbour, Wishart had reckoned *Carnarvon* would be allowed now. Lucky devils . . .

Noon: and the force was 85 miles from Alexandria, 215 from Scarpanto. A north-west wind, which had been no more than light airs an hour ago but had already increased to about Force 3, was putting a lop on the sea's surface, pushing up small white-edged waves through which *Tuareg's* stem smashed continuously with spray streaming back across her foc'sl. Wet steel gleamed in the sun, and the spray was brilliant white; the sound of it lashing across the gunshields and superstructure was a constant drumming. The wind was still rising and it was driving wisps of cloud across the high blue of the sky.

Rum had been issued, and one watch sent to dinner. Tony Dalgleish was at the binnacle, and Chalk had just gone down; he'd been up with a file of official correspondence with which there hadn't been time to bother when they'd been in harbour. No time, and even less inclination . . . Nick reached for a cigarette, as *Tuareg* swung to a port leg of the zigzag pattern. He'd slid the case back into his pocket and pulled out his lighter when, behind him, Dalgleish barked, "Alarm starboard—aircraft—green five-oh—"

Nick was off his seat, his thumb on the alarm button, sending morse "As" racketing through the ship. He'd yelled at Mason, the signalman on watch, "Red flag—hoist!" Houston told him, "Junkers 88s, sir. Flying right to left."

"Yes, I see them." Black against the blue, and flying at this moment through shreds of cloud. They *had* been flying from right to left—westward—but they were turning to port now, this way. They'd probably been on a sweep, just hoping to run across some target. Six of them. He'd been holding the binoculars one-handed while he used the other on the action stations buzzer, but that was finished now, the ship humming and clattering with movement as her crew closed up, and he had both hands free. Pratt was at the binnacle, Dalgleish had gone aft, and Houston was dragging his dead weight up to the director tower, where his team were already busy, with "A" and "B" guns' barrels lifting and traversing outwards on the bow. Six 88s were *not* anything to get worked up about—not after the experiences of recent weeks—but they would already have wirelessed a sighting report to their colleagues on Scarpanto and to the other airfields, and that was something else again.

Huntress—on *Tuareg*'s starboard quarter—opened fire. Too soon, Nick thought. Waste of shells. Houston was holding his fire, but the guns were following director and on target, their barrels still moving slowly upward and inching left, tracking the black twin-engined bombers as they droned in towards the ships.

You could imagine the scene on Scarpanto, when the sighting report came in: the ranks of yellow-nosed 87s, their pilots racing out to them . . . Fire-gongs: the double, tinny clang, and immediately the head-splitting crash as the four-sevens fired. Fumes choking for a second, clearing immediately as the wind and the ship's forward motion whisked the stink aft and away. Shell-bursts opened ahead of the attackers: *Huntress*'s had seemed to be on the right from this angle, which meant short, but Houston had put his straight under the Germans' noses. They'd begun to weave, the formation splitting as they dodged and bucketed. The Glen ship had opened fire, and now *Afghan* had too: two bombers were going for the big ship in the centre, putting themselves into shallow glides and crossing in the sector between *Huntress* and *Tuareg: Tuareg's* rate of fire increased sharply as Houston gave up his controlled shoot and switched to barrage, browning the sky ahead of the Junkers' dives.

Bombs away . . .

The other four were boring in, flak all round them, black crosses plainly visible on white panels on wings and fuselages. Bombs leaving them now—leaving two of them just as the first ones raised thick humps of sea astern and on the quarter of the Glen ship. Rather like shallow-set depthcharges exploding, only smaller in diameter. More bombs coming now, from the last two attackers: a double line of splashes rose astern again, well clear. Compared to Stukas these 88s were so unfrightening that they were almost benign. The first lot of bombs must have fallen on *Glenshiel's* far side, hidden by her not inconsiderable bulk. All six Junkers had banked away to starboard after their attacks, and all six were still in sight but nobody was wasting ammunition on them now; they were drawing together, gradually re-forming as they flew away north-westward at about two thousand feet.

The red flags were sliding down. Pratt suggested, "Just a curtain-raiser, I suppose."

Nick had got through to Dalgleish, on the telephone to the after-control position. "We'll remain at first degree, Number One."

It would mean action messing for the watch who hadn't fed yet. Even those who'd been sent to dinner probably hadn't got much of it inside them before the buzzers went. But this sort of thing was Dalgleish's problem. Nick lit the cigarette which he'd been about to light when Houston had spotted the bombers; he'd taken his first drag at it and he was letting smoke trickle gently from his nostrils, deliberately relaxing while he had the chance, when Yeoman Whiffen reported, "Red warning flag on *Glenshiel,* sir!" Turning, he put his glasses up—to the danger sector, the starboard bow: he saw them at once, fine on that bow, high up, a big crowd of them. Stukas—as evil-looking as ever.

Guns were already following the director to that alarm bearing. The Stukas were flying south. Nick tossed his ill-fated cigarette away to leeward. They were flying across the force's bows, from right to left. They'd circle, he supposed, and attack from the port side on a northward—homeward—course, using the sun behind them to blind the gunners. There seemed to be a couple of dozen of them in roughly equal groups, two groups at different heights. No—*three*. There was a third lot behind the higher one, on a closing course towards the others as if they'd been out on their own. A sky sweep, and homing now on the target they'd found; about thirty bombers in three groups of ten. He'd been wrong with his mental picture of Scarpanto: these things must have been in the air long before the 88s had arrived.

Houston was telling the four-sevens to load with long-fused barrage. Nick was watching that force of bombers as it crossed ahead, circling its intended victims; he was thinking that with eight hours to go before the light went, if the Luftwaffe was going to hound them in this kind of strength they'd be bound to draw *some* blood. Better not to dwell on it too much: best to live from one minute to the next, from one attack to another. Although one might imagine that now the bastards had located them, going by recent Aegean experience the attacks might soon become continuous—the kind that poor *Gloucester* and *Fiji* were subjected to, the kind that made ABC recall *Glenroy* yesterday. Cunningham wouldn't want to recall this expedition if he could possibly get it through: after the *Glenroy* business he'd be under enormous pressure from London to get these troops in.

All right, come on, let's get on with it . . .

Vultures still circling: mean, sharp-eyed, crossing the ships' line of advance and edging round, moving down the port side now. Pratt muttered, "Wonder what it feels like. They must know *some* of 'em won't get home."

Each would count on it happening to the other man, Nick guessed. And they'd be thinking of killings and Iron Crosses, not of their own casualties. Yeoman Whiffen reported, at Nick's elbow and with his tin hat at a rakish angle over his bony face, "Signal from *Glenshiel* to C-in-C, sir, repeated *Ajax: Under attack from Ju88s, in position—*"

That would have gone out ten minutes ago. Nick nodded. "Thank you, Yeoman."

"Sir."

Tin hats, binoculars jutting below them, revolved slowly as the bomber force drew aft down the port side with the sun flashing on a wing here, a tailplane there. Guns traversing too, loading numbers peering out round the edges of the gunshields, hands shielding narrowed eyes against the sun. Pompom gunners squinting upwards, rotating themselves on their seats as the whole mounting swivelled, turned by handwheels rather like pedals on a bicycle. *Tuareg* seesawed rhythmically, splitting the choppy sea and spraying it out on either side as her bow dipped smoothly into it, smashing the waves one after another without noticing them, flinging sea back over her foc's'l and the for'ard guns. Everything white and blue gleaming in the wetness of salt spray, the shine of painted steel. The bombers were far out beyond *Afghan,* who was on *Tuareg's* beam; farther out and two cables' lengths astern, *Highflier's* single-barrelled four-seven mountings were cocked up, waiting, ready on the target: one group of which seemed for a moment to be stationary, suspended in mid air, floating . . . Then Nick realized that they'd turned inwards—while the other groups continued steadily from right to left. The batch who'd turned were splitting up: separating, some of them climbing . . .

"What the hell?"

Bombs were falling, over there. Out there halfway to the horizon, over no kind of target, he saw a desultory rain of bombs. And Stukas climbing, swirling out in a general break-up of the formation. He moved his glasses to the left again: a thought had occurred to him, an explanation of the Stukas' strange behaviour, but he wasn't putting any trust in it, no more than he believed in fairies. Settling his binoculars on the other two groups of Stukas, the ones who'd flown on down the port side, he saw them turning in now: the far-back lot were all over the place but two other groups of ten were turning to attack.

A Stuka out of that mix-up on the beam was falling, streaming smoke. And another—watching it, he was beginning to believe in fairies after all—exploded, sending a third over on its back and spinning downwards. Others scattering in all directions: and he saw another in flames, gliding seawards.

"All guns follow director. Red barrage, stand by!"

Highflier and *Afghan* had opened fire. But the second group of bombers seemed to be in trouble now—as if they'd caught the same infection. Bursts of HA shell were to the left, ahead of and below the flights approaching from the quarter: looking up at his own ship's director tower Nick saw Houston shifting left as well, swinging about ten degrees and settling on that left-hand attack. And the reason was—extraordinarily, but beyond doubt now—

Pratt began it.

"Sir—I hesitate to suggest such a thing, but—"

"We've got an air force."

"Thank God. Thought I was getting DTs or—"

Tuareg opened fire. But Pratt hadn't been seeing pink elephants, he'd been seeing Hurricanes. And Stukas were falling like autumn leaves. At one point he saw four dead ones in the air at the same moment: all burning, going down. Poetry of motion, he thought, beauty unsurpassed: but the left-hand flight was coming over now and all the ships were in action, barraging ahead of it as it approached. To the right, three Hurricanes were making hay, making the Stukas look as clumsy and as vulnerable as barnyard fowls, as helpless as the half-drowned sailors they liked to shoot at in the water. No time to watch that circus, though; weaving, dodging bombers were overhead, *Tuareg* throwing up a short-fused barrage now, all four destroyers putting an umbrella of shellfire over *Glenshiel,* whose own guns were shrouding her upper decks in smoke. Shooting into the sun, which the enemy was trying to make use of; pompoms opened up just as the first siren-screams rose to cut through the din of gunfire. Glancing to the right he saw a Hurricane chasing a Stuka in a shallow dive: he saw the blast of the fighter's guns, bits flying off the bomber. Come-Uppance Day, he thought, glimpsing it in one ecstatic glance: looking back quickly at the danger zone he saw a Stuka picking *Tuareg* for its target, flipping over at this moment into its dive: he was already at the binnacle, displacing Rocky Pratt. The attack was coming from the port side, from high up across *Afghan*.

"Port twenty-five."

"Port twenty-five, sir!"

Turning his ship into the direction of the attack. Guns pounding solidly: and he heard, as one bomber pulled out of its dive and curved away from *Glenshiel's* bow through the gap between *Tuareg* and *Huntress*— out of his sight as it passed astern—the new Vickers guns' strident blare. He hoped *Huntress* wasn't in the line of fire of one trigger-happy RNVR sub-lieutenant. He was watching the Stuka, its dropping, screeching, vulturish descent.

"Midships!"

"Midships, sir . . ."

By turning towards it he was making it dive more steeply: break its bloody neck, if it could be persuaded to go just a *little* steeper . . . Or else make it let go of its egg from high up, with consequently poor aim, before *Tuareg* passed under the line of steepest-possible trajectory.

"Steady as you go!"

"Steady, sir!"

The bomb fell clear of the thing's spread legs. Tumbling in the sun: one thousand pounds of high explosive gathering the pull of gravity while the Stuka pilot fought to defeat that same pull, the aircraft flattening and shell-bursts and close-range fire all around it as it pulled out high and the bomb went wide. Nick called down to CPO Habgood, "Starboard fifteen." *Tuareg* was right ahead of *Glenshiel* after that swing off to port, and he had to get her back into station. There were Stukas in all directions, gunsmoke, shell-bursts, noise. The one who'd attacked so ineffectually was legging it away northwards, half a mile away and about five hundred feet above the sea. *Tuareg* heeled to port as she turned to regain her position in the screen. A Stuka was dropping on *Glenshiel*— it was through the barrage and only close-range weapons were shooting at it as it came on down, down . . . Bomb leaving it now: and the Stuka was sliding away to port, banking as it dragged its yellow nose up, and flames streamed suddenly from that raised starboard wing: then he'd lost sight of it in smoke, and he'd no idea where the bomb went. Gunfire was easing off: *Tuareg* had just ceased fire altogether. The only Stukas in sight were three scurrying northwards with two Hurricanes in pursuit.

Sixteen-thirty: with four and a half hours of daylight left, the ships were alone again. Two Hurricanes had stayed with them for about an hour after that air battle, then another had arrived and that pair had departed. The single aircraft had been relieved by yet another, after another hour, and he'd been the last. End of luxury, of the sensation of being pampered.

Three times during the afternoon enemy reconnaissance machines had come to look at them. Twice Hurricanes had chased the snooper away, and once it had been shot down. But the Germans would know that when the force got to a certain distance from the desert airfields the fighter escort would be withdrawn; once a recce flight came and found them unescorted, it wouldn't be long before the dive-bombers returned.

There was quite a lot of movement on the ships now. The wind was Force 4 and the sea was up to match it. But it seemed to have got no worse during the past hour; if it stayed like this and there was some degree of shelter inshore, it ought to be possible to get the troops in.

On his high stool, Nick drank tea and munched biscuits. Pratt came up from the chart, bringing a tea-mug with him. He murmured, looking round at the sea's frothy, jumpy surface, "Might be a bit tough for the landing-craft, sir?"

"They'll have to cope with it. It's important to get this lot ashore."

The appearance of the Hurricanes might have been an indication of the importance attached to it. For the sake of the cut-off Retimo garrison, presumably. A garrison—Wishart had said—that included women, for God's sake: an Aussie field hospital with twenty or thirty nurses in it, evacuated from Greece. Well, they'd be worth their weight in gold, no doubt, but there'd be all hell to pay if they couldn't be got out when the crunch came . . . There'd been a heated exchange of signals, Wishart had told him privately, between Whitehall and ABC during the last day or two; the C-in-C had had to point out that the Navy wasn't afraid of incurring losses, only of losing so many ships that there'd be too few left operationally fit for the Eastern Mediterranean to be held. Then Malta would fall, and Suez would be lost, and the Levant, and the whole Middle East and its oil . . . London still seemed blind to the facts of life in terms of air power and the lack of it. One trouble was that "Tiger," the big Malta convoy operation, had succeeded; it had only got through by a fluke of weather, but as a result of it London—or Churchill, anyway—did believe in miracles and the performing of the impossible.

Wishart had mentioned the hunt for *Bismarck,* too. The entire Home Fleet was at sea, and so was Force H from Gibraltar. *Hood* had to be avenged. Britain and the Empire were fighting the war alone: the German propaganda machine under Dr Goebbels was going full blast—*Bismarck* was unbeatable, cock of the oceans, and where was the Royal Navy? The world sitting on the sidelines had to be shown *Bismarck* destroyed and Goebbels answered. Here and now as *Tuareg* and her consorts zigzagged towards Crete and prepared to receive the Stukas, the job was to get *Glenshiel's* troops ashore in Plaka Bay: but at the back of one's mind there was also a picture of the bleak Atlantic weather and the great ships dipping through it, searching for a needle in that enormous haystack.

The Stukas didn't come until half past six. When they opened the attack, which was to be non-stop from that time on, the ships were about one hundred and forty miles from Scarpanto and the same distance from their destination. The first sign of the ordeal that was coming was not the usual cloud of dive-bombers but, on the starboard bow, a single twin-engined aircraft which Houston identified as a Heinkel. It came in to a range of about six miles, flew parallel to their course for a few minutes, then swung away and dwindled towards Crete. Nick sent the ship's company to action stations, knowing what must be coming.

"We'll get the full weight now." Pratt said it, behind Nick, to Ashcourt.

"Unless they've also found *Ajax* and *Dido,* perhaps."

Ajax, Dido, Kimberley, and *Hotspur,* heading for the Kaso Strait and about two hours astern of this force, would be on the quarter to starboard and roughly sixty, seventy miles away. From the Scarpanto Stukas' point of view one target might be about as attractive as another, since both would be at about the same radius from their base. They'd more than enough aircraft to take on both targets, anyway.

Nick saw them first, ordered the red warning flag to be hoisted and alerted Houston to that bearing—fifty degrees on the starboard bow, about due north and the direction of Scarpanto. A cluster of black specks, high, crossing an area of clear blue. About a dozen, he thought. But after about a minute Houston called down his voicepipe to the bridge that there was another bunch not far behind that first one.

And there was another behind *that,* although it wasn't visible yet. Ten minutes later, by which time it was obvious that the action was going to be continuous until darkness came, no one bothered with the reporting of new formations as they came into sight. The Stukas were coming in a constant stream, a dozen or sometimes eighteen or twenty at a time, with only a few minutes' flying time between waves.

Nick guessed how it was going to be. He slid off the seat and went to the binnacle.

"I'll take her, Pilot."

Pratt made room for him. The navigator's tin hat was green with a red-and-yellow unit flash on it; it had been left behind by some pongo in one of the Greek rescue operations.

All the ships' guns were poking skywards and on the bow, waiting.

"Red barrage—load, load, load!"

Nick heard, from "X" gun, the clangs of the first fused rounds dropping into the loading-trays and then the thuds of the trays as they were swung over to the guns' breeches.

"Signal most immediate from *Glenshiel* to C-in-C repeated *Ajax,* sir: *Stukas approaching in large numbers from Scarpanto. My position 160 Kupho Nisi 95.*"

"Very good." He called up to the tower, "Harry, if this becomes as fraught as it looks it might, you'll probably be better off with the after guns in local control."

"Aye aye, sir. May I see how it develops?"

"Up to you entirely."

But dividing the fire-control would make it easier to ward off more than one attacker at a time. Otherwise Houston would need eyes all round his skull and two separate brains. Nick glanced at Pratt: "D'you agree with *Glenshiel's* position?"

"Near enough, sir."

The last time Lorrimer had sent such a signal, the reply had come in the form of three Hurricanes. You couldn't hope for anything of that sort here, though, so much farther from the desert. That signal had been only to let ABC know what was happening, and to warn the cruisers who were heading towards Kaso.

Tuareg was rolling now as well as pitching. It didn't take much to make a Tribal roll, on account of the rather high centre of gravity. He could hear the sea's drumbeats slamming against her stem, the rush of water heaving and thumping against her sides as she drove through it, the roar of the ventilator fans and the wind's howl in the foremast rigging. Within seconds these familiar sounds would be drowned in the noise of battle.

"Signal flying from *Glenshiel,* sir—*Negative zigzag.*"

"All guns follow director. Red barrage: stand by—"

"Signal's down, sir!"

Tuareg was on her mean course at this moment. He told Habgood,

"Stop the zigzag, Cox'n. Steer three-one-oh." The Stukas, a squad of them in four flights of three, were bouncing about in the wind. He watched through his binoculars as they rose across the sky, in and out of whorls and streaks of fast-driven cloud.

At 7:40, *Glenshiel* was hit for'ard. The assault had been continuous, with bombers overhead all the time and no moment when planes weren't diving to attack, bombs in the air and others bursting in the sea.

Glenshiel's forepart was in flames. The ship's course into the wind had helped the fire to take hold, and now it was expanding it, driving the flames aft. Bunting was running to her foreyard: Whiffen, with his glasses on the flag-hoist, bawled through the noise of gunfire, "Red one-eight, sir!"

An about-turn. To give Lorrimer's people a chance to get that blaze under control, of course. Then they'd turn back, press on towards Crete. Turning stern to wind would confine the fire to the for'ard end of the ship, where it could be got at with foam and hoses. He saw the string of flags drop: Whiffen saw him see it, which saved him the effort of making himself heard again above the din. Two Stukas were diving on *Glenshiel* and one on *Tuareg:* but there wasn't anywhere you could look in the sky without seeing at least one yellow nose. As he bent to the voicepipe he felt the jar of a bomb exploding in the sea somewhere abaft the beam: he called down, with his mouth inside the wide funnel-top of the pipe, "Starboard twenty!"

All the ships were under helm, reversing course. A "red" turn was a turn on your heel, an immediate about-turn instead of the follow-my-leader kind that would have been ordered with a blue pendant. The figures one-eight meant 180 degrees, right round. *Tuareg* and *Afghan* would find themselves astern of *Glenshiel* now, with *Highflier* and *Huntress* roughly on her beams. *Tuareg* rolling like a bottle as she turned broadside-on to the sea: a bomb plunked down on the quarter, raising a mound of erupting sea so close that her stern almost swung into it before it collapsed. All the guns were firing, and their barrels would be about red-hot by now: four-sevens, pompoms, point-fives, and the new Vickers GO too: those Vickers pans had been loaded with one tracer bullet to every five others, which were a mixture of armour-piercing and incendiary, and the tracer made their double streams of shot easy to identify. It also allowed the gunners to "hose-pipe" their shot on to the targets.

"Midships!"

"Midships, sir . . ."

Habgood's tone in action became so calm that he sounded like a man drifting into sleep. Nick told him, "Steady on one-three-oh degrees."

"Steady on one-three-oh, aye aye, sir."

Pratt was talking into the plot voicepipe, telling Sinclair, the CW candidate, to get the ARL plot-table going. Then he'd be able to adjust his dead-reckoning position by however much this course alteration put them off the track. A Stuka had gone straight into the sea, between *Tuareg* and *Huntress*. *Huntress* had a three-inch AA gun mounted where her after set of torpedo tubes had been removed, and she was making good use of it. There was already less smoke coming from *Glenshiel's* fire: with any luck they'd be able to get back on course quite soon. To be going the wrong way like this felt like conceding victory to the Stukas, and any delay to the schedule would mean that tomorrow morning the force would be in range of the bastards for longer than they need have been. And by tomorrow morning ammunition might not be all that plentiful. A bomb was coming down from a Stuka that had broken off its dive high up: Nick had done a deep knees-bend to the voicepipe. "Port twenty-five!" Another yellow-faced horror up ahead, half obscured by shell-bursts and just tipping over now into its dive: *Tuareg* swinging hard a-port, listing and rolling violently, swinging halfway back then rolling again to starboard so far over you'd imagine she'd turn turtle. The bomb had raised the sea off the starboard bow and the other Stuka had corrected the direction of its dive: coming from the bow, screaming in as the first swept out of it, low to the surface of the sea . . . "Midships. Starboard twenty-five."

Flags on *Glenshiel:* it was the same hoist as last time, red one-eight. They'd beaten the fire, then.

"Executive, sir!"

Tuareg already had full starboard rudder on as she fought round across wind and sea, sheets of water flying as she turned, to head in towards the diving Stuka. "Midships!" That dive was close to the vertical. Any steeper, the pilot wouldn't be coming out of it. *Come on, just a little more . . .* Pratt's mouth was opening and shutting as he pointed: all one could hear was gunfire and sirens, the fast booming thuds of the pompoms and the higher racket of point-fives: the Stuka which Pratt was pointing at was coming in a shallow dive straight towards the bridge. Pompoms switching their attention to him now: and the German's machine-guns spitting yellow flame . . . "Starboard twenty-five!" One bomb was falling from the Hun he'd been trying to push into a vertical descent: he hadn't pushed him far enough, unfortunately; the hideous thing with its black-cross markings was pulling out, arcing upwards and away through woolly-looking shell-bursts. The other one almost on them now, pompoms and other close-range weapons blazing right in its face and *Tuareg* turning fast right under it: Pratt lurched sideways, cannoning into Nick then throwing his arms around the binnacle, sliding down on to his knees. There was blood all over Nick's left side. "Midships."

"Midships, sir."

Pratt had toppled, gone over on his back; half his face was missing. Nick saw that Ashcourt was at the voicepipe to the plot, which was the way to contact the doctor or one of his first-aid parties. PO Whiffen was kneeling in Pratt's blood. *Tuareg's* swing was easing too fast, and he ordered ten of starboard wheel to get her round to the course of three-one-oh. *Glenshiel* wasn't much more than halfway round: he saw a bomb-splash go up very close to the big ship's starboard side, and the Stuka, breaking away over the top of *Huntress,* burst into flames. Tail down, stalling, about to fall into the sea. Several more overhead, one in its dive above *Glenshiel* and the next wave coming up from the direction of Scarpanto.

"Steer three-one-oh, Cox'n."

"Three-one-oh, sir . . ."

They were taking Pratt down on a stretcher. Gallwey, with "MO" stencilled on his tin hat, was standing in the middle of the bridge, swaying against the roll and pitch, staring up at the weaving Stukas with his mouth open. Nick shouted, "Go on down, Doctor!" and Gallwey turned, only half hearing: Nick was already busy again with another attack developing, a Stuka starting into a dive from right astern. "Port twenty-five!" The doctor was moving away, still staring upwards as if he couldn't believe what he was seeing: and the Stuka pilot had shifted his aim, hauling his machine to port as he saw the start of *Tuareg's* swing. Waiting now, counting seconds, to get the timing right . . . Quick glance away towards *Glenshiel:* there was one going down on her too: but nothing else, only this one immediate menace to his own ship that he could see. The after guns were shooting at it, while "A" and "B" barraged over the assault ship.

"Midships."

"Midships, sir . . ."

"Starboard twenty-five."

"Starboard twenty-five—"

"Bring her back to three-one-oh, Cox'n."

Gallwey had left the bridge. Pratt's blood was everywhere. The Stuka attacking *Glenshiel* was through the layer of exploding AA shells, and the other one's bomb had missed to port of *Tuareg* by about twenty yards as she swung hard a-starboard. That one on top of *Glenshiel,* though— he saw its bomb fall away, the first slow-looking moments of its drop, the Stuka itself roller-coasting up and away on the other side. Lorrimer had put his wheel over, but the broad-beamed assault ship wasn't as manoeuvrable as a destroyer was . . .

"Course three-one-oh, sir."

A sort of cloud—like the dust from a beaten carpet—rose over *Glenshiel's* foc'sl as the bomb plunged into her.

Waiting for the explosion, eruption deep inside her. Glancing round:

no other immediate dangers. There'd still been no visible explosion. Men were running for'ard along the assault ship's upper deck: her forepart was already blackened from the earlier fire. *Tuareg's* guns and all the other destroyers' guns as well were barraging at Stukas circling and dodging high overhead: seven or eight of them, but nothing diving at the moment: then he saw two of them push their noses downward. Farther back, another squad was approaching from the north-east. Darkness was the only hope of an end to this, and darkness was still the best part of an hour away.

"Yeoman!" Whiffen saw him beckon and hurried across the bridge. "By light to *Glenshiel: Are you all right?*" Silly question, he thought: still, let it go . . . He saw Ashcourt, and beckoned *him:* "Sub, you're navigator. Get the DR up to date from whatever Sinclair can tell you." He saw a Stuka on the bow tilt over, pointing its nose down at *Tuareg,* and as he bent to the voicepipe the thought flashed into his mind that it was no wonder ABC had recalled *Glenroy* and company yesterday . . . He waited with his face down at the pipe, staring up under the rim of his tin hat at the down-rushing bomber, and not liking it all that much.

"Starboard twenty-five."

"Starboard twenty-five, sir . . ."

"Reply from *Glenshiel,* sir—" Whiffen bawling into his ear—*"One in forepeak failed to explode. Hold your breath while we perform extraction."*

The Stuka was angling off, adjusting its aim to *Tuareg's* use of rudder. Nick ordered, "Midships. Stop port. Port twenty-five." He nodded to the yeoman of signals, looked back at the Stuka and saw its wings tilt again: he thought it was because it was coming in a comparatively shallow dive that it could keep adjusting its aim like this: perhaps he'd passed the port helm order a bit too soon. Reaching for the telephone to the ACP: "Number One, can you shift the pompoms to this fellow on the bow?" He'd hung up without waiting for an answer. "A" and "B" guns couldn't have elevated enough to reach it, and if he checked the swing again he'd have been playing into the German's hands: with one screw stopped she was fairly whizzing round, heeling hard over.

Pompoms suddenly: and point-fives, and the distinctive tracer-streak of the starboard Vickers GO. The Stuka was diving right into those converging streams and he was being hit, smoke and flames gushing suddenly, bomb released and falling short, the pilot trying to level out . . .

"Midships. Half ahead both engines."

"Midships, sir . . . Half ahead both, sir. Both telegraphs half ahead, sir. Wheel's amidships, sir!"

"Starboard fifteen."

"Starboard fifteen, sir."

"Steer three-one-oh. How are you doing down there, Cox'n?"

"Fifteen of starboard wheel on, sir. Steer three-one-oh. Happy as larks, sir . . ."

A Stuka was going for *Glenshiel,* who at the moment was on *Tuareg's* quarter, but Dalgleish had shifted his guns to it. The local-control arrangement seemed to be working rather well, Nick thought. He saw some men on *Glenshiel's* for'ard well-deck: putting his glasses on them he saw they were bringing out a Neill-Robertson stretcher, the kind you could strap a wounded man in to pass him through hatchways or down into a boat. They were taking it to the ship's side: tipping it over, letting the whole stretcher go . . . He realized they must have had the unexploded bomb in it. He looked up and around, at a sky still full of Stukas, smoke, shell-bursts; two more 87s were diving towards *Glenshiel:* there were others higher, circling, watching for openings, he supposed. Ammunition ought to last out until sunset, with luck, but there'd be precious little for any sustained action of this kind tomorrow. One Stuka above *Glenshiel* had let go its bomb high up, but the other in contrast was pressing its attack right home, diving straight into the umbrella barrage and through the streams of close-range stuff: and still intact, still diving . . .

Bomb released. The Stuka was pulling out rather gradually: scared perhaps he'd tear his wings off.

A spout of sea leapt up, right against *Glenshiel's* starboard quarter. Its blast flung one of the landing-craft upwards, wrenching the for'ard end from the davit: what was left of it dangled from the after davit, and the ship's side was blackened, its paintwork scorched and smoking. There'd almost certainly have been some damage done inside, from that one. Now there was another Stuka diving at *Tuareg* from astern: Nick was at the voicepipe, watching it come down . . . A minute later, when the bomb had thumped into the sea and Habgood was bringing the destroyer back to her course, he found *Glenshiel* out on the quarter, much farther away than he'd expected. At the second glance he realized her speed had been cut by half.

"Starboard fifteen."

To close in, get back to her. A light began to flash from that high bridge; this would be a crucial signal. He had one eye on that fast-winking lamp and the other on the Stukas. Leading Signalman Mason was at the starboard ten-inch, taking the message in. A Stuka right in the sun was tilting into its dive, and the fresh team, refuelled and bombed-up in Scarpanto, was just arriving.

Starboard shaft damaged. My best speed now 10 to 12 knots.

In other words, the end. Victory to the Stukas . . . No bad dream to be shrugged off, it was reality. They'd have to turn around, admit defeat, get as far south as possible during the dark hours, pray for fighter cover some time tomorrow.

"From *Glenshiel,* sir—"

"Yes, I read it." That one had gone for *Afghan,* but two more of the circling vultures were going into their dives now. Having hurt *Glenshiel*—her sudden slowing would be obvious to them—it would be her they'd concentrate on now. Vultures plummeting, shrieking, scenting victory and blood. *Glenshiel* couldn't possibly reach Plaka Bay with the troops now. At 12 knots it would take ten hours from here, it would mean arriving in full daylight. Lorrimer had begun to flash again: that last signal had only answered Nick's question, but now he'd had time to confirm the damage and it was obvious what he was about to say. The only thing he *could* say—turn about, withdraw.

CHAPTER EIGHT

·   ·   ·

The thought came to him suddenly, mainly out of distaste for the prospect of conceding victory to the Luftwaffe, that perhaps there *might* be some way . . . The light was still flashing from *Glenshiel*. Lorrimer would be talking plain horse-sense, not wishful thinking: Nick told himself he was being silly to allow himself the luxury of imagining that anyone could wave magic wands. Merit lay in knowing when you were beaten: in not throwing away lives and ships when there wasn't a hope in hell of—

"From *Glenshiel,* sir: *It appears we have no option but to withdraw.*"

Peculiar signal to make . . . "Port twenty." Stuka coming. He beckoned to PO Whiffen, without taking his eyes off that yellow nose. "Pad, Yeoman!" Signal pad, on which to take down a reply to Lorrimer—who was delaying the decision, inviting the submission of ideas. Crouching by the voicepipe and watching that foul thing hurtling down at his ship, Nick wondered whether the troops *might* still be got ashore . . .

"Ready, sir." Whiffen, with the pad, right beside him. When he'd told him to stand by he hadn't known what message he'd be dictating to him: only giving himself a moment's grace, as Lorrimer indeed had given himself some latitude by not having passed the about-turn order yet. But it came now, born of necessity and urgency: Lorrimer could accept it or reject it, might spot some weakness in the proposal that he hadn't yet seen for himself.

"Midships." He heard Habgood's acknowledgement and added, "Stop starboard. Starboard twenty-five."

"Stop starboard, sir. Starboard twenty-five . . . Starboard engine stopped, sir. Twenty-five of starboard wheel on, sir . . ."

He tapped Whiffen's pad. "To *Glenshiel: Submit it should be possible after dark to transfer all troops to* Tuareg, Afghan, *and* Highflier, *using your landing-craft.* Huntress *would escort you homeward.* On completion of landing opera-*tion I would withdraw at full speed rejoining you during forenoon tomorrow.*"

With that engine stopped she was fairly spinning round. He called down, "Half ahead both engines," and asked the yeoman, "Got that?"

Whiffen began to read it back: Nick cut him short. "Send it, quickly." Before Lorrimer ordered the reversal of course: once he'd passed the order it would be less easy for him to accept this proposal. It wouldn't be *easy* to accept it anyway: the weather would make the transfer of men to the destroyers and also their landing in Crete a fairly tricky busi-ness, and it wouldn't be helped by the shortage of suitable boats. Another drawback, perhaps in the long run the biggest, was the splitting-up of this force before the inevitable air assault tomorrow morning. He had suggested *Huntress* as the assault ship's escort because she had that high-angle three-inch gun.

"Ease to ten degrees of wheel."

"Ease to ten, sir!"

He was reducing the amount of rudder on her, but continuing right round, which was the shortest way back now to the course of three-one-oh. The bomb had gone wide and it was *Glenshiel* who was get-ting attention now. Lever, the killick signalman, was passing Nick's message, *Glenshiel*'s lamp winking acknowledgement word by word. One Stuka diving on her: several more weaving about above the barrage, waiting to pick their moments. Nick thought Lorrimer *might* accept this plan: the fact he hadn't already hoisted a "red one-eight" signal did sug-gest reluctance to throw in the sponge. "Midships. Steer three-one-oh."

"Three-one-oh, sir . . ."

"Two four-oh revolutions."

Lever reported that he'd passed the message: Nick heard Habgood's, "Two-four-oh revs passed and repeated" and he thought, *Poor old Pratt* . . . *Glenshiel* was flashing: Lorrimer hadn't taken long to sort out the pros and cons. *Tuareg* was steadying on course again, the course for Plaka Bay alias Ormos Plaka: dipping to the head sea, bridge aslant and wet as he looked back across it at the Glen ship, at that dot-dashing light: then quickly upwards again and all round, for Stukas.

"From *Glenshiel,* sir—"

"Port twenty. Three hundred revolutions." He stayed close to the top of the pipe with his eyes on a Stuka that had seemed to be going for *Huntress* but was now aiming itself at *Tuareg.* A quick glance towards the yeoman: "Well?"

"Message reads: *Concur with your 2027. Transfer of troops will take place at 2200 without further signal. I will stop but maintain steerage way on course 045 degrees. One destroyer at a time is to come close into my lee with scrambling nets down port side. On completion of transfer of approximately two hundred and twenty men to each of your three ships you are to proceed independently in execution of previous orders.* Time of origin 2036, sir."

"Midships!" Gunfire thickening again, pompoms joining in. "Starboard twenty-five!" In less than half an hour, he thought, watching the bomber rushing down, it would be dusk. Plenty of time between then and 2200—10 pm—for Dalgleish to make arrangements for the reception of the troops, and by that time it would be fully dark. One thought of "the troops"—a mass, khaki-covered, seasick . . . As well to remember that they were also men, individuals, lives, people with other people who loved them, worried about them . . . He shook the thought away: what he had to do now—when his eyes and mind had a moment clear of Stukas—was work out some orders to be passed to *Afghan, Highflier,* and *Huntress.*

Darkness was a blessing, a priceless benefit, resting to the mind and soothing to the spirit . . . *Tuareg,* with her quota of troops safely inboard now, nosed out around the assault ship's bow, feeling the effect of wind and sea immediately as she left the patch of shelter.

"Steer three-oh-six."

"Steer three-oh-six, sir!"

"Cox'n, you can take a few hours off, now."

"Aye aye, sir. Thank you, sir."

A relief quartermaster would already be down there with him, ready to take over. The ship wasn't at action stations, but Nick had wanted that expert hand on the wheel during the transfer operation at close quarters with *Glenshiel*. He'd want it again in a few hours' time when they got in towards the landing place.

Tuareg was rolling and pitching, sliding her foc's'l into the black water and flinging it back in white sheets at the bridge. Astern, hidden now behind *Glenshiel's* bulk as Lorrimer held her broadside to the direction of wind and sea, *Afghan* was getting her troops up out of the plunging landing-craft while *Highflier* waited for her turn and *Huntress* circled on anti-submarine guard. Darkness was velvet, a surrounding comfort: it was only when it came down around you that you realized how much you'd come to hate the daylight. Checking the luminous face of his watch, Nick saw that it was now 10:25. He heard arrivals in the bridge behind him: then Dalgleish announced in his clipped, dry tone, "Lieutenant-Colonel Oswald, sir."

A tall figure groped up beside him. "Commander Everard?"

"Welcome, Colonel. Your men being made comfortable?"

"Absolutely, thank you. Good as the Ritz any day." The colonel laughed: he had a young man's voice, Nick thought. These Special Service warriors did tend to get promoted young, he'd heard. The soldier added, "Even if a few of us do have a touch of *mal de mer.*"

According to a report from Mr Walsh, who'd been helping Dalgleish during the embarkation, half the pongoes had been "puking like cats" as they came aboard. Possibly an exaggeration: but it couldn't be too pleasant for them, even less so if they had to land and go into action in that condition.

The colonel told him, "I've a message from Captain Lorrimer. He wanted me to tell you that your idea for carrying on like this is absolutely bang-on, and he's grateful to you for coming up with it. He wishes you the best of luck and says for God's sake get a bloody move on."

Nick had every intention of getting as much of a move on as he could. But the inshore work wasn't likely to be all that simple.

"*Afghan's* closing astern, sir."

"Very good." One more to go. He told Oswald, "I'm praying we'll find some shelter in Plaka Bay when we get there. If we don't, we won't get you ashore. It's quite a wide bay, but it doesn't go far in, and the only bit clear of rocks is right in the centre at the back end. It'll mean one ship going in at a time, taking it in turn. In calm weather we could probably do it faster, but with this wind and in the dark—well, we'll see how it is when we get there."

"I'm sure you'll do the best you can for us."

"Another problem is we only have ships' boats, not landing-craft. In this ship we've one motorboat and two whalers." He looked round into the dark of the bridge behind him. "Number One? Listen—Ashcourt can take charge of the boats, this time. I want one whaler each side of the motorboat, and all three lashed together. It ought to make for stability, so that even if it's a bit bumpy inside we could still load all three boats to something like their life-saving capacity. Then we'll put the whole lot ashore in three trips."

The soldier murmured, "More of a business than I'd realized."

"Depending on what it's like inshore, I'll get as close to the beach as I can. Number One, work out how the boats are to be secured together, and set up whatever gear you need. Ashcourt'll need a few good hands with him. And think about capacities—it may call for four trips, not three."

"Aye aye, sir."

"And I'll want an anchor ready for letting go. I'll need Chalk up here with me: and I think Houston should stay up top, in case we run into any opposition, so either Mr Walsh or the buffer could take charge for'ard. Up to you. But now take Colonel Oswald down to the wardroom and give him a large whisky, on my wine-bill. Ditto his officers." He told the colonel, "Sorry I can't join you."

Houston muttered, when Dalgleish had led their guest away, "Likely to be an awful lot of dampish khaki socks . . ."

·   ·   ·

At 0148 Cape Littino was abeam to starboard at a range of five and a half miles, the high ridge of land behind it a black interruption to the starry sky. With this wind and the cloud-patches they'd had earlier Nick had entertained faint hopes of cloud-cover for the return journey tomorrow, but it didn't look now as if they'd get any.

"Sharp look-out to starboard now, Sub."

He'd said it to Chalk but the gunner, Mr Walsh, also grunted an acknowledgement. Nick had sent Dalgleish, Houston, and Ashcourt to get some sleep: he didn't need them at this stage, and rested men would be more use later than tired ones. He himself had been off the bridge for only about five minutes—when they'd buried Rocky Pratt, at midnight. He doubted if he'd be leaving it again before they were back in Alexandria.

The reason he'd called for a sharp look-out on the starboard bow was that eight miles after Littino was abeam they'd be coming up to the Paximadia Islands, rocky outposts of Crete which were the reason for his having led the flotilla this far out. He reckoned to have the islands two miles on his beam at ten minutes past two. It was part and parcel of the same thing: he'd needed the running fix on Cape Littino so as to be sure of passing at a safe distance from the Paximadias but also in sight of them, in order to use them as a point of departure for the fifteen-mile run from there to the landing spot. The Sailing Directions suggested no landmarks in or near Plaka Bay, and it was essential to arrive at precisely the right bit of coast.

He moved out to the side of the bridge, and trained his glasses astern. He could see the splodge of whiteness that was *Afghan*'s bow-wave: it changed shape, expanding and contracting as her bow rose and fell in *Tuareg*'s wake. The destroyers were in close order, only cable's-length gaps between them. He came back to the binnacle.

Mr Walsh asked him, "What's the height of this rock supposed to be then, sir?"

"About eight hundred feet."

"Eight twenty-seven," Chalk corrected him.

The gunner muttered, "Oughter be stickin' up like a sore what d'you call it, then."

Chalk picked them up at that moment: "There they are! Green five-oh, sir!"

"Well done, Sub."

The islands were abeam at eight minutes past two. He brought *Tuareg* round to 326 degrees.

Fourteen and a half miles now, from that turn to the entrance to Plaka Bay. He had it clearly in his mind's eye, an entrance two miles wide between Cape Stavros to port and Kako Muri—whatever *that* meant—to starboard, and he wanted to take *Tuareg* in just slightly to the left of centre. He'd memorized the land heights behind the bay and on each side of it, too, and this would be a help when he got in there.

"Messenger—"

"Sir?"

"Shake the first lieutenant and Lieutenant Houston and the sub-lieutenant. Then go aft and tell Colonel Oswald that disembarkation will commence at 0240."

Two-thirty am. It was Sunday now, 25 May.

"One-four-oh revolutions."

Salt-washed rocky headlands lifted on either bow, and a welter of foam boiled right across where *Tuareg* was heading. The offshore wind was strong and gusty, and the general run of the sea was from the west and along the coastline.

"One-four-oh revolutions passed and repeated, sir."

CPO Habgood was back on the wheel now; Nick was taking his ship in alone while the other two waited close offshore. Dalgleish had the boats and gear organized and a scrambling-net ready at the ship's side, ready to be cast loose, with men standing by to help the soldiers over the side with their weapons and equipment as soon as the boats came alongside the net.

"There'll be a crosscurrent, Cox'n, by the looks of it, as we enter."

"I'll be lookin' for it, sir."

Might turn out to be bloody awful, in there. On the other hand, it might be easy. *Tuareg* was acting as guinea pig for the others, and it wouldn't be very clever to have beaten the Stukas and then end up on the rocks.

"Steer three degrees to starboard."

"Three degrees to starboard, sir . . ."

Due north, that would make it. *Tuareg's* stem was moving up close to the welter of sea that was pouring over itself in a sort of tumbling action from around the left-hand promontory. Entering it—now . . .

"Course north, sir!"

She was being pushed round to starboard: swing increasing fast, Habgood grunting curses as he got hold of her head and yanked her back like a wayward horse. She was as much as forty degrees off course before he got her under control.

"Carrying port wheel, sir."

"You'll have to lose it quickly as we get through this."

"Aye, sir . . ."

A few miles inland and on either side, rising ground loomed high across the stars. Wind was gusting through the gap between those mountains: it would be blowing clear across the island from Retimo.

Chalk's attention was on the whirring echo-sounder. According to the chart there'd be plenty of water here, but local charts weren't detailed or reliable. And there'd very likely have been silting, in recent years.

Ship's head swinging away to port: Habgood whipping off the port rudder she'd been carrying, then hauling her back to her course of due north.

Ahead, conditions looked patchy: more sheltered than it was outside, but with a ground-swell and areas of whitened surface where wind-gusts from gaps in the mountains scored it. He guessed there'd be a circular flow around the bay, probably an eastward or south-eastward set so far as *Tuareg* would feel it. Likely as not a strong one . . . The most obvious hazard was over to starboard where a long spur of rocks a mile inside the headland extended south-westward from the shore. Through binoculars Nick could see a heave and swirl of broken water close inshore: but it was in two separate areas, and where the land came out in a flattish promontory between them might be a likely aiming spot for the boats. For want of an alternative, it would have to do: as long as they could get in that far, across however much of a current there might be. Lacking time as well as alternatives and information, you couldn't dither: you had to make a quick choice, then stick to it. He reached for the telephone to the after-control position, where Dalgleish would be waiting to hear from him.

"Number One. I'll be stopping in about three minutes' time. The landing area for the boats will be where our stem will be pointing when we stop—a minor promontory with broken water to each side of it. Due north, distance about one cable when we stop. Tell Ashcourt to look out for an easterly set, could be quite strong."

Dalgleish would start getting the boats down close to the water now. One whaler, being the seaboat and having Robinson's disengaging gear on its davits, would be slipped quickly, with a bang, actually dropped into the water. But the other one and the motorboat would have to be lowered right into the sea before their falls could be released: an extra two or three minutes, because the weight had to come off the falls before the pins could be unscrewed. And every single minute counted now. From one problem to another: first it had been the Stukas, then the uncertainty of shelter from the north-wester, and now it was time: which made a vicious circle, bringing one back to Stukas—tomorrow morning's. Four return boat trips, each taking, say, fifteen minutes including loading and off-loading time, were going to fill an hour. Then if he sent the other two in here together—there'd be room for them, and if the weather didn't go mad suddenly it would be safe enough—that would add another hour. So—0445 at the earliest, before the job was finished and he could start getting off the coast again. One hour after 0445 would be 0545 and daybreak, Stuka time . . .

It wouldn't do.

"Yeoman." Whiffen appeared quickly out of the darkness behind him. Nick told him, "Take this down." Whiffen was moving to his hooded signal table on the starboard side. "To *Afghan* and *Highflier: Join me now. Enter at slow speed with caution for tide-rip off Stavros point and stop near me one cable south of landing beach. Commence landing troops immediately on arrival.* Got that?" Whiffen, scribbling rapidly, said he had. Nick added, "Blue shaded lamp. You'll raise them somewhere astern."

It was going to crowd the place, but it would save an hour. He called down, "Stop both engines."

"Stop both, sir!"

"How much water, Sub?"

"Six fathoms, sir."

"Good." At the voicepipe again: "Slow astern together." Just to get the way off her. He told Chalk, "White houses off to starboard—see them?" Chalk said yes, he did. "That's a village, marked on the chart as Plakias. Use that and the edges of the headlands for shore bearings." Into the pipe: "Stop both engines." He added to Chalk, "When we drift I want to know which way and how fast."

Engine and ventilator noise died away. From the back of the bridge he could hear the rapid clack-clacking of the shaded Aldis lamp, and from down near the boats orders, voices shouting to each other. It was 0246 now: it would be at least an hour before he could hope to be getting under way again.

"We're drifting astern, sir. South-east—quite fast, sir."

"Slow ahead starboard. Port ten, and steer three-one-five, Cox'n."

One engine slow ahead, and her nose straight into it, might hold her. He told Chalk, "Watch the bearings constantly, now." He could have been anchored, but time and his instincts were against it. He sent the messenger, Crawford, down to Dalgleish to tell him that he was stemming the tide on 315 degrees—for Ashcourt's information.

The other two destroyers were in position with their boats in the water by 0301. *Tuareg's* own boats had returned by that time, crabbing awkwardly across the current, for their second load. Nick had his glasses on *Afghan,* and felt considerable relief when he saw her motorboat and two whalers draw away and head for the shore—in a slightly circular route, as they found out about the crosscurrent. From down on the iron deck he heard Dalgleish yell, "Carry on, Sub!" That was the second lot of soldiers going in. Should complete by 0400, with luck: but it was the performance of the slowest ship that would count. *Highflier's* motor-cutter was away now, thick with men and towing a whaler that looked dangerously low in the water. Now there was nothing to do except hold the ship in her position and wait for the boats to reappear.

He'd increased the revs slightly on the starboard screw, and he thought he'd got it about right now. The other two ships were to starboard and slightly on his quarter: they were coming back to where they'd started from, having both drifted astern to start with and then woken up to what was happening.

"Are you watching that bearing, Sub?"

"Yes, sir. We're all right, still."

Nick put his glasses up, searching for the boats, wanting to see them coming *now* . . . But it was deep shadow in there under the loom of the mountains. You could see where the water was broken and where it wasn't, but that was about all, except for the mountains themselves against the sky and those white cottages.

Chalk had taken a closer look, thinking better of what he'd said a moment ago . . . "We're—about one degree *inshore* of it, sir!"

Nick bent to the voicepipe. "Down four revolutions."

Boats were approaching . . . And a second lot to the right: one of the others catching up a bit . . . The time was 0319. *Tuareg* was mov-ing quite a lot to the ground-swell but it was also getting noisier and he thought the wind was freshening, humming and whining in the shrouds. He thought he'd probably been lucky to get in here now and not any later, when slightly worsened weather could have changed the situation quite dramatically. So long, he thought, as it doesn't happen before we finish. When the boats came alongside this time it would be the halfway mark, so far as *Tuareg*'s soldiers were concerned. And that was at—0323 . . . About forty minutes since they'd started, so adding the same time-lapse again you could still reckon on completion by 0400. Allow another twenty or thirty minutes for the others, and it would be 0430. Not much better than the original estimate, the one he'd thought to improve on by bringing them all in here at once. One hour of darkness was all they'd get, for putting distance between themselves and the Cretan coast.

Then, at 0348, four minutes after the boats had left with the fourth and last party of soldiers, *Tuareg*'s motorboat broke down.

Going by the timings of the first three runs, the boats should have returned one or two minutes before 4 am. They arrived at fourteen minutes past, in tow of *Highflier*'s motor-cutter. It had been coming off from shore, seen *Tuareg*'s contraption being carried away rapidly south-eastward on the current, chased after it and caught it, towed it inshore to off-load, and then brought it back out to the ship. It was now a quarter past four, and *Highflier*'s cutter still had two more parties of men to land.

At *least* an extra half-hour . . . Nick forced himself to stay calm, control jumping nerves. *Afghan*'s boats, meanwhile, completed their landings and embarked *Highflier*'s final load, so that the last two lots of soldiery in fact reached shore practically simultaneously.

Nick had turned *Tuareg* around while her boats were being hoisted and secured, and he was in position to lead the others out of the bay.

"Boats are coming from shore, sir!"

"How many?"

"Both lots, sir, I think . . ."

His fingers were drumming on the binnacle: he caught them at it and stopped them. It felt as if he had wires inside his brain, all strung tight. *Too* tight: and it wouldn't do, a man who was too tense and too tired was a man who made mistakes.

"Cox'n, is Leading Seaman Duggan there with you?"

"Aye, sir, he's here."

"Put him on the voicepipe, please . . . Duggan?"

"Yessir?"

"I meant to ask you earlier—who won that darts match?"

"We did, sir."

"Well done!"

"Thank you, sir."

Nick straightened, checked the time. Four thirty-one . . .

"Three-one-oh revolutions."

"Three-one-oh revolutions, sir!"

That was Leading Seaman Sherratt on the wheel now; one watch had been stood down and CPO Habgood would be getting some well-deserved rest.

"Three-one-oh revs passed and repeated, sir."

Afghan and *Highflier* were in station astern of *Tuareg*, on course 143 degrees. Thirty knots, those revs should provide: he'd have liked to have made it 360 and squeezed an extra 2 or 3 knots out of her, but 30 was *Highflier*'s best speed.

It was a quarter to five. The two hours inside Plaka Bay had felt like two weeks. Now Plaka was astern, Alexandria three hundred miles ahead. One hour of darkness, therefore, then dawn and a whole day within easy distance of the Scarpanto airfield.

There was satisfaction in having got the troops ashore, particularly as the wind was rising astern of them now, nearer Force 5 than 4. He'd thought it had been past its peak, but he'd been wrong; and he doubted whether the three destroyers who'd been taking a similar batch of commandos to Selinos Kastelli would have got them in. It was right on the island's south-west corner, with no kind of shelter at all; the full strength of wind and sea would be sweeping along that curve of coastline.

The Paximadias were twelve miles ahead. Ten miles beyond them Cape Littino would be abeam, and course would be altered to 130 degrees—adjusted for the one-knot easterly set—the straight heading for Alexandria. There'd be an eight-hour gap, roughly, before he'd catch up with *Glenshiel* and *Huntress:* eight hours during which each small force would be on its own. Just about all the losses so far had been from small, detached forces . . .

He was tired, suddenly: or suddenly conscious of being tired. It came from this temporary relaxation of the tension, probably; for about fifty minutes one could *afford* to feel tired. Better make the most of fifty minutes, he thought. There was a day of Stukas coming now; then a quick turn-round in Alexandria and another job to be done, troops to be taken in or brought out. Before much longer it would be all one way—out.

He got into his chair. He'd expected to do no more than doze, but he slept at once, and dreamt. Fiona was there somewhere, and he was reaching to her: touching emptiness: but then it switched, and he was at Mullbergh with a high wind in the trees outside the window where they were dining—Paul and Jack on his left, Sarah stiff and old-maidish on his right, staring disapprovingly at Paul. Jack was talking on and on, sounding pompous and condescending, making sneering remarks about submarines, and Paul was watching him across the table with an air of guarded reserve, silently critical. Nick urged Paul, "He isn't like this really, you know. He's like you and me. It's only the effect this old bitch has on him, don't you see that? Damn it, he's your *brother*—"

"Five-thirty, sir . . . Captain, sir?"

The dream had changed. That wasn't Paul's voice.

"Sir, it's half past five!"

He didn't believe it. It was obviously part of the same stupid dream. He'd only just slumped down and shut his eyes.

"Captain, sir. About time for dawn action stations."

It was Tony Dalgleish beside the chair. *Tuareg's* dark bridge and the noise of sea and wind, the roar of the ventilator fans. Wind and sea were still astern, he knew it immediately from the motion.

"Right. Thank you, Number One."

"Here's some kye, sir. I think the cox'n got at it."

Nick took the mug of cocoa that Dalgleish was offering him, and sniffed at it. Rum. Illegal, of course. He straightened in the chair. "My compliments to the chef."

Daylight growing: with the coast of Crete thirty miles to the north, Scarpanto sixty north-eastward. All three ships were rolling and pitching as the eastern sky turned rose-red and its glow spread across the lively, wind-whipped seascape. Stars were fading rapidly in a clear dome of sky, and the destroyers astern were plunging end-on shapes wedged in high-curving, flying sea.

"Signal to us, sir, from C-in-C!"

PO Whiffen was beside the chair, his jovial face redder than usual from the wind. Ashcourt was beyond him at the binnacle, where Pratt should have been. Nick missed Pratt's stolid, pragmatic personality. He told Whiffen, "Read it to me, would you." He was watching the sky, the eastern and north-eastern sectors in particular, the direction of Scarpanto and of the rising sun. It was already three-quarters daylight and he doubted if they'd be kept waiting long.

"To *Tuareg,* from C-in-C, repeated—"

"Just the message, Yeoman."

"Aye, sir . . . *Report position course speed and whether troops still on board.* Time of origin—"

"All right. Here." He slid off the seat, beckoning Whiffen to join him at the chart, so that he could give him their position. He hadn't intended to break W/T silence at least until the enemy had found him, by which time it wouldn't have made any difference, but now he'd have to. He could understand ABC wanting to know where his ships were, anyway, and presumably the army command would want to know what had been done with their commandos, too . . . The position was 237 Kupho Nisi 50: course 130, speed 30. He added, for Whiffen to scrawl on his pad: *Landing operation was completed at 0430.* "Send that, Yeoman. To C-in-C and the same repeats." The "repeated" addresses were authorities to whom the signal was sent for information; in this case they included

Glenshiel and the force that had been sweeping Crete's north coast during the night—*Dido* and *Ajax* and two destroyers.

It was fully daylight now. Leaning against his chair he studied the horizon and the sky. Nothing: except for the sun coming up red and angry, rather like a hot tomato. He got through to Dalgleish at his station aft, and told him to have one watch piped to breakfast. "While you're at it, tell McEvoy I'll have mine up here, would you."

"Think our friends may be busy elsewhere, sir?"

It was possible. *Dido* and company would be somewhere in the Kaso area.

At 0640, by which time he'd had his breakfast and there were still no bombers, another signal arrived from C-in-C. Nick was ordered to turn his three ships north-eastward and join up with the cruiser force— *Dido* and *Ajax*—which was now steering south-west out of the Kaso Strait. The force was also to be joined by three other destroyers, *Napier*, *Kelvin,* and *Jackal,* who were on their way north from Alexandria.

He went to the chart and marked the rendezvous position on it. The new course would be 050 degrees, which required an eighty-degree turn to port. He told Whiffen, "Hoist eight blue, Yeoman." Back in his chair, he thought about this change of plan: that—probably—it meant reprieve. He'd have his destroyers in close company with the cruisers and their batteries of high-angle AA guns in about one hour flat. And today's chances had been slim: *now,* he could admit it. When one thought about what had happened to Mountbatten's ships . . .

"Answering pendants are close up, sir!"

"Haul down." He told Ashcourt, "Come round to oh-five-oh."

Jack Everard had got all the information he'd come down to the plot for. He shoved the notebook into his pocket, yawned for about the tenth time in the last half-hour, and went back to the bridge. He told Napier, "We were right, sir. Should sight them any minute now, probably fine on the port bow."

He'd had no sleep at all last night. He felt all washed out: and for the best of reasons. Inside the condition of physical exhaustion, he'd never felt so good in his life. Or so—*dumbfounded* . . .

Carnarvon had sailed from Alexandria at 0800: the sailing orders had come late at night, when Jack had been ashore on night leave expiring at 0600 . . . Ahead of the cruiser a destroyer, *Halberdier,* was zigzagging and pinging for submarines. There was a long swell running and she was making heavy weather of it: each time she plunged her bow down into the sea you expected to see her screws come right up out of it, but each time they just stayed hidden. She and *Carnarvon* were making 18 knots; one full day in harbour, plus last night with the engineers working until about midnight, had got her back into running order.

"We need a good long spell in dockyard hands, sir." Buchanan, the engineer commander, had warned his captain this morning when they'd been coming up the swept channel out of Alex. "In anything like normal circumstances I'd have to tell you she wasn't fit for operations. So if you *can* keep the revs down, sir, treat her gently—"

"Depends on the enemy, Chief." Napier had shrugged: Buchanan hadn't told him anything he hadn't known already. "We shan't dash about when we don't have to . . . But look here, Chief, you've done extremely well, you and all your people. The C-in-C's pleased as punch, I can tell you. D'you realize that in just three days he's had two cruisers and four destroyers sunk, and one battleship, two cruisers, and four destroyers badly damaged? Every ship he can get, he needs."

"Argument rather on my side, sir, if I may say so. I mean for treating her like an old lady with a weak heart."

She certainly wasn't a *young* lady. But you wouldn't have thought there was anything weak about her, looking down on her forepart as she smashed powerfully through the long, blue-white swells, heading out north-westward to meet the crippled assault ship *Glenshiel* and bring her back to Alexandria. *Glenshiel* had caught a packet yesterday, when she'd had brother Nick's destroyers with her, and this morning she'd already fought off three separate attacks by Junkers 88s. She was down to 8 knots, now.

Fullbrook, an RNVR lieutenant, was just handing over the watch to Tom Overton. Old Tom, for God's sake, who *did* have interests other than golf—as Jack had witnessed, last night . . . Overton met Jack's eyes, and winked: Jack nodded, still astonished by everything that had happened, and thinking of a girl with blue-black hair who was the cousin of another rather like her but more beautiful and a few years older, this older one being Tom Overton's girlfriend and the wife of a very rich French-Egyptian. Overton beamed at Fullbrook: "All right, dear boy, I have the weight." The weight of the watch, the ship, he meant. But Alexandria was an extraordinary town: and it had taken on entirely new fascinations now for Jack Everard, Lieutenant, Royal Navy.

Napier was looking at him, seeing him lost in daydream. And he could, just about, have fallen asleep on his feet, gone on dreaming . . . He went down to the chart table instead, pulled the log towards him and leafed through the signals on it.

The ones directly affecting *Carnarvon*—the changed rendezvous position when *Glenshiel* had reported her latest speed reduction, and the assault ship's signals about air attacks and requests for fighter cover—fat chance she had of *that*—were familiar, things he'd worked with during the forenoon. But there was also one from C-in-C to brother Nick in *Tuareg,* ordering him to join the cruiser squadron up near Kaso: the cruisers were being sent back up through the straits for a second night's sweep of the north coast, a repeat of last night's operation. It would be a day or two before *Tuareg* could be back in Alex, then. All the talk was of evacuation: in the Union Club last night, for instance, in the crowded downstairs bar where Jack had started his evening with Overton . . . It was no secret that the fighting was going badly: troops were holding out strongly at Heraklion and at Retimo—although at Retimo they were said to be cut off—but at Suda and in the Maleme-Canea area, which was where it really mattered, the situation was reported to be hopeless. The Germans were pouring supplies into Maleme airfield in Ju52 transports, so that hour by hour the balance was tipping further in their favour.

Other signals: *Isis, Hero,* and *Nizam* were returning from their attempt to land commandos at Selinos Kastelli. Bad weather had forced them to turn back; *Nizam* had lost both her whalers in the heavy seas. But *Tuareg* and company must have got their troops ashore: brother Nick, Jack thought wrily, coming up to scratch—as usual . . . Meanwhile *Glenroy* would be sailing later today for Timbaki, escorted by *Coventry* and two destroyers: she'd been turned back from a similar operation a couple of days ago. And last, but very far from least, a battle squadron under Vice-Admiral Pridham-Whipple was sailing from Alexandria at just about this moment, escorting the carrier *Formidable* for an air attack on Scarpanto airfield. The carrier's escorting force consisted of the flagship *Queen Elizabeth,* her sister-battleship *Barham,* and eight destroyers.

At lunch yesterday in the wardroom, Jack had remarked to Tom Overton, "Rather funny exchange of signals, our skipper's and *Glenshiel*'s on the way in."

Overton hadn't heard about it. Jack told him about Fifi and the Auberge Bleu. Overton chuckled: "Great spot, the old Auberge."

"Oh, d'you know it?"

He wouldn't have thought nightclubs were the first lieutenant's line of country. Overton had murmured, "Used it once or twice, you know."

Then they'd met in the evening, in the Union Club. Jack had gone ashore with Willy Irvine for a drink and a snack, a change of atmosphere. Leave had been granted until 0600 Sunday morning; the ship was "under sailing orders" but no specific orders had been received by the time he'd come ashore, and the engine-room department had still been at work down in the bowels. So she hadn't even had steam up, and no early departure had seemed likely.

In the bar he'd found himself standing next to old Tom. *Carnarvon*'s first lieutenant had a glass of Stella beer in his sunburnt fist: Jack had looked at it in surprise.

"I agree. This horse is not fit for work. But the night is yet young, dear boy, and at this stage easy does it, eh?"

"I dare say, if you're making a night of it." He wondered if Overton played golf in the dark. Luminous balls? He laughed, spluttering into his gin. But Overton ignored that: he was looking at him rather intensely as if he'd just had some bright idea. "Everard, I say."

"What?"

"Did I understand you to say that you had never sampled the pleasures of the Auberge Bleu?"

"I haven't, no."

"Like to? Tonight?"

"Right ahead. Just her masthead."

Glenshiel had been spotted from the director platform ten minutes ago but now Commander Bell-Reid had sighted her from the bridge. He added, "You can see her spotting-top when she rises on a swell or we do. *There*—"

"Yes." Napier, ramrod-straight on his seat, had got on to it too. There was a certain relief in having made the rendezvous with the assault ship before the bombers came back to her.

Then they had the destroyer, *Huntress,* in sight too. A quarter of an hour later, when they were at close quarters and *Carnarvon* was being put about to turn in astern of *Glenshiel,* Jack could see the assault ship's fire-blackened upperworks, bomb damage aft, several landing-craft shattered in their davits and paintwork scorched black from near-misses. He could imagine her as she'd have looked yesterday evening, on fire, and this morning with the 88s' bombs raining down around her: for all that, she'd got off lightly. With only one destroyer in company, and so sloweddown that from the bombers' point of view she must have looked like a sitting bird, at their mercy . . .

No—not mercy. You couldn't use that word, here in the eastern Mediterranean in the spring of 1941. Certainly not in relation to Stuka pilots. And despite that, last night one had—he thought, *It's incredible* . . . To think of himself last night in that nightclub, and later in the small hours in the cousin's bed: and this wounded ship struggling south while others nearer to Crete waited for the dawn and for the arrival of the bombers: there was a harsh incongruity, a sense of two identities, two worlds.

Napier had given the yeoman a signal that was to be flashed to *Glenshiel's* captain but not recorded on the log: *Fifi is filing a paternity suit. Now which way do you want to go?*

Overton chuckling at the binnacle, looking round at Jack . . .

At the Auberge last night he'd been a different man entirely. His girl—she'd be about twenty-eight or -nine, he guessed—had turned out to be about the most beautiful woman Jack had ever seen. In a city of beautiful women, she outshone them all. The cousin, Gabrielle, could have walked into practically any room and stopped the conversation, but beside Tom's girl she'd been eclipsed, made to look quite ordinary. She wasn't ordinary: when her cousin was out of view she was sensational. And very lively, warm, outgoing: within minutes they'd been having fun, and even right at the start there'd been an edge of tension, expectation . . . Overton quick-witted, amusing, taking it for granted that he should have this extraordinarily beautiful, extremely rich man's wife hanging on his words, taking no notice of anyone but him . . . And again, thinking back to it, he was struck by the nightmarish contrast—the girl's lips and lithe, sweet body, enclosing arms, whispers in the scented darkness and the first faint light of dawn outside—dawn that had also begun to light this long rolling swell and the bomb-scarred ship, the battle raging in the north.

At 1800, when they'd brought *Glenshiel* to within 75 miles of Alexandria, they met the battle squadron on its way out north-westward for the attack on Scarpanto, and *Carnarvon* was detached to join it. Jack's mind stayed full of the girl: his memory of the extraneous events which followed was like a film shown fast but with occasional stills of incidents and conversations that weren't necessarily of particular importance. There was the run northwards, *Carnarvon* acting as AA guardship and stationed between the battleships and *Formidable: Queen Elizabeth* impressive in her dazzle-camouflage, with the vice-admiral's flag at her foremasthead and a huge ensign flapping at the main. He was watching her through binoculars when Overton asked him, just before they closed up for dusk action stations, "Wish it was this time yesterday, Jack?"

Lowering the glasses, he shrugged.

"Don't tell me you didn't enjoy yourself."

He took a breath. "No. I won't tell you that."

"Seeing her again, d'you think?"

He had to. He said, "Of course."

"She won't always be available, you know. Matter of luck and timing."

"What d'you mean?"

Action stations: the Marine bugler, Sykes, splitting the air with it, and the same call floating from the flagship and from *Barham* and the carrier. It felt good, he remembered, being part of such a powerful force—and being on the offensive, too. It was a disappointment to learn next morning that the twenty-three-thousand-ton aircraft carrier had only ten operational aircraft with which to attack the hundreds on Scarpanto and then fight off the inevitable retaliatory attacks. At dawn action stations on the Monday morning—it was 26 May—he watched *Formidable* turn into the wind to launch her aircraft. Two of the ten that took off turned out to be defective and had to land-on again, but the other eight, four Fulmars and four Albacores, formed up and winged away towards Scarpanto. All eight returned, with reports of Stukas destroyed on the ground and damage inflicted on the airfield installations. They had to get airborne again almost at once, as the Stuka counter-attacks began to come in; and at about the same time the battle squadron was joined by the cruisers *Dido* and *Ajax* and destroyers which included *Tuareg, Afghan,* and *Highflier.*

Thinking about Gabrielle—between Stuka attacks, and sometimes even while they were in progress—Jack wished his involvement with her hadn't stemmed from Tom Overton's affair with another man's wife. That was a bit over the odds, he felt; it stuck in the gullet, rather, and he was aware of having consciously to turn a blind eye to it.

Still fighting off Stukas and 88s, the fleet withdrew south-westward.

Then at noon there was a signal ordering them to provide cover for *Glenroy,* who was trying to run troops up to Timbaki, and course was altered to due west. At 1320 a force of twenty Stukas arrived from the direction of the desert, and attacked, most of them going for the carrier while she was still in the process of getting her fighters up. She was hit by two bombs and badly damaged, and at the same time the destroyer *Nubian* had her stern blown off.

If a girl went to bed with you so readily, the very first time you met her, did it mean she'd do it with anyone?

Of course it didn't. He told himself not to be stupid, not to waste time thinking about it. It kept him awake, though, even when he was dog-tired.

Glenroy had been badly mauled by the bombers: she'd been forced to turn back again without getting her troops ashore. Air power, nothing else, was allowing the Germans to pour their troops in and keep British reinforcements out. Nothing was going well: if you faced it squarely you had to admit that all the Navy was doing was losing ships . . . Destroyers were oiling from the battleships during the 26th, that Monday. It was at dusk that evening that *Formidable* was detached to limp away to Alexandria. At daylight on Tuesday the 27th the battle squadron was ordered to close in towards the Kaso Strait again, to cover the withdrawal of *Hero, Nizam,* and *Abdiel,* who'd run the gauntlet with commandos and ammunition into Suda Bay and were now bringing out about a thousand other personnel who weren't needed on the island. But the battle squadron was still a couple of hundred miles short of Kaso, just before 9 am, when a mixed force of Junkers 88s and Heinkel 111s attacked. Jack saw the almost solid descent of bombs: it was a well-executed, highly-concentrated attack, and the battleship *Barham* got the worst of it. One bomb hit her on "Y" turret; near-misses, enormous blasts of sea flinging up close beside her, holed and flooded two of her anti-torpedo bulges. She took on a list, and had a fire inside her which her ship's company were fighting all that forenoon.

He could imagine what it must be like inside there, in those cramped, smoke-filled compartments, airless, suffocating, and the fire taking hold and spreading . . .

"Everard—are you in love, or something equally ridiculous?"

He looked round quickly. The commander, Bell-Reid, was glaring at him from a couple of feet away.

"The plot is calling, Everard." Bell-Reid pointed. "The plot voicepipe?" It was right beside him. He hadn't heard a thing. He answered it now, and Midshipman Brighouse, who was taking a turn as his Tanky, navigator's assistant, had some footling thing to ask him. He gave the snotty a short answer.

Bell-Reid growled at him as he straightened from the voicepipe, "Ever since we left Alexandria two days ago, Everard, you've been giving a close imitation of a dying duck in a thunderstorm. Are you sick?"

He shook his head. "Perfectly fit, sir."

"Woman trouble?"

"No, sir." There was no trouble that couldn't be solved by getting *back* to Alexandria.

Bell-Reid muttered, "Well, pull yourself together, for God's sake!"

At least he'd had the decency to keep his voice down . . .

At 1230, the C-in-C recalled the whole force to Alex. Jack's last memory of that trip—the last still picture in the blur of ships' movements, signals, Stuka attacks, and the sickening sight of bomb-bursts—was of Petty Officer Hillier's face as he goggled at a signal which he'd just removed from the pneumatic tube. Hillier was yeoman of the watch. It was early afternoon, and the battle squadron was steaming southwestward. He'd been taking the signal over to Napier, unfolding it as he crossed the bridge: glancing at it, he'd stopped in his tracks, mouth open.

Napier asked him, "What is it, Yeoman?"

"Sir, they've—" Hillier gulped, swallowing emotion. "We've sunk the *Bismarck,* sir!"

In Alexandria, Aubrey Wishart left ABC in the Operations Room and went down the passage to his own office. The wires had been humming all day between this headquarters, Army HQ in Cairo, and the Chiefs of Staff in London.

Wishart picked up the telephone and asked the exchange to connect him to the extension which was Rear-Admiral Creswell's office at Ras-el-Tin.

"Creswell."

"Aubrey Wishart here. It's on, Hector."

At the other end, George Hector Creswell took a deep breath. "It" meant the lifting of twenty thousand troops from Crete.

"Right. Thank you."

He put the phone down, on a battle lost.

CHAPTER NINE

·   ·   ·

"Something wrong, Nick?"

It was stuffy in the day-cabin, despite open scuttles: all they seemed to let in was the smell of Egypt, and Egypt's flies. The urgency now, the need to be seeing to about forty things at once in order to be ready to sail again at dawn, might be adding to the sense of airlessness. And he didn't want to seem fidgety to Aubrey Wishart, who must have had a thousand matters to deal with but had still found time to call by and see him.

He answered that question: "Not . . . necessarily." He'd had a feeling there *would* be a letter from Fiona, this time. He told Wishart, nodding at the totally uninteresting mail scattered on the table, "I'd hoped for one that isn't here, that's all."

"When you get back on Thursday"—Wishart smiled: genial, confident—"she'll have written then, old lad."

"Well." He glanced at her portrait. "I hope so."

"*That* one, eh?"

"She's stationed in London. MTC. Since that bloody awful raid three weeks ago, I haven't heard from her."

"Mails are fairly erratic, you know."

"Mr Gieves gets his bills to me regularly enough." He flopped into the armchair facing Wishart's. There wasn't time for this kind of chat, for talk of personal matters and the outside world. They mattered as much as they ever had, but here and now they had to be pigeon-holed: to get back to the real world, or be any use to Fiona—if she'd let him— he had to see this through first. It wasn't going to be any joy-ride.

Tuareg had entered Alexandria with the rest of the force a couple of hours ago; they'd oiled and then shifted to a buoy, and now as daylight faded they were taking in ammunition from a lighter on the starboard side. On the other side there was a lighter with stores and fresh provisions, and a water-boat beyond it. Lights had been rigged on the upper deck and the work would be going on for some hours yet; then there'd be an interval in which to get some rest before sailing at 0600 for Heraklion via the Kaso Strait.

The object of this expedition was to lift forty-five hundred men, the entire garrison of Heraklion, from under the Germans' noses and into destroyers and cruisers between midnight tomorrow and 2 am on Thursday the 29th. Embarkation would have to be completed by 2 am, or the warships with their loads of soldiers would be caught by daylight on the wrong side of Kaso.

He reached over with a light for Wishart's cigarette. This was the evening of Tuesday, 27 May, but it felt as if it could easily have been last Friday, when he'd sat in this same chair and Wishart had filled the one he was occupying now; the ensuing days could have been one long disjointed dream. Another dream haunted him too, when he let it: that apparently inconsequential one of Jack and Paul at Mullbergh. He had a sense of important things left undone: of time running out, no chance now to put matters on any better footing. He or Jack or both of them might so easily not survive this next phase of the battle—survival even this far seemed vaguely surprising—and he'd have liked to have cleared things up, at least to have had a shot at bridging the gulf between them.

Too late now. And even with time and opportunity, he knew it might well have been a wasted effort. He shook it out of his mind again . . . "It's good to see you, Aubrey. I hope one of these days we'll be able to spend more than five minutes talking to each other."

"Not this evening, anyway." The admiral shot a glance at his watch. "As I need hardly tell you, there's a lot going on. I'm on my way over to Ras-el-Tin, actually. Main reason for stopping was, as I said, to tell you that having got those chaps ashore at Plaka Bay has impressed ABC considerably."

"I was lucky. The weather only just held up long enough." He changed the subject. "Who's this navigator I'm getting?"

"*Masai*'s. A VR lieutenant, name of Drisdale. Smeake says he's good."

"And what's the overall pattern for the evacuation, can you tell me that? Apart from tomorrow's outing?"

Force B, the ships heading for Heraklion tomorrow, was to be commanded by Rear-Admiral Rawlings with his flag in *Orion*. There'd be three other cruisers—*Ajax, Dido,* and *Carnarvon*—and the destroyers *Tuareg, Afghan, Decoy, Jackal, Imperial, Hotspur, Kimberley,* and *Hereward.* But the Tribals and *Carnarvon* wouldn't be embarking troops; they were to sweep north of Heraklion to fend off interference by Italian torpedo-boats.

Wishart told him, "Mostly it'll be from Sphakia on the south coast. All the troops from the Suda-Maleme area have been told to fall back across the island to Sphakia, and the first lift will be tomorrow night, same time as yours on the other side. There'll be a bigger one the second night—six thousand men, it's hoped—and about another three thousand on each of the two nights after that. There's also Retimo . . ." He frowned. "That's much less simple. We want them to pull out and get across the Plaka Bay, but so far it hasn't been possible to get a message through."

"No W/T there?"

"There's no military wireless anywhere, old lad. All army communi-

cations for some time now have been passed through our NOIC Suda—
one Captain Morse. He's now shifting to a cave above the Sphakia beach,
and the pongoes are setting up their HQ there with him. But we sent
a Hurricane with long-range fuel tanks on it, to drop a message to the
Retimo garrison, and nothing more's been heard of it. We've twice tried
sending submarines in, too; but the Eyeties are patrolling that coast with
their torpedo craft every night, and we damn near lost the first boat we
sent in. The second simply didn't get her landing-party back. And as you
know we're having to use every submarine we've got, to sit on the
Italian ports in case they get a rush of blood to the head and send their
fleet out—"

"The people I landed at Plaka may have fought their way through.
Would they know what's wanted?"

"Well." Wishart spread his large hands. "They were to secure the
route. There'd been no order to evacuate, though, at that stage."

"Retimo's where you said the field hospital is. All those women?"

Wishart took a long drag at his cigarette.

"Nick, it's a bugger." He shook his head. "Yesterday General Freyberg
reported that the Suda troops had reached the limit of endurance. It's
the air thing again, you see . . . Only hope, he said, was withdrawal to
the south coast. He also reported Retimo cut off, Heraklion surrounded.
Same day, Churchill signals Wavell: *'Victory in Crete essential, keep hurling
in all you can.'*"

"Are they mad, in London?"

Wishart shrugged. "They don't know their arses from their elbows.
Wavell explained it to them yesterday, though, in words of one syllable,
and they do seem finally to have glimpsed the realities of the situation.
Better late than never." He slapped his hands down on his knees, and
stood up: a bulky, towering man. "I'm off now. Late already. Nick, don't
worry about that girl. She's *much* too pretty to come to grief."

On deck, ammunition boxes were being slung up out of the lighter
on the torpedo davit, and seamen working at high speed under the
direction of Petty Officer Roddick were uncasing the shells and cordite

charges and sending them on down to the shellrooms and magazines. Pompom and point-five ammunition went straight down in its boxes, except that on the gun platforms gunners squatted, loading belts. Mr Walsh was darting to and fro, ticking off items on his clipboard, and on the other side of the ship CPO Habgood and assistants were doing the same with sacks and crates of stores. Up ahead of the stores lighter, the water-boat was just casting off. Dalgleish had a stranger with him, an RNVR lieutenant with a beaky nose and deepset eyes: a cadaverous, gloomy-looking man. After Wishart had left, Dalgleish introduced him to Nick.

"Lieutenant Drisdale, sir, formerly of *Masai.*"

Most of *Tuareg*'s officers would already know Drisdale, of course, and it would make things easy. Nick asked him, "Are you an experienced navigator?"

"One year in *Masai,* sir, and before that I was in a minesweeper."

"Glad to have you, anyway." He looked at Dalgleish. "Ashcourt could show him where everything is . . . You'll find all the corrections are up to date, I expect, Drisdale. Pratt was a very conscientious fellow."

"Yes, sir." Drisdale nodded. "A very nice one too."

There was a letter to be written, to Pratt's family.

Redmayne, the engineer, was waiting to have a word with him. And PO Whiffen, the yeoman, was hovering with a log of signals. A lot of the routine stuff wasn't transmitted but came by hand, on paper. Too much paper by half: and there wasn't time now to bother with anything but essentials: there was a fresh and mounting sense of urgency as the new task loomed.

Jack Everard had gone ashore, to collect new charts, replacements for worn-out ones and also some inshore charts that weren't in the folio and might be needed in the course of the evacuation. His most pressing need, in fact, was to get to a shore telephone.

While they were looking out the charts he'd asked for he borrowed an empty office with a phone in it, lit a cigarette to calm his nerves, and then asked the dockyard exchange to get him Gabrielle's number. Her telephone was ringing, ringing . . .

"*Oui?*"

"Gabrielle?"

"Who is it who asks for her?" French, and female, but not Gabrielle. Some visitor to the apartment . . . He spoke in his own halting, Dartmouth-accented French, "This is Jack Everard. May I speak to Gabrielle, please?"

She laughed, as if he'd said something funny. Then she said, "Oh, *Lisa* . . . It's Martine here, my dear."

"I don't understand, I'm sorry. Martine—"

Martine was Overton's girl. She broke in, in that rapid French gabble, "Lisa dear, how sweet of you to ask us. Gabrielle and I would *adore* to, but I'm so terribly sorry, you'll have to do without us. Her beloved is returned, you see, *and* my own, and—"

"Beloved? Who—"

"Oh, you're right, these husbands *do* get in the way." She'd laughed again, and called out to someone else in the room: a string of French, with more hilarity mixed up in it. There was a man's voice then, from some distance, and then—his nerves jumped—Gabrielle's, unmistakable . . . She'd laughed too, and answered—incomprehensibly. Martine said into the phone, "I'm truly sorry, Lisa, joking apart. Both our wretched husbands are insisting we must dash away with them to Ismailia. So Lisa, pet—"

"Look, my name is *not* Lisa—"

Shriek of laughter: "But we know this so *well*, my dear!" He could see that lovely, laughing face: and somewhere in the room behind it he could imagine Gabrielle's too, Gabrielle asking her cousin with the enquiry in those wide, dark eyes of hers, who this really was . . . "Lisa, do you hear me? Are you still there?"

"What?"

"I said Gabrielle would like a little word now."

"Hello?"

"Gabrielle, what on earth is—"

"I'm so sorry, my darling. We'll be away at least a few—well, I suppose as much as a week, or—"

"Husband?"

"Oh, never mind that. What's a little week matter? In about seven or eight days I shall be here again and this wretch will have deserted me again, and—oh, just one moment . . ." He heard the man's voice, closer now: then Gabrielle's quick, high note of protest: "You certainly may *not* speak with her! All you wish to do is flirt, and I won't have it! Lisa, goodbye, darling."

Click. She'd hung up.

Gabrielle had a husband?

She'd gone to a lot of trouble to keep it quiet . . . In the boat again, on his way back to the ship, he tried to remember details: how, for instance, there'd been no signs of a man's clothes or shaving gear, anything masculine at all. In fact the apartment and its decor and atmosphere had been so entirely, positively feminine that no such possibility had occurred to him. Of course, he hadn't looked inside any cupboards . . . Had she worn rings? Yes, he remembered a small clicking shower of them on the glass top of her dressing-table as she'd shed them.

Another man's wife?

Overton wasn't in the wardroom, and Jock McCowan said he'd gone to turn in early—most people had. So tonight he couldn't question him about Gabrielle. Couldn't do a damn thing—not for eight days. Or seven . . . But—he put the question to himself, and shirked answering it—would he go to see her then? Ring her, in a week's time?

He'd been privately censorious of Overton's affair with a married woman; he'd been careful to ignore it. That had been the first step—looking the other way because if he hadn't it might have upset his own apple-cart. Now, the *second* step?

He was in the chartroom, stowing away the new ones. Then he went on to the dark and empty bridge to change the one on that table, the chart for the Alex-Kaso run tomorrow. He'd put the light on, pulled the old chart out, and begun to roll it, glancing at its clean replacement: he was looking at the Kaso Strait, with Scarpanto like a lizard flanking it to the north-east. Tomorrow—by this time tomorrow night, he thought—we'll have fought our way through that gap. Touch wood . . . The mental shiver told him that he was tired and that it would be sensible to turn in. He put his hand to the light-switch, and his eyes went back to the charted shape that was Scarpanto: it was truly lizard-like, reptilian, and you could think of its Stukas as reptiles too, the spawn of that large, sprawling parent—poisonous, yellow-faced, massed and waiting for the victims . . . Crossing the bridge with the rolled chart under his arm he paused, leant there for a moment, looking over towards the destroyer moorings and all around the big, quiet expanse of harbour. Lights burned on ships still ammunitioning or storing. Others besides the Heraklion force would be sailing in the morning: there was to be a lift at the same time from Sphakia on the south coast, a small one presumably, only destroyers. Reflections of those lights grew out like spears across the dark water: a snatch of music in the breeze was from one of the French ships, lying demilitarized with only skeleton crews on board. A sentry's hail of "Boat aho-o-oy!" was answered by a shout of "Guard!" Guard-boat doing its rounds: the officer of the guard from the duty battleship toured the harbour several times during the night to check there was a sentry awake and alert on each ship's upper deck.

Turn in now, he thought. He pushed himself off the side of the bridge, headed for the ladder. He'd have to be up by 5:30; and for some time after that there might not be many opportunities for sleep.

Gabrielle, married? Just—amusing herself, then?

He woke—shaken by the snotty of the watch at 0530—with the same thought in his mind, and a strong desire to talk to Overton about it. But he wasn't able to until late in the afternoon, just after 1630, by which time the force was only a hundred miles from Scarpanto. They'd been zigzagging all day with revs for 23 knots on, making good 20 on the mean course, and there'd been no sign of the Luftwaffe. The four cruisers were in line ahead, the flagship *Orion* leading and *Carnarvon* bringing up the rear, and the eight destroyers were spread in a screening arc across the line of advance, wing ships tailing back far enough to be on the flagship's beams; on the starboard side of the screen the wing ships were *Tuareg* and *Afghan*. It was an arrangement that made sense, since the Tribals were to be detached, with *Carnarvon,* after dark and after they'd all passed through the Strait. While the others raced westward to Heraklion, these three were to diverge north-westward and patrol a line 25 miles north of the evacuation port. Then they'd rendezvous with the main force north of Kaso at 0430, for the run south.

At 4:30 pm Tom Overton had come up to confer with Tyler, who was officer of the watch for the First Dog, about some change in the watchkeeping roster. Conference over, he'd drifted across to the side of the bridge and begun to fill a pipe. Jack went to join him: it was the first time he'd seen Overton today when there hadn't been other people hanging around.

Overton looked up at him. "May this peace and quiet last, eh?"

"Fat chance . . . Tom, I . . . er . . . went ashore last evening, to get some charts. Happened to find myself near a telephone, with a few minutes to spare, so . . ."

"Tickled to hear from you, was she?"

"Her husband was there with her."

"Crikey!" The pipe-stuffing stopped for a moment. "Who did you tell him you were? You should always have some yarn ready, you know."

"You aren't surprised, then."

"How d'you mean?"

"You knew she had a husband, didn't you?"

"My dear boy, most of them do have. I suppose if I'd *thought* about it . . ."

Bell-Reid shot a hard look at the pair of them as he stalked past, heading towards Napier in the front of the bridge. "Shall we close the hands up, sir?"

"I suppose we should." Howard Napier lowered his glasses, and checked the time. Now he was looking round for his navigator . . .

"How far are we from the Kaso Strait, Pilot?"

"About . . . ninety miles, sir."

"We *had* better, then." He nodded to his second-in-command. "Close 'em up, please, John."

Bell-Reid swung round: "Bugler! Sound action stations!"

Just before 5:00 the red flag ran up to *Orion's* yardarm, and within half a minute the cruisers were doing a controlled AA shoot at a flight of three Italian high-level bombers. Their pilots seemed more interested in survival than in getting their bombs anywhere near the ships: as the last bomb splashed into an area of unoccupied salt water, Drisdale spread his arms horizontally and intoned, "Wide . . ."

Despite his appearance of deep gloom, Drisdale had been *Masai's* resident comedian. So Dalgleish said.

"Should we remain closed up, sir?"

"Until dark, yes," Nick answered Dalgleish over the telephone to the ACP. "Better lay on action messing, for supper."

To port, *Orion* was a handsome sight. Low, powerful-looking with that single wide-based funnel, four-inch AA batteries abreast it, main armament of six-inch turrets fore and aft. *Ajax,* famous for her part in cornering the *Admiral Graf Spee* at the battle of the Plate in December 1939, was *Orion's* duplicate. Astern of her came *Dido,* elegant-looking with the two slightly raked funnels and the tier of three for'ard turrets, two more aft. By contrast *Carnarvon,* plugging along behind those three, had a decidedly old-fashioned look about her. But her engineers seemed to have done a thorough job in record time on those recently defective engines of hers. Nick saw tin hats in her bridge, in place of white caps: so she too was staying closed-up at action stations.

"Alarm starboard! Green four-oh—Stukas!"

"Red flag, Yeoman!"

But *Tuareg* hadn't beaten the flagship to it: *Orion's* red warning signal had shot up just at that moment. All the fleet's guns swinging round and lifting . . .

•   •   •

"*There*, lad!"

Mr Walsh yelled it as he grabbed the killick torpedoman's shoulder, pulling him round and at the same time pointing aft—at a single Me109 coming at them from astern at wavetop height, now rocketing upwards to sweep over *Afghan* with its guns flaming: *Tuareg* next in line on that same flight-path . . . Overhead, the rising note of a Stuka's siren suggested that a co-ordinated attack might be developing. The torpedoman bent his knees, settled the stocks of the twin Vickers against his shoulders, took aim: the Messerschmitt was coming straight towards the ship, so there was no deflection. Walsh had shown the other Vickers gunner the target: he was a torpedoman too, and he was on it, whipping round and sighting and opening fire in one swift movement. Two double streams of tracer were flying at the fighter's nose, and point-fives joining in now, too, from farther for'ard. The German didn't like it, he was banking away, twisting his plane to starboard, dragging it up and round with flames visible inside it then gushing out, streaming right to the tail with the black cross on it: the Messerschmitt went over on its back before it hit the sea, sea leaping in a long, low, moving fountain as it skidded in upside-down. Cheering from the guns' crews aft: and the pompoms were thundering at the Stuka—which was pulling out high, letting its bomb go wide. But the leading torpedoman was pointing, his mouth open as he shouted—inaudibly, the words drowned in noise. Mr Walsh saw what he was pointing at: a bomber going down nearly vertically at the destroyer *Imperial*, out ahead. She was under helm, and nearby ships were barraging to keep the attacker high: *Imperial* had no pompoms, only point-fives. The Stuka pilot seemed to know it and to be taking advantage of it, plummeting down through the canopy of shell-bursts—still diving . . .

They saw the bomb detach itself: and the Stuka levelling, not far above the sea's brilliant blue. The bomb burst just about alongside its target: a mountain of sea shooting up right against *Imperial*'s stern. Almost for sure, she'd be stopped by that one . . . But she hadn't even faltered.

The waterspout had crashed down across her afterpart and she'd steamed on out of it. Mr Walsh shouted in Dalgleish's ear, "'Ighly adjacent, that was!" He was scanning the sky again, getting ready for the next attacker.

Nick checked the time: an hour had passed since *Imperial* had survived her near-miss, and the force was still intact, well inside the Kaso Strait and with land in clear sight to port. They were up to schedule, maintaining the ordered speed of advance under constant, concentrated attack. It was astonishing, he thought, that ships could be bombed so determinedly for so long and that none of them should be hit: should *yet have been* hit . . .

"Port fifteen."

Attending to business: turning towards the direction of a Stuka's dive, and looking all ways at once. It was rather like a game of squash, except that if you missed a squash-ball it didn't kill you.

"Midships."

The attack had been going on for three hours now. Another half-hour and the sun would be sliding down behind the Cretan mountains. Thirty minutes, and several bombs per minute . . . The Stuka was hidden in shell-bursts: emerging now, yellow snout bright with the sun's glint on it. He watched it closely and at the same time retained a peripheral awareness of the possibility of being jumped on simultaneously from another direction. The Stuka boys had evidently been putting their cropped heads together, planning synchronized attacks; he'd seen it half a dozen times in the last hour.

Bomb releasing *now* . . .

"Stop starboard. Starboard twenty-five."

Spin her away from it: and with a quick glance round at sea-level for the positions of other ships, all of them dodging bombs. *Tuareg's* thumped in thirty yards to port, close enough to feel the jar of its explosion through the wood grating under his feet.

"Midships. Half ahead both engines."

"Midships, sir. Half ahead both, sir . . . Wheel's amidships, sir . . ."

Lilting tone: a voicepipe litany. Nick told him, "Port fifteen. Steer three-two-five."

The sky over the cruisers was filthy-grey with shell-bursts. High up and to the west, flying north, he saw the group of Ju88s which had attacked from astern a few minutes ago. Their bombs had gone down like rain on the other side of the cruisers, a long grove of splashes with the last ones rising only a short distance astern of the destroyers in the centre of the screen. Perhaps one small miscalculation—of wind or drift—had made the difference between that clear miss and having all four cruisers hit or near-missed. Pilots had problems, no doubt, but from down here it looked as if it ought to be so easy . . . "Starboard twenty."

He was pleased with his ship's gunnery performance. Separating the control of the guns was paying off, in terms of flexibility, and also he'd been impressed by the way they all united, as if all the gunners' brains were connected telepathically—when one particular attack looked more threatening than others.

"Midships."

It left him free to concentrate on handling the ship . . . *"What?"*

Drisdale repeated, "Eighty-eights coming up astern, sir!"

He nodded, concentrating on this Stuka. In any case you couldn't dodge the high-level attackers as you could the point-blank rushes: luckily they weren't as accurate in their aim, either. The 88s were getting round astern of the northward-moving force and attacking on their homeward course towards Crete—or Greece, wherever their base was . . . The sun was inching down: and the Scarpanto Stuka base was now less than forty miles away. Wouldn't it be shaming for the arrogant, murderous bastards to have so many ducks waddling through their backyard and not be able to hit a single one of them?

Don't count on it, he thought. Still fifteen or twenty minutes of light, or partial light, left.

"Port twenty-five."

"Port twenty-five, sir . . . Twenty-five of port wheel on, sir!"

Bomb on its way down. One single Stuka, about an hour ago, had let go five small bombs from one dive. An experiment, presumably, that hadn't come to anything. Several times he'd seen two bombs, though, two splashes, probably two five-hundred-pounders instead of the more usual one-thousand-pounder. Splash going up now, nicely clear to starboard; he called down for the rudder to be centred, then shot a glance at the compass to see how far round he'd come: then, looking up, he saw one of Drisdale's 88s trailing black smoke like a scar across the sun.

Within a few minutes the lower rim of that sun would touch the mountain peaks. Stukas were still coming up from the Scarpanto direction, perhaps desperate for last-minute success. At this moment three were diving on the cruisers: on *Orion*. Gunfire increasing, shell-bursts thickening over the centre: he took his eyes off it, aware of the danger of looking at one sector for too long, and glanced round for nearer threats. The sky was colouring as the sun sank and the blackness of the mountains made them seem to lean out across the sea: there was violet growing, and deep blue, a whole spread of colours deepening and blending, flooding outwards; over the other horizon, the Scarpanto side, first stars were pinpricks in a darkening sky. The colours growing out from behind the mountains were mixed rose-pink, gold, and violet. Gunfire was at a peak again, the Stukas' sirens screaming through it, and the action was all concentrated in the centre, against the garish backdrop. Nick swung around with his glasses trained to starboard, swept to the right into dimmer, opalescent light that was fading and at the same time reflecting—from the sea's surface probably, the image refracted in layers of warm air—a distillation of the colour in the west: through it, *in* it, he saw the Savoias, five or six of them, sneaking in towards the ships like big wave-hopping moths.

"Alarm starboard—torpedo bombers, green nine-oh!"

He added, for Houston's benefit, "Flying right to left, Harry, angle of sight zero—"

"Director target! Red barrage—"

"Starboard twenty-five." The guns were swinging around and depressing at the same time as layers and trainers followed the pointers in their dials. Clang of the fire-gongs: the four-sevens flamed and crashed, the amount of flash showing how dark it was getting suddenly. This turn towards the bombers would shut "X" and "Y" guns out of the action but it would also help to avoid any torpedoes which the Italians might already have dropped. He saw one Savoia pulling upwards and banking, sheering away to the left and its torpedo dropping very much askew: to the right a flare-up, one plane hit: *Afghan*, astern, had joined in, and that burning plane had flopped into the sea . . . . "Midships."

"Midships, sir . . . Wheel's amidships, sir." Gun-flashes and shell-bursts were bright now as night closed in. A fire burning on the sea was the wreckage of that Savoia: the attack had been broken up and the others had disappeared, but they might be circling for another attempt in some other sector and Nick had a signalman flashing to the flagship: *Savoia bombers attacked with torpedoes and some may still be with us.* Over the rapid click-clacking of the signal lamp he heard Houston's order to the guns, "Check, check, check!" A sudden silence had allowed him to hear it— the Aldis lamp, and Houston's voice from the tower carrying down the voicepipe. No targets, then: it was bewildering, after so long. He said into the voicepipe, "Port twenty," and the yeoman reported, "Message passed to *Orion*, sir."

The wind was right ahead, on this course. Spray swept over constantly, whipping like hail over the glass wind-deflector on the leading edge of *Tuareg's* bridge; binoculars needed frequent wiping.

Ajax had been near-missed and damaged in that last Stuka effort against the cruisers. She'd reported damage that included a fire and twenty men wounded, and Admiral Rawlings had detached her with orders to return to Alexandria.

Now it was 2200, 10 pm. Half an hour ago *Orion* and *Dido* and the other six destroyers had increased to 29 knots without zigzag and headed west for Heraklion; *Carnarvon* had turned off on to a course of 281 degrees, maintaining revolutions for 23 knots, and *Tuareg* and *Afghan* had taken station 30 degrees on her starboard and port bows respectively.

Nick asked Drisdale, "What time should we raise Ovo Island?"

"About 2300, sir. It'll be abeam at a quarter past."

"And the turning spot?"

"Near as dammit 1 am, sir."

Pretty well what his own mental arithmetic had already suggested. If it hadn't been, he'd have checked Drisdale's figures. There was to be a small adjustment of course when they passed Ovo Island, in order to reach the ordered position of 35 degrees 45 north, 24 degrees 50 east; then they were to turn and patrol a line due eastward, which would cover the approaches to Heraklion from the Milos direction. Then at 2 am they'd turn south-east, eventually rejoining the rest of the force at about 4:30 just north of the Kaso Strait.

Presumably some Intelligence source had suggested that interference by light surface forces was to be expected. The Italians certainly *had* had some destroyers at Milos—which was where they'd mustered those caïque-borne invasion forces—and MAS-boats in the Dodecanese, Scarpanto, and elsewhere. With the evacuation starting, they *might* decide this was the time for some offensive action—such as catching *Orion* and company speeding eastward, loaded with battle-weary troops.

Tuareg and *Afghan* were primarily the patrolling force. *Carnarvon* would have been added to the party in case they failed to link up with the main force before daylight; then they'd have the AA cruiser's guns to protect them, and some chance of getting through. And *Carnarvon's* limited speed would also have earmarked her for this job: she couldn't have kept up with the others on their fast passage from Kaso to Heraklion and back.

Ajax's departure wouldn't affect the operation much, Nick thought. Forty-five hundred men, which was the maximum number of troops expected to be there for lifting, could easily be fitted into two cruisers and six destroyers. Rawlings would miss *Ajax's* firepower when the air attacks began again in the morning, but that was about all; the admiral had been right to disembarrass himself of a lame duck at this early stage, because the one thing the evacuation force could not afford was to be slowed down.

Twenty-three-forty-five: the main force would have reached Heraklion and the first ships ought to be inside the little port by now. Twenty-three-thirty had been the estimated time of arrival, based on departure from Cape Sidaro after the passage through the Kaso Strait. Jack Everard came up from the chart, and answered a question Napier had put to him half a minute ago: "Exactly thirty miles to go, sir."

Thirty miles to the western end of their patrol line, to the point where they'd change course to east. At this moment, Heraklion was twenty miles to the south: and those thirty miles, at 23 knots, would be covered in one hour and a little over twenty minutes. They'd been intended to reach the turning point at 0100, so in fact they were about twelve minutes astern of station.

It didn't much matter, Jack supposed. And just as well it didn't, because there'd have been no question of speeding up. According to Tom Overton there'd been a decidedly frosty exchange between Napier and his engineer commander on the subject of maintaining these revs all through the night—all through tomorrow as well, come to that. In Alexandria, Buchanan had agreed that there was no reason to expect problems now; he'd been proud of the way his staff had coped with the earlier difficulties, and confident the repairs would hold out. Napier had reported accordingly, and *Carnarvon* had therefore been included in the operation. But a short while ago Buchanan had started worrying again and brought his worries to the captain, who had—according to Overton—blown his top. Buchanan had been sent off with a flea in his ear and instructions to look after his own problems.

Jack had been down in the plot, clearing up Midshipman Brighouse's inept attempt at working out some earlier star-sights; Overton had been on the bridge when he'd come back to it.

He hadn't reopened the subject of Gabrielle: and Overton had seemed relieved that he hadn't. It was in his mind all the time, though . . . Morally, there was no doubt what he ought to do: and the urge to cut adrift wasn't just a moral thing either, it was the fact of having been deceived, tricked into this. And that telephone call: the husband unsuspecting in the background and the women laughing—worst of all, making him a party to that laughter. Unless he cut loose, he *would* be a party to it.

But—not see her? Ashore in Alex in a week's time would he be capable of not calling her?

Carnarvon ploughed on, deeper into the black Aegean.

"Captain, sir . . ."

He was awake at once, hearing Dalgleish telling him that it was ten minutes past two and that they were coming up for the next alteration of course.

"Right. Thank you."

"Kye, sir. Just common or garden, I'm afraid."

"Can't always be lucky, can we?"

He'd dreamt he'd had a letter from Fiona; it was disappointing now to know it had been a dream. He sipped his cocoa and thought about their position now, the distances and the timing of the rendezvous with Rawlings's ships down near Kaso before daylight.

They'd reached the north-western limit of the sweep at thirteen minutes past one, and altered course to 090 degrees, in accordance with operation orders. At 2:15, by which time they'd have been steaming due east for an hour, they'd be coming round two points to starboard for the two-hour leg down to Kaso. According to the orders there was supposed to be some fighter cover over the Kaso area at 0530, but Nick thought he'd believe that when he saw it. Long-range fighters from the desert, they'd have to be—or imaginary ones from never-never land.

Coming to the end of the west-east patrol line didn't mean the screening job was finished. All the way down to Kaso they'd still be to the north of the evacuation force, covering it against surface raiders.

Dalgleish called suddenly, "Signalman!"

"Aye, sir . . ."

Dalgleish told Nick, who still had his nose in the cocoa mug, "*Carnarvon's* flashing, sir."

That blue lamp would be winking out the order for the change of course. When they'd turned, Nick thought, he'd go back to sleep.

A thump in the port side of *Carnarvon's* bridge was a signal arriving up the tube. Petty Officer Tomkins, yeoman of the watch, retrieved it and took it to the hooded signal table.

He read it out to Napier. Flag Officer Force B was announcing that the Kaso rendezvous was to be delayed by one hour, from 0430 to 0530.

Napier gave it a moment's thought. Then he asked, "To what speed can we reduce now, Pilot, and keep that rendezvous?"

About 17 or 18, Jack guessed, as he went to the chart to check on it. He also guessed that the question of rpm and Buchanan's fears must have been worrying Napier all this time. At the chart table, he found they could come down to 16 knots, and he reported this to Napier.

"Yeoman. Make to the destroyers: *Speed 16.*"

Probably it was taking longer than the admiral had expected to embark the troops. The ones ready for embarkation when the force had arrived would be taken aboard fast enough, but the soldiers actually holding the perimeter against the surrounding Germans would only be able to slip away in small groups, a few at a time. And it was possible, Jack guessed, that with the wind as strong as it was the cruisers might not have been able to get inside that very small harbour; then they'd have to lie off while the destroyers ferried soldiers out to them.

Napier cut into his thoughts: "You'd better get some sleep, Pilot."

At 4:11, Jack woke with the bridge messenger bawling at him from the chartroom door, "Captain wants you on the bridge, sir!" Flinging himself off the settee, he realized that the ship was rolling—which she hadn't been when he'd turned in—and also, judging by the vibration,

that she was again doing something more than 20 knots. His first thought
was that perhaps they'd run into some Italians and turned to engage or
chase them: but there'd have been an action alarm, in that case . . . He
was on the bridge within seconds: Napier told him, "We're on two-
four-five, Pilot, 23 knots. Altered three minutes ago. You'll see some signals on the log. Get an up-to-date DR on, will you?"

PO Hillier gave him the signal log, and he took it with him to the
chart table. The first thing was to establish the dead-reckoning position
and mark on the new course, extending it south-westward. Then, to find
out what it was all about.

The signals told the story clearly enough. One: *Imperial's* steering had
failed: she'd run amuck, just before 4 am. A total breakdown. *Imperial*
was the destroyer who'd been near-missed last evening and seemed none
the worse for it, he remembered. When her rudder had jammed,
Rawlings's ships with the troops from Heraklion on board had been
steering east at 29 knots. Two: *Hotspur* had been ordered to take off
Imperial's crew and sink her. Admiral Rawlings was continuing eastward:
with his ships full of troops he'd have no option. But he'd reduced speed,
so that *Hotspur* should catch him up later—with any luck, before daylight. Three: *Carnarvon* and the Tribals were steering south-westward now
to provide cover to *Hotspur* as she withdrew alone, with two ships' companies and an unspecified number of troops on board.

Following that misfortune, it made good sense. But at about 4:30,
when he was fiddling around with courses and distances at the chart,
Jack saw that *Carnarvon* and her destroyers had no hope at all now of
getting through the Kaso narrows before dawn. The same, of course,
applied to *Hotspur.* There'd been that earlier delay of one hour, and now
another ninety minutes had been lost.

At 0446 the order came to alter course and withdraw towards Kaso.
Hotspur had torpedoed *Imperial*, and was on her way. There was to be a
rendezvous two and a half miles north of the Yanisades lighthouse at 0545.

"Course, Pilot?"

He was at the chart, getting it . . . "One-oh-two, sir."

Napier gave Hillier, the yeoman, a course-alteration signal for the destroyers.

At 23 knots, by 0545 they'd be several miles short of the rendezvous position. The run to it was 25 miles, and it was now 0450. They'd be three or four miles short. Jack reported this to Napier; the captain nodded, but did nothing about calling for more speed. He had accepted, right from the beginning, Buchanan's prognostication that if he exceeded revs for 23 knots she'd almost certainly bust a gut.

Now, they'd be entering the Kaso Strait at dawn. It wasn't good, but it was less bad than it had looked a short while ago—being caught well this side of the bolt-hole. And if the promised air-cover should by chance materialize, all might yet be well. In fact it would be absolutely marvellous . . . Jack put the time of the alteration, and a reading of the Chernikeeff log, in his notebook. The time, as *Carnarvon's* wheel went over, was 0452.

At 0503, the port engine stopped.

CHAPTER TEN
·   ·   ·

Light grew like a cancer in the east. Guns were cocked up, trained towards that brightness: from the destroyers' bridges binoculars swept horizon and sky: on the gun platforms men in tin hats, lifebelts, and anti-flash gear had their eyes fixed on the coming of a day that no one wanted. *Carnarvon* was struggling eastward at less than 7 knots, on one engine and carrying enough rudder to counter the single-screw operation. She was a cripple, painfully dragging herself across the sea: you could think of a mouse being played with by a cat, with no chance of escape but still trying to get away, following blind instinct but aware of the imminence of a savage clawing. Waiting for the cat . . .

There was a faint chance of escape, perhaps, if they got that engine going. At any minute her engineers might work the miracle: after three-quarters of an hour of "any minute now . . ." The Tribals zigzagged, using their Asdics and watching the sky, that streaky silver leaking up from behind a mauve horizon. Twenty-eight miles eastward, according to Drisdale's calculations, the rest of Force B would be just about entering the Kaso Strait, and *Hotspur* would be rejoining, panting up from astern into the shelter of the cruisers' guns.

Drisdale murmured, with his glasses on *Carnarvon*, "Glad I'm not a plumber." By "plumber" he meant engineer; Nick had glanced at him and away again, not understanding what else he meant. Drisdale added, "Thinking of *her* blokes. Slaving away at that engine, with everyone else cursing at 'em to get a bloody wriggle on—"

"Red flag on *Carnarvon!*"

Ashcourt had reported it. Instinctively you looked for a threat in the east, where both the sunrise and Scarpanto were. All Nick could see in that sector was an irritatingly *pretty* sky.

"Alarm port, red seven-oh, 88s!"

"Starboard fifteen." To get closer to the cruiser. "One-four-two revolutions." Fifteen knots, that would give him. He put his glasses up and found the bombers: there were two flights each of four aircraft, flying on a course of about 130 degrees at something like five thousand feet. He told Houston, up the voicepipe to the tower, "Open fire when you're ready."

When they're in range, he'd meant; but if they held on as they were going they'd pass about a mile astern. Going somewhere else, perhaps. Could be: that course would bring them over the Kaso Strait, if they held to it . . . But one flight of four was veering off, swinging away to port. Nick told CPO Habgood, "Midships. Steer one-double-oh." Then, glancing round at Ashcourt, "Keep your eyes peeled on the sun while I watch this lot."

"Aye aye, sir."

Tone normal: eyes slightly more expressive. Ashcourt had had enough experience of battle recently, of this kind of battle, to realize they'd be very, very lucky now to get away intact. It wasn't just a threat from those four bombers, or from those eight, but from the hundreds that would be coming very soon. The ships had been spotted—which had been inevitable, but it had happened sooner than it need have—and one of them was lame, and the Stuka base was only sixty miles away.

You could see the land clearly now, from south-east to south-west, and the sun's first rays were spotlighting the higher inland peaks. The nearest bit of coastline was a promontory called Spinalonga, ten miles away. One lot of 88s seemed to be going straight on, still, while the other four aircraft circled round astern: if they kept circling they'd be coming up on the port beam in a minute.

"Alarm ahead—Stukas! Right of the sun—"

"All guns follow director. 'A' and 'B' with red barrage—load, load, load!"

The 88s were coming up on the port quarter in a loose straggle and in shallow dives: ahead, the Stukas were above the sun and hard to see. Nick heard the fire-gongs from down for'ard as Houston launched an up-sun barrage from "A" and "B" guns, leaving "X" and "Y" in the control of PO Wellbeloved from the open-topped HA director-rangefinder up behind him. All noise now . . . Stooping near the voice-pipe with his eyes slitted against the glare, watching for Stukas attacking, he heard *Carnarvon*'s guns and *Afghan*'s: then Ashcourt's noise-piercing yell, "Alarm port! Port quarter—Messerschmitts!" Nick had the ACP telephone—fumbling it as he still watched for Stukas . . . "Port quarter, Messerschmitts!" The racket of a fighter's engine confirmed it: an Me 110 out of nowhere, blasting across ahead and banking round to starboard towards the cruiser: and others were over her already in swallow-like swooping rushes, one bomb just short then one hitting near the base of the foremost funnel: there'd been a flash and a burst of smoke and debris and now a plume of smoke trailing back. Stukas coming now—and *they*, like the Messerschmitt fighter-bombers, were also going for *Carnarvon*. She'd been hit again, for'ard, and the last of the

Messerschmitts had straffed her bridge with its guns. Stukas' sirens swelled
in triumph over the bedlam of gunfire. A spout of sea rising close to
the cruiser's quarter was a bomb from an 88: she seemed to stagger as
a second struck her, right aft. The raised four-inch gundeck amidships—
the gun-mounting on it—had been blown clean out of her in the blast
of yet another hit; and she was on fire aft, more bomb-spouts rising on
the far side of her, in the sea but near enough to hurt. One Stuka was
diving steeply at her, another close behind it, both sirens screaming: the
first one's bomb tumbling clear, shining as it turned over in what looked
like slow motion with the new day's brilliance flashing on its fins. New
day dawning in a rush of disaster, precipitate and stunning, a nightmare
bathed in sunrise, drowned in noise. *Carnarvon* lay stopped, stricken, like
a boxer overwhelmed before anyone had heard the bell for the new
round: you had an urge to appeal to some non-existent referee, ask for
a new start . . .

"I'll see if I can find him, sir." Jack heard himself shout it over the thunder of guns and the howl of Stuka sirens. Napier looked round with a
suggestion of a smile that was noticeable because this wasn't much of a
time for smiling. He'd nodded. *Carnarvon* was on fire and had some
flooding on the port side aft, several other areas of damage below and
above decks, and Stukas still swarming over. It was eight or ten minutes
since the first bomb had hit.

It was Bell-Reid, his second-in-command, whom Napier wanted
found. He'd glanced round, as Jack moved away: "Clear the bridge!"

There was a general movement to obey: look-outs, signal staff, mes-
sengers. Willy Irvine nodded at Midshipman Wesley: "Go on, Mid." Jack
stopped at the plot voicepipe to tell young Brighouse to clear out too;
going on aft to the ladder he found himself joined by McCowan,
Clutterbuck, Midshipman Burk, and the rest of the director's and ADP's
crews, who'd been ordered down when the power circuits had failed.
Clutterbuck shouted in Jack's ear, "Last man over the side's a sissy!"

Pompoms and point-fives roaring: Jack hurried on down into the ship, and Napier, glancing behind him into the near-empty bridge, found Able Seaman Noble, his servant, still standing there.

"Away you go, Noble!"

"Ready when you are, sir."

Napier told him, "I'm waiting for news from the commander. You carry on, now."

"All the same to you, sir, I'd as soon as—"

Both men staggered as the ship lurched from an explosion. You could hear the rising shriek of another diving Stuka. Noble shouted, "Oughter blow up your lifebelt, sir." Pointing at Napier's dark blue covered Mae West.

Napier looked down at it and nodded, and one hand moved to free the inflation tube. The other gestured brusquely: "Off the bridge, Noble. Do what you're bloody well told, will you?"

Jack had gone down two ladders: to the lower bridge, then to the level of the for'ard gundeck. Now another, to the foc'sl deck: and another still, to the upper deck but under cover, inside the foc'sl deck's shelter. It felt as if he was forcing himself to keep on going down. Men were mustering in here by divisions, here and up for'ard in the seamen's messdeck; until the order came to abandon ship, it was healthier to be under cover. Down again: the PMO and the younger doctor, Holloway, were using the lower-deck crew space as a dressing-station and operating theatre. There'd been casualties among ammo-supply and damage-control parties, and there were sights one tried not to look at; on the upper ladders Jack had heard McCowan say that two of the four-inch guns' crews had been wiped out.

Several minutes ago Napier had given the order to prepare to abandon ship, but he'd been unable to contact the commander, Bell-Reid, who'd gone down earlier to visit various trouble spots and should have reported over the sound-powered telephone from the lower steering position. That was on the platform deck, almost in the bottom of the ship and vertically below the bridge. In the lower deck, emergency lanterns glowed, hoses had been run out and men were struggling to manoeuvre stretchers up through hatches, through thickening smoke and the reek of fire, the ship's compartments booming and shuddering to bomb-explosions in the sea around her. Like a dark, noisy, enclosing cavern. Damage-control parties were getting out, getting up towards the air and daylight: they'd been told to, with the stand-by-to-abandon order. Buchanan, the engineer commander, was on his way up to report to Napier; Jack asked him if he'd seen Bell-Reid, and he had not. When the commander had gone down, *Carnarvon* hadn't been in quite as hopeless a state as she was now; the only fire inside her then had been the one right aft, and Buchanan had still been trying to get her engines going. While there'd been that degree of hope, plus the expectation of getting her under control in emergency steering control, there'd been no talk of abandoning her. Everything had got much worse very quickly: in something like six minutes she'd been hit by four more bombs, there'd been an explosion in No. 1 boiler-room, the steering-gear compartment right aft had been wrecked and flooded, and a fire somewhere between No. 2 boiler-room and the for'ard engine-room was threatening the midships four-inch magazine. That magazine should have been flooded by now, but no report had reached the bridge.

On one of the ladders, Jack met a stoker petty officer named Berwick. He asked him if he'd seen the commander anywhere.

"Can't say I have, sir."

"He was supposed to be going down to the lower steering position, I believe."

"Ah, but we shut it off, sir, that section . . . *Christ*, then—"

"Why did you—"

"Fire, sir, very fierce, started in the LP supply room—so the 'atch over that lobby—"

"He may be down there." Nightmare, suddenly. But real: and he was in it. With the peculiar feeling that he was down here on his own orders, his own victim . . . "Listen, Spo—if we can't open that hatch, we could get to him from aft along the lower passage. With a couple of hoses going to hold the fire back—"

"What's the fuss, Everard?"

Commander Bell-Reid: and he had his doggie, OD Webster, trotting faithfully at his heels. No need for the rescue attempt, then: relief was huge. The stoker PO actually laughed with the relief of it: Bell-Reid glared at him, and Jack explained, "We thought you'd been shut in, sir, in the lower steering position. We were working out how to try to get you out."

"Very civil of you." Bell-Reid nodded. "Thanks. But where the hell's Overton, d'you know?"

"Afraid I don't—"

"Mr Overton's dead, sir." Berwick added no detail. Jack gave Bell-Reid the message he'd come down to deliver: "The captain's anxious for you to get in touch, sir. He sent me to find you. He's ordered stand-by-to-abandon-ship, and—"

"I know *that*, damn it." But with telephone circuits mostly dead it was hard to know who knew what. Bell-Reid had spotted someone he wanted: he shouted, "Mr Brassey!"

Brassey was a warrant officer, gunner. A scrawny man with skin like yellow parchment; he looked now as if he'd just been down a coal-mine. Bell-Reid asked him, "Is the bloody thing flooded now, or isn't it?"

"What I'm after, sir. Should'a been, but I just got the buzz there's lads in there wounded."

"Inside the magazine?"

"I dunno, sir, but that's what I 'eard. If it's right I could use some 'elp."

"How did you hear it?"

"Young Clark, sir. He's a good 'and but he was—well, shook up. And he couldn't shift 'em, not on his own. Weren't making all that much sense like, sir."

Bell-Reid looked at Jack.

"Give Mr Brassey some support, Everard?"

He nodded. "Aye aye, sir."

It hadn't been his own choice, this time.

"There's your help, Mr Brassey. Get it flooded double quick. If it blows up she'll go down like a stone before we've got the wounded out of her. Petty Officer Berwick here'd like to go along too, I expect."

How men might have been wounded in a magazine deep inside the ship, without the magazine itself having exploded, was a mystery. But with fires near it, it did have to be flooded, obviously ... "Here, Everard!" Bell-Reid called him back, handed him a box; there was a hypodermic in it and a flask of some fluid. "Morphine. Up to that mark *there* is one effective dose to kill pain. All right?"

He nodded, stuffed it inside his shirt so he'd have his hands free. Blundering aft through smoke, darkness, and the noises of the tortured, dying ship. *Sinking* ship. Well, not yet: there *might* be time to get down there, do whatever had to be done and get back up again. *Don't think, just do it* ... The only torch they had was Mr Brassey's: they were three decks down and moving aft along a passage that ran down the ship's side—the starboard, higher side—flanking the two boiler-rooms and engine-rooms. It was narrow, and with the list on her the deck slanted so that their shoulders bumped along the inboard bulkhead as they moved from one watertight door to the next, having to stop to open each one and then shut it again behind them. The farther aft they got the hotter and smokier it was: it was the eye-watering, lung-racking reek of burning paint, corticene, rubber. The bulkhead on the left, the inboard one, was hot to the touch. Behind him, Berwick called out something about smoke-helmets in the damage-control headquarters beside the engineers' store—*if* the damage-control parties hadn't taken them all up top with them when they'd evacuated. But that meant lower deck, back aft. There was a transverse bulkhead with the wardroom and officers' cabins aft of it, warrant officers' mess and gunroom—the gunroom being an unusual feature in a cruiser of this class—this side of it, and various offices and stores for'ard of that before you came to the marines' mess-deck. Smoke-helmets were going to be a necessity: Jack already had a wadded handkerchief—cotton-waste, Berwick had—to breathe through, and they were going to have to get right inside the magazine, which extended down into the hold and had the seat of the fire somewhere close to it. The noise of the guns was muted this far down, but each near-missing bomb was like a kick in the head.

Carnarvon lurched suddenly, just as they were getting through a door: it was as if there'd been a big shift in ballast that had increased the list to port, and the heavy door swung back on the gunner. Brassey cursing: the stoker PO shouted, "Now then, 'old steady there, old girl!" Keeping his own spirits up . . . A bulkhead had gone, probably, letting sea flood into another section of the stern. For one blind moment Jack did let himself think about it, *feel* it: the hatches and ladders overhead, hatches slamming and ladders twisting under distorting strain as one end of her filled and the sea rushed thundering through. He knew what it looked like from outside, but here he was *in* it; he could have let his nerve go, turned and made a break for it; but he'd allowed himself that flash of imagination deliberately, to prove to himself he *could* master it, and he'd already wrenched his mind to another area—to the fact that there were wounded men down here, helpless men who'd drown like kittens in a sack if they weren't brought out. Behind it was a memory— it would last him all his life—of the Dutch transport *Gelderland*, with men waving from her scuttles as she sank. He'd regained purpose, balance, a sense of direction and of urgency outweighing fear. Breathless still, and shaking inside, but it was the answer, the antidote to fear, having purpose and having to concentrate on the detail of achieving it: it enabled you to tolerate the fear, live with it.

Through what seemed like hours . . .

They got two wounded men. Flash or blast—Mr Brassey reckoned— had passed down the shell-hoist from the midships four-inch mounting to the ammo lobby 25 feet below it. A single shell had exploded in there, probably in the arms of the handler. It had blown that one man to pieces, plastering him over the lobby's bulkheads, and badly wounded two others inside the magazine. One had had an arm torn off and one side of his head scalped to the bone, the other multiple punctures and broken ribs, perhaps lethal internal injuries. The morphine acted quickly, but getting them up and out of the magazine and then out of the flat up to the next deck wasn't easy. It was greenhouse-hot, stifling, the deckheads raining condensation. The fire had reached the battery rooms, and the switchboard room was a furnace behind its clipped steel door. The way up from this section was by a vertical steel ladder to an armoured, watertight hatch in the deck above: up there, they were above the edges of the fire. Berwick had left a hose running, to safeguard the line of retreat; the canvas of the hose was steaming from the deck's heat and the water might have been gushing from a hot tap. But worst of all, they found that the fire had broken through on the starboard side, upwards from below to this higher level: the realization that there'd be no getting back the way they'd come hit all three of them at about the same moment.

Berwick had opened the magazine flood-valves: she wouldn't blow up now, not from *this* cause: and now they'd got the two wounded men up, dumped them for a moment in a swirl of hot water that reddened around them. Like corpses: and by flickering yellow torchlight their rescuers looked to each other like ghouls: bloodstained, sweating, filthy. Bombs were still exploding and close-range weapons were in action, but it sounded as if all the four-inch had been knocked out. Or no ammunition getting to them now.

Jack took Brassey's arm and tilted the torch upwards so its light would shine on the underside of the big armoured hatch at the top of the next ladder: there was a manhole-size smaller hatch in its centre, oval-shaped and held shut by the usual heavy clips. Steel an inch thick. Brassey grunted, "*You're* a big bastard, Spo." Berwick went up the ladder, Brassey shining the torch up past him at the hatch. He got two of the clips off: then the third wouldn't budge as easily. Jack thought, watching upwards, *It's got to* . . . Berwick was straining at it now, using all his weight and grunting with the effort: he was braced with his feet well apart on the ladder, shoulders bunched, both fists locked on the handle of the clip.

He was a very powerfully built man: Jack knew that if he couldn't move it neither he nor Brassey need even try.

"Sledge-'ammer." Panting, chest heaving, Berwick stared down into the torch beam. The ship rang from an explosion for'ard. She'd go— they all knew it—at any moment: there'd be a movement, a sudden shift in her angle in the water, and she'd go in one swift slide. Berwick said, "Won't do it wi'out a sledge."

"Won't do it, then."

Brassey stared at Jack. He looked like something dug up out of a wet grave. The stare dredged an alternative, the only one, out of Jack's mind.

"We'll have to try to get for'ard up the port side."

The low side, where the flooding was. Berwick was clambering slowly down the ladder. Brassey growled, "What if it's up to the fuckin' deckhead?"

The answer was, *Then we shan't get through*. There was incipient terror in his mind but he had a hatch jammed shut on that too. And he'd told himself, while he'd been waiting in an agony for Berwick to open the other one, that you could drown outside the ship as easily as inside. All right, so in here you'd be trapped, you *were* trapped, but—

Shut up . . .

The ship had a pronounced list already, and she was deeper by the stern than she had been when they'd started this. That port-side passage *might* be flooded right to its roof, and even if it wasn't, if she tipped over by another degree or two when they were in it, they'd *stay* in it. But with that hatch stuck—you could guess, from bomb-damage up top when the mounting itself had been blown over the side and flash had penetrated to the magazine—there wasn't anything else left to try.

"We'll be lucky, you'll see." He told them, "Let's keep close together. Mr Brassey, you come in the middle with your torch. I'll go first with this chap." The man with no left arm: the badge on the remaining one was a star with the letter "C" in it, marking him as a cook.

"Might bloody fry before we're swimmin'." Getting aft, out of this lobby, Brassey meant.

Water swirled steaming on the deck. Water from the shattered stern would drown the fires eventually, but by that time it wouldn't do anyone any good, she'd be on her way to the sea-bed. Meanwhile in the wet area where flooding had approached the edges of the fire and where damage-control parties had had hoses running to cool decks and bulkheads, it was less fire than progressive scorching, smouldering, heat, and fumes. A battle between elements, and the sea would win it: in the end, the sea won everything. They'd left the smoke-helmets one deck down, he realized . . . One-handed, he dipped his handkerchief in water and held it against the lower half of his face: he needed the other hand for steadying the cook, who was across his shoulder in a fireman's lift. He was soaked in blood from him already, and moving into greater heat, through the short midships passage between the two fan rooms and then turning right out of it, down the slope with really blistering heat radiating at him now, truly man-burning heat, and paintwork beginning to bubble on the bulkheads.

On the port side he found himself moving into water that was knee-deep, thigh-deep, then up to his waist, and over it: by the time he was actually in the passage and had turned for'ard it was around his chest and the man he was carrying had his face an inch from the darkly swirling surface. He was unconscious now: he might even, for all Jack knew, have been dead. The length of the passage they had to get through was something like a hundred feet, he thought, with four watertight doors which he'd have to open and Berwick shut again behind them. Brassey's torch-beam glinted on the water, throwing grotesque shadows on white-enamelled bulkheads as they shuffled forward: Jack burdened, sticky with the cook's blood, trying to keep his breathing slow and even, forging slowly through black water that deepened as they got nearer to the ship's middle section where her beam was widest. First door now. He spread his feet on the slanting deck, got the cook well balanced across his shoulder so as to have his hands free for working off the clips. If she listed one degree more, he thought, it would drown them. *If* . . . The knowledge was in Brassey's face too, close up beside him: yellow, blood-streaked, smoke-blackened here and there from some earlier excursion. Easing the last clip off, he felt the pressure of the water on this side of the door and above its two-foot-high sill forcing it open, away from him. The weight on the clip made it hard to move and he had to hammer at it now with the heel of his hand: but if it had been a door that opened the other way, *this* way, nobody could ever have opened it against the pressure. *Christ*, he thought, *but we're lucky* . . . The clip banged up and the door crashed open: water was sluicing over the sill like a river over a weir, deluging into the next section, foaming and roaring. His ears ached from the rise in pressure: he shouted, turning and at the same time bracing himself against the flood's pull, "Shut it quick as you can, Spo." Berwick wouldn't manage it until the level on the other side had risen so that the flow slackened; by that time, with luck, it mightn't be at much more than sill-height. But the door had to be shut behind them: it would have been a relief to have simply hurried on, but you had to think of the risk of a new flood pouring up behind them from the stern. Air out, water in: if all these doors were open at once it could send her to the bottom. They were all through, and Berwick was leaning hard against the door, Brassey helping to support that other wounded rating. The flow of water was quite gentle already, and Jack hoped that at the next door it might even be contained by the sill.

"Next section ought to be dry, I'd say."

"Like *I'd* say I oughter be 'ome in me bed." Like a dog snarling, only it had been intended as a smile, Jack thought. He told him, "You may not have noticed, Guns, but so far we're doing pretty well."

Even in this section the water was only going to be about three feet deep at the higher end: so there'd be a little to spill over at that next door, but it was a terrific improvement. In fact it felt like a miracle. *Touch wood* . . . There wasn't any, only enamelled steel. *And don't get too cocky too soon*, he warned himself. She could still go in this next second: roll over, or there'd be a split, a suddenly collapsing bulkhead, the roar of inrushing sea: Berwick had the door shut and a clip on, and they began the wade to the next door, which was in the bulkhead that made the after end of No. 2 boiler-room. The water was about eighteen inches higher than the sill and there was that much to cascade through, but it amounted to nothing much, because it was pouring from a short section of passage into a long one. The air was cooler too. It was about 45 feet to the next bulkhead, the one dividing the two boiler-rooms: he'd stopped there, waiting for the others, and the man on his back said, "Florrie—Christ's sake, Florrie luv, what y' *doing?*"

Brassey said, "Takin' 'er knickers off, I shouldn't wonder." He cackled with laughter. "Come on, Spo, let's get a bloody—"

A deep *boom* from aft: a shudder that ran right through her. He felt the deck angle more as her stern settled. He was wrenching at the clips: he shouted, "Leave it open! *Run!*"

Still one more door.

This wasn't a cave they were trying to get out of: it felt like it but it was a steel carcass hanging at the top of three hundred and fifty fathoms of sea. And it *would* go soon: you could sense or feel how it was just hanging, how the next thing would be the stern-first slide, the fast and sickening slipping-away you'd seen quite a few times now. He had the clips off the last door, and it wasn't opening. It was stuck. He couldn't—

"Bloody 'ell—"

Brassey had pushed up beside him, added his not very considerable, scrawny frame to it. Muttering obscenities . . . Stoker PO Berwick suggested mildly, "Let *this* dog see the bone, sir?" Jack edged one way, Brassey the other, and Berwick came in between them. Now five men's weight—including the unconscious ones on their backs—still wasn't moving it. But there was a deep rumbling noise from the stern and the door gave suddenly, swinging open . . .

"Go on, Spo. Straight up top!" Another, similar rumble: it could only be water breaking through her, and he thought, *Here it comes* . . . He'd guessed all along they'd never get away with it, hadn't he? "Carry on, Mr Brassey. See you somewhere."

Slitted eyes gleamed out of the fiendishly ugly face. Brassey growled,

"You're a right good 'un, Everard." Then he'd gone through into the lobby where the up-ladder was.

"Starboard twenty-five, sir . . ."

CPO Habgood sounded as calm as always. Nick told him, "Two-five-oh revolutions." There'd been another upheaval or explosion in *Carnarvon*'s stern, but she was still afloat. There must still have been a lot of men to come out of her. A Stuka's bomb missed to starboard, the fountain of it breaking right across her: she'd go at any moment, and in the circumstances he knew what he was going to have to do. Nothing he did would save her, and if he stopped to pick up survivors he'd as likely as not lose his own ship and another two hundred and thirty lives, quite probably adding *Afghan* and *her* two-hundred-and-thirty-odd to that. And the survivors he rescued would simply be sunk twice instead of once.

The facts were simple, but the decision wasn't easy.

A Stuka was aiming itself at *Tuareg*. "Midships." He had Dalgleish on the ACP telephone. "Get the lashings off half our Carley floats. Stand by to ditch them when we're closer."

He bent to the voicepipe again.

"Meet her."

"Meet her, sir . . ."

"Steady!" Yellow beak predatory, loathsome: but it was pulling out, high among the shell-bursts, tracer curving away short of it. Its bomb had seemed to start with a slanting trajectory to port: when it had splashed in he'd put on wheel to close the cruiser. Drisdale was pointing: at more 88s arriving . . . "Port fifteen." The bomb had gone in forty yards away. Another Stuka was about to start its dive: and there'd been another hit, in that second as he glanced at *Carnarvon*, in her bridge. He'd seen it and flinched from it . . . "Midships." Then, into the telephone, "Stand by to ditch the floats."

"Standing by, sir."

Chalk's voice, very calm. *Carnarvon* was almost right over on her side and men were sliding down the exposed slope of hull. The cruiser had got her own Carley floats over and he saw some boats in the water too: the Stukas and Messerschmitts weren't likely to leave them alone for long. In fact there—now—a Stuka flying low, parallel to the ship's side, guns flaming . . . The spectre behind his eyes was of his own elder brother, 25 years ago, in a shattered, sinking cruiser: David starkly mad, jabbering incoherently. Memory wrapped in shame and infinite regret was heightened by knowledge now of personal responsibility: what you'd made yourself, you couldn't blame, couldn't stand aside from . . . "Stop both engines!"

His own voice had passed that order. *Tuareg's* screws would stop now—were stopping—but she still had a lot of way on, pitching as she drove up towards the expanding area of survivor-dotted sea. The gleam on the water and the stink was oil-fuel. He told Chalk over the telephone, "Scrambling-nets both sides!"

Chalk was yelling the order to Dalgleish. The nets were rolled up and lashed along each side of the iron deck; all you had to do was cast off the lashings and they'd tumble down . . .

"Slow ahead together."

Chalk reported that the nets were down.

"Ditch the floats."

Dropping them out here rather than closer in where they might fall on top of swimmers. From all round the ship's afterpart the heavy lifesaving rafts were toppling over, crashing into the sea. The guns were engaging yet another Stuka that was going for *Carnarvon.*

"Stop both."

"Stop both, sir."

"Port twenty."

There was a group of about twenty men on and around one of the cruiser's own floats: they were waving and cheering as *Tuareg* slid up towards them. But thinking more clearly now, he knew he had no business to be stopping, risking his own ship and all her company. That group around the float would be all he'd take: twenty-odd out of nearly five hundred. No business to be taking *any* . . . From the foc'sl break a heaving line soared out and fell across the float; they'd got hold of it, and now the men on *Tuareg's* deck would haul them in alongside. Nick was looking round for Stukas, shocked at the wrongness of his decision: but it hadn't been a decision, only an unthinking reflex. He shouted to Drisdale, "Tell me when I can move!" The navigator raised a hand in acknowledgement, and leant over the side of the bridge to monitor the rescue operation. A Messerschmitt 109 swept low over the sea, firing bursts at floats and the heads of swimmers. Bombs from some Ju88s were raising mounds of sea around the foundering ship's hulk: men would die from the shock-waves of those explosions.

"All inboard, sir!"

"Half ahead together. Three-six-oh revolutions. Starboard twenty-five." He felt sick. A Stuka was diving on *Afghan; Afghan* lay stopped, as *Tuareg* had been, and *Tuareg's* four-sevens were barraging over her.

"Yeoman"—he had to yell into PO Whiffen's ear—"make to him: *Course one hundred, speed 34 knots, executive.*"

Dalgleish reported by telephone, "We have 23 survivors on board, sir. No officers."

Nick passed the phone to Ashcourt and told the coxswain, "Steer one-oh-oh degrees." *Afghan* was getting under way, circling to starboard through a man-dotted sea, bow-wave rising as she picked up speed; and Houston was shifting target to a new group of Stukas approaching from right ahead, high above the sun.

Napier had been killed when a Stuka's bomb had hit the bridge, and the fire from that hit was still blazing, would be until she sank and the sea put it out. You could feel the heat from it down here on the upper deck beside the starboard whaler's davits, where the last of the wounded were being got away. Jack and Brassey had been helping with them, getting them aft to this point and then down the side to waiting Carley floats. The whaler itself had been lowered fifteen or twenty minutes ago when the order to abandon ship had been given, and the system—

presided over by Bell-Reid—was that a stretcher with a man in it would be lowered from the for'ard davit and the empty stretcher brought up again on the after one. There were several stretchers in use, so it wasn't too slow a process. Jumping ladders had been shackled together and hung over the side, resting on its slope, and men at intervals on the ladders were guiding the stretchers as they came slithering down.

It was nearly finished now. At the ship's side, Bell-Reid asked one of the men who'd brought the last customer, "How many more?"

"Three, sir. One's strapped in an' ready, then two to go." The SBA turned back, to re-enter the ship through the door under the foc's'l break.

Brassey sloped in after him. "I'll give 'em an 'and inside."

It wasn't all that safe *outside*. One man had been shot off the ladder, and another killed on the upper deck, both by Stuka machine-guns.

Bell-Reid helped to detach an empty Neill-Robertson from the after fall. Then he leant over the side, and called down to the two men on the ladder to go on down, get away. Straightening, he told Jack, "You go down, steer the next one when it comes, then carry on. Someone else'll replace you." He'd turned to Fullbrook, the RNVR lieutenant. "You too. And well done, both of you."

Jack was about a quarter of the way down the ladder when the ship began to move. Bow rising: then the ladder began to slide, scraping across the ship's side as she tilted. This time she wasn't fooling. And old Brassey was inside her—and Bell-Reid, Melhuish, half a dozen others. Above him Fullbrook shouted something, but a Stuka was roaring over and the shout went with it: next moment something came crashing down past him and it was Fullbrook, jumping . . . Jack looked down, saw where he went in, saw also an area of sea clear of heads or floats: *Carnarvon's* long bow was lifting, lifting faster . . . He twisted himself round on the ladder and pushed off from it in a sprawling sort of dive.

"Course one-four-six, sir."

It was the course for Alexandria; and the first 25 miles of it, starting now, was the run through the Kaso Strait. At the moment *Afghan* was more or less back in station astern; both ships had been dodging like woodcock under the Stuka rushes.

They *might* get through. It was possible—given an outsize allowance of continuing good luck.

The sun was well up now. Sidaro had been abeam before 0700 and they'd held on to the old course for two miles beyond that in order to clear Elasa Island at a safe distance. Ahead, about 25 miles south-eastward, a discoloured patch of sky like a dirty thumbprint on a glass marked the position of Force B—Admiral Rawlings with *Orion* and *Dido* and destroyers. Force B was just about out of the Strait now; and a signal from the admiral to C-in-C a quarter of an hour ago had reported a near-miss on the destroyer *Hereward,* and that she'd been slowed down. She was dropping astern and the rest of the force was pressing on, under constant attack.

One more carcass to the vultures. Alone, a single destroyer couldn't possibly survive when it was already winged.

For the moment, *Tuareg* had no bombers overhead. It was the first respite since the attacks had begun on *Carnarvon* at first light, and you could bet it wouldn't last many minutes. But even *one* minute gave you time to draw breath, gave guns' crews a chance to clear the gundecks of shellcases, ammunition-supply parties to get more shells up and into the ready-use racks.

Unfortunately it also gave you time to think.

"We seem to be still here, sir. Once or twice I didn't think we would be."

Dalgleish had taken advantage of the lull to come up on the bridge. He was offering him a cigarette.

Nick took one. "Thanks."

Dalgleish said quietly, "About *Carnarvon,* sir. Difficult to know how to say how *bloody* sorry—"

"All right." He shook his head: he knew how well-meant it was, but . . . he didn't want it. "Thank you."

"I promised some of the lads, sir—they wanted me to tell you how they felt."

"Thank them for me. Number One, are you doing something about organizing breakfast?"

"Sandwiches and tea, sir. I've sent cooks to the galley . . . I'd better get back aft—"

"Alarm port! Stukas, red nine-oh!"

"Signal, sir—"

"Give it to the navigating officer." How *they* felt . . . They meant it kindly and he appreciated it, but none of them could even begin to guess at how *he* felt. He had his glasses on the new attackers: about a dozen of them, in three flights. And any moment now, back to routine . . .

Drisdale told him, "*Decoy*'s been near-missed, sir. Speed of the force is reduced to 25 knots."

Afghan had opened fire: now *Tuareg*'s guns crashed: Nick lowered the glasses from his eyes, watched the ugly-looking bombers spreading out for their attacks. The near-miss on *Decoy* was an ill wind: they'd be catching up at an extra five sea-miles per hour now. It wouldn't be anything like *safe* down there with the admiral but it would be less *un*safe than it was here. Pompoms had opened fire and the whole circus was in action: diving, shrieking bombers, guns thudding, crashing, flaming. *Afghan*'s pompom flashes were mixed blue and white. Some of the pompom belts would have been reloaded during that lull: they were two-pounder shells, each the length of a man's forearm, and handling the belts was heavy work. They'd put more tracer into the point-five belts now, taking that tip from the point-fives' little brothers farther aft. Same family name of Vickers. *Tuareg* heeled as he turned her hard a-port and a bomb thumped in to starboard: each one that was dropped could be the one that would hit or near-miss, stop her, give her to the pack to finish off: behind recognition of that distinct possibility was an out-of-focus image of *Carnarvon* on the sea-bed with two thousand feet of water over her. "Midships."

"Midships, sir . . . Wheel's amidships, sir."

"Starboard twenty-five."

Glimpses: of *Afghan* away to port with two Stukas going for her at once, *Afghan* heeling so far over under a lot of helm that he was looking almost straight into her bridge; a bomb-burst flinging up sea ahead and *Tuareg* driving through it, dirty water drenching down on them, swirling down through the gratings; Drisdale doing a little dance, shaking first one foot then the other, his white buckskin shoes filthied from that torrent. Cursing: and PO Whiffen advising him in a piercing yell, "Shouldn't a joined, sir!" Then the far-off sight of a destroyer on her own, steaming towards Crete under a cloud of shell-bursts, bombers trailing her like flies. That would be *Hereward,* closing the Cretan shore to give her soldiers and ship's company a chance of reaching it when she sank. *Four* Stukas now attacking *Tuareg: Afghan* helping with her pompoms: *Afghan* with all her guns poked up and flaming, defiant, angry-looking, beautiful. The Stukas seemed to be ganging up against one ship at a time, and each time you came out of one of the onslaughts it was a surprise to find you'd got away with it.

At 0730 Houston had Force B in sight from the director tower. Even from the bridge you could see the bombers over them, a constant procession of them to and from Scarpanto. Soon afterwards, a new signal to C-in-C reported that *Orion* had been near-missed and damaged and that the force's speed was now 21 knots. *Orion*'s captain had been severely wounded by a Stuka's machine-gun bullet. Nick remembered that fighter cover had been promised for 0530 over this Strait. But at that time Force B hadn't been *in* the Strait: the fighters might have come, found no ships to cover, flown home again? Then he remembered: Rawlings had signalled that one-hour delay, last night . . . Anyway, the only fighters here had black crosses on their wings.

"Flight of 88s coming up astern, sir!"

Ashcourt: he had a telephone, at the back end of the bridge, to the point-fives and the for'ard pompom deck, and he was directing them to fresh targets after each one had passed over. He was spotting for himself and also getting reports from the tin-hatted look-outs each side of the bridge.

"Midships."

"Midships, sir . . ."

You lived by the minute but you had to reckon on hours, on a day-long battle. Dodging, you held as closely as you could to the south-easterly course, getting back to it each time as soon as possible. Every yard made good in that direction was a *good* yard. Habgood had reported the rudder centred: Nick told him, "Starboard fifteen. Steer one-four-six." He was watching one that looked like attacking at any moment. Up ahead there seemed to be a lull, with Force B's ships in sight now from *Tuareg*'s bridge and pushing on under a clearing sky-cap, an absence of shell-bursts or attackers. One quick glimpse through binoculars had told him this: another now confirmed it. Bomb-splashes rising like geysers between the two Tribals were from the Ju88s, three of them at about five thousand feet. That Stuka was going for *Afghan,* not *Tuareg: Tuareg*'s pompoms and point-fives flaming at it. And it was the last of them: there was nothing up there now but the muck hanging, shredding away in the wind. One Stuka, its bomb somewhere in the sea, was departing, and gunfire had petered out.

Peace was uncanny. There were ship and sea noises instead of the roar of guns: there was time to take note of being alive, ships unharmed, on course, catching up on the main body up ahead. Blue sky, blue-and-white sea, *Afghan* sleekly impressive as she wheeled back into station.

Swimming slowly: becoming aware of himself doing it—of having been doing it, semi-consciously, for some time. Cold water. *Very* cold.

"Give us a tow, sir?"

A Carley float, thick with men, and other men in the water round it holding on. A few of them laughed at the comedian's request, and the same man called, "We could accommodate one more, sir."

It was a kind thought, but the float was already overcrowded. He

swam on, looking for a float where there *would* be room for him. He'd
been pretty well whacked out before this swim had started. Oil in the
water here: the sea was loppy but it was probably the oil that was holding it down, preventing the small waves from breaking. The waves were
high enough to prevent one seeing far, though: a radius of five to ten
yards, he thought, was about his field of vision.

Clutterbuck swam into it. Blinking steadily: he'd lost his spectacles,
poor chap. When he saw Jack, he stopped swimming.

"Why are you going that way, Everard?"

"Good as any, isn't it?"

"Ah." An eyebrow lifted. "You pays your money and you takes your
choice . . . Hey, look out!"

An aircraft was approaching, low. Jack waited, just dog-paddling
slightly, otherwise motionless in the water, and the thing roared overhead. Live men attracted bullets, he'd seen that time and time again.
There was aircraft noise a lot of the time but it was mostly high up, and
one had only to be careful of the low ones or of a circler that might
be looking for something to use its guns on. Wavetops were breaking in
his face: he was out of the oil-patch, then. Clutterbuck was swimming
slowly away, going towards the sun; it was easier to go the other way, so
it didn't blind you. Might have suggested that, if one had thought of it.

Brassey's face, Brassey's rasping voice: *You're a right good 'un, Everard.*

As if he hadn't reckoned on living: and at that, he'd most likely reckoned right. But frankness in the face of extinction—things not matter-
ing that *had* mattered, rank-consciousness no longer operating. Face like
a squeezed lemon with stubble on it, a man with a lifetime of naval service behind him calling you a right good 'un, for God's sake . . . The
mind roamed free while the body remained trapped in the swimming
stroke and another aircraft zoomed low somewhere close: the sudden
stammer of its guns came like torture to the brain, as if the brain could
feel the bullets that would be ripping into helpless swimmers or a
crowded float. He'd stopped moving again while it passed, until the
sound had faded. Not all that many of the pilots did it, and perhaps only

a minority of them enjoyed the killing, but there had to be a fair proportion of psychopaths up there, he thought.

Getting bloody tired. Waves breaking in your face didn't help much, either. Might be why Clutterbuck swam east? The hell . . . Poor old Brassey: right good 'un *he* was . . .

He'd stopped swimming, his body telling him it was a pointless as well as painful exercise. Slumping with his face down in the water: holding his breath and then expelling it through pursed lips as the sea washed over him. All that exertion earlier . . . Drifting into thoughts of brother Nick: whether he and his destroyers had got away with it, or been sunk too. Aircraft noise again: he pulled his face up, gulped air mixed with salt water: it wasn't a low-flyer, he thought, not one of the blood-lust merchants, just one passing over. Keep swimming, you've had your rest. Swim all the way to that—

All the way back to Gabrielle. Of *course* he'd ring her . . .

That *boat!*

Making his eyes focus: one hand up quickly to clear them. It was a whaler he was looking at, clinker-built, greyish-blue, full of men. But room for more, he thought, certainly for *one* more. It was rising and falling, rocking, by no means overfilled. He'd turned himself towards it, water breaking in his face again in stinging whiteness, and one man in the boat had seen him. He was pointing, shouting.

Three yards—or ten, it might have been. Some of the men were trying to paddle the boat towards him with their hands. No oars, then. The one who'd spotted him was standing, leaning forward with his hands on the boat's gunwale; he seemed to be about to launch himself over, come and fetch him. Talking over his shoulder to a stir of men behind him as the boat rocked over.

"Hang on there, sir, I'll—"

It was young Brighouse, for God's sake. Beside that first chap: Brighouse was clambering over, coming for him. Pausing to shout, "Shan't be a jiffy—"

Roar of an aircraft engine suddenly very close: a fighter dipping, swooping at the boat. He heard the hammering of its guns, saw flashes, a wave broke in his face. The Messerschmitt had swept over, banked in a sharp turn, engine-noise thunderous as it hurtled over in another pass. He was face-down in the sea, jarring underwater thumping in his ears. Head up again, sucking at the air: noise fading . . . The boat lay a few yards from him, broadside-on and low in the water with its upper strakes in splinters, no sign of human movement in it. One man's body was slumped over the bow, head and shoulders in the sea as if he'd been trying to drag himself away.

"*Dido,* sir . . ."

Nick couldn't pay attention to whatever his navigator was telling him. He was aiming *Tuareg* at a diving Stuka. Stooped above the voicepipe, ready to jink her away when he saw the bomb coming. A quick glance now, though, at Drisdale—he was staring out towards the cruisers—and back quickly to face this obscene attacker.

The lull was over and the storm had broken. *Tuareg* and *Afghan,* rejoining Force B, were thrashing up into station on the wing of the destroyer screen, under waves of attacks by 87s and 88s. During that lull the Luftwaffe must have been reorganizing, girding themselves for this all-out assault. Nick had thought he'd seen concentrated attacks before: but *this* . . .

The bomb was falling away from that shrieking, spread-legged horror.

"Port twenty-five. Two-four-oh revolutions." He looked over at the cruisers, saw more diving Stukas, ships' guns all flaming up into the permanent haze of smoke, the self-renewing clouds of shell-bursts. There was something wrong with *Dido's* for'ard guns, though: he put his glasses on her, and saw that she must have been hit on her B turret. She had three twin turrets for'ard, and in the turret in the centre one of the pair of barrels simply wasn't there, the other was twisted up, bent nearly double.

Bomb-splash to starboard. "Midships."

"Midships . . . Wheel's amidships, sir."

"Starboard fifteen."

"Alarm astern—Stuka!"

He could hear its howl rising over the din of gunfire. Even now *Carnarvon* was in the back of his mind, a shattered hulk in the deep-sea darkness. Habgood had reported 15 degrees of starboard wheel on: he told him, "Increase to 30 degrees of wheel. Three-six-oh revolutions."

"Stone the crows . . ."

Back aft, Mr Walsh had grabbed Dalgleish's arm, pointing: at a Stuka diving vertically on *Orion*. Literally vertically: like a dart dropped out of the sky. Dalgleish had to look away, attend to other business, barrage-fire from "X" and "Y" guns at a flight of 88s coming up on the quarter: Mr Walsh goggling, seeing the bomb come away and the Stuka go straight on, straight into the sea in a huge fountain-splash right ahead of her. The bomb burst on her A turret, turret dissolving in flash and smoke, then the smoke clearing to show that pair of guns wrecked and naked to the sky, the turret's armoured casing blown right off. *Orion*'s B turret had been knocked out too, in the same explosion: so now she had only her after six-inch turrets and the midships four-inch mountings on each side. None of that "A" turret's crew could possibly have survived.

Dalgleish was looking over at the flagship now: he hadn't seen it happen but he could see the results of it now. The sudden roar of pom-poms and point-fives brought his attention back to things close at hand: a Stuka that had attacked *Dido* and levelled out down on the sea was racketing clumsily up across *Tuareg*'s stern, exposing its whole disgusting underside as it banked and lifted. *Tuareg*'s close-range weapons—*Afghan*'s too now—were all at it, seeing the chance of a kill and wanting it, *needing* it . . . You could see the tracer converging, hitting, the little flashes and then the start of fire as the incendiary rounds ripped in, and the Stuka was suddenly a flying torch with a German frying in its cockpit: Mr Walsh hit the port-side Vickers GO torpedoman on the back—"'Old your fire, lad!"

Bullets and shells were precious, not to be wasted. There'd be hours of this yet, before they got out of the Stuka radius.

Battling southward: still praying, minute by minute, for the promised air support.

Orion's captain had died of his wounds at about 0930, soon after she'd been near-missed in a multiple attack. Now, just over an hour later, here was another one: eleven Stukas were going for the flagship. They came over through a heavy barrage, dipping their yellow snouts one by one and close on each other's tails.

A minute later, from *Tuareg's* bridge the flagship was invisible among the bomb-splashes, her seven thousand tons and five hundred and fifty feet of length completely hidden in the bomb-churned sea. Nick thought, *She's gone* . . . As if the whole world was going, piece by piece. All the guns in all the ships barraging to protect her: and the Stukas still getting through. Then she was in sight again, steaming out of the holocaust: but stricken, swinging away off course with smoke pouring out of her. Steering gone, or jammed: out of control and badly hurt. Some of those bombs must have burst inside her, and she had more than a thousand troops on board as well as her own complement of about six hundred.

"Port fifteen. One-eight-oh revolutions."

All the other ships were turning, dropping back to stay with the flagship. You could imagine the struggle inside her, the desperation to smother fires, tend wounded, get her back into control. You had to try *not* to think about the troop-filled messdecks.

Jack Everard lay across the whaler's bow, resting on a dead man's body, half in and half out of water. He'd clawed up over the body, using it as a bridge while the whaler tipped, heavy with sea and dead men inside it.

Sea washed red over and around the bodies. There were about eleven of them. The boat had been riddled with bullets and it was waterlogged, waves slopping over the shattered gunwales; the weight of the bodies inside it was lessened by the fact they'd all been wearing lifebelts, some of which had not been punctured. It was also the reason for a few of them floating near the surface, only barely restrained by the top edges of the boat as the whole mass lurched sluggishly to and fro.

The only face he could recognize was that of a leading signalman named Durkin. He lay on his back, partly supported by an inflated Mae West, and as the boat and its contents rocked so did the killick's head. When it faced to its right it looked quite normal, but each time it flopped over you could see where the back of the head had been smashed. Durkin's head wasn't the only thing you didn't want to look at twice.

There was no reason for it, no way to understand it, no advantage to anyone in these men having been turned into corpses. With time to think, not much strength in him for the moment, and the horror all around him, under him, Jack wondered whether the Messerschmitt pilot could have explained it.

Brighouse, the snotty, wasn't visible. He'd be in the sea, Jack guessed. Brighouse had been in the act of climbing over the side to come and help him; he'd have been hit then and gone on over, and if his Mae West had been perforated he would have sunk. They floated afterwards, brought up after a certain time by the expansion of internal gases.

He'd got his breath back, more or less. He shifted, to get himself up higher and look around. The whaler's bow went down deeper and the body under his left knee shifted: he had nearly all his weight on the other foot, on the top of the stem-post. The boat was like a half-rotten log, only just on the positive side of neutral buoyancy. There were two drowned or shot men not far away, supported by their lifebelts and with waves breaking right over them, but neither of them was small enough to be young Brighouse. The best thing to do now, he decided, would be to get these bodies out of what was left of the whaler. If its timbers remained buoyant it would be better than nothing to hold on to.

*   *   *

Orion was turning back again, recovering. She was magnificent, Nick thought: a wounded lion refusing to lie down and die, crawling back into the fight.

"Midships, sir!"

"One-four-two revolutions. Steer one-four-six."

The destroyers were gathering round their flagship, and *Dido* had dropped back too. The Luftwaffe was at this moment conspicuous by its absence, but it was likely to return at any moment. When it did, *Orion* would have her hand held tightly.

Italian MAS-boats—torpedo craft—might pick up *Carnarvon* survivors. The MAS-boats, one had heard, had saved a lot of men from other sinkings—from *Gloucester* and *Fiji,* for instance.

Drisdale was looking at him expectantly: as if he'd said something to which he now expected a reply.

"Say something, Pilot?"

He'd shaken his head. "Only being wildly humorous, sir."

"Sorry I missed it." He put his glasses on *Orion* again: she'd just spewed another cloud of yellow smoke from her funnel, and her speed had dropped to almost nothing: you could tell at once by the way her bow-wave dropped. He cut *Tuareg's* speed to match: the others were all doing the same, and watching for the flagship to gather way again.

Still no Stukas.

"How far are we from Scarpanto?"

"Hundred and twenty miles, sir."

At noon, two Fulmars appeared from the direction of the desert. It was a marvellously comforting thing, to see aircraft that weren't enemies. They stayed with the ships for about an hour and then flew south again. *Orion* was still in trouble, with sudden speed variations and gushing multi-coloured smoke; each time she slowed the whole force fell back, clustering around her, praying she'd get going again and knowing she might not. Junkers 88s attacked at 1300, and again half an hour later, and the last attack came at 1500—by which time the force was only about one hundred miles from Alexandria. Several of the destroyers in the screen had been damaged by near-misses. Most of the ships were very low in ammunition: *Orion* had only a few rounds left.

"It's a mercy the Luftwaffe decided to call it a day, sir."

Dalgleish said it, after he'd leafed through the signals on the log. *Orion* had two hundred and sixty dead inside her, and rather more than that number wounded. Nick was thinking of a letter he was going to have to write, to Sarah. Saying . . . what? *I had no option but to leave our son to drown.*

Who'd understand it, who hadn't seen this kind of war? Sarah, of *all* people?

CHAPTER ELEVEN

•   •   •

When he woke, opening his eyes slowly to the growing Aegean light, it took a few moments to remember where he was and what had happened.

Pain in his back: he shifted, easing himself over on the caïque's hard timber, and immediately the young Italian began jabbering at him. He hadn't got as far as remembering the Italian until he heard that voice start up again. He was up on the cabin roof, grinning like a wolf.

Jack sat up. "Morning, Alphonso."

Gabble-gabble-gabble . . . Alphonso—whatever his name was, Alphonso suited him and he didn't seem to mind being called it—had sprouted more black beard during the dark hours. He'd been on this caïque when Jack had seen it and eventually decided to leave the whaler's wreckage and swim over to it. He hadn't realized until he got quite close to it that the caïque was wrecked too; it had been hard to make out what it was, and he'd studied it for a long time before he'd started out, wondering how long the swim would take him and whether after he'd committed himself to the transfer it might start moving away. In fact it had been closer than he'd guessed, and it wasn't in any condition to move except by drifting. Its hold, occupying about half of its normal below-water bulk, was full of water, the bow actually under water and gunwales awash from right for'ard to about amidships; only the stern part was dry. There was a wheelhouse-cabin, and a lower cabin down a short ladder from it, and also an engine space right aft; these were sound and watertight and were providing the buoyancy for the caïque to remain afloat. The engine was smashed; he'd been down there yesterday before the light went, and it looked as if there'd been some kind of internal explosion.

The Italian had helped him aboard, over the gunwale amidships—which was more or less at water-level—and then up to the stern. Treating him like some long-lost brother, or at least as a welcome guest. He'd given him bread, cheese, and a cup of peculiar-tasting wine. Greek, probably. It had come out of a very large, wicker-covered jug; if it was full there'd be about three gallons in it.

Alphonso was round-faced, soft-looking, not at all badly fed. About twenty or twenty-one, probably. He was beckoning to him now, wanting Jack to join him on the cabin-top. And why not: there'd be more of a view from up there. He stood up, looking round at the sea as the light of a new day grew across it. It was almost fully daylight: roughly as it had been yesterday when the assault on *Carnarvon* had begun.

He clambered up to join Alphonso, who greeted him with easy friendship. Looking around from this higher viewpoint he could see nothing floating, no boats or Carley floats to interrupt the bright gloss on the sea's surface. To the south the mountains of Crete were pink-washed in the lifting sun; they seemed closer than they'd been last evening.

Fiona had written, *I have been in contact with someone at the Admiralty whom you do not know—incidentally he's a friend of Jane Derby's, not mine—and he swears that up to this moment of going to press a certain destroyer and its captain*

*are in perfect nick. (No pun intended.) So what the hell is said person doing
ignoring my letters? No answers to the last three, and really it's a bit damn
much, I sit here writing my heart out and not a word from you for week after
week. How do you think I was feeling, before Jane went and found this out for
me? How do you think I feel NOW, you rotten swine? What is it, some
Egyptian belly-dancer? If it is I'll get myself sent out there somehow and dance
on her belly and on her boyfriend's with my Army boots . . .*

"Clear this away, sir?"

He glanced up at Leading Steward McEvoy, and nodded. "Yes, please."
"This" meant the breakfast things. Outside on the iron deck the hands
were being detailed for the forenoon's work. Last night had been spent
in the usual way—oiling, ammunitioning, and storing—and *Tuareg* with
others would be sailing at noon for Plaka Bay.

They'd entered Alexandria yesterday evening at 8 pm. *Orion* had had
only eight tons of fuel and two six-inch shells remaining. Below decks
she was a shambles, a butcher's shop.

He left the table, to get out of the steward's way. He'd answered Fiona's
letter last night, with a telegram saying, *Just received your first letter for a
month. Have written innumerable times and will write again now. Love, Nick.*

He hadn't in fact done much letter-writing lately; he'd been waiting
to hear from her, and he hadn't wanted to express anxiety as forthrightly
as she'd done now. That angry and possessive note, faintly disguised as
humour, brought feelings into the open, where until now neither of
them had wanted—or allowed—them to be. In a way, it was rather marvellous.

But he had to write to Sarah too. It was a hellish job to face: not
only because of what he had to tell her, but also because there was not
the slightest point in even trying to express, to Sarah, his deepest,
sincerest feelings. Nothing he could say to her, now or at any other
time, could help the situation; it was a fact of life that one had to face,
accept . . . Beside that unpleasant prospect, Fiona's letter—this flimsy
sheet of pale blue paper in his hand—was a life-saver, one item of relief
and pleasure to rest the mind on. It was also thrilling, wonderfully

promising for the future; if it hadn't been for the loss of *Carnarvon* and the odds-on death of Jack Everard, Sarah's son, he'd have been glowing with it. And it *was* marvellous . . .

Wasn't it?

If there was going to be a future—yes. He had a stronger motive for personal survival now: so yes, it was terrific . . . But this was hardly a time for counting chickens. In the past fourteen days, the Mediterranean Fleet had been reduced to just one quarter of its operational strength; and there were still thousands of soldiers to be brought out of Crete. You couldn't last for ever. Any more than a tossed coin would always fall the same way up. There was a certain amount of skill in avoiding bombs, but there was a damn sight more luck in it than skill.

While Force B had been lifting men from Heraklion on Wednesday night, four destroyers had been at Sphakia landing rations for fifteen thousand troops and taking off an advance party of seven hundred and fifty. The Australian destroyer *Nizam* had been near-missed during the withdrawal. Also on Wednesday Force D—comprising the Australian cruiser *Perth,* assault ship *Glengyle,* AA cruisers *Coventry* and *Calcutta,* and three destroyers—had sailed from Alex; they'd have been taking a biggish load of troops from Sphakia during this past night, and now, this morning, they'd be fighting their way southwards. Then in about an hour Force C again—*Napier, Nizam, Kelvin,* and *Kandahar*—would be sailing; and at noon *Tuareg* and *Afghan* with two H-class were to set off for Plaka. With so few ships intact, nobody could expect much let-up; nobody was asking for it, either.

It was a bit much to believe that Fiona, bless her heart, had written *three* letters that had gone up in smoke. He guessed that in the last few weeks she'd have been waiting to hear from him—just as he'd been waiting to hear from her.

A knock on the cabin door announced PO Whiffen, with the signal log. He announced, tucking his cap under his arm as he came into the cabin, "There's an 'immediate' to us, sir."

It was the one on top. Their sailing orders were cancelled. *Tuareg* and the three others who'd been earmarked for the Plaka Bay lift were to remain at immediate notice for sea.

"Ask the first lieutenant to come and see me, would you."

It would be diplomatic, he knew, for him to go over to the depot ship and call on RA(D), the Rear-Admiral (Destroyers). But in the present state of upheaval RA(D) had been spending a lot of his time at sea commanding cruiser forces, and he wouldn't be an easy man to find or have much time to spare. Also, Nick's position was an irregular one, since he was neither commanding a flotilla nor attached to one, and as CO of a private ship he had no natural direct access to the rear-admiral. The division of four ships of which he'd have been senior officer on the cancelled Plaka expedition was only a temporary grouping of bits and pieces: for whatever job replaced the Plaka one they might well be split up again. Another point was that in *Woolwich,* however helpful RA(D)'s staff might be, he wasn't likely to get much of a clue as to what was happening: it was from Gabbari, from ABC's War Room, that the decisions were coming now.

So thank God for Aubrey Wishart and the Old Pals Act.

"Want me, sir?"

"Come in." Wishart would be just about standing on his ear, at this stage. He'd sent Nick a very hurried, private message last night about *Carnarvon,* but obviously the staff was being worked 24 hours a day. But then—he was a *very* old friend . . . Nick was lighting a cigarette, and he offered Dalgleish one. He'd seen him briefly earlier on, on the quarterdeck at Colours, before he'd come in again for breakfast. He told him, "Our trip's been cancelled. No midday sailing. But we stay at immediate notice."

"As Mr Walsh would say, sir,"—Dalgleish expelled a cloud of smoke—"'Stone the perishin' crows' . . . The evacuation can't be *over* yet?"

"Some snag at the place we were going to, I'd guess." A snag like the Germans getting there first, perhaps. He added, "I'm going over to

Gabbari to see if I can find out what's cooking. I'd like the motorboat alongside in"—he checked the time—"at a quarter past nine . . . How's Redmayne getting on?"

"Still hard at it, sir. I don't know, I'll—"

"Tell him I want to hear from him before I leave the ship, would you."

Some of the nearer misses had shaken things up in the engine-room, and Redmayne and his staff had been working down there all night.

"Admiral Wishart will join you shortly, sir."

"Thank you."

The marine orderly went out and shut the door, leaving Nick in Aubrey Wishart's office. He'd waited in the lobby, to start with, while Aubrey had been contacted in the War Room.

Lighting a cigarette, he stared down at the now familiar pattern of Chart 2836a—*Grecian Archipelago, Southern Sheet*—which was spread on a trestle table. Crete—Kaso—Scarpanto: for an age now it seemed one had lived with this picture. Leaving it, he sat down in the visitor's chair, took Fiona's letter out of his pocket and re-read it. It was possible, he thought, that she was pulling a fast one: that she hadn't written at all—for some reason at which it might be unwise to guess—and so he hadn't either, and now this was her way of breaking the deadlock?

She'd sent him a copy of *The Last Tycoon* by Scott Fitzgerald, she said. An American edition. He wondered where she might have got it from.

Wishart broke in like a charging elephant.

"Did you get my note, old lad? More sorry than I can say. We've had no news about survivors—if that's what you've come about. But a lot of 'em are sure to be picked up, and we *wouldn't* hear, not for a while."

"No, I realize—"

"It was a pretty dreadful spot you were in. You did the right thing though, Nick." He flopped into the chair behind the desk, and glanced at his watch. "Anything I can do for you, while you're here?"

"Yes, please. Tell me why my trip to Plaka's been put off, and what *is* lined up for us."

Wishart's smile faded. "You've bust in here just to ferret that out? Not about *Carnarvon?*"

"I wouldn't have expected you to have news of survivors yet. But we're all getting a bit frayed around the edges, and if we could know how long we're likely to be here in Alex—"

"Christ Almighty!"

"What?"

"I think you've got a bloody nerve, that's what!"

No smile.

Nick stood up. He said quietly, "I'm sorry. I hadn't intended—"

"Really, a *bloody* nerve!"

Wishart was right, of course. He did have a bloody nerve. He nodded. "Yes. Very sorry, Aubrey. I'll—"

"Look, sit down." Aggression had faded into sudden weariness.

Nick said, "No, you're perfectly right, I should have thought before I—"

"Sit *down,* damn it." Wishart was pointing at the chair. He looked exhausted. "We're *all*—frayed round the edges, aren't we . . . ? I'll tell you what's happening, Nick. Otherwise I suppose I'll never get to meet that slant-eyed female who's on display in your cabin . . . Heard from her yet?" Nick nodded: Wishart smiled. "Told you so . . . Now, listen. We aren't sending you to Plaka Bay because it seems the information we had yesterday was all balls and there won't be any troops there to lift. We're getting a lot of conflicting reports. For instance NOIC Suda, from his cave at Sphakia, told us there'd be ten thousand men for Force D to embark last night; then the Army said there'd be only two thousand plus stragglers, and no hope of holding out until the night of the 30th— tonight—so last night's lift would be the final one. Cutting confusion short, Force D is now on its way back here with six thousand soldiers on board, and there'll be certainly one more lift, possibly two . . . *Perth,* incidentally, was near-missed about twenty minutes ago, and she'd had one boiler-room knocked out. We're risking lives and ships—soldiers' lives as well as sailors', once they're at sea—and the dividend isn't always clear. You saw what it was like, on your own last trip, and it's getting worse every hour."

"Arliss is sailing now for Sphakia?"

"Yes." Captain Arliss, RAN, was commanding Force C from his destroyer *Napier.* "And subject to developments it's likely there'll be one last, bigger lift tomorrow night. If it's approved you'll probably sail at dawn tomorrow with *Phoebe*—flying Admiral King's flag—plus *Abdiel* and a bunch of whatever destroyers are still seaworthy by then. That's what you're being held back for now. Satisfied?"

"Grateful for the information. And I do apologize—"

"It's a damn shame about Plaka. But obviously we can't send ships out to get bombed when it's unlikely there are any troops to bring off. And the north coast's finished now, of course; Kaso's a closed door."

"What happens to the Retimo garrison, then?"

"They remain there." Wishart looked down at his hands. "With orders to capitulate—if we can get an order to them, which so far's been impossible."

"The field hospital, and its nurses?"

"There's nothing we can do, Nick. They shouldn't have been there in the first place, mind you. When they were pulled out of Greece they were supposed to come back here; some mix-up stuck them in Crete, and by the time we heard of them—well, Retimo was already cut off."

"So we have to leave—what is it, twenty women—"

"Nearer thirty. Plus the wounded men they've been nursing."

"We leave thirty women in a garrison that's about to be overrun by Nazi paratroops?"

"Nobody likes it, old lad." Wishart's large, tired face was rather like a Saint Bernard's, nowadays, Nick thought . . . "ABC is very deeply concerned about it. Apart from one's personal feelings, I can tell you—in confidence—that it's being alleged in very high places that we aren't getting enough Aussies out. This is being hung round ABC's neck, and obviously he'd give his back teeth to bring out more. Point of fact, there were five Australian infantry battalions in Crete to start with, one has already been lifted from Heraklion and two others are now on their way—or will be—from Sphakia. Leaving two out of five, and they're shut up in Retimo, or possibly between Retimo and Plaka. The RAF's sent planes to drop messages at Retimo no less than three times now, and so far as we know not one of the messages has got there. Hence the fact they haven't pulled out to the south coast as ordered." He sighed, looked at his watch again. "ABC's got Prime Ministers and all sorts of people yammering at him. I suppose they have to clear their own yardarms before the Press starts on it and there's some political storm back home. What's more, they don't seem to have heard about the girls yet. And we're helpless, Nick, we can't do a bloody thing!"

"No hope of another shot at getting a message in by submarine?"

"Pointless." The big man got up, lumbered over to the chart, and Nick joined him at it. "However—just to show you we aren't absolutely stupid here, I'll tell you, for the record, that I've arranged for another boat to be off Retimo tonight. *Tamarisk,* from this Alex flotilla. She's been doing a cloak-and-dagger job up in Vari Bay." He pointed: Vari Bay was in Greece, about ten miles south of the Piraeus. "Consequently she has commandos with canoes on board, so she could have been used for a Retimo reconnaissance. In fact, we've decided against it . . . She's had an interesting patrol, though. She sank a steamer and two caïques full of Germans about *here*—and had a look right inside the harbour at Milos Island, and one or two other places, and found them all empty. They did have MAS-boats at Milos, but obviously they've brought them farther south now. And hence the little troop convoy—Huns are bringing 'em down straight from Greek ports, instead of mustering them at Milos."

Being an old submariner himself, Aubrey Wishart was proud of his fellow submariners, and inclined to ramble on about their exploits. Nick brought him back to the subject.

"Why would it be pointless?"

"Because it's too late for any troops there to get across to Plaka Bay—which was the purpose of contacting them. And there's no question of any more runs through Kaso. There's simply nothing to be gained."

"You couldn't bring the women out by submarine?"

"For Christ's sake, Nick, talk sense. You know the size of our boats. Thirty women—even if we could get them off from shore? In what—canoes, one at a time? Not to mention the wounded—and they'd as likely as not be unwilling to just walk out on them . . ."

"Yes. I see . . ."

Something Wishart had said a minute ago was fermenting in his brain. He was probing, worrying at it: and his nerves jumped suddenly.

"The enemy's moving reinforcements down by sea from Greece?"

"From the Piraeus." Wishart nodded. "Long haul, but safe for them now."

"Into Suda, I suppose."

"They may be using Heraklion as well."

"But Suda'd be the main base for their destroyers and MAS-boats." He ran his finger around the crescent-outline of Crete, Scarpanto, Rhodes. "This is their front line now. North of it, up here, anything of ours that moved they could bomb the hell out of. So they'll forget the backwaters, concentrate on securing Crete."

"We'll be operating submarines up there, of course."

"This one—*Tamarisk*—she'll be off Retimo tonight, and you can get a signal to her when she surfaces after dark?"

"It's already drafted, I imagine."

"Recalling her to Alex."

"Precisely." Wishart checked his watch for the twentieth time. "And *now,* Nick—"

"Could we sit down for a minute?"

"Christ Almighty!" Wishart, flushing, pointed at the wall. "My boss is in there with two generals and one air vice-marshal, and he's expecting the Prime Minister of New Zealand and Field-Marshal Wavell at any minute. London's screaming its head off, our ships at sea are being bombed round the clock, I've given you ten minutes I can't spare, and—"

"Give me two more." He wasn't apologizing this time. "I believe I could get your women and wounded out of Retimo. Two minutes, to tell you how?"

It took four minutes. Then another at the chart, checking distances and times. Finally Wishart threw down the dividers.

"It's bloody chancy. I think it's probably idiotic. But if ABC agrees, and you pull it off, you could ask for the Crown Jewels."

"If I was looking for rewards I'd settle for a flotilla. In point of fact it looks like a job worth doing."

"I'd guess you'll be getting a flotilla in any case. If ABC didn't have such an enormous load you'd probably have it already." Wishart stopped talking. He stared at Nick for a couple of seconds: then he nodded. "Wait here. I'll see if I can get a word in."

Nick sat down, lit a cigarette, went on thinking about it. It *was* risky: there were certain things that could only be left to chance. But nowadays you were taking a gamble every time you poked your ship's nose out of harbour. You took an almost suicidal risk when you tried to pass through Kaso in daylight. Risks were commonplace, routine: and he didn't think his plan was all *that* chancy. It was unconventional, certainly.

He sat back in the chair, thinking about details. He'd smoked three cigarettes before Wishart came back.

He looked grim. Bearer of rotten news, Nick guessed. He was well aware there could be some fundamental snag he'd overlooked, and that ABC's hawk eye would have spotted it right away. Or the hawk eyes of the Chief of Staff or Staff Officer (Operations) . . . He got up, watched the rear-admiral push the door shut and move over to the desk.

He cleared his throat.

"We are to work out an operational plan. You and I. Then the Staff will look it over. To start with"—he sat down, reaching for signal pad and pencil—"let's decide what orders we'll ask S/M(1) to pass to *Tamarisk* when she pops up at 2200 tonight." By S/M(1) he meant the commanding officer of the 1st Submarine Flotilla. "*Tamarisk's* CO is a Commander Rivers, by the way. Got a cigarette?"

"Here—"

Wishart used Nick's lighter. Then, leaking smoke from his nostrils, he pointed the cigarette across the desk. "Nick—hold on tight to that chair, will you."

"Why?"

"So as not to fall off it. Listen—I'm instructed to inform you that the 37th Destroyer Flotilla is now reconstituted. It consists of *Tuareg* as leader, with *Afghan, Highflier,* and *Halberdier.* Captain (D) is Captain Sir Nicholas Everard. To be precise, *acting* Captain, since this'll need a rubber stamp from the Board of Admiralty. Now, let's get down to your hare-brained scheme . . ."

He was back at *Tuareg* at 11:30, climbing the gangway into the screech of the bosun's call. The news had come aboard ahead of him: there'd been a signal from C-in-C to RA(D) repeated to various people including D37, which now meant Nick Everard. On the quarterdeck, faces were smiling as the call's wail died away.

"This is terrific, sir!"

"Glad you think so, Number One. Any problems here?"

"No unusual ones, sir."

"Chief?"

Redmayne had washed the oil off, he noticed. "Top line, sir."

"Well done." He asked Dalgleish, "Did you get a message about COs coming aboard at noon?"

Dalgleish nodded. "Your steward's preparing for them, sir."

He'd invited the captains of *Afghan, Highflier,* and *Halberdier* for a midday gin. The gins would in fact be small ones; the object was to give them a preliminary briefing on tomorrow's operation. Written orders wouldn't reach them until shortly before sailing time; there had to be a lot of information from the submarine, *Tamarisk,* before details could be established, and they wouldn't get her report much before dawn tomorrow. But the basic plan was worked out, and there were certain preparations to be made now.

He told Dalgleish, "If you're happy to, you can pipe a make-and-mend." A make-and-mend was a half-day free of work; it was a term deriving from older times, when such occasions were used by sailors for making and patching their clothes. "But no shore-leave. And there's one job—some stores to be drawn. Paint and timber." He enjoyed the look of mystification that crossed his first lieutenant's face. It was reflected in some others too, notably in CPO Habgood's and in the buffer's, PO Mercer's. He asked Habgood, "All right, Cox'n?"

"Yessir. And if I may, sir, on be'alf of chief and petty officers and all the ship's company, I'd like to offer most 'earty congratulations."

Mercer growled, "Hear, hear, sir."

"Thank you very much, Cox'n." He glanced at Mercer. "You'd better stick around, Buffer. First Lieutenant'll have a job for you in a minute."

"Paint and timber, sir?"

"Right." He looked at Dalgleish. "Come and have a word, Tony, would you?" They went round to the starboard side, and in the screen door; in the day-cabin he pulled out some sheets of Wishart's signal pad on which he'd made various jottings. He asked Leading Steward McEvoy, who was mustering glasses near the pantry hatch and had the whole cabin shiny-bright, "Are we allowed to sit down in here?"

"Och, I might permit it, sir."

"Very kind."

"Like tae say congratulations, sir."

"Thank you. Sit down, Tony. Smoke?"

"No, thank you, sir." Nick was aware that he himself had been smoking far too much, lately, and that he'd have to cut it down. *After* this jaunt . . . He saw that Dalgleish had a notebook and pencil ready: he told him, "What we need is—in total, to take into account whatever's on board already—paint, as follows . . . Black, six gallons. Red, four gallons. Green, four gallons. White, also four. And have them ready before we sail in two separate lots of each colour, each lot one half of the total quantity." He waited while Dalgleish wrote it down. From the far side of the cabin Fiona's eyes were fixed on him, and he wondered whether she'd have had his cable yet. He told Dalgleish, "Make sure we've got a dozen wide paint-brushes. Widest obtainable. And the other item is timber. We need one dozen planks twenty-five-feet-long, and about six fifteen-feet-long. Usual sort of planks, about a foot wide."

Dalgleish listed it all.

"The depot ship's been warned they're to meet our requirements without argument, by the way. Have Mercer start checking on what he's got already—get it done with, then he can enjoy his make-and-mend . . . But also there'll be some crates of medical stores arriving, and a lot of cots or camp-beds. Gallwey can take charge of the drugs and stuff; stow the beds aft somewhere. That's the lot, and if you're back here before my guests arrive I'll give you a glass of gin."

"I'll make it snappy, then." Dalgleish got up. "Actually the wardroom would very much like the pleasure of your company this evening, sir, to wet the fourth stripe. Would you honour us with your presence, sir?"

"If I'm not summoned ashore, I'd like nothing better. Thank you . . . Look, one other thing. Tell Drisdale he's to check that we have chart 1658 on board, and that it has any recent corrections applied to it. It's a large-scale plan of Suda Bay."

"Suda!" Nick just looked back at him. The first lieutenant nodded. "Aye aye, sir." He added the chart number to his list.

That might provide a good red herring. Leading Steward McEvoy had visibly absorbed it. It so happened that chart 1658 had the Suda Bay plan as its main content, but it also had plans of five other places including Retimo, alias Rethimnon.

Let not the left hand know . . . Nearer the time, he'd tell them. News travelled on the winds—on the khamsins, mistrals, gregales. One man's ignorance could mean another's life.

He was positively enjoying this. His own plan, and his own flotilla about to put it into action. Unless of course whatever *Tamarisk*'s landing-party reported put the kibosh on it. The submarine's signal, which would come at some time before dawn tomorrow morning, would be the trigger to action. Or the other way about, the stopper on it. Nick was due to go ashore at 6 am to Wishart's office at Gabbari: by that time they should have the answers. But he felt guilty for enjoying the prospect of this . . . "lunatic operation," Wishart had called it at one stage. Smoking now, prowling the spacious day-cabin, pausing at a scuttle to watch a felucca sliding past with its lateen sail barely holding any wind, then stopping to look into Fiona's eyes: thinking about *Carnarvon,* about the letter he had to write to Sarah. Did he *have* to describe all the circumstances, including the fact that by his own decision he'd had to steam away from her survivors?

Yes. Fiona told him flatly, *Yes, you do.*

It wasn't a job to funk. It wasn't anything to be ashamed of—unless you *did* funk it. And it was a fact that, by and large, the odds were in favour of survival, in warmish waters . . .

There'd be a heap of problems facing him when he got back from this jaunt. Assuming the mantle of a Captain (D) meant taking on a mass of administrative work. It meant embarking a staff—with consequent crowding of wardroom and cabin accommodation—of specialists: flotilla torpedo officer, communications officer, and so on. And a secretary, a paymaster to cope with the paperwork. Extra communications ratings—both V/S and W/T—and a PO steward in McEvoy's job, damn it . . .

Fiona's look was expectant, demanding. He hadn't noticed it until this moment, but he knew what she wanted. He nodded at the portrait, and murmured, "I'll write to *you* this afternoon."

"Sir?"

McEvoy was looking at him enquiringly down the length of the cabin. Nick thought it might be possible to push him—McEvoy—through for the PO's rate. Something to discuss with Dalgleish . . . He admitted, "I was talking"—he touched the frame—"to her."

"Oh. Aye." Unsurprised. Setting the Angostura and lime-juice shakers on the silver tray, near the new bottle of Plymouth gin. He nodded. "I'd not blame ye for *that,* sir."

• • •

The caïque had been drifting south-eastward, Jack thought, and was now in a different current that was taking it more or less due south. A finger-like object on the horizon—it had been to the north of them when he'd first seen it and now it was about north-west—was almost certainly Ovo Island, which he knew was about fifteen miles north of Malea Bay and had a one hundred-and-seventy-foot light-tower on it. He guessed they'd either drift ashore somewhere in the Malea Bay or Cape St John area, or be transferred to the western-flowing current as they came nearer the coast. If that happened they might run ashore on Standia Island, or pass it and carry on for sixty or seventy miles to Suda Bay.

He and Alphonso were keeping off the cabin-top now, because three times Messerschmitts had buzzed them, obviously looking for signs of life—in order to end it if it existed, presumably. From the caïque's stern-sheets, where they spent most of their time now, they could dive into the cabin and out of sight at the first sight of an approaching aircraft. Alphonso seemed to have no illusions about the Luftwaffe, even if they were his country's allies.

Through being taken sparingly, the bread and cheese were lasting well. Alphonso was a generous host, taking it for granted they'd go halves whenever they allowed themselves a snack or a drink of wine. The bread was hard, like grey rusk, and the cheese was made from goats' milk: no mistaking *that* rank flavour. In the circumstances, no objecting to it either.

Apparently the caïque had been attacked and damaged by a British submarine. Jack had asked Alphonso what had happened—by pointing at the sky and at the caïque, making aeroplane and machine-gun noises, and so on. Alphonso had shaken his head, gabbled away in Italian: then, remembering that Jack couldn't understand him, had sprung to his feet and embarked on an elaborate charade. First he'd used his hands in the sea over the caïque's side to indicate the surfacing of a submarine. *Boom* . . . A ship blown up: then he began to fall about, jumping up and falling down again, in one place and then another. A lot of men falling dead: passengers: soldiers? Alphonso drew a swastika in the salt crust on the cabin door. Then, pointing at himself, he went through the motions of diving overboard and swimming. Looking at Jack: eyebrows raised to ask him, *understand?* He began a new mime: of a man resembling Jack—he pointed at him—coming aboard. From the submarine, it had to be. Going down for'ard to the hold which was now flooded: doing something or other: then coming aft here and down through the trap-door into the engine space. Alphonso dropped down into it and showed Jack the damage he'd already noticed: smashed machinery, holed and charred deckboards. Jack guessed that an officer from the submarine had boarded this craft in order to place charges, which would be the simplest way to sink a ship built of heavy timber, but hadn't found any heavy, movable object with which to tamp down the stern charge. So the force of the explosion had been dissipated instead of directed down through the bottom. And of course the bottom would be particularly strong here, reinforced to carry the engine's weight.

Back on the caïque's stern, Alphonso had finished his story. First, a couple of *boom-booms:* then he'd shown the submarine gliding away: gone! Flashing smile from the narrator. Then himself swimming, and climbing back on board. Heaving objects overboard: dead German soldiers was a fair bet. Finally Alphonso climbed to the cabin roof and reclined on it. He spread his hands: understand? Jack had given him a standing ovation. Then he'd had to tell *his* story. Himself in a big ship—spreading his arms and looking upwards and from one side to the other, to suggest its vastness. Alphonso got that all right, and he was enjoying this game like anything. Jack gave him Stukas swooping, guns shooting up at them, bombs whistling down, bombs bursting all around him, Alphonso was screaming with laughter, rocking to and fro. Jack swimming, climbing aboard . . . Alphonso, having laughed himself almost sick, clapped him on the back and shook his hand. He wasn't at all a bad companion to be stuck on a half-sunk caïque with.

· · ·

At about 10:30 pm, Nick added the final lines to his letter to Sarah. He'd redrafted it twice: it still wasn't perfect, but it would have to do. He addressed it, and added "sender's name and address" to the space on the back, remembering as he did it to write "Capt." instead of "Cdr."

He'd already written to Fiona: he'd done that before he'd gone along to the wardroom to "wet his stripe" and accept his officers' hospitality at dinner. He'd told her nothing about his promotion; there was only that small panel on the back to catch her eye and frustrate her with the lack of news of it inside. She'd have to write back immediately now, to question him about it.

From outside on the quarterdeck he heard the quartermaster of the watch give a sudden, high-pitched yell: "Boat aho-o-oy!" Challenging some approaching or passing ship's boat in the darkness. The answer came immediately: "Aye aye!"

It meant two things. One, the boat was coming to *Tuareg:* otherwise the answering cry would have been "Passing!" Two, the boat was carrying an officer of wardroom rank, a lieutenant or above, but not a ship's captain or an admiral. If whoever was arriving had been junior to a two-striper, the answer would have been "No, no!", while a commanding officer in the boat would have produced the name of his ship, or for an admiral a yell of "Flag!"

Nick was about ready to turn in, but he waited to see what this might be about. Hoping his guess would be right . . . He heard the boat coming alongside; Harry Houston, officer of the day, had been fetched from the wardroom to receive the visitor. There was a murmur of conversation out there: and presently a knock on the door of the day-cabin.

"Excuse me, sir." Houston's bulk filled most of the frame. "Officer with a message for you from Gabbari."

"Bring him in."

An RNVR paymaster lieutenant came in sideways around Houston. Removing his cap, he handed Nick a brown OHMS envelope with

BY HAND OF OFFICER stamped across it. Nick thanked him. "Who are you?"

"McCartney, sir. I work for Admiral Wishart."

"Lucky man."

"Yes, sir. I'd sooner have a sea job, though."

The tone had suggested it wasn't an entirely casual observation. Nick took the envelope and tore it open: he murmured, "So would Admiral Wishart." Then he read the brief, handwritten note.

Our signal was passed and acknowledged at 2210. See you here at 0615. A.W.

He nodded. "Thank you. There's no answer."

At this moment, *Tamarisk* would be moving in towards the coast at Retimo, running on her diesels and trimmed-down so as to present as small a silhouette as possible. Inside her, the commandos would be blacking their faces, checking weapons, and readying their canoes. And depending on what they learnt ashore and then reported, there would or would not be a lift from Retimo tomorrow night.

CHAPTER TWELVE

· · ·

He'd got her in his glasses: a black hump in the dark, quiet sea on *Tuareg's* port bow. And she must have picked them up at about the same moment: he'd only just settled the glasses on her when the challenge came winking on a blue-shaded lamp. Leading Signalman Lever was beside him in the front of the bridge and he had *Tuareg's* shaded Aldis ready: he was aiming it, with his eye to the back of the sight on it, and now he was clicking out the reply, the recognition letters for this watch.

"Yeoman—pass astern 'S' for sugar."

"Aye aye, sir!" Three blue flashes was the code in the operation orders for *I am stopping engines.* Lever reported, "Challenge answered, sir."

"Make to him: *Please transfer passengers over my port side.*"

The lamp began to click again. It was a quarter past midnight—Sunday morning now, the first day of June. The rendezvous had been ordered for 0020 (with the object of making it by not later than half past) so they were five minutes ahead of schedule; it should be easy enough now to embark the commandos and get under way again by the half-hour. *Tamarisk,* her job completed, would continue her delayed return passage to Alexandria.

The calm conditions were ideal. If there'd been any sea running this transfer would have had to be done by boat, and it would have taken longer. Timing, keeping right up to the schedule, was vital to the plan.

"Message passed, sir."

"Stop both engines. Where are the others, Pilot?"

"Hauling out northwards, sir."

The other three were to patrol to seaward while *Tuareg* picked up her passengers. Nick trained his glasses on the submarine again. Last night she'd landed her commandos at about midnight and embarked them again a few hours later, and before she'd dived for the daylight patrol she'd signalled the report that Wishart had shown him before breakfast.

Reconnaissance completed. Approximately eight hundred personnel including twenty-six nurses and two hundred and thirty wounded will be ready for embarkation from sandy beach between longitude 24 degrees 29 point 1 and point 3 east 0130/1 June. Beach party will be transferred at rendezvous as ordered.

It had been a huge relief, getting that message; not only for the sake of this operation, but because of earlier failures to contact the garrison by submarine.

"Slow ahead port, slow astern starboard." He was turning the ship, to make it easier for the submarine to come alongside. There'd be no need to secure her: she'd only be there long enough for four fit men to rush over. "Stop both engines."

"Stop both, sir . . . Both telegraphs to stop, sir."

Just abaft the beam now, the submarine was a low black silhouette, its length shortening as it turned. Bridge and conning-tower were easy enough to see, but you needed to look hard to make out the low, dark line of casing that swelled upwards at the bow, a curve up over the for'ard torpedo tubes. Evil-looking object . . .

"Take over here, Pilot."

Drisdale came up beside him at the binnacle, and Nick moved to the side of the bridge to watch *Tamarisk* slide up out of the night. Down on *Tuareg*'s waist PO Mercer and his gang would be ready with a plank to shove over; and Rivers would probably only lay his bow alongside the destroyer, because amidships the bulge of the submarine's saddle-tanks would make for a wider gap to bridge.

The flotilla had come up from Alexandria on a course that would have taken them to Plaka Bay if they'd continued on it; if a Luftwaffe scout had spotted them, it would have seemed they were heading for somewhere on the south coast. In fact no German had come anywhere near them: they'd had cover from Fulmars to start with, and then Beaufighters. How the aircraft had been spared to work with ships was something best known to ABC, air command in Cairo, and possibly a Dominion prime minister or two.

Tamarisk's forepart slid up to overlap *Tuareg*'s quarterdeck. The submarine was at a slight angle to the destroyer: Rivers was keeping his screws well out and his tanks clear of any bumps. Men were standing on the casing, ready to come over: there was a forward-rushing swirl of sea as her screws went astern and stopped her, then a warning shout and a thump as the end of gangplank banged down to bridge the gap. The men were moving to it: the first one hesitating for a moment, making sure of his balance then coming swiftly across. A voice called, "Everard?"

Nick shouted back, "Yes. Rivers?"

"Morning. Listen—you've got *five* passengers. Extra chap's a leatherneck who says he knows you."

That would explain itself in a minute, no doubt. Nick called, "Many thanks for your help!"

"My pleasure. Good luck now!"

The men had all come over and the plank was being dragged back. A couple of submariners were retreating along their casing towards the conning-tower. And the submarine was backing off, white water lathering through the widening gap. Nick told Drisdale, "Half ahead together, three-one-oh revs." The course from here would be due west to clear Cape Stavros, with small alterations later to bring them down to the coast at Retimo. It was twenty-five minutes past midnight: so they were right on the schedule, so far. As *Tuareg*'s screws began to drive her ahead he aimed his glasses out to starboard and saw *Afghan* leading the other two down on a converging course to get back into station.

There was a clattering at the back of the bridge. Dalgleish announced, as he came for'ard, "Captain Brownlees, Royal Marines, sir."

Brownlees . . . He remembered: the marines they'd landed on the other side of Retimo, to relieve German pressure on the Retimo airstrip: Brownlees had been OC *Tuareg*'s detachment. They'd been one of a flotilla of four Tribals then: looking back on it, it seemed like a year ago.

"I gather I should congratulate you, sir."

"Very good of you. I expect you've had a rough time since we last saw you. Perhaps you'll tell me about it later. Who have we here, now?"

"Lieutenant Haggard, Lieutenant Scott, Sergeants Davies and Foster, sir." They all shook hands. Haggard said, "I'm in charge of our party, sir. We brought Captain Brownlees out, though, with the idea it could be useful to have a Retimo local, as it were."

"Might well be. Do you people need feeding, or anything?"

"We've been very well fed, sir, thank you."

"Then we'll go down to the chartroom and tie up loose ends. Number One, stay up here, will you? Sub," he told Ashcourt, "we'd better have you down there." He explained to Haggard, "Sub-Lieutenant Ashcourt will be in charge of our boats . . . Lead on down, Sub, and I'll be there in a moment."

There was one hour to go before 0130, when the boats' keels were due to scrape on sand. Then one hour for the embarkation. It would mean smart boat-work and no delays at all. Joining them presently in the chartroom he asked Haggard—recognizing him by his shape, which was short and square—"The extent of the beach, according to the signal, is about three hundred yards. Right?"

The commando nodded. He had close-cropped ginger hair and a face that suggested he laughed a lot. "Wider than that, actually, but that's a stretch where your boats can get right up to the sand-shelf instead of sticking fifty yards out. We gave you the location, incidentally, in case something went berserk and we missed this rendezvous."

He and Wishart had guessed it. And of course they *could* have made the lift without these men's help; it was just easier with guides who'd already been there. And he had another use for the commandos, at dawn, which as yet they knew nothing at all about . . . Ashcourt had spread out the Retimo chart: Nick reached for a pencil to use as a pointer.

"Embarkation beach—here to here. We'll use the whole length of it. The advantage is that our four ships can stop at the three-fathom line at hundred-yard intervals, giving the boats bags of room to get to and fro without getting in each other's way. It should speed things up, and time is a very important factor on this one."

Lieutenant Scott nodded. "We'll organize our Aussies into four widely separated queues. Nurses and doctors with wounded will come first."

"Do they realize ashore we'll be showing no lights at all?"

"Very much so." Brownlees said, "If you showed any they'd quite likely shoot them out. They've had Germans heavy-breathing in their faces for quite a while now; the bastards are very close all round them. Also, they put up a starshell or two every so often. We may very easily get some interference."

"Let's hope we don't . . . Is eight hundred the sum total?"

"For lifting, yes. By no means the total garrison. For the reason I've mentioned, mostly—there's constant pressure on the perimeter and the blokes holding it simply couldn't move."

"Will they capitulate in the morning?"

"Well." Brownlees shrugged. "It's a decision for their commander.

None of them *wants* to surrender. They reckon they could hold on for ever. They question why *anyone* should be jagging in."

"The CO's an Aussie?"

"Certainly. There aren't more than a dozen of my lot left. My colonel was killed three days ago." He leant forward, to the flame of Ashcourt's lighter; Nick had passed his case round. "If the Hun does catch on to the fact we're pulling out and starts making a nuisance of himself, I take it you'll want to join in with your ships' guns?"

"Only if we're certain they know we're there. And not if we can possibly avoid it. Nine-tenths of our chances of success depend on them *not* knowing we're here. Didn't that come across in our signal to *Tamarisk?*"

Hammond nodded. "Loud and clear."

"I'm only talking about what *could* happen." Brownlees breathed smoke out. "The principle's accepted—we try to do it softly, softly. But *if* it blows up in our faces, you'll want to know where the Hun positions are. I've got it all marked out on this, anyway." The map he pulled out of his pocket looked as if it might have been used for wrapping fish and chips. "Shall I transfer the essentials to your chart?"

"That could be useful. Thank you. But I want to make this point about secrecy very strongly to you. Wouldn't be much point crowding people into ships just to be drowned when the Stukas come looking for us at dawn, would there?"

Sergeant Foster nodded. "*There's* a thought, now." Davies muttered, "Sooner *not* think about it, thanks." Nick was saying to Ashcourt, "If you've any questions to ask them about the beach and approaches, Sub, now's your time. After that I've something quite different to talk about."

He checked the time. It was 0040. But the point he'd made about not being caught by the Stukas: he didn't think any of them had really followed the implications to where logic took them. Dalgleish had, though. When Nick had been explaining the operation to him, here in the chartroom early yesterday, when he'd got to the point of 0230 being

the latest they could afford for departure from Retimo with the troops
on board, Dalgleish had gone on staring at the chart for about half a
minute. Then he'd reached for the dividers and checked the distances
from Retimo to Kaso and from Retimo to Antikithera. Then he'd looked
puzzled, and gone through his throat-clearing routine.

"Hesitant as I am to look on the gloomy side of things, sir, or quib-
ble over paltry detail—if we leave Retimo at 0230 and leg it away at
30 knots, won't we be on the wrong side of Kaso at sunrise?"

There'd been a lot of gunfire ashore, to the west and south: machine-
gun fire and heavier explosions—mortars, he guessed, but there were no
soldiers up here now to ask.

"Course two-oh-oh, sir."

Drisdale was stooped at the pelorus, watching bearings—a church
about two hundred and fifty yards inland of the beach and the dome
of Retimo's ancient fort off to starboard. The town, or village, was built
on an out-jutting piece of coast with a little harbour tucked in this side
of it; it was a tiny harbour without quays or any jetty and apparently it
was always silting up. Drisdale said quietly, "Bang on for the approach,
sir. Perfect."

"Slow together."

Aware of how close the Germans were, you tended to speak in whispers. The quiet area behind the beach was if anything more worrying
than the more lively western sector: you found you were waiting for
the silence to be shattered . . .

A mile offshore he'd positioned himself so that—by running in on a
course of two hundred degrees with that church exactly ahead, its spire
even at that distance easy to pick out with binoculars—when he stopped
her and sent the boats away Ashcourt would only have to steer for the
church and he'd hit the beach right in the centre of the strip they were
going to use. *Afghan* was slanting out to starboard now, on *Tuareg*'s quarter, and the other two were diverging to port: when they all stopped

roughly on the three-fathom line, their boats would have about five hundred yards to cover. *Tuareg*'s were already manned and lowered almost to the water.

"Fifty yards to go, sir."

Drisdale had only the dome's bearing to watch; Nick, conning the ship in, was keeping the church dead ahead.

"Stop both engines."

"Stop both, sir . . . Both telegraphs to stop, sir."

"Thirty yards . . . Twenty . . ."

"Tell 'em to stand by, Sub." Chalk passed the order by telephone to the for'ard pompom deck. Drisdale intoned, "Ten yards—"

"Slow astern together."

"In position, sir!"

He left the screws working astern for just a little longer, to get all the way off her.

"Stop together. Away boats." He told Drisdale, "Watch that bearing like a hawk."

The boats would be in the water now, and their crews would be securing them together: at any moment they'd be moving off towards the beach. He could see the other ships' boats in the water too, but *Tuareg*'s had a bit of a start on them. Time—exactly 0130.

"Boats are on their way, sir!"

So were *Highflier*'s. She was lying on *Tuareg*'s port side, *Halberdier* beyond her. *Afghan*'s boats moving away inshore now: and *Halberdier*'s. Not bad at all.

Seconds ticking by . . . Drisdale was muttering numbers to himself at the gyro repeater. Nick imagined that the waiting troops would be formed up in one mass: there'd be an initial delay while Brownlees and the commandos split off the first four loads, but by the time the boats went in for their second loads things should be better organized. Embarking lame men and stretcher-cases would be a fairly slow process, naturally.

He'd told Brownlees and the cut-throat merchants, half an hour ago and after the details of this bit of the operation had been settled, "When we clear out from Retimo, we're going to take an island."

Oh-one-forty-eight: one lot—all women and wounded, Dalgleish had reported—had been embarked, and the boats had gone inshore again. Fighting was heavier now—judging by noises and flashes—inland and to the right, the west. It was too close to feel comfortable about, even if it might be farther inland than it seemed to be. Nick asked Houston up the voicepipe whether he could see anything ashore.

"Only when flares and things light bits up, sir. I'd guess most of the action's five or six hundred yards behind the town."

It was rising ground there, but not all that steep: if an enemy had a sea view at all it would be from several miles away. There was a modest hill about three miles inland, and a lower one to the right, but the real heights on this slim waist of the island were near the south coast, the Plaka-Timbaki area.

Drisdale was putting the port screw ahead, to maintain the position. The drift was north-westward, and every few minutes there had to be an adjustment. He put his glasses up towards the beach again: things were going to have to speed up, now. Otherwise—

Drisdale had called down quietly, "Stop port."

There was no "otherwise" about it. The time-limits were rigid. The next part of the operation, nearly a hundred miles away, had to be completed by first light: hence the need to be off this coast by no later than 0230. There were forty minutes left and three round-trips still to go . . .

"There, sir!"

Chalk was pointing. "Bit off to the right—"

"Must be *Afghan*'s."

"No, sir, hers are in sight too—to the right again."

"Are we in position, Pilot?"

"Within a few yards, sir, yes."

And the boats were swinging round: Ashcourt must have just seen the dark shapes of the ships and realized he'd gone off course. Oh-one-fifty-two: he'd be alongside now in . . . say, five, six minutes. It would take a few more minutes to get his passengers inboard, and it would then be just past the half-time point, with two more trips to make. Perhaps it wasn't as bad as he'd thought: perhaps they *would* do it in the time. He wondered how the women were settling into his quarters back aft.

Hare-brained . . . Aubrey Wishart wouldn't be getting much sleep tonight. If Ashcourt hadn't mucked this trip up they'd have been inside the schedule. There was nothing in hand for this kind of cock-up, or for any more of them: they'd started off five minutes to the good and now that had been thrown away.

A starshell broke overhead. He'd heard the thump of it bursting, and looked up just as the bleak magnesium brilliance sparked and expanded to flood the whole coastline, seascape, town, beaches, ships . . .

Drisdale muttered, shielding his eyes, "That's torn it."

Like a false daylight: shiny sea with boats chugging towards their ships, weighed-down, slow with their loads of passengers, sitting ducks if anyone was there to shoot at them. Nothing was happening for the moment, though, except the flare hanging right overhead, drifting lower and slightly westward on its parachute. Its stark brightness made the scene unreal, unnatural: light too bright and shadows too black, one of those nightmares when you were held in treacle or your limbs wouldn't move. He heard the motorboat's engine as the three linked boats ran in alongside: an Australian voice bawled, "Put the bleeding light out, Ethel!"

He didn't get a single laugh.

The flare died. Suddenly, as if it *had* been switched off. Odd: the British kind burned right down to the sea. The Aussie called, "That's my girl!" A gush of men's laughter rose as the boats bumped alongside.

Last trip now: and it was 0225. All four ships' boats were inshore. *Highflier's* had had a slight lead when they'd last been in sight. *Tuareg* had lost ground—probably impeded *Afghan's* boats too—through Ashcourt's earlier misjudgement.

Anyone could make mistakes: the trouble was that *everyone* could pay for them.

The shore action was still heavy, but sporadic and still mostly behind the town. The Germans must have been trying to light up some shore sector, not the sea, with that starshell.

"*Highflier's* boats are in sight, sir."

Whiffen had spotted them, on the port bow. Drisdale was checking *Tuareg's* drift, bringing her back into position for the umpteenth time. Whiffen added, "And again. *Halberdier's*, sir."

"Boats in sight starboard bow!" Chalk, this time. They'd be *Afghan's* over there: Ashcourt surely couldn't have done it *twice* . . . Sweating with impatience, Nick reminded himself that Brownlees, who was to command the next phase, was coming off in *Tuareg's* boats on this last trip and that he'd have wanted to see the others get off the beach first.

Afghan's boats were well out now, two-thirds of the way to her.

"Time, someone?"

Leading Signalman Lever told him, "Half past, sir."

Should have finished: should be clear, getting off the coast . . . Houston was calling "Bridge!" into the voicepipe. Nick ducked to it. "Captain."

"Our boats are in trouble, sir, I think. About halfway out or nearly, and stopped. I'd guess the motorboat's seized up again."

Jesus Christ Almighty . . .

"Bearing now?"

"Just about right ahead. Bearing now is—one-nine-eight, sir."

"Distance?"

They're roughly halfway, sir."

Two hundred and fifty yards, say . . .

"Slow ahead together." He straightened. "Chalk."

"Sir?"

"*Run* to the first lieutenant. I want two strong swimmers ready on the foc's'l with all the grass line we've got, and power on the capstan to haul the boats in when the line's fast. When I'm as close in as I can go

I'll give them a shout, and they're to wait until they get it. Understood?"

"Aye aye, sir." Chalk was throwing himself down the ladder at the back of the bridge as he yelled it. Whiffen reported, "Torch flashing from the boats, sir!"

"Don't answer it." He wasn't flashing lights that could be seen ashore. The engines were going slow ahead: he told Habgood, "Steer one-nine-eight." Then to Drisdale, "How close in can I get without going on the putty?"

"Another half-cable, sir. *If* the chart's reliable."

It probably wasn't: he recalled the stuff about silting on this coast. But you had to take your chances. He told him, "Watch your bearing on the dome and tell me when I must stop."

"Better just check it." Drisdale dived for the chart alcove. The other destroyers' boats were all alongside their respective ships, or at least so close as to be hidden by them. Nick told Whiffen, "Blue lamp to *Afghan* —and don't let any of it leak shorewards: *Proceed in execution of previous orders.*"

"Aye aye, sir!"

Drisdale had done his checking and he'd put the bridge messenger, Crawford, to watch the echo-sounder: he himself was back at the pelorus. "Three degrees to go, sir." Chalk came back, out of breath. Nick told him, "Keep a look-out for'ard; tell me when they're ready on the foc'sl." He called down, "Stop starboard."

"Two degrees to go, sir."

Chalk reported, "They're on the foc'sl, sir."

"How much water under us?"

The messenger said, "About four feet, sir."

Nick had remembered that he had one hundred and eighty or so extra men on board. Extra bodies, anyway. She wouldn't be drawing *less* than usual.

"Stop port." He asked Chalk, "D'you know who the swimmers are?"

"PO Mercer and Leading Seaman Sherratt volunteered, sir."

Nick guessed, focusing his glasses on the boats—they'd swung broadside-on now, and the torch was still flashing seawards—that the swim would be roughly a hundred yards. But Mercer and Sherratt could manage more than that, he thought, rather than have their ship smash her Asdic dome on some obstruction. "Slow astern together."

"Still one degree to go, sir."

She still had forward way on, too, and he aimed to take it off her. Grass line was actually coir rope, made from coconut fibre and so light that it floated. Paid out properly from the foc's'l it wouldn't impose much drag, if any, on the swimmers. He'd called for two of them in case one got into any difficulty.

"Ship's stopped, sir."

"Stop both engines." He shouted at Chalk, "Go!" and Chalk yelled it down to the dark foc's'l; a second later two splashes were clearly audible. Action behind the beach now: it seemed to have spread this way from the area behind the town . . . "What are the other three doing, Yeoman?"

"Moving off, sir. *Afghan's* turned round and the other two's getting round astern of her."

He went to the front of the bridge, and put his glasses on the boats. Fireworks flickered along the coastline: flashes of small-arms and machine-gun fire. Drisdale reported, "Bearing's steady, sir, and there's three feet of water under the sounder."

They were all right as long as they didn't drift sideways: on either side there could be shallower patches, silt deposits.

"How's the ahead bearing?"

"As it should be, sir."

Chalk began suddenly, "I think—"

Then he was silent. It had been wishful thinking, and he was thinking better of it. It was never difficult to imagine you were seeing what you were waiting to see.

Minutes passing. *Slow* minutes . . .

The torch from the boat flashed slowly and clearly, O . . . K . . . Nick shouted down at the foc's'l, "Heave in!" and Dalgleish's "Aye aye!"

floated back to him. The sky had been lit for a second by an explosion among the houses: now it was dark again and he was temporarily blind from it. He told Chalk, "Nip down and remind the first lieutenant to bring the tow in very steadily with no jerks or straining. Otherwise the grass could break." The breaking-strain of coir was only one-quarter that of hemp: Dalgleish wouldn't be unaware of it but it could be as well to remind him. Nick checked the time: twenty minutes to three. By cracking on full speed, 34 or 35 knots, he'd catch up on the flotilla's 30 or 32. But they'd only just beat the light: in fact they might *not* beat it, now. It was a three-hour passage to that deep harbour in Milos Island.

En route, there'd be some painting done.

He was awake: what had woken him was the lurching and scraping of the caïque running aground on rock. It had roused Alphonso too: he was panicking, in Italian.

"All right, all right . . ."

The sunken forepart seemed to have anchored itself: the caïque had been swivelling on that pivot so that the stern was now pointing at the land. He could see it through the darkness—high, and higher still behind that, a hill or mountainside blacking out the stars. Alphonso was still chattering like an excited monkey: he told him, feeling the total contrast of his own Britishness, "Wait a mo'. Steady on. *Attendo—momento!*"

He had no idea what time of night it was, except that he felt as if he'd slept for a long time.

Sorting out some stars, he got his bearings roughly. This had to be an east-facing coastline they'd fetched up against: and that made sense, because at dusk they'd been moving into a westerly drift. The only place that fitted this was the shoreline south of Cape St John, in the Gulf of Mirabella.

The distance to the actual shore and from where the caïque had stuck on its submerged rock was hard to make out, in the dark. It might be two yards and it could be twenty. But the thing was, obviously, to get ashore, before the caïque either washed off again or sank: more likely,

both. Five, ten yards, he thought. The sea was washing regularly over a
rock ledge there, sluicing over and pouring back each time in a minia-
ture white waterfall; it might be an easy place for getting out.

"Come on, Alphonso." He sat on the transom, swung his legs over;
there was a list on the caïque and he was at the lower, starboard side.
The sea felt warmer than it had when he'd last been in it: probably
because the night air was so cool. Alphonso hung back, muttering what
sounded like a prayer. Jack reached back, grabbed a handful of his shirt
and tugged at it. "Come on. *Venez. Allez oop!*" Alphonso pulled back,
protesting. "All right, suit yourself, I'm off." He let himself down into
the sea; he was expecting his feet to touch bottom, but they didn't. He
let go of the transom, dropped right in and began to swim; he was
climbing up on to that shoreside ledge when he heard a splash and then
gasping noises as Alphonso floundered after him.

"Time now?"

"Five-thirty-six, sir."

And as near as damn it, daylight: except that the bulk of Milos Island
close to starboard was keeping the flotilla in shadow as they raced northward within spitting distance of the rocky coast. Black, forbidding: it
didn't look like a place the Venus could have come from. It would look
prettier, no doubt, when the sun was up and shining on it, and by that
time they'd be tucked away inside the inner harbour, the landlocked
dead-end of the splendid bay called Ormos Milou which was in fact
the ancient crater of a volcano.

He said to Dalgleish, "We're going to make it by the skin of our
teeth."

"Please God."

"Let's not rely on him *too* heavily."

Drisdale said, "Time to come round, sir."

"Bring her round, then."

And the three other destroyers would follow, one after the other heeling as they put their rudders over to turn in *Tuareg's* gleaming wake.

She'd only caught them up at a little after five, about ten miles south of Psalis Point. Now at 32 knots, creaming up along the sheer black coastline, they were about to round the corner which the chart called Akra Vani. Then they'd turn again, first east and then south-east to enter the bay, which might or might not have Italian destroyers or MAS-boats in it. He'd suggested to Dalgleish that they shouldn't try to saddle the Almighty with too much responsibility for the outcome because he had a feeling that the Deity's concern might be more for grand strategy than for tactics. Saint Paul, after all, did find himself having to "cast four anchors out of the stern and pray for the day" when he arrived at Malta, and even for the Saint that prayer neither brought the day any closer nor saved the ship from being wrecked. He shouldn't have got himself on to a lee shore in a force 8, that was all.

Any more than Nick should have allowed his flotilla to be half an hour behind schedule, the one thing he'd sworn must *not* happen.

"Course is oh-six-five, sir."

Akra Vani would be abeam in about one minute, distance four hundred yards. Then they'd alter round again. There was plenty of water here and it was safe enough, but so close to the rocks 32 knots felt like an enormous lick of speed. It was necessary, and so was corner-cutting, if they were to have any chance at all of getting in there before the enemy knew they'd arrived. He wondered if there might be anyone up on those slopes to see them, see the rushing ships and the white bow-waves curling, the wash rolling away powerfully and fast to break in surging foam along the steep-to, rocky coast. In the villages—one hamlet at the little harbour and the main village higher up, inland—there'd be *some* kind of garrison. Probably Italian, possibly German. He'd gone into the idea of putting landing-parties ashore on their way into the bay, to take the main village from its rear, the north-west, but he'd decided against it, for several reasons that still seemed sound. Primarily because of the delay involved and the difficulties of finding a landing-place on that area of coast; and as things had turned out, there certainly wouldn't have been time.

The cape was abeam. He nodded to Drisdale's unspoken question, and said again, "Come round." Drisdale called down for 15 degrees of starboard wheel.

Growing light showed them the entrance now, a gulf about two and a half miles wide narrowing to no more than one mile farther in. In just a few minutes they'd be tearing through those narrows into what would then be a widening, figure-of-eight-shaped harbour, a wonderfully sheltered and spacious bay which the enemy had used as an assembly point and jumping-off place for those caïque convoys which the Navy had broken up or turned back. Nick's plan was a gamble on the theory that now the Germans had Suda Bay, and there was no Royal Navy north of Crete to threaten their south-bound convoys, they'd have allowed Ormos Milou to relapse into the peace and obscurity from which they'd disturbed it.

He was also gambling on the accuracy of Intelligence reports which indicated an almost total lack of liaison between the Italian navy on the one hand and the Luftwaffe and Wehrmacht on the other. And on one other hope: there'd been an incident recently when German aircraft had attacked an Italian destroyer. There might still be minimal contact between the Master Race and its lackeys, but it was a reasonable bet that after that fuss the German planes would shy away from Italian markings.

All the same, a week ago there'd been five Italian destroyers in this harbour. And the flotilla ought to be making a quiet approach in semi-darkness, not galloping in in broad daylight.

"Midships."

"Midships, sir . . ."

The water was absolutely flat. *Afghan* under helm astern of him, tucking her forefoot neatly inside *Tuareg's* outdrifting wake. *Highflier* about to follow round . . . Behind him Brownlees, the captain of marines, said, "I'll go down and get my chaps ready, sir."

"Good. Best of luck."

"Steer one-one-oh."

Dalgleish suggested, "Cable party, sir?"

"Have them piped, but only to stand by down there." He looked round, and beckoned to Ashcourt. "We're cutting this so fine I shan't anchor until the boats have got to the jetties." He thought, And *that's* if there's no shooting . . . But it was the racket of cables running out and waking the garrison from its beauty-sleep that he was thinking of—as well as counting on there being no Italian ships in the inner harbour. If there were, nobody ashore would sleep on much longer. He told Ashcourt, "Muster your cable party behind 'A' gun, to start with."

"Aye aye, sir."

"And watch out for the wet paint. We don't want Mercer's artistry all buggered up."

Ashcourt would be taking charge on the foc's'l while Dalgleish got the motorboat away with 25 Australian soldiers under their own lieutenant and with Captain Brownlees and Sergeant Foster as well. The two commando lieutenants and Sergeant Davies were now in the other three destroyers as liaison officers between Brownlees and the three other detachments of the landing-force. There'd been written orders for the soldiers in each ship, but the commandos had been used to explain Brownlees' own intentions for when they got ashore. There'd be roughly a hundred men landing, more than enough to take and police the two villages and keep the lid on tight until dusk this evening.

Dalgleish said, "I'll go down now, sir."

"Yes. Tell Mr Walsh to train the tubes out on both sides."

"Aye aye, sir."

Guns' crews were closed up, circuits tested, ammunition-supply parties standing ready. The ships would be stopping to send their landing-parties away in less than ten minutes. Running straight into the gulf now, and daylight reaching down inside the bowl of hills.

"I'd like to come round a bit more, to hug that next point, sir."

He nodded. "All right."

"Starboard ten."

"Starboard ten, sir!"

"Steer one-two-oh."

Nick hoped the artificers' night's work on the motorboat was going to prove effective . . . The point Drisdale was about to embrace was called Akra Kalamaria. And the time was 0544, already a quarter hour past the deadline for having all four ships at rest in the inner harbour looking like Italians, and the soldiers in possession of the harbour village—Adhamas—and of the larger village of Milos a mile and a half up the road.

The paint was spread in three colours—green, white, red, the colours of the Italian flag—right across the foc'sl of each ship, and duplicated on their quarterdecks between "Y" gun and the depthcharge chutes. It had been done in a hurry and in the dark on the way up from Retimo, and as artwork it might be a bit rough, but it should pass inspection from the air. Planks had been put across the painted areas so men's feet wouldn't smudge them, particularly on the foc'sls during the anchoring.

Akra Kalamaria was two hundred yards abeam to starboard. And on about red three-oh, up on the hill and right against the background of brightening eastern sky, he saw the village: houses, two church spires . . .

"Yeoman, hoist the Italian ensign."

"Aye aye, sir!" They were all ready with it: almost in the same breath Whiffen confirmed, "Eyetie flag's up there, sir."

"Very good." He didn't particularly want to look at it. "Now make to *Afghan: Will postpone anchoring until boats have reached shore.*"

Oh-five-forty-seven: the point coming up to port now was called Bombairdha. Just around it—they'd be turning to port, circling it—was the anchorage and the harbour, with two jetties of sorts. The nearer one would be used by *Afghan's* landing-party, who were to take control of the waterfront and the houses near it, and the other three contingents would land at the eastern jetty, which was where the road up to Milos and to its subsidiary village of Tripiti started.

Chalk said, "Mr Walsh reports tubes trained out both sides, sir."

"Very good."

He hoped there'd be no use for them. He'd know in about ninety seconds' time.

•   •   •

Jack had been right when he'd guessed they'd landed on the western shore of the Gulf of Mirabella. It was getting light now and he could see the Spinalonga peninsula offshore to the south, and the little islet this side of it. Here, behind them, a spur of mountains ran south-westward and another, less dramatic, formed a coastal ridge. Calm sea, with nothing in sight on it except the wreck of their caïque a few yards away, edged a high, stony landscape which would become a hot one when the sun was up.

Alphonso sat hugging his knees, facing the sunrise and Jack Everard. He was silent, for the first time since they'd become shipmates. Perhaps he was realizing that now they hadn't the sea to isolate them and to contend with, they'd become part of the world again and therefore enemies. But they still had needs in common: food, drink, perhaps shelter. The biggest difference between them would be that Jack's ambition was to avoid meeting Germans, while Alphonso would probably like to find some.

Quite a *large* difference, when you thought about it. It would be sensible, Jack thought, for him and Alphonso now to go their separate ways. He bent down and offered his hand.

"So long, Alphonso. *Au revoir. Bon chance, amigo.*"

Alphonso shook his hand warmly enough, and with a flash of the old happy smile, but there was still cogitation in progress behind those dark brown eyes. Jack had just done his own thinking: it would be a good idea, he'd decided, to head for the south coast. If there was any evacuating still going on that would be the likely area for it. Alternatively one might be able to pinch some sort of boat and sail south. To kick off with, if he followed the shore of the gulf until the coastline curved east, then he'd be able—with luck—to find a way on through or over the mountains, and he'd have to chance his luck along the way in the matter of food and drink. Water, he supposed, would be the most important thing.

He'd gone about five yards before Alphonso caught him up. Jack stopped, looking round at him and frowning.

"Me go. You stay. Or go *that* way."

He tried to mime it, putting the flat of his hands towards Alphonso as if to bar the way to him. But this was the sort of game the Italian enjoyed. He was smiling, pointing south and nodding violently, then pointing at both himself and Jack, linking them together. Then he was going through the motions of eating, stuffing food into his mouth and chewing, and taking a drink—he was thinking of it as wine, by the way he smacked his lips—again, apparently it was something they were going to do together.

"Alphonso, I believe you're bonkers."

Nodding, laughing . . . "*Si, si!*"

He gave up, started off again, trailed by his Italian. Ten minutes later, he saw the houses. A hamlet—a fishing village, perhaps—there were boats and nets. He stopped to let Alphonso catch up with him. The sight of the white houses—cottages—obviously pleased the Italian: he started towards them at a trot, and Jack followed. He thought they might at any rate get a drink of water.

An old woman, in black and with her head covered rather like a nun, turned and scuttled away round the back of the first house as they approached it. Alphonso laughed, turned to wink at Jack, then walked up to the front door and knocked on it. Jack stood waiting, glad to have Alphonso take the initiative now, a dozen yards behind him. He was conscious of looking like a tramp: bearded and none too clean. Well, say like a shipwrecked RN lieutenant. Alphonso looked like a circus acrobat down on his luck.

Right behind him, a harsh voice barked some sort of question.

Jack turned quickly, startled. A man of about thirty, brown-skinned and heavy-set, a peasant or a fisherman, had materialized from God only knew where. He repeated the same question: in Greek, presumably, or Cretan. Jack waved a hand towards the sea, then pointed to himself. "English navy." He made a swimming motion, and the man nodded, jerked his head in a beckoning gesture and then turned away. Jack, trailed again by Alphonso, stumbled after him along the uneven, stony path. If anything wheeled moved here it wouldn't be more than a donkey-cart. At about the third house, which seemed to be a small farm or small-holding, the man turned in and beckoned again. He led them past the house, heading towards a barn, and when he got close to it he waited for Jack to get there before he pushed the door open and went in.

Hard-baked earth floor: circular, a threshing-floor. But there was a big rough table at the back, with glasses of wine and a stone jug on it, a group of people vague in the half-light. Early in the day for boozing, he was thinking: then he'd focused on the people. A corporal with a New Zealand shoulder-flash, a dark girl—Cretan, he guessed—and a solid-looking male local who might have been the girl's father. She looked about seventeen.

The corporal, surprisingly, got to his feet. The girl half-smiled, dropped her eyes. The man who'd brought them in was explaining something to the other one. The girl looked up again, and as Jack met her eyes the smile came back. He said, "My name's Everard." His epaulets marked him for *what* he was. He added, "I was sunk in the cruiser *Carnarvon* three days ago. What's the form here?"

"We're foraging." The corporal held out his hand. "I'm Chris McGurk. Glad to meet up with you, Lieutenant, sir. This here's Maria. We come down on the scrounge—they're s'posed to be gettin' us some fish. Stuck here till it gets dark again now, can't bloody move in daylight." He pointed at the Cretan. "We're with *his* lot, dozen of us, up in the mountain there. He's her brother—Nico, he's called." The girl was attractive, in a direct, uncaring way. Long skirts and shapeless wrappings, but she'd have a good figure, he guessed, under all that. The corporal said, "The *Carnarvon*, you said? We got a rum little bloke with us, name of Brighouse . . . he come off—"

The brother interrupted, muttering in his own language; he'd lifted one hand, to point. Eyes followed the thick, pointing finger to Alphonso.

"Hey. What's *this?*"

They were all staring at Alphonso. Jack said, "He answers to the name of Alphonso. Unfortunately I can't speak Italian and he doesn't understand a word of—"

"*Italian?*"

The brother looked suddenly very angry. Corporal McGurk had a
Luger in his fist and it was aimed at Alphonso. The Cretan reached
across, grasped its barrel and pushed it down. He growled something to
the other man, the one who'd brought them in. Alphonso found himself grabbed suddenly from behind: both his arms were twisted up behind
his back, and his young, swarthy face in its fringe of black beard was
screwed up in pain. The brother spoke again, and the other one turned
Alphonso round and rushed him out: he'd found his voice and he was
protesting, pleading in shrill Italian. Nico touched the corporal's gun
again: "No shoot. Shoot no good." He touched his own ear. "No good.
Germans come."

"Yeah. Okay."

"Okay. Good!"

"Look," Jack told the corporal, "he's perfectly harmless! He and I have
been sitting on a half-sunk caïque together for three days and nights,
he's really—"

"Save it, Lieutenant." McGurk nodded at him. "Believe me, it's best."
He looked away, staring up at the rafters, and began to whistle between
his teeth. Jack came to life: "Christ, they aren't going to—"

Alphonso screamed. The sound came from somewhere round behind
the shed: then it cut off abruptly. The girl leant forward, crossing herself
and whispering. The corporal explained, "We're liable to be hunted. We've
no choice, sir." Maria's brother leant over to pour Jack a glass of wine.

The director-tower voicepipe called; Nick answered it, and Houston told
him, "Harbour and anchorage is empty, sir."

From up there he could see clear across the point of land. Nick
straightened from the pipe, and glanced at his navigator; Drisdale said,
"Phew . . ."

They could have wiped up a few destroyers or MAS-boats; normally one would even have hoped to find some, but noise and fireworks were very definitely to be avoided if possible in this operation. Perfect peace and not a raised voice anywhere was what was wanted. There might quite possibly be a radio set with a German or Italian operator up in the village; to find such a radio and destroy it was a priority job for the landing-parties. *Tuareg* swept past the point, and Nick said, "I'll take her now." He called down, "Port fifteen."

The inner harbour gleamed like an enclosed lake on a gentle, dewy morning. Light pouring over the eastern hills confirmed that it was completely empty: there wasn't even a caïque afloat in it.

"Midships."

"Midships, sir!"

"Yeoman, pass the signal for: *Am stopping engines.*" He stooped to the pipe again: "Steer oh-six-eight."

Afghan would come inshore of *Tuareg,* as she closed in to her own landing-place.

"Message passed, sir!"

"Slow together. Sub, tell Mr Walsh to train his tubes fore and aft."

It was like a picture postcard: Shabby little fishing harbour, wisps of chimney smoke, some old lobster boats moored close inshore. *Afghan* was hauling out to port and slowing, her boats lowered close to the water and her waist crowded with khaki and tin hats. Once they'd got control of the place the soldiers were to lie low, stay inside the houses.

"Stop together."

"Stop together, sir . . . Both telegraphs to stop, sir."

The ships were rolling and pitching as their own wash overtook them: they'd entered at high speed and over the shallows it really stirred things up. Another forty or fifty yards and he'd stop her, about one cable's length from the jetty. There wasn't a sign of life anywhere, except for bluish smoke drifting up in still air.

"Slow astern together."

"Tubes are trained fore and aft, sir."

Sand-stained water swirled up *Tuareg*'s sides as her reversed screws took all the way off her.

"Stop both engines." He glanced at Chalk. "Away motorboat."

Nine minutes to six. She was still bucking around, to her own and other ships' disturbance of the water. But apart from that it was as smooth as glass, and barring enemy interference it promised to be a very quiet, peaceful day. The messdecks would be jammed solid, and therefore hot, but exhausted men wouldn't find it impossible to sleep. Half of the main-deck crew space had been screened off as a hospital; the nurses had Nick's quarters aft, and Aussie officers had the wardroom. The two doctors who'd come with them were being accommodated in Gallwey's sickbay. Upper decks were to be kept clear; close-range weapons' crews would stand normal watches but keep under cover, out of sight. It was all in the orders.

"Motorboat's alongside, sir."

The other destroyers' boats were in the water too, but it would be five or ten minutes before the troops could be ashore. That wasn't long, but if the Luftwaffe chose to pay a visit now, saw the ships lying off and the soldiers landing, the Italian colours might not impress them all that much. This should have been finished before daylight.

Waiting: controlling impatience. The ship's movement was lessening as the water calmed. He glanced at Drisdale. "If we wanted to look one hundred per cent Italian we'd have chickens pecking around on the quarterdeck."

"Might get some from shore, sir?"

Drisdale had taken it seriously, for God's sake . . .

"Boat's left the side, sir!"

About bloody time . . . He bent to the pipe: "Slow ahead port. Starboard twenty." She was in as good a spot as any, and it would leave plenty of room for the others to anchor to the north-east of her in a line parallel to the waterfront: all he had to do was turn her round and drop the hook. "Stop port. Midships." *Tuareg* was already swinging nicely. He told Chalk, "Up here, Sub, and tell the cable party to stand by."

Afghan's boat had reached the nearer landing-place. He asked Drisdale, "How much water?"

"Seven fathoms, sir."

Two shackles of cable would be plenty, then. He stooped: "Slow astern together."

"Boats are at the other jetty, sir."

Troops would be landing, hurrying up towards the village. So far, so good . . . He was waiting to get some sternway on her, so as to lay the cable out neatly ahead of the ship. "Stop together." He told Chalk, who was in the front of the bridge with an arm raised for Ashcourt to see from the foc'sl, "Let go!" Chalk dropped his arm. Nick heard the clink of a sledge-hammer knocking the slip off, and then the roar and clatter of chain cable running out. His mind was moving on, meanwhile, to the next stages . . . The landing-parties would re-embark at 9:30, by which time it would be dark enough, and by 10:00 he'd have his flotilla outside and well clear. The black paint would be used then, for blanking out the Italian colours while the ships sped south across the Aegean; four hours at 30 knots to Kaso, with another three and a half hours southwards from the Strait before the blessed darkness lifted. By sunrise they'd be not much more than two hundred miles from Alexandria, and there'd be Beaufighters to meet them.

In Alexandria, please God, there might be news about *Carnarvon* survivors . . . He told Chalk, as he heard the cable's rush slow and then stop, "Tell him to veer to two shackles, and secure."

"Aye aye, sir!"

He had his glasses on a column of troops doubling up the road. With the delay he'd run into, he thought he was extremely lucky to be getting away with this. Touch wood . . . Dalgleish said, beside him, "Captain, sir. Deputation here from the medical party. You did say as soon as we'd anchored—"

"What?"

Lowering the glasses, turning: Dalgleish had an Australian major with him—a doctor—and two Australian-uniformed females. The one pushing forward beside the major was short, stocky, decidedly plain. The other—

He took his eyes off the other one, as the major said, "Wanted to say how grateful we all are, Captain. I'm sure you're busy; we'll clear off again now, but—"

"Captain—you've done us proud, you really have, sir."

That had come from the short, thickset woman. The other, who was willowy with light brown hair and a distinct resemblance to Ingrid Bergman, only nodded as she looked at him very directly out of wide, grey, appraising eyes. About twenty-eight, he guessed: and what a business for someone like her to have been through, for heaven's sake . . . Then he was telling them, "Kind of you to feel like that. But—" he shrugged, shook his head. Dalgleish shouldn't have let them up here this soon, and there wasn't time for speeches. Nick told him, "See they have everything they need." The Bergman-type girl hesitated as the others turned away: she asked Nick quietly, "Tomorrow—at sea, if it's okay— could I come up here? Little while, just to see how—"

"You'd better," he warned her. "If you don't come up of your own free will, I'll send an armed escort to collect you."

"Cable's secured, sir."

"Thank you, Sub." Surprise on young Chalk's face. The girl had paused at the ladder-head, looking back at him across the bridge: and Fiona would have her eyebrows raised, he guessed. But what was Fiona doing with her spare time—except not writing letters?

Boats were returning to all the ships. Signalmen had been landed with the soldiers, sailors with battery-powered Aldis lamps and semaphore flags; there'd be some "all-clear" messages soon, please God . . . Beaufighters in tomorrow's dawn: he warned himself, *Better not count chickens. We can't have all the luck.* He yawned—and caught himself in the act, realizing how tired he was. Then a follow-up thought hit him—a really marvellous one: once those signals had been made there'd be no reason at all why he shouldn't retire to his sea-cabin below the bridge, and sleep like a dog all day.

POSTSCRIPT

. . .

There was no last lift from Retimo (or Rethimnon). There was no 37th Destroyer Flotilla, cruiser *Carnarvon,* destroyer *Huntress,* assault ship *Glenshiel,* nor transport *Gelderland* either. But all the other ships mentioned in the story were present and engaged in the operations as described.

"There is rightly little credit or glory to be expected in these operations of retreat," wrote Admiral of the Fleet Viscount Cunningham of Hyndhope in his autobiography *A Sailor's Odyssey.* He also said, during the course of the evacuation of Crete, "It takes three years to build a ship, but three hundred to build a tradition."

The tradition held up. And bringing sixteen and a half thousand soldiers out of the island cost not only ships but the lives of two thousand men of the Royal Navy. With the greatest respect for the memory of ABC, *I'd* say there was glory.

—A.F.

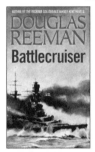
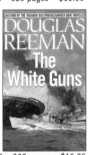